COMPOUND FRACTURES

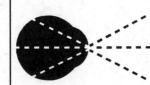

This Large Print Book carries the
Seal of Approval of N.A.V.H.

COMPOUND FRACTURES

STEPHEN WHITE

THORNDIKE PRESS
A part of Gale, Cengage Learning

GALE
CENGAGE Learning·

Detroit • New York • San Francisco • New Haven, Conn • Waterville, Maine • London

GALE
CENGAGE Learning®

LIBRARY OF CONGRESS CATALOGING-IN-PUBLICATION DATA

White, Stephen, 1951-
 Compound Fractures / by Stephen White.
  pages cm. — (Thorndike Press Large Print Core)
 ISBN-13: 978-1-4104-6032-5 (hardcover)
 ISBN-10: 1-4104-6032-0 (hardcover)
  1. Psychotherapists—Fiction. 2. Therapist and patient—Fiction. 3. Suspense fiction. 4. Large type books. I. Title.
 PS3573.H47477C66 2013b
 813'.54—dc23   2013028748

Published in 2013 by arrangement with Dutton, a division of Penguin Group (USA) LLC, a Penguin Random House Company

Printed in the United States of America
1 2 3 4 5 6 7 17 16 15 14 13

To my readers

[It's] the greatest poison in the the world.
One drop could kill you.

Ivy Baldwin

PROLOGUE

DOCTOR LILA

One session stood out. It was our second.

I have replayed the session in my head at least ten times. It was when my perspective changed. The day I got suspicious. On occasion I went back over it to see if there was a nuance I missed. Other times the loop replayed itself, an earworm, a melody my memory couldn't cut loose.

It's not in my personality to recall moments of assurance with much clarity. What I tend to recall vividly are my doubts and my fears. That therapy loop earned the replays because it was the session when my doubts and my fears began to crystallize, when I went from thinking that I might be in over my therapeutic head to wondering what the hell I might have gotten myself into with Dr. Alan Gregory.

Or as I called him, my patient.

■ ■ ■ ■

My name is Delilah Mary Travis. My friends call me Lila. Most of my patients call me Dr. Travis, or Delilah.

Alan Gregory called me Lila. But we weren't friends.

It was the third week of January. The session had been fitful. I felt no rhythm in his words.

As the end of our time approached I said, "I don't know what happened that morning. The day of the fire. The morning of the shooting. Moment by moment. You may think I know. You may wish I knew. You may want to proceed as though I know what you need me to know. But I don't know."

He didn't reply. That happened frequently with us.

During Alan's previous visit I'd asked him why he'd picked me to be his therapist. He said it was because he wanted a therapist he didn't know — he knew almost everybody in Boulder — and because someone he trusted had once said good things about my work. I'd asked him why he didn't go to Denver; there had to be therapists there he didn't know. He said it was too much for him then. An almost three-hour round-trip?

He said he couldn't do it.

I began to think he'd been less than honest. I began to believe he chose me because I was inexperienced. He thought he could manipulate me.

I said, "I imagine it will be tender for you, sharing the story. But at some point you will need to tell me those details."

He stood. His timing was impeccable; he rose within seconds of the precise forty-five-minute mark. As a therapist he had sat through a million forty-five-minute hours. After the first few thousand or so he'd undoubtedly internalized the session interval.

I had not. My hours in the consultation chair were still in high triple-digits. The clock I relied upon was digital. It was not visible from his seat.

"Who does, Lila?" he replied. "Know? What happened, I mean."

Who knows? You're going existential about that? You were there, I wasn't. If I had been there I would know what the hell happened.

I kept the rant to myself. I said, "Are you unsure what happened that day?"

No dissociation, please. I don't have the chops for fugue. Not your fugue.

His face adjusted into an expression I couldn't interpret. He had a few of those. Then he said, "Am I 'sure'? A lot of cer-

11

tainty is squeezed into that syllable. Certainty is elusive for me. Death? Certain. Everything else? Uncertain."

God.

"Okay," he said. "Here's part of what happened that morning that you don't know. That maybe no one else knows." He took a deep breath. "My wife was in my office to caution me about a development in a case she was working. When she came to see me she didn't understand the implications of what she had learned. She thought she did, but she did not. She was being generous, maybe loving — I go back and forth about that — by warning me about legal action that was coming against someone I know."

"Legal action?"

"Taking that person into custody. For questioning. Or arrest. Like that."

"Thanks," I said. Why I thanked him I did not know.

"I told her that if she were to start arresting people she would have to begin by arresting me."

I was disbelieving. I'm sure I looked it. I said, "You?"

He said, "It's complicated. This may help: After Lauren told me what she was about to do, I knew the time had arrived to reveal some secrets I'd been keeping from her. I did that — I revealed some things I had done."

"Things?" *Jesus.*

"Acts."

That sure clears things up. I said, "You're being vague."

"Intentionally. I am revealing I have secrets, but I am not revealing those secrets."

"Trust?" I said. Not exactly a therapeutic reach on my part. It was like a meteorologist forecasting rain seconds after she opens her umbrella.

"Yes. Lauren recognized the implications of what I told her. I knew she would, but I had hoped that my admission might alter the tilt of her heart. In my favor."

To him, his failure to trust me required no exploration. I felt it as a wound.

"I was wrong," he said. "Lauren was angry. Not understanding. All that my revelation changed for her that morning was her thinking about whom to arrest."

Alan Gregory was one of those people who confused me when he told me things intended to alleviate my confusion. By then that wasn't news for me.

I said, "She was going to arrest you? When she was shot?"

"Not at the beginning of her visit but, yes,

by the end. When she was shot."

His shoulders fell. Some amount of tension disappeared from his temples and his jaw. He seemed relieved to have breached this wall with me. We made brief eye contact. The intimacy of it all stunned me. Part of me melted with his glance, as though for that instant alone our arteries shared the same pumping heart.

He shook his head, as though he were as amazed as I was. His breath was shallow. "That morning? The fire up the street? Don't forget the fire."

My breathing was shallow, too. The mirroring was not intentional. No, I had not forgotten the fire.

In a way that I don't think I had ever felt before in my time as a therapist, I was aware that a patient was sharing a dangerous secret with me. Not just a sensitive truth — that's routine — but a dangerous one. Dangerous for him. And possibly dangerous for me.

Alan Gregory woke to foreboding every morning of his life. To help him I would need to understand his foreboding. Perhaps even to feel it.

I said, "Could you please sit back down, Alan?" If he considered me a peer he wouldn't put me in the position I was in. I

14

knew that. I didn't like it.

"Our time is up," he said.

I swallowed a sigh. "That's my call. This is my office. I am your therapist." I shouldn't have had to remind him of that. We'd work on that issue later. The list of what we would work on later was becoming unwieldy.

He nodded. But he remained standing. He seemed more paralyzed than defiant.

"Your wife was about to have you arrested for what?"

"Something serious," Alan said. "A felony. I can't discuss it."

"Can't?"

He sat down. "I will tell you what I told Lauren that morning: my caution has to do with clean hands." He looked at his hands as though he couldn't not look at his hands.

With monumental self-control I managed not to look at my hands. I was aware that his wife was shot not too many moments after he told her whatever he told her that morning. Apparently about clean hands.

"Yours?" I asked. "Your clean hands?"

He stood back up. "No," he said. "Yours."

That did it. I looked at my hands. I said, "Sit, please." He didn't. *Shit.* "She had a reason to arrest you? The felony?"

"Yes. Definitely."

"You say 'definitely' yet you continue to

15

be vague. You seem to be admitting . . . what, guilt? Yes? Are we talking about trust again? Right now? Between you and me?"

Air escaped his nostrils in a little huff. "Guilt? No question. Right and wrong. Morality? That's murky. Between us? Of course it's about trust."

He paused. I look back now and I wonder about that pause. I think he was telling me something. But I was missing it.

He tried to explain. "Trust is not only an issue between you and me. It was there between my wife and me. Maybe it is there between my friend — or friends — and me. There is a lot on the line here beyond my mental health. Culpability. Survival. Freedom. All of those."

Before I could acknowledge that gravity, he refocused on the mundane. He said, "We need to talk about your notes. Session notes, process notes, whatever. And supervision."

What? "Please sit. If you don't I am going to have to stand." He sat. I said, "Thank you. What about supervision? What about my notes?"

"Are you being supervised on this case?"

I had never before been asked that question. Few patients know that supervision — oversight of a treatment by a senior practitioner — exists as an option for their therapist. But Alan Gregory knew. He was one of those senior practitioners. In Boulder he was a supervisor.

"This therapy?" I said. "With you?" He nodded. "No. I am not being supervised."

"If you change your mind — about supervision — will you agree to inform me? I can't have what I tell you leave this room. Not even to a supervisor. Clean hands?"

"That's irregular," I said. "You know that."

"It's essential. Without that assurance, I can't proceed. Won't."

"I need to think about it. We can discuss it next time. What about my notes?"

"I would like you to make them sparse," he said.

"Short? Or, or lacking detail? What kind of sparse?"

He nodded. Then he shook his head.

I made a *so-WTF* face. If I'd had a supervisor she would have been directing me to continue to work on maintaining a therapeutic expression. They all did.

He said, "Lacking content. No names. No facts. No he-said, I-said. Process? Go to town. Whatever's helpful."

"I don't show my clinical notes to anyone, Alan. Ever. You don't have to worry."

His eyes were dismissive. "I wouldn't be here if I thought you would. I am concerned

17

about people who would look at them without your consent."

I felt a chill. *Huh?* I looked at my hands again.

He said, "You may not have experience with those people. I do."

"I don't," I said. With another patient, I would not have admitted that. Alan Gregory was not another patient.

"Those people may know that I am coming to see you for therapy," he said.

It is typically no more a presence in my body than my liver, but my heart suddenly became an entity in my chest. *Bump-bump. Bump-bump.*

I began to question things I should have questioned sooner. My mind reassembled fragments and pieces he had allowed to leak out along the way.

A wildfire. Arrest. A gun. Shots in the back. A witness. His partner. A felony. A little boy. Trust. A leg wound. A wife in ICU. A cabbist.

Oh shit. And . . . holy shit. The felony. Trust. Guilt? I realized what he was admitting to me. I began to speak. My breath caught in my throat. I tried again.

I said, "You had a motive? That morning? To shoot your wife, didn't you?"

"If you choose to stop treating me, I understand."

18

"I asked you a question," I said.

Bump-bump. Bump-bump.

He looked out the window. "My request about your notes?"

Jesus. Did you hear what I just asked you? "Uh, I will be careful. I will take a look at what I've written. Next time we can talk about what I decide about shredding and starting over. Did —"

"Handwritten or digital?" he asked. "Dictated? I hope you don't have them in the cloud."

"Handwritten."

"If you shred, it needs to be cross-shred, not strip-shred. Separate the confetti into piles. Dispose of the piles in different places. Or set the shreds on fire. Either works."

My patient wanted me to torch my notes. I added paranoia to his differential diagnosis. *Great. This is great.*

"Alan, did you have a motive to shoot your wife?"

Without any further hesitation, he said, "I did. That's the problem. At some point, they'll figure that out. He certainly will. And he won't let go. That, by the way, is the exact sort of thing that can't go in your notes."

He?

Bump-bump.

19

1
BEFORE THAT MORNING

SAM AND LUCY

"The dead guy? He was, what, a psychologist or something? Psychiatrist?"

Sam Purdy didn't reply to the man's questions. He introduced himself curtly, slammed his car door, and took a few steps away.

The detective had responded to the call on Prado expecting to see a familiar house. But the house was gone. He walked up near the edge of the debris and faced the wide *V* that Eldorado Canyon carves into the Front Range of the Colorado Rockies.

Sam was aware that he shouldn't be able to see Eldorado at all. The damn house should be in the way.

The last time Purdy had been on Prado was the week of 9/11. In 2001. Since then Prado had been but one tile in the mosaic that made up his 9/11 grief and confusion.

The damn void changes everything. I can

see things I couldn't see.

Sam wanted to chew on that. To weigh the possibility that moving beyond the old grief — he hadn't — might require his willingness to see things that weren't visible before.

The RP, the reporting party, had a different idea. The man, fit and gray, stepped in front of the detective, blocking his view. "Took you long enough to get here. I called 911 like three hours ago." The man's thumbs were tapping at his phone, a touch screen the size of a slab of Spam. "Two hours and thirteen minutes to be precise. I started my phone's stopwatch." He held it up in case the detective doubted him.

Purdy sighed a sigh of capitulation. "This is your property?"

"In six months it'll be my castle. Where you been?" The man tapped his wrist. "Time is money."

Purdy noted the absence of a watch on the tapped wrist. He said, "This? Not an emergency. And this? Not a conversation. I ask questions. You answer them."

The man nodded. Sam refocused on the absent house. He wasn't done reflecting on absence and opportunity. Not even close.

The RP couldn't stay quiet. Purdy tuned back in as the man said, ". . . have to admit that this is big. You guys missed the gun. Could it have come after? No way. You're going to have to, what, reopen? Is that what you say? Big deal." Sam watched the man punctuate his self-congratulation with a tightened fist and a muted arm clench, mimicking Kobe after a clutch three.

The guy had no way to know that Sam hated Kobe Bryant like he hated jock itch.

Sam moved a finger to his lips. In a low voice he said, "Quiet. Shhh."

The ensuing peace lasted no more than half a minute before the man blurted, "I love northern light. It's soft. You have any? At your house?"

The question left Sam at a loss. In Sam's world, if you have southern light and you turn around, you get northern light. How could a house have one and not the other?

The RP brought his outstretched hands together above his head. He slipped one foot from a sandal and shaped the arch to the other leg's knobby knee. "Six months from now? Maybe seven. Ten? Kitchen there. Study here." He indicated floor plan features with thrusts of his head. "This wall glass, triple-paned. Ceilings, twelve feet. I was thinking fourteen, but — Trim? Beetle-kill, painted. No VOC. LEED Platinum or Diamond, whatever is best. Can houses get that? My kid has allergies. Hell, my dog has allergies. I want the best LEED."

The guy said "LEED" and Sam understood him. That told Sam two important things about himself. It indicated he was conversant with contemporary environmental building standards. And it meant maybe he'd been in Boulder too long.

"The vista will do all the heavy lifting. Across the mesa. Flatirons at dawn? I'm up early. You? Cannot wait. No sun in my eyes. Not a ray. Pool table there. No shadows." He cackled in anticipatory glee.

Sam wondered if there were people troubled by shadows on their pool tables. His friends, Alan and Lauren, had a pool table in a room that faced west. *Has Lauren been bothered all these years by shadows? At least she's had the good sense not to bitch about it.*

"Sounds sublime," Sam said. Faking interest in rich people's concerns had long been a reflex for him. He thought the time had come for rich people to feign interest in his problems. He was still waiting on that.

He faced the homeowner. "What did you touch before I got here? Be specific."

The man's pace of speech went from zero to sixty in two seconds flat. "Bricks. Sorting bricks. Kicking bricks. Stacking bricks. Saving bricks. See that? Four-by-four-by-eight. Two of those. One, two. Four-by-four-by-eight-by-two. That's two hundred fifty-six bricks. I'm on my way to four stacks, four-by-four-by-eight-by-*four.* Five hundred and twelve." Deep breath. "Bricks." During a second inhale he pointed in the direction of the neat piles on the edge of a driveway that led to the slab for a garage that was no longer there. "That neighbor — Thomas? Tomás? I don't know — asked for bricks from the demo. His house was built in the late fifties, same as this, maybe same builder. He's old. Thomas, not the builder. Builder's probably dead. He wants a patio wall or a barbecue or — Who cares? I was being helpful. Sure. Sure — Also trying to prevent NIMBY problems. Two birds, five hundred and twelve stones. Yah!"

Sam's on-the-fly diagnosis was that the RP operated in too many simultaneous dimensions. Sam blamed that, too, on Boulder. He'd seen it take down lesser men.

Sam asked, "Were you wearing those gloves?" Work gloves were tucked in the man's belt. Canvas. Leather. "When you touched the bricks."

"Yes."

"Sure?"

"Yes."

25

"And the gun you found? What about the gun?"

"No."

"No, you didn't touch it? Or no, you weren't wearing the gloves when you did?"

The guy pulled out his phone, began pecking with two thumbs. "I saw the gun when I lifted a brick. Took a photo. Here it was when I found it. There. See? Then I called you guys. Two hours and thirteen minutes later —"

"Yeah, got that part. Show me the gun." The man led the detective near the edge of the debris. He pointed at the revolver. Sam said, "So, when we run prints we won't find yours? No stray DNA? We won't see any disturbance in the dust that shows you moved the gun?"

Purdy detected some hesitation. *Damn.* "Want to change your story, Mr. . . . Picker?" He recalled the man's name from the call he got from dispatch.

"It's Pichter, like *pitcher* in baseball, but in a Jumble. And it's not a story."

In a Jumble? "Let's walk through it one more time, Mr. Pichter. So I understand."

"Like you're slow?" Mr. Pichter said, stretching the last vowel a couple of beats.

Purdy sucked his tongue to the roof of his mouth to keep from saying what he was

26

thinking. It worked. "Sure," Sam said, "like I'm slow." Old-time Iron Rangers could turn a vowel into a fable. Sam did that with the *o* in *slow.* "You never lived here, Mr. Pichter? In this house. Yes or no."

"Got it thirty-two months ago. Short sale. Good deal, not a great deal. Land plus plus plus. I mean, this location? Let's be real. Wanted a lot on this side of Prado since . . . for — uh-uh — ever. Who doesn't? Had a tenant until Easter. Young guy. Does disaster response for State Farm. Tornados, fires, floods, hurricanes, whatnot. Not a lot of earthquakes lately. What's that about, you think? Huh? Since he left, vacant. Approvals and permits? Pain pain pain. Delays — cost of money alone — twenty grand. That's with interest rates in the crapper." He shrugged a what-are-you-gonna-do shrug.

Sam was speechless.

Jumble Guy wasn't. "Luck? Me? Don't feel bad for me. I've had my share. I got a shitload of Apple when it was sixty-eight. Not in sixty-eight. *At* sixty-eight. It's my iStock. And my brother-in-law got me a hunk-hunka of the Chipotle IPO. My brother-in-law? Burritos? I like Mexican food even less than I like him. Now I'm rolling in the tortillas. Get it? And" — he held up his phone — "I'm an Android guy. Ha."

When the 2008 crash came, Sam learned that his retirement funds were invested in GM, some squirrelly mortgage bonds, and AIG. *This assbite is sitting on a golden throne of Apple and the Chipotle IPO. Now he's building a McPalace on Prado. Yeah,* Sam thought, *life is fair.*

"The demolition was when?" Sam asked.

"Yesterday. Front loader had a hydraulic failure. They'll be back to finish tomorrow first thing in the A.M."

Purdy returned his gaze to the cleft in the Rockies. Eldorado was sucking in the afternoon shadows as though it were a black hole. He turned his body right to face the mesa that rose up from South Boulder Creek. He shifted his focus back to the debris to try to digest anew the tragedy of demolishing what for over half a century had been a solid home. *What a waste. Oh well. Money does what money does.*

Sam squatted to examine the revolver, a Smith & Wesson .38 Special. He guessed it was an Airweight, though he'd have to move a brick to be sure. It sat among chunks of mortar on the old concrete hearth. The gun was why he was there.

He was tempted to get all self-critical about not looking up the damn chimney back then. The week of 9/11.

But that was a week he'd been looking for terrorists, not for guns in chimneys.

He stared at the revolver for half a minute praying it would speak some truth to him. It didn't. It was a common enough handgun in a place he'd almost given up expecting to see one.

Sam used his cop voice, absent any Iron Range embellishment, to say, "No. Sir."

"No what?" Jumble Man replied. His reply was naïve and hopeful, as though he anticipated learning something interesting about the .38 he'd discovered in the rubble of the chimney of the house he'd just knocked down.

"No, your demo crew won't be back tomorrow."

Sam used his radio to request forensic support just as his partner was rolling her vehicle to a stop directly behind Jumble Guy's dusty Porsche SUV. Lucy's phone was to her ear. Sam knew she was running the Porsche's plates. She nodded a greeting. Sam nodded back wide-eyed — a silent caution to her to be careful about Jumble Guy.

The man saw it all. "What? Who's she? Come on, guy. Let's work this out."

"Detective Purdy. Not 'guy.' That's Detective Davenport. Don't even think about calling her 'girl.' Won't go well for you."

29

"I got a schedule. Cleanup in the morning, excavators in the afternoon. The diggers won't break ground without a clean lot. Form guys on their heels. Then concrete, with a pumper. You know what a pumper costs? For a day? Foundation insulation, plumbing rough-ins. The plumbers were so hard to pin down. We're drilling halfway to hell for the thermal heat." He clapped his hands three times. "Bam. Bam. Bam. Bam. Schedule is king. *King.*"

Sam considered pointing out that there had been three claps but four *bams.* And only two kings. He didn't. He said, "Bummer."

Jumble Guy said, "I didn't have to call. I was being a good citizen. That should be rewarded."

Sam smiled. "You're going with that? I'll make sure it's in the report. We give citations sometimes. To good citizens. You could hang yours near your pool table. In the room with the northern windows. The one with no shadows."

"I did not have to call."

"But you did. Now? This is a crime scene. Pretend there's yellow tape everywhere the house you hated used to be. Your job? Stay outside that tape."

"Give me a break."

Sam thought about it. Rejected it.

He asked, "Do you know what *prado* means?"

Jumble Guy mistook the question for a quiz, with a prize he wanted to win. He said, "In English? Damn, I should know that. My own street name. I give up, what does it mean?"

"I don't know," Sam said. "My Spanish sucks. Do you know anything about Ivy Baldwin? From way back?"

Jumble Guy made a face that exposed too many teeth, like an aggrieved rodent. "Who's she? I don't know her. Is that one of my new neighbors? I only know Thomas. Tomás. The brick guy. Come on. One more. Give me an easier one."

Sam kicked at a broken brick. "Never mind," he said. "You lose."

2

"How do you see it, boss?" Lucy asked.

Sam made a noncommittal puffing sound through pursed lips. Pichter had started taking pictures of everything in sight with his damn phone. Maybe even video, which meant audio. Sam was behaving as though he was about to be on YouTube.

One night shortly before Sam met Ophelia he'd descended into a funky muse about the actuarial likelihood that his lifetime could end up being split almost evenly between two centuries, the twentieth and twenty-first. By the time his lubricated lifespan contemplation neared completion, Sam reached a subjective conclusion that of the two centuries he would inhabit, the twenty-first was not shaping up to be his favorite.

What happened on 9/11 was one of the reasons. YouTube was another. Sam had developed a persistent fear of becoming a trending topic on YouTube. He knew whatever video of him might captivate a YouTube audience would not reflect well on his character.

"Nothing coherent." Sam answered Lucy's question in a low register so that Jumble Guy couldn't eavesdrop.

She gave Sam a chance to go on before she said, "This all happened *that* week, Sammy. I didn't work this case with you, so you're going to have to explain why finding a gun here all these years later is such a big deal."

Sam turned his back on Jumble Guy. "The scene inside this house was an epic mess. Body cooked for three days before we got it. Which was after raccoons came in through a doggie door and did their gnawing thing." Sam pronounced *gnaw* with a hard *g* as though the word had two distinct syllables. Lucy had known Sam forever but even she couldn't tell whether he had mispronounced the word or if he was making a point. "Maybe a coyote, too. Don't recall the details. Wild things. By the time I walked in? What the deceased most resembled was a gunshot victim a few days after zombies had feasted on his flesh."

"Nice image. Thank you for that, Sam."

"Welcome. But we never found a gun."

The last time he was here, all those years earlier, he had thought of Lucy as his young partner. *Damn. The woman is almost middle-aged. How the hell did that happen?*

She said, "Now you have your gun. That's good, yeah?"

"You would think. But this pistol comes with a surprise — that skinny chain you see on the trigger guard. That's a complicating factor."

Lucy had noticed the chain. She had a ready explanation. "Maybe whoever stashed it wanted to make sure it didn't fall out of the chimney. Used the chain to keep it up there. Away from the kids."

"Say that's right. But if this was a self-inflicted wound — which is where I had my money back then — how did the gun get back up the chimney? How does that happen?"

"So now you're thinking homicide?" Lucy knew that a change in manner of death from suicide to homicide would turn this old case into a cold case.

"The death has been 'undetermined' all this time. Nobody ever got off the fence. Back then it looked like suicide, it smelled like suicide. If it had been a zombie it would have walked like a suicide. But without a weapon nobody would make the call."

"Watching a lot of zombie shit on cable with Simon lately, Sam?"

Sam grinned. "We bond over it, do Netflix marathons. Father, son, the living dead. That week, Luce? Nothing was clear. This death just got tossed into the big pile of crap that wasn't clear."

"Where was the dog? There was a doggie door. Whose dog was it?"

Sam was stumped. "I don't know. I don't . . . know. Vic's or his roommate's, I guess."

"Any gunshot residue on the vic? Did he pull the trigger?" Lucy asked.

"Inconclusive, like everything else. Found residue, but some of the essential locations were . . . gone."

"Gone? What does that mean?"

"The wild things. The vic was the feast. The guests were moveable."

"Yuck again, Sam," Lucy said. "You been practicing grossing me out?"

"A little bit." He smiled.

"Spatter? Was it consistent with suicide?"

"I don't recall it being inconsistent. What this didn't look like was terrorism. That week, suicide was not priority one. That week, the rest of that year, we were chasing terrorist ghosts."

"Hey," Lucy said, "we've both seen citizens hide guns in funny places. Inside a flue? If the fireplace was no longer in use, why not? I've seen stranger stashes. Maybe this was just a gun stash some citizen forgot about. Unrelated. Or, we could get lucky and lift some latents off the gun. If they're the vic's —"

"You feel lucky, Luce? I don't. Prints or not, if the gun was stashed back up that chimney, then it wasn't the suicide weapon. A guy can't shoot himself under the chin and then put the pistol away in some hidey-hole. Right?"

"Fair assumption. If this was the gun, then someone else was here."

"But . . . the crime scene guys said the scene was not disturbed by people. Just critters. Who would know a guy had a gun stashed up the chimney? Guy who put it there. Who else? Other people who lived here? Maybe."

"Another fair assumption." She watched his face, hoping for an indication of his mood, before she put a hand on each of his shoulders. "You really want to dig this up, Sam? The heroes died that week. The rest of us? We didn't have a great week. You don't need to make this perfect. I haven't been hearing any clamor for a new conclusion."

"I should forget it?"

"I'll write an addendum about finding the handgun, put it in the file. We move on. Catch us some new criminals."

"Ballistics?" Sam asked.

"Was there a slug for a match?"

Sam shrugged. "I don't recall. Probably."

"Shit, who cares? I vote to let it go. We have two different armed robbers out there right now that need arresting. That's what we should be doing. Not this."

"You really think it's two different assholes, not one?" Sam said. "Captain's sure it's one."

"He's wrong. That surveillance video shows a pistol with a wood grip. Second holdup? A witness says no wood grip. Different weapons mean different assholes. You can make that one of your infamous second rules. I'll pretend you made it up."

"Let's stick with one crime at a time, Luce." Sam gestured at Jumble Guy. "Today we got us a .38 on a chain. We also have one nightmare RP; he's like a rodent with ADD. I probably shouldn't have pissed him off. You watch — he won't let this go." Sam squatted near the hearth. "What do you make of the chain?"

Lucy did yoga regularly, though not religiously. Not quite as often as Sam ate meat with nitrates, but close. When she bent from her waist to examine the gun, Sam found himself becoming annoyed at the posture she adopted — mostly because he hadn't been able to approximate that position since the death of disco.

He used his pinky to indicate the trigger guard of the revolver. "The gun wasn't hung from the chain. It's *attached* to the chain. It's locked on with a bolt and a wing nut. You ever see someone attach a gun like that?"

"Rhetorical? Why wouldn't that chain interfere with the trigger action?"

"It's tight and forward on the guard. Look how long the chain is." He stood to chase the path of the chain into the mess of bricks that had tumbled down around the revolver. "Three feet or so here, give or take. Four there." He pointed. Took a half step. "Over this way, five. Under the flue, back out, eight, ten, twelve maybe? More?" He looked at Lucy. "Why hide a gun in a chimney at the end of a chain that long?"

Lucy said, "To reach the chimney cap? It had to attach somewhere, either the flue or the cap, right? Did you find the other end? Is there a hook?"

"Haven't gotten that far." The end of the chain disappeared beneath broken bricks and cracked mortar. While Lucy snapped photos, Sam pulled on a glove and used his index finger to shift a brick to one side, exposing the end of the chain.

Lucy said, "Fuck, there it is. That hook is crimped onto the chain. No way to hang that onto the cap. There has to be more. Move those two bricks next."

Sam stood. His spine crackled like it was made of caramel corn. "I have to start doing crunches," he mumbled.

Lucy said, "What?"

Sam wasn't ready to bend over again. He said, "Ophelia thinks I cuss too much. I'm working on it. You should, too."

Lucy said, "Fuck that. But I like Ophelia, Sam."

"You know she's older than me? First time I've . . . been there."

"Been where?" Lucy turned away. She didn't want Sam to know she was smiling.

"Been involved with a woman who's older."

"So? You'll die first anyway. The way you fucking eat."

Sam laughed. "You do cuss a lot."

"I haven't liked most of your girlfriends. I can't think of a single one I liked before Ophelia."

"Not Carmen? I thought you liked Carmen."

"Not even a little."

"Huh. You would have liked Dee."

"Dee? That mythical preggers sprite from back East? When was she your girlfriend? In a wet dream?"

"She wasn't. Not, you know . . . well, at all. We had — Don't know why I said that. We both like Ophelia. Maybe my search ends there."

"Don't blow this one like the others, Sam. The tits on Ophelia? Woman her age? You'd be a fool."

Sam laughed before Lucy did. Everybody had an opinion about Ophelia's breasts. Sam was used to it. Kind of.

Lucy lowered her upper body to get even closer to the end of the chain, balancing her weight on her left foot while allowing her right leg to float behind her as yoga ballast.

"Now you're showing off," Sam said.

"You think maybe that hook was part of a bungee?" Her index finger was inches from multiple frayed lengths of thin deteriorating elastic bands that extended out from the hook that had been crimped to stay fixed on the end of the chain.

"Now that you mention it, I am thinking that."

40

Lucy said, "Well, that means —"

A brash, husky crack of thunder erupted from the direction of Gross Reservoir. A brilliant flash of lightning followed before Sam could even begin counting. Lucy tumbled onto her back from the shock of it all. Sam offered his hand.

While they'd been distracted by the gun on the chain, the sky above the Front Range had turned the gray of bad dreams. "You got a tarp in your car?" Sam asked. "We should cover what we can for the crime scene guys. There has to be another end to that bungee someplace in the debris. Don't want it floating away during a monsoon."

Lucy was on the run toward her vehicle. She called back, "You have noticed that the crime scene guys are almost all women now? Yes?"

"I have not. I'm thinking that noticing that would be sexist. Wouldn't it? Or am I missing something about the nature of the progress you've been wanting me to make?"

Lucy opened her mouth. She didn't know how to respond.

They used some of Jumble Guy's carefully stacked bricks to secure Lucy's tarp in place. By the time they finished, rain was falling in fat drops. Lucy was a step behind Sam as he dashed to his Cherokee for cover.

41

Sam said, "Most days I love the monsoons. And we need the rain. But then most days I'm inside and I don't worry much about being hit by lightning."

Lucy was trying to remember the last steady downpour. She couldn't. Red Flag Warnings had been posted since spring along the entire length of the Front Range. Boulder County was kindling. Everybody knew a wildfire was coming. A bad one.

She said, "The gun is a gun. Vic was shot, there had to be one. That chain, though? There didn't need to be a chain."

"Chain makes it a puzzle, Luce. You know me, I like the puzzles. But a bungee? Bungee makes it goofy. Let's say you're a guy crazy enough to stash your pistol in the chimney. Why not just run the chain to the top? Why add a bungee to the mix?"

"At the risk of sounding obvious, it makes the contraption spring-loaded," Lucy said.

"Does. The handgun would disappear up the chimney right after you let go. Or after you died. Again, why? Why would somebody shoot himself and want the gun to disappear?"

"To fuck with us," Lucy said. "I hate it when citizens fuck with the cops."

"Language, language," Sam said. "A disappearing gun? I've been doing this a long

42

time. But that's a first. Goofy, like I said."

"Rain's stopping," Lucy said. "We got, what, three minutes of monsoon? Nada."

"It's so dry," Sam said. "We're going to get a fire soon. You watch."

They got out of the car and began to remove the tarp. Sam said, "Have you heard the old stories about Ivy Baldwin? What he did up here? In Eldorado?"

"Amazing man," she said. "No, astonishing man. Hard to believe what he did."

"Do you think he really did what they say? Crossed that canyon on a wire?" Sam pointed to the canyon. "Has to be half a mile across. Quarter mile up."

"Absolutely. I have pictures in a book at home. Guy named Ed Tangen took a lot of photos of him."

"No net? Dozens of times? For real?"

"He even did it in his eighties. He was eighty-two, I think, the last time. My grandfather met Ivy once at Elitch's. He used to perform there when it first opened."

"Damn." Sam got quiet for a moment before he asked, "Do you know what *prado* means? In Spanish?"

Lucy said, "Means 'meadow.' "

"Huh. Wouldn't have guessed that. Thought it meant vista, or view. Or foothills maybe."

43

"And that," Lucy said, "is why there are fucking dictionaries."

3
AFTER THAT MORNING

ALAN

Lauren had planned her own service. The document describing her wishes for what would take place after her death was in the shared file where we stored our wills in our home office. The file was marked WHEN I AM DEAD in block letters.

I had not known she had given her funeral any thought, but I was grateful for the road map she left behind. It allowed me an interlude when I would not need to make important decisions. When the time arrived I would hand off the funeral directions to her sister Teresa, who was eager to be useful.

Lauren's death was an anticlimax. I had stepped into the kitchen for a glass of water. When I came back she had ceased breathing. Stopped living. Begun being dead. Just like that. I wasn't at her bedside when it happened.

The feelings that were so overwhelming to me that morning, the morning she was shot, all came back with fresh intensity. I sat alone with her and cried.

I felt some anger. But I felt mostly sad. And very much alone.

The only person in the house with me was Sofie, Lauren's teenaged daughter from Holland. Sofie had arrived in Colorado only two days before. That was when she and I met. Sofie was a revelation to me. She entered our fractured, wounded family with grace and familiarity, almost as though she were reentering our family, naturally finding her place in seams and gaps that I didn't perceive until she filled them.

She heard me crying beside her mother's body. She joined me. We sat for a while, crying together, arms around each other.

To comfort me and maybe herself, she told me stories about her mother's visit to the Netherlands.

Teresa gave me instructions. Because she thought I'd forget, she emailed me schedules. And she texted me reminders about the schedules. She told me what time to be ready to leave the house, when to have the kids ready to go. I did my best to comply.

I texted her back so that she didn't have to text me again.

Grace wanted her sister, Sofie, not her aunt Teresa, to help with her hair. But it was Teresa who told Grace she couldn't wear that to this, or vice versa. I was grateful for Teresa's help with the daughter wrangling. I would have given in to Grace on everything.

Had someone asked me before — before that morning, the morning everything changed — I would have guessed that Lauren would choose cremation. As with so many other things having to do with the end of our lives together, I got that part wrong. The final remembrances were to conclude with a traditional motorcade — a couple of black limousines chasing a black hearse — to a cemetery for an old-fashioned hole-in-the-ground burial.

Teresa guided me into place near the gravesite with the frustrated resolve of a choreographer who was exasperated with her most-challenged student. The Indian summer sun shone brilliantly in the southwest sky. I stood where Teresa put me, a half-dozen feet back from a dark pit excavated in a slightly uphill expanse of gray-green turf.

I called her back. I said, "Please. One

thing?" I asked her to have the cemetery staff remove the turf-hued carpet from around the mechanical apparatus that would lower the weight of my wife's coffin into the earth. I was certain that Lauren would not have been pleased by the faux-grass accompaniment.

A man from the cemetery rolled up the grass rugs. The unadorned hole looked like a scar in the earth. That felt right to me. The day was about raw dirt.

Around me were my children.

I was grateful. For them. For their lives. For their presence in mine. For the support they didn't know they gave. In that moment, and forever, for the chance to support them.

Around us, mostly behind us, but some on each side, and a few dozen more across the way, were a hundred people, give or take. I only glanced up at their faces a couple of times. I saw many strangers. *How could that be, that so many people I don't recognize want to see my wife's body lowered into the ground?*

Once I learned of Lauren's wish that she be buried, I'd made a guess that the grave-site she preselected would be in the shade of a tree, or on a north-facing slope. It turned out that I got that wrong, too. After years of avoiding sunshine as a reluctant

48

homage to the multiple sclerosis that had plagued her since shortly before we'd met, she wanted her body to disintegrate for eternity in as sun-washed a spot as the high plains could provide. Damn the summer heat. Damn the UV rays.

Lauren also surprised me by identifying a friend — someone I wasn't sure I had met, a woman she had once volunteered with somewhere — to act as "spiritual presence and guide" at the final service at the cemetery.

If forced to rate it before that morning, I would have placed Lauren's spiritual inclinations at no higher than a two on a ten-scale. I allowed that it was possible that I had that wrong, too, about my wife. The cynical side of me entertained and then rejected before finally accepting the alternative conclusion that, should there turn out to be an afterlife, my wife wanted to have greased the skids. Just in case. Maybe.

When Lauren's friend stepped forward to begin her role as our spiritual presence, and to guide us, I tried to match her face with a name. I thought Teresa had told me that her name was Crystal. But she introduced herself to us mourners as Clover.

Clover spoke for a few minutes. Nothing she said registered. It was babble; her words had nothing to do with Lauren's life. She concluded by looking up at the sky with great drama. She announced that Lauren had asked that a song be played before she was lowered into the earth.

I didn't know what the sky had to do with it. But I had woken that morning determined to be well behaved. The determination was essential because I didn't feel at all like being well behaved. In fact I was fighting a strong urge to be a requiem rebel.

Lauren's MS had left her music averse for the last years of her life, but she had chosen to have music played when she could no longer be discomfited by it, just as she had wanted the sun to shine when its heat could no longer create any havoc for her.

The song she had chosen for the end was "The Weight" by the Band.

I don't read music. I don't understand the structure or the nomenclature. I feel music like almost everyone else. But I don't feel music like my daughter feels music.

Immediately after the initial chord of the song called the gathered to attention, Gracie broke into dance beside me. For the first few measures my daughter's movements were confined to some restrained motion of her feet and her lower legs — like an Irish step dancer warming up for something big.

50

I just need some place/Where I can lay my head.

I could tell by the hushed intake of collective breaths from the mourners, and from Aunt Teresa's suddenly wide eyes directly across the way, that Grace's dance performance was indeed an impromptu addition to the festivities and not part of her mother's detailed going-away choreography that I had not been tipped off about.

For those first few measured steps Gracie held my hand as she danced, but that didn't last. She shook off my fingers as her feet began to move faster, and her hips began to lift higher, and her arms began to drift until they found the parts of the melody they were seeking. Her long fingers, no longer tethered to me, extended out and up to meet the power she was feeling that came from some essential force, somewhere else, or somewhere deep inside her, as music begot motion.

My impulse was instinctive: To stop her, to protect her. To lean over and whisper, "Not here, honey. Later. You can dance later. All you want." But I didn't. Gracie had a need to dance right then. She had every right to dance. Lauren, I wanted to believe, had chosen to have music at the burial for Grace.

51

In case her daughter had a need to dance.

Grace displayed no self-consciousness during her graveside recital. She could have been dancing alone in our basement.

I expected the dance to stop shortly after it began. My initial thought was that Grace had memorized a few steps, a little jig that would serve as a bugle blow to announce a change in phase of the ceremony. I thought the dance would be confined to the solitary square meter of ground beside me.

The early moves were indeed regimented — in the sense someone had probably danced them before Grace danced them — but soon the steps became free-form and freeing. Once she got going I felt certain that no one had ever danced the moves that Gracie did that day. I watched in awe and admiration as my daughter's coltish legs bounced into motion I had never seen before.

Gracie cried as she danced. The tears began to form right from the first note, from her first step. She never sobbed; the tears fell silently, dripping down her cheeks and off her chin. But hers wasn't a sad dance; she moved with exuberance that she intuitively matched to the circumstances. She lifted my mood as she captured the essence of the parts of her mother that were never anchored to this earth by her illness.

It was a lot to ask from a little girl's graveside dance. But I thought Gracie pulled it off like a pro.

As the lengthy song wound down — "The Weight" is a dirge, not a ditty — she reached out and took my hand again. Taking her father's hand was not an act of supplication on Grace's part, nor was it a bid to seek a closing canopy of paternal security.

She was inviting me to join her in the celebration of her mother's life.

I can't dance. My daughter knew that better than anyone. But there, beside my wife's open grave, with my daughter's hand in my hand, I began to dance in front of the assembled mourners. I danced with Grace until the music that Lauren had chosen stopped on the precise note where she had chosen to stop it.

Gracie wasn't done. She kept on, extending her dance for a few more measures as she heard personal notes that no one else in the cemetery could hear. Her final movements, her final tribute, took place in stunned, and stunning, silence.

When she was done, she exhaled audibly. Some of the fallen tears hung poised on the curve of her chin, waiting to drip to the ground. Then she stood still again beside me, her back straight, as tall and proud as she had ever been. I fell to my knees and hugged her. Her tears wet both of our faces.

Grace's dance spoke about conclusion and finality and passing so succinctly that I would not have wanted to be the person forced to use words to try to say the same thing, next. "That was beautiful," I whispered to her.

Around us, people were applauding.

4

In the back of the car on the way home for a final reception I had my arms around two of my children.

Sofie sat up front. She was feeling her way that day, hovering in the shadows. She had asked to sit behind the kids and me at the cemetery. She told me in advance that on that one day she did not wish to be a curiosity to people who remained unaware of the slice of Lauren's history that included her birth.

In my heart Sofie was already one of my children. God, my kids. My salvation. We had a life to build together without their mother. They got me out of bed in the morning. They gave me a reason not to end the day in a chemical stupor.

At times I was disbelieving about what had happened — *how can this be true, how can this be my life?* — but I didn't feel sorry for myself. I was determined that the moment should be profound for us. That it should honor an end. And that it should announce a necessary beginning. If I could do that, I told myself, I might sleep.

Ha. I didn't sleep at all that night. Or the night after.

The night before the funeral was the first time that I dialed Diane's cell phone number since that morning, the one when she stepped into my office and shot Lauren in the back. I was a bit of a coward; I made the call from a blocked landline that identified me as PRIVATE CALLER.

I wanted to ask Diane why she killed Lauren. I did not know the answer.

I also wanted to ask her how she was doing, or scream at her that she was getting what she deserved. As the phone rang I was unsure what I would ask.

She didn't answer; the call rolled over to voicemail. If she had picked up, I might have killed the call. I would have felt like killing something. If I ran into Diane on the street, I would have to choose between slapping her across the face and strangling her.

Or giving her a hug.

I remained confused about that morning. Everything else? All the anger and despair and hope and promise was there in the morning, and again on the morning after that. For days I searched for the sign of a new beginning. After a week or so I stopped looking. I feared that a new mundane was settling in, which meant that I would need to create my own new beginning.

Did I have the resolve, the will, the energy, the vision, to pull that off?

No. But I had the kids. I would do it for them. With them.

A friend who had recently managed to create a lucrative new career from the ashes of the 2008 financial collapse had told me that "personal reinvention is an underappreciated skill."

It was apparently my turn to learn if she was right.

5

The day after the burial I began to get phone calls about Gracie's dance.

Producers. Local TV at first. I politely declined their requests for interviews.

By late morning a new set of phone calls began to arrive from bookers with the national morning shows. *Today, Good Morning America, Fox & Friends.* By that afternoon, a booker from *Ellen* was on the line. Then one representing Katie Couric. Others of a similar ilk soon followed.

After I declined the bookers' overtures I would hear from their producers. Further declinations earned me calls from the shows' executive producers. The executive producers all wanted the same thing the bookers had wanted, which was the same thing that the local producers had wanted.

They wanted Grace. They wanted to fly Gracie to New York or to LA to be on their shows. They wanted to be first.

I asked each of them why. Partly, I asked for my amusement. Partly, I was wondering if I was missing something. No one had a good answer for me beyond a reference to her celebrity on YouTube. As in "YouTube, you idiot."

"What she did was so special," one insisted. "People need to meet her, to know her," another one said. She said it three times during a breathless one-minute plea.

All I could think was *No, they don't.*

The next day at 7:12 A.M. — I allowed that it was 9:12 Eastern — the reality show bookers and producers started calling with their pleas.

Gracie could have a special onetime appearance on *Dancing with the Stars.* Or do a solo while the judges deliberated something else — I didn't know what — on *So You Think You Can Dance.* Perhaps Grace would be interested in submitting a video for consideration on *America's Got Talent?*

The producers sensed my reticence before they felt my resolve. To forestall that resolve they offered me an opportunity for a conversation with the talent, as though my determination could be erased, or my parental judgment demolished, by the chance to have a breathless chat with Nigel Lythgoe. I thought they'd made him up, but he was a real person. I checked Wikipedia.

Gracie was aware of her nascent Web fame. Her friends showed her the YouTube video hours before I learned that someone at the funeral had recorded it. My daughter was a trending topic on Twitter — the hashtag was #dancinggravegirl — before I had scrambled to sign up for access to Twitter, long before I figured out what a hashtag was, well before I began to comprehend why or how my daughter had been assigned one, or how I could track what was happening to my daughter's sudden damn fame online.

Jonas became my guide. That was nothing new. Jonas was often my guide.

Grace was conflicted about it all. She liked the attention. Celebrity was a big deal for Grace and her friends.

Like the producers and the bookers, though, Gracie could sense my reluctance. She could tell that I didn't want her to dive in.

At dinner two nights after Lauren's funeral, Jonas and Sofie and Gracie and I spoke about the flood of invitations I had been juggling for Gracie to appear on national television. Sofie answered Grace's questions about what all the attention might mean. Whether it would be fun. Sofie's cross-cultural perspective was incisive. Her birth father worked in national news production in Holland. Sofie had an intuitive feel for the enchantment and for the potential pitfalls.

She was, I thought, beautifully jaded about it all. I could feel her bias — she was a skeptic — but Gracie seemed immune to skepticism, which was worrisome to me as the conversation progressed. Jonas stayed quiet. Until the end of the discussion.

At the very end Gracie asked Jonas what he thought. Actually, she didn't ask on her own. At the very end I suggested she ask her brother what he thought. I was hoping for some help. Until then Jonas had been acting as though the whole conversation was an annoying intrusion into what otherwise could have been a perfect evening to write line after line of code in C++. I thought the language was C++. I was unsure.

Once his silent grousing was complete, he said, "They care about you because you danced at Mom's funeral. Not because you danced. Not because you're great. I mean you're okay, Grace. At dancing. That's not it.

"But the next time, if you do what they want you to do, if you dance on TV, there

won't be a funeral. You'll just be a girl dancing by herself on TV. It won't be the same.
Not for you. Not for any of them. Not for
the people who see you who have already
seen you dance on YouTube.

"When everything is over they'll be done
with you, and I think you'll wish you never
did it. What you did for Mom was kind of
great. I don't want you to wish you never
did it."

I loved the fact that when Jonas dissed his
sister he usually squeezed a compliment in
there, too. He was a young master of the
spoonful-of-sugar diss.

Gracie looked at Sofie. Sofie nodded.
"Our brother is smart. Next time — if you
go on those shows — you'll just be a girl
dancing. It won't be special the second
time. Not for you. Not for anyone watching
who has seen the clip."

Jonas said, "You don't want to go on those
shows anyway, Grace. They're lame."

Grace said, "They're not lame."

Sofie nodded. She was agreeing with
everyone, all at the same time. She was
blessed with the kind of personality that allowed her to get away with it.

Seeing Sofie in action, I became hyperaware that I wasn't. Blessed with that kind
of personality. I recognized, too, that that

was important to know. Going forward.

The family discussion ended. I hoped that the impact of Gracie's brush with quasi-fame would fade within days.

Again I was wrong. The echoes that continued to sound were not at all what I was expecting. The ones that were most surprising came from the bell that would be rung 2,763,912 times on YouTube.

Some people I once knew were among the bell-ringers.

6

During the earliest hours of the blurry day after the one when Lauren was shot, I had called Grace and Jonas to the hospital so that they would have a chance to say good-bye to their mother, who I thought was dying imminently. They arrived in the darkness with a police escort arranged on the fly by Sam Purdy's partner, Lucy.

I should not have been surprised that Lauren and I were out of synch. Even at the end, about her death. I was not surprised that Lauren was stubborn until the end. Three more vigils would follow that first one, but Lauren didn't get around to dying until twenty days later. At no time during those twenty days did anything resembling hope emerge about her condition. She lived tentatively but tenaciously, furiously, and sometimes even frustratingly. But she lived in biological definition only. Her brain stem barked orders none of us heard and her organs did what they could to fulfill those orders.

I wondered if anything else was going on with her. Consciously. The kids wondered. Our friends wondered. But the machines said no. The doctors said no.

My heart said no, too. I didn't feel her presence.

I sat with her and spoke to her for hours every day, mostly sharing old memories and asking new questions, but she showed no indication that she heard any of it.

She never talked back, or shifted her eyes, or squeezed my hand.

She farted once when Grace was with me. About most things Grace was open-minded. She said she thought the fart meant something. I suggested that it did not.

I talked with Lauren about my love for her. How it felt different at the end than it did at the beginning. I told her I wished she could tell me more about her love for me. Whether it felt different at the end than at the beginning.

I became adept at keeping her nails trimmed and polished the way she liked. I brushed her black hair but no matter how much I brushed it, I couldn't keep it from losing its luster. I was diligent about keeping her lips moist, and her cuticles creamed, because she'd always despised them to be dry. I rubbed her feet until the Colorado calluses on her heels became supple for the first time in years.

Each day I would spend minutes or even hours looking for meaning and metaphor in her apparent determination to stay alive, but I never found anything that convinced me that what I was seeing was anything more than evolution and biology and chemistry at work. I never once managed to discover any comfort in allowing myself a short or long flight toward a fantasy that my wife would recover and rejoin me. And the kids.

I knew from the moment that I accepted what had happened that morning that I wasn't awaiting a miracle. I was awaiting my wife's death.

I was not eager for it. I never prayed for it. I never felt impatience about it.

What she proved to me at the end was that her belief seemed to be that life itself could be more important than living. But she never proved to me that was a good thing.

Visitors came and went for the first week and a half at the hospital, for the last ten days at our home under the care of hospice. Given the circumstances — news and rumors that Lauren had been shot for no sane reason by my best friend spilled like flood-water across the Boulder Valley floor — almost everyone who visited approached the tragedy with befuddlement and the kind of curiosity that causes even kind inquiries to end up misshapen by careless words and by the aftereffects of intoxicating gossip.

During the hospital visits neither her friends, nor my friends, nor our friends, knew what to say. I did. I came to know what to say. I would greet the visitors warmly, take their hands in mine, and thank them for coming.

I was delighted to see some of the visitors. Too few, probably, but that was me.

By and large, the people I was happiest to see were the people whose grief about Lauren's condition was as real as my own. The people whose confusion about fate and finality was as real as my own.

I found myself most confused by the people who seemed to believe they under-stood what was going on. They baffled me.

After the awkward first few minutes that most of Lauren's visitors would spend either staring at my unresponsive wife or doing everything they could to avoid looking at my unresponsive wife, I would inevitably be ready for the well-meaning guests to leave.

Some sensed it. They left. I thanked them, again, for coming. I completely empathized with their instinct to be by her side, even momentarily, and I sympathized with the helplessness they felt while they were actually sitting at her unresponsive side.

I never thanked the guests for leaving quickly, but I felt gratitude for that, too. I let each visitor know how much Lauren would appreciate her time with them.

Others would arrive at Lauren's room like pilgrims. They came with a certainty that a hospital visit had to be of some predetermined length in order to count on some ledger kept somewhere. About such things. When people with that mind-set visited we would sit on opposite sides of Lauren's bed and pretend that she wasn't there while we conversed about something that wasn't important, or that we couldn't influence.

The weather. The wildfires. The coming solstice. The damn Broncos. Global warming was a frequent topic.

Or we'd talk about things that were important but weren't germane. My kids. Their kids. The looming holidays. The future.

And politics. Politics it turned out was a safe topic at the bedside of a coma victim. Religion? Not so much. Who knew?

At ten minutes, or fifteen — whatever

time-target they'd arrived with in their minds — the ledger could be marked. The visit counted. The pilgrims would discreetly check their watches or the clocks on their phones and realize they were free to leave.

I thanked them for coming. If they had handed me a document to verify their efforts, I would have gladly stamped it for them. Added my initials.

Among the first visitors was her assistant at the DA's office, Andrew. Andrew's family's roots were in Eastern Europe. His surname was a jumble of consonants that I had learned to pronounce only from hearing Lauren's repetitions. I couldn't recall ever seeing his name written out.

I had no idea how to combine consonants to make them sound like his last name. If God announced to me that Lauren would rise from her bed if only I could spell Andrew's surname, Lauren would have expired among the ruins of my misordered consonants.

Andrew missed Lauren. He arrived at the hospital carrying calla lilies, one of her favorites. Andrew said, "She loves these."

"She does, Andrew," I said, choking back tears. I hugged him. In an almost whisper, he said, "When the time comes, I will bring her things from the office for you. I have them set aside at my apartment. Some of them are personal. Things she had going."

As we talked I learned that his family was from Hungary, a few dozen kilometers from the Buda side of the Danube. He tried to help me spell his last name by teaching me a trick to remember the order of the consonants. I memorized the mnemonic, but then the vowels tripped me up.

Before he turned to leave he reached into a lapel pocket and pulled out a deep-red Field Notes memo book. I recognized it instantly. He said, "This one is blank. From the stash I kept for her. If you run across a yellow one of these, would you let me know? I number — numbered — and dated them all for her. To keep track. A yellow one is missing. It was on her desk. That morning."

"Did you say yellow?"

Lauren was addicted to the tough little notebooks. She liked that they were flexible and almost flat, that they fit anywhere — whether in a slender purse pocket, or the back pocket of her tightest jeans — and she liked that they were graph paper, not lined paper. For Lauren, having MS and writing between lines didn't get along. For Lauren, double vision, flawed dexterity, and the tiny keyboard of her smartphone often combined to create frustration. She carried two Field Notes notebooks with her most of the time. The red ones were for work. The blue ones were for family. One of each was always close by — in her purse, or by the kitchen phone, or on her bedside table — often paired by a rubber band.

In the blue Field Notes she would jot down changes or additions to the family schedule that she would later add to the big calendar on the fridge, or thoughts, or personal things she was eager to recall. A brand of body lotion she wanted to try. Grace's new friend's mother's name. Jonas's math teacher's email. A Christmas gift idea for the kids that came to her in July. A wine she liked. A promising recipe. Her determination to eat more chia seeds.

In the red Field Notes — those were the work versions — I never knew what she wrote. Work things. Privileged things. Those thoughts were not intended for my eyes.

We had each, always, respected the sanctity of the other's work.

Andrew confirmed he'd said "yellow." I said, "It wasn't with her when —"

Andrew rescued me from having to complete the sentence. "No, she'd left it with me, to transcribe some notes and look into something, before she went to your office.

71

That's how we worked. She would put my initials on certain pages. I would take the information from those pages to put dates on her calendar, or add phone numbers or email addresses to her contacts, or to call someone with a follow-up on a subpoena or a warrant or a legal question about a case, or to get back to a detective about a witness statement. But when I got back to the office after the Dome Fire evacuation, the yellow notebook she had given me before she went to see you was missing."

I clarified. "I knew about the system with the red notebooks. She did something similar herself with the blue ones at home, late at night in bed. Were the yellow ones" — I did not recall ever seeing a yellow one — "for work, too?"

Andrew said, "Not exactly. They were something else she was doing. The yellow ones were for ongoing . . . projects."

"What category? Blue was home. Red was work. Yellow was . . . ?"

"Yellow was . . . work, but not quite work. Okay? If you see it, please let me know. I don't think she would want it missing."

Andrew's visit that day was followed by a group visit from most of the infield of Lauren's old softball team. The hospital chaplain interrupted that gathering. He was

72

certain he could be of some help to Lauren. I wasn't. So certain.

On another day, with less on my mind, Andrew's missing Field Notes puzzle might have stuck in my brain as important. That day it didn't.

Not much was sticking in my head those days.

Herding visitors felt really, really important.

7

Sam had been with me at Lauren's bedside the first night, the one that the doctors initially expected her to die. The doctors had been wrong. It happens.

He came by to visit again a few days later. During Sam's first visit at the hospital he was my friend, in all good ways. During the second visit he was my partner in crime. As we hugged — so not Sam's thing — he whispered, "Let's walk and talk. Come on. Follow me. Shhh."

We walked corridors, then up two flights of stairs. When I would begin to speak, Sam would shake his head. We'd walk a little more. I would try again. He would indicate *not yet.*

Like my wife, the old hospital was waiting to die. Like my wife, the old hospital felt, even smelled, like it was waiting to die. A new facility was being constructed across town.

I was aware that, unlike my wife, Community Hospital would have a second life.

Sam and I finally found our way into an empty room at the end of a long corridor. The rooms in that wing were mostly occupied by elderly people with recently replaced hips or knees. He closed the door. We walked into the adjoining bathroom. He closed that door. He turned on the water in the sink, then opened the faucet inside a shower that was spacious enough to wash a motorcycle, and then he flushed the toilet.

The toilet flushed as though it were tasked to evacuate a large swamp in a single flush.

The cacophony of mini-Niagaras around us created a curtain of white noise. Sam said, "The DA knows something. A little of it? Almost all of it? I don't know. Is he guessing? I don't know. I'm hearing things second- or thirdhand, but I don't have any eyes on this. I'm pretty sure the DA has a subpoena out, maybe even a warrant, and —"

"Which DA? Elliot? Or Weld County?"

"Our DA. Boulder. Elliot."

Figured. *Shit.* "For Frederick?"

"Yeah. I guess. Sure. What else?"

"You said 'warrant'? Are we going to be arrested?"

"A warrant would be for surveillance,

though a subpoena might suffice, depending. One of us, both of us, I don't know. My guy didn't know. But he thinks it's our phones. That would be the warrant, but it may just be electronic communications, which we — I mean cops — can do with a subpoena, or even less. We have to assume that Frederick isn't dead."

He flushed the toilet again. The suction created back-pressure in my sinuses.

The *Frederick* Sam was alluding to wasn't a guy. It was a town. The town where Sam had staged a murder so that it looked like a suicide over three years before. The victim, a woman Sam had dated, was planning — imminently — to kill our kids. Sam's. Mine.

I had been a willing conspirator after the fact. As the ensuing months became years, Sam and I grew complacent, thinking we'd gotten away with it. Our complacency was long gone. The possibility of fresh surveillance underscored our vulnerability.

He went on. "We — you — have to assume they're listening to us when and where they can. Phone, email, text? Possibly. With your mobile? If you don't want them to be able to track you with GPS, you have to turn that function off on your phone. If you don't want to be tracked by triangulation from cell towers, you have to turn your phone off completely. Power it down, or pull the SIM card. At least put it on airplane mode. If you're feeling completely paranoid, yank the battery."

I was suddenly feeling pretty close to completely paranoid. I said, "Really? They do that? They track people that way?"

" 'They' is me," Sam said. "And, yes. We do. It's not complicated. What you call your smartphone, we call our target's 'tracker.' If your particular provider is cooperative when we request information, we can know things about you that you don't know about yourself. Where you've been, who you've talked to, who you text. How many times you stop at Liquor Mart, or go to McDonald's. GPS tells a lot of stories."

"My provider? Is it one of the cooperative ones?" Sam didn't reply. "Are they — you — allowed to do that? Track people that way on their . . . what, trackers?"

Sam puffed out his cheeks. Then he said, "There are safeguards. But we have workarounds, ways around the safeguards. Let's say there are occasional abuses. Safest thing for you? Get a burner. Use it for a while. Toss it. Get another."

"I don't know what a burner is. And what's 'a while'?"

"A burner is to a cell phone what a throw-down is to a piece. Provides anonymity."

What? A small part of my cortex went up in flames. I thought I could smell the neural smoke. "Not a good moment for analogies, Sam."

"A burner is a cheap prepaid phone. Cheap makes it disposable. Lie about your name when you buy it, use cash, and it's anonymous. That defeats surveillance. It's the opposite of a tracker. We don't know it's yours, so we can't follow it. Or you."

"Where would I get one?"

Sam scratched behind his ear. He flushed the toilet again. "I hear they're available at convenience stores. Gas stations. Walmart."

"Walmart? You hear? Do you have one?"

"Never mind that," he said. "Let's say you don't get a burner. If we can't meet face-to-face and you need to talk to me, call my cell three times in a row from a public phone. Hang up after one ring. I'll call you back at that location as soon as I can get to a pay phone. Same for me if I need to reach you."

"What about at home? Can we talk there?"

Sam's new girlfriend, Ophelia, lived across the dirt lane from the kids and me in Spanish Hills. On nights when Sam wasn't being single dad to his son, Simon, at his little bungalow a few blocks from the hospital where we were speaking, he could reliably be found in Ophelia's doublewide, yards across the lane from my family.

"The scenic overlook on 36 gives them line of sight to the lane. Line of sight allows photography and maybe even directional mics. I don't think they'll do that, but . . . hell, you never know. If Elliot has a bug in his ass about this . . ."

"Sam, I wasn't there — in Frederick — when that woman died. I was in New Mexico with Jonas. I can't be a suspect in Elliot's eyes. I have an . . ." My mind had latched on to the word *burner* and wouldn't let in the new word I needed.

"The word you're looking for is *alibi* and, no, you don't have one."

"I was in New Mexico with a witness. That's the definition of an alibi."

"The kid in Frederick? Elias Tres? Remember, he's raised doubts about the day Currie died. There are people in Weld County who think the kid is right, that the coroner was wrong. That means that there are people who think that the date of her death is off by one day. Add that day into the equation and you were back from New Mexico with Jonas. Your alibi could evaporate."

"Are you telling me that Elliot thinks I

killed her?"

"I don't know. What I'm telling you is that I don't think you can count on having an alibi. Time of death — her day of death — is in flux."

I felt bewildered. *Flux* didn't sound like a real word. I repeated it a few times in my head but kept thinking it had something to do with plumbing, which made no sense. Sam asked me if I was okay. I didn't think it wise to reveal the whole *flux* problem I was experiencing.

I said, "My car just *happened* to be in Frederick that night?" That was a cheap shot. Sam nodded his acknowledgment. "It was there because you drove it there, Sam." He nodded again. I had tears in my eyes. "I don't need this right now."

"The grief?" he asked. "How is it going?"

I had no answer for him. I still felt more shock than sorrow.

That would change.

"Me?" Sam said. "I'm finding it's important to pay attention to what I can see because of the void. The things that are apparent because of what's gone."

Those words made no sense to me either. They became part of the *flux* conundrum I was experiencing. I told him I was glad he was finding that helpful.

Sam said, "Remember clean hands? I got your back, Alan. Don't forget that. I know you got mine. You start to fall? I catch you. I start to fall? You catch me. Right?"

I flushed the toilet. *Swoooosh.* I said, "Sure. That's the deal. I need to get back to Lauren." He didn't move out of my way. I changed the subject. "Yesterday? Lauren got a get-well card from Michael McClelland. How many times do we have to stop him? What happens the one time we fail?"

McClelland was the man who had sent the woman in Frederick to kill our kids. He was in state prison. He created his mayhem by proxy.

Sam's shoulders dropped. He was so concerned with dodging a current bullet, he hadn't thought about the likely future bullets that would come our way from McClelland.

I needed Sam right then. More than ever. But I was growing concerned that the moment our interests failed to coincide about what happened that night in Frederick, I would lose him. As a friend. As an ally.

The consequences of losing him could be catastrophic. I had lost too much already.

I squeezed past him. On my way back to Lauren's bedside I tried again to understand what Sam meant about seeing things because of the void. I got nowhere.

I feared Sam was getting ready to wash his clean hands. Of me.

I gradually reached an acceptance that Lauren's death might not be imminent. I knew she would die. I knew she would prefer to die at home.

I moved her to Spanish Hills so she could feel some solace and some familiarity before she died. I made room in the master bedroom for a hospital bed. I used our savings to pay for twenty-four-hour care.

Kind, generous people from hospice became my angels by keeping her in comfort while she got around to dying at home.

She would die, I knew by then, at her own pace.

8

SAM AND LUCY

Lucy took the empty stool next to Sam at the bar. They each said, "Hey."

She asked, "You see Alan?"

Sam said, "He's at the hospital almost all the time. I just left him. Lauren is waiting to die. Alan is waiting for something. It's all so sad I don't know what to say."

She pointed at Sam's pint glass. "Buy you another?" Sam was finishing his first.

"Love one."

Meeting for a beer had been Lucy's idea. She had chosen the bar. Sam knew immediately that Shine wasn't his kind of saloon the way kale isn't his kind of food. Sam figured she had dragged him to Shine to broaden his experience, which she considered her duty, or merely to irritate him, which she considered her prerogative. She nodded at the bartender, raising two fingers.

"They make their own beer, Sam. It's

pretty good."

"In Boulder everyone but us has a Ph.D., and just about everyone makes their own beer. I may be the only guy in town who exclusively drinks other people's beer."

"Feeling cranky? Maybe I can help. I went back and read the ME's Prado report. Vic had a freshly broken index finger on his left hand. A twisting injury. Spiral fracture."

"Well," Sam said. "That is interesting. He was a southpaw. Huh."

"Excuse me? Spiral? Twisting? I'm thinking the damn bungee," Lucy said. "Like his finger got caught in the trigger guard. You know, after."

"That's interesting, too."

"And we got ballistics back on the handgun," she said.

Sam said, "Took them long enough."

"Prado isn't exactly high priority. People are on vacation. The gun was a mess. Required rehab before they could examine it."

"I was talking to Ophelia about Prado," Sam said. "She thinks the roommates were gay. I didn't give that a thought. It's been only a decade, but it's a different world."

"World didn't change," Lucy said. "Maybe you did. Would it alter your view of the case?"

"Lovers' quarrel? Wasn't on my radar then. Tell me about the ballistics. Tell me something that makes me happy about Prado." He drank a third of his beer.

"First, I got you a present. On eBay." She placed a padded envelope on the bar.

Sam slid an old postcard in a protective sleeve from the envelope.

Lucy said, "That right there is the one and only Ivy Baldwin, on his high wire, back in the day. 1906. 1908. I'm not sure which. Early on."

"No shit? Wow. Look at him. Look . . . at . . . him. How high up is he?"

"Almost six hundred feet. And the wire is almost the same distance across. No fucking harness. He falls, he's toast. No, maybe more like butter. Or jam."

"No harness? If he did that today he'd get a two-hour special on ESPN. Prime time. He'd be a sensation. Jimmy Kimmel would love him. He'd make Ivy a regular."

"You are right, Sam Purdy."

"This is really sweet of you, Lucy. Did this postcard cost you a fortune?"

"Your mother taught you better than to ask questions like that."

"Thank you. I'm touched."

"My pleasure." She waited until he returned the photo to the envelope before she

85

went on. She said, "Jumble Guy? Did you hear? He actually scratched his way up to the LT's office. Turns out the guy is almost connected."

Sam snapped his head in her direction. "Jumble Guy talked to our lieutenant?"

Lucy said, "Jumble Guy is demanding — *demanding* — that we clear his name."

Sam found that so funny he snorted beer out of his nose. They lost a minute arguing about whether the white shit floating on top of Sam's pint was beer foam or snot.

Lucy pulled the ballistics report from her shoulder bag. "Yada, yada. Science, science. A lot of numbers. Boilerplate. Dot, dot, dot. Drumroll." She mimed a drumroll.

Sam thought her mimicry was more Revolutionary War marching band than anything rock 'n' roll. He said, "Not in the mood, Luce."

"You never are. I didn't pick you to be my partner because you're fun."

"For the record, Lucy, I picked you."

"The first time. After your suspension? I did the picking. But whatever." She shook the pages. "The ballistics are of no help. It's a sign from the universe."

"What kind of no help?"

"The not-conclusive kind."

"Really? Fu —" Sam said.

Lucy said, "Fu — ?"

"This whole case is not conclusive. But what exactly? Slug fired from the revolver we recovered on Prado doesn't match the slug from the guy's skull?"

Lucy said, "On further review they decided the original slug is too damaged for a comparison."

"No equivocation?"

"None." She placed the pages in front of him with dramatic deference, as though Sam were Richard Nixon and she Rose Mary Woods in a hoop skirt. "Carson wrote the report." She stabbed at the final paragraph. "You know Carson. The man hates inconclusive. Even when things are inconclusive. If he says it's inconclusive it's really, really inconclusive."

Sam gave no indication he'd noted any irony in Lucy's Rose Mary Woods–ish obsequiousness. He dug his reading glasses from his shirt pocket. He found the end of his nose on the first try. Then he turned back to the first page, skimmed it, and went back to the second. To himself, as much as to Lucy, he said, "We don't even know if our gun is the weapon that killed our guy."

"It's a reasonable assumption. Especially given the bungee and the vic's broken index finger. The twisting injury? That's great evidence. Can I summarize what I think we know?" Sam didn't reply. Lucy interpreted his silence as license. "We know a long bungee was hooked over the top of the chimney cap. The bungee was attached to a chain that was bolted to the trigger guard of the handgun Jumble Guy found. The gun probably hung a few inches above or below the flue. Someplace the vic could reach it."

"What don't we know?" Sam said. He was still examining the beer foam for snot.

"We don't know whose gun it was, why it was hanging in the chimney, or who put it there. And we don't know how the vic got the gun."

Sam said, "The vic, Luce? He had a name. Marshall John Doctor. He was a twenty-nine-year-old psychologist who treated children, abused kids. Worked at the Kempe Center. He had a family in Oregon. I bet they loved him."

Lucy leaned back in reaction to Sam's soliloquy. "Okay. Noted." She hesitated before she added, "So the guy was 'Doctor Doctor'? I didn't put that together. Wonder if his patients called him that. You ever read *Catch-22*? Probably not your kind of book."

"I read it. People have stories. Vics have stories. The people they leave behind have stories. He was Marshall John Doctor,

Ph.D. We get disrespectful sometimes. Both of us. Usually it's good, cuts the tension. I don't mind. But not this time."

Lucy waited for a punch line. One didn't arrive. "Is this an Ophelia influence?"

"This is me talking," Sam said. "Me."

"Bullshit. That woman has you whipped." Sam checked to see if she was smiling. She was. She said, "You are whipped, Sammy. Can we be done with this case? Or are you going to ask for budget to look for DNA from that revolver? A little blood or tissue around the muzzle?"

Sam couldn't tell if she was joking. "Wait. Latents or trace?"

"Off the handgun? No trace. Only latents were Jumble Guy's. Partials. Index finger and thumb. They couldn't lift anything old. Too much time and exposure."

"He touched it? I knew he touched it." Sam sighed. "Are we done? Yeah. No. After all this time? I don't know. Probably not. I should let this go, right?"

"Probably." She spun on her stool. "The ballistics is good news in a way. If the gun matched the slug, we'd have to figure this out. Without a match, the gun is an artifact. We can leave Prado where it is. Manner stays undetermined. Life goes on."

"Tell that to the broken trigger finger,"

Sam said. "The twisted broken trigger finger. You were checking on the handgun registration. Anything? Background check?"

"Almost forgot. I found the original owner, but it doesn't add much." Lucy pulled another sheet of paper from the file. "Gun was purchased new from a reputable dealer in 1988 by a fifty-three-year-old woman in Iowa. I ran her. She had a couple of cute priors — one for shoplifting some fancy panties from a local ladies store, and one for disturbing the peace at a funeral — before she died in 1998.

"There's no record of what happened to the gun after her death. Or to the fancy panties, for that matter. No hits on the weapon between the date of purchase and now."

"She have a name?"

Lucy looked. "Beulah Baxter. Of the Donnellson, Iowa, Baxters."

Sam snorted. No beer exited his nose. He said, "Second rule? Of guns?"

"Oh great, here we go," said Lucy. She'd grown wary of Sam's second rules.

Sam used his pronouncement voice. He said, "The lives of guns are like the lives of people. They often don't get interesting until after they leave home."

"You just come up with that?"

He said, "Ms. Baxter's death in 1998? Cause? Manner?"

"Negative on the nefarious. I ordered a death certificate, which hasn't arrived, but the woman at the county clerk's office told me on the phone that Ms. Baxter's demise was purely organic — some rare cancer."

Lucy was holding the remaining sheets of paper from the thin file she had put together. Sam held out his hand. All of the records had originated in the predigital age. Lucy handed him the printed versions of records that someone had photocopied from the originals before somebody else had scanned them into cloud eternity. Included among the papers were the original handgun registration form and the amusing rap sheet from Iowa with the arrest for the fancy panties.

Sam shuffled through them twice. "Absent DNA or a miracle, we basically have a dead end on the weapon after it was purchased in 1998?" Sam asked as he scanned the pages. "Over a decade of dead air?"

"The purchase was in 1988. Beulah died in '98. We assume she had the gun in between, but we don't know that for sure. But we do know where the gun's been since September of 2001, Sam. It's been hanging in that damn fireplace on Prado."

"Couldn't the gun have been put in the chimney sometime after Doctor's death?"

She made a face. "That's possible, in the sense that anything is possible. Likely though? I think the big question is how the gun got from Iowa to Boulder after it left home to begin, you know, its interesting life back in 1998."

He said, "I was hopeful on the ballistics." He ran his hand over the top of his head as though it were a bowling ball and he was desperate to locate the finger holes in the dark.

Lucy could tell that Sam was contemplating the wisdom of a third beer. "Drop this, Sam. Let it go. And no more beer. You're driving. Two's enough."

"What? A deal? Do me this: Go to the archives. In person. I want to see any photos we have from the scene. All of them. Autopsy, too. That finger? Definitely. Damn. Wait — No. No trail, Luce. No requisition. Take cell phone photos of the file. We can work from those for now. If there's nothing there, there's nothing there. I'll drop it."

Lucy gave it some thought. Then she nodded. "Deal."

"It's better if people don't know what we're after. Be as discreet as you can be."

"What are you thinking, Sam?" She waved

the bartender off.

"There was some screwy stuff with this case. Until I know what it all means, until we decide to follow up on it or not, I don't want anyone to know that we're looking."

"What was screwy?"

"Did I tell you I got reassigned after one day?"

"You didn't. That explains all you don't know."

"Deputy DA Crowder got reassigned, too. One day. Now, the damn bungee. The broken finger? Mostly the whole disappearing gun thing. Screwy."

"It was that week, Sam. Explains a lot."

"And — and — the 911 call was anonymous, Luce. From a pay phone."

"Somebody didn't want to get involved. Happens all the time, Sam."

"Or maybe somebody didn't want us to know he'd already been there. That happens all the time, too. If we can find that person, we might have a witness. Maybe put this to bed for reals."

Lucy packed up the evidence. Sam gazed around the room as though he had just sat down and recognized the peculiarity of his surroundings. He said, "Is this place like a yoga bar, Lucy? Is that what this is? Is that some new . . . thing I don't know about?

Half these people look like they're dying for a chance to roll out their mats and break into a child's pose. The other half look like they just finished meditating."

She laughed. Then she said, "Shine is about nourishing, Sam. In all ways."

"God help me," Sam said.

"That too," Lucy said. "That too."

9

ALAN

Sofie's presence was a godsend. After the funeral she asked her adoptive parents and her birth father, Joost — he was the family emissary who had accompanied her to Boulder at the beginning of the visit — to permit her to stay through the end of the year so she could spend time with her American siblings.

The Dutch parental council unanimously consented.

I had wanted to dislike Joost, but I couldn't. Sofie's biological father was a decent, straightforward man who obviously loved his daughter. That he'd held my likely naked wife in his arms only a few years before was a definite limiting factor in any future friendship for him and me. In the grand scheme of my life right then? I would deal.

Thanksgiving passed. I had no trouble

finding things to be thankful for. I tried not to focus on the things I was furious about. But the rituals that November?

I couldn't face them. No turkey for us. I grilled quail. I was amazed at how little meat there was on each quail. I should have marinated an entire covey. Or two coveys. If he were in the right mood Jonas could consume an entire covey in a sitting.

I began thinking that I needed to regroup in time for December's celebrations.

I forced myself to find the resolve to try to mount a decent Chanukah for Jonas and a decent Christmas for Grace. I enlisted Sofie's help; she got into the spirit with, to me, unfamiliar Dutch gusto. I surfed the wake of her enthusiasm as we decorated the house. Sofie highlighted some alluring cultural touches from the Netherlands.

By the first of December the family room was blue and white and red and green all over. Festive? Kind of. Confusing? Absolutely. In a good way.

Sinterklaas arrived in Spanish Hills before Chanukah, which arrived that year long after Santa Claus showed up in the malls, but well before Christmas morning. Black Peter's arrival was a revelation to me — his dark Dutch holiday role felt custom-made for my mood — but I never really understood his cultural significance in Holland's version of the Nativity. Sofie stayed up late with me on Christmas Eve. I drank. She didn't. For me, it was an opportunity to get to know her better. That part was great. She saw the time as an opportunity to explain Black Peter and the role of Sinterklaas, but I'd had too much warm whiskey and I never quite got it.

Sofie baked a pastry called *kerstkrans* and a treat called *letterbanket.* Gracie assisted with the baking and spent an afternoon learning folk dances from her sister.

In another time, in other circumstances, the version of the holiday that we created that year would have been magical. But it wasn't another time. The circumstances weren't other; they were what they were. The holiday was interesting and ever distracting, but not magical. Better than I had any right to expect, but not magical.

Someone was missing. We didn't pretend otherwise.

One mid-December evening as we built up toward the clash of observances by juggling a growing number of cultural and religious symbols, the family celebration became too much — too ecumenical, or too multidenominational, or too pan-cultural. The menorah was beside the tree under the mistletoe above the wooden shoes placed just so on the edge of the hearth a few feet below the stockings hung by the chimney with care.

Jonas, who was born with a gift of clarity that I cherished, stopped his sisters as they were singing a carol that night — Sofie had arranged the song partly in Dutch, partly in English, with the chorus in Norwegian. I asked about the Norwegian. She explained that she liked the way it sounded.

Jonas stood before the second chorus of the folk song. He waved his arms and he said, "Wait, wait. What exactly are we celebrating? Right now, this very minute."

I opened my mouth to try to provide an answer and realized that I had no idea what we were celebrating. We just were. Because the calendar said it was time. And because we had a disparate but united family ensemble that allowed us to have a prayer of pulling it off. Together.

As our energy evaporated and the evening wound away, I got the kids to bed. Then I retreated to lie alone on the bed that I had shared with my wife. I was still prone there when I awoke in the middle of the night.

It was the first time I had fallen asleep in our bed since that morning. The one when

Lauren was shot. I couldn't get back to sleep.

The next morning I woke, as usual, in the guest room bed.

That was when I decided I needed to get back to work.

Or that I needed help. Most likely, I needed both.

My front-page notoriety, along with my long sabbatical from my practice, had left me with a fractured referral base and few active patients. I couldn't manufacture new patients but I was sure I could find myself a therapist. I knew a lot of therapists.

But I wasn't quite ready to be in therapy. That's what I kept telling myself.

10

Two days after Christmas Sofie found me in the master bedroom. The bedroom door was open, but she'd said, "Knock knock." Actually I thought she said, *"Klop klop."* When she stepped in I was standing in front of the open door to the walk-in closet.

I was tempted to ask her for a lesson about the differences in everyday onomatopoeia in English and Dutch. The inclination didn't last. I knew I lacked the requisite brain cells, language skills, and attention span.

I didn't have to say a thing to her about what I was doing in the closet. Or about how I was feeling. She recognized the hopelessness and the sadness in my eyes. She volunteered to help.

She was the perfect person for the job. She had a dog in the hunt. And that dog, as with all things Sofie, was well behaved. Sofie also possessed a natural talent to manage the other dogs already barking around my ankles.

Sofie was mine, yet she wasn't. Her very existence expanded my idea of family. Technically, as my wife's daughter from a time long before we'd met, she was my stepdaughter. But I was, at best, father number three to Sofie. Her birth father remained much involved in her life, and she continued to live with and be raised by adoptive parents I had never met, whose love for her was apparent in every breath she took. I felt such gratitude to all of them, the generous, loving people in Holland who raised her so well. I didn't know how I could have made it through the crisis without her presence in Colorado.

Sofie devised a plan on the spot. One of the things I was learning about her was that she usually had a plan. The first step in Sofie's plan involved making Lauren's things visible. That meant emptying the closets and the drawers and the boxes. Sofie gathered Lauren's hanging clothes and sorted them into categories that made sense to her. She set up tables in the bedroom for folded clothes and displayed all of my wife's things so that I could see each item.

The most organized portion of Lauren's closet had always been the section reserved for her footwear. Neat shelves below eye level displayed her current seasonal favorites. Well-marked boxes on high shelves identified other pairs — by date purchased, by type, sometimes along with a photo of the shoes. For our purposes, Sofie removed from the closet for display only the left shoe from each pair. She lined them, neatly nested together, against the floorboard on the longest wall in the bedroom.

I thought the many left shoes resembled a company of disembodied Rockettes in the midst of a right-leg high kick.

Sofie pinned Lauren's jewelry on a big board of pine — she fell into Dutch to identify the specific lumber for me — that she pulled from Peter's old wood shop. She hung the jewelry items with pushpins that became, for me, a connect-the-dots timeline of my marital relationship. I remembered every piece I had given to Lauren, when, and why.

Sofie neatly folded the lingerie. Altogether it took up remarkably little space. Seeing it in piles, with any anticipation of seeing it on my wife's body gone, the lace and silk had no allure for me.

Lauren had owned two dozen hats. I hadn't known that.

She'd had four canes. I had known that.

Sofie took a simple cardboard box and lined it with foil wrapping paper from the holiday just past. Some things went straight into that box. Sofie's decision making was not clear to me. I was fine with that.

She proposed a strategy. First, I would choose the sentimental pieces that I wanted to save for sentimental reasons. Whatever I would like, for whatever reason I would like it. Next, Gracie and Jonas would get to pick some things for themselves. "How many?" she asked me. I chose the number ten. Each of the kids, Sofie included, would find ten things they wanted, alternating turns.

"No," she said. "Grace first ten, then Jonas ten. Then me. Ten. That's best."

"A compromise. Alternate the first turn, so everyone gets a favorite. Then each of you pick nine." Sofie assented.

When the time came to do the choosing, I knew Jonas wouldn't select anything. I would pick some things for Jonas if and when he got stumped. Sofie volunteered to help me with that.

"Once the kids are done," I said, "you may take what you would like. You are almost her size. Take whatever you like, whatever you will wear. Whatever you will treasure. Whatever will help you remember her the way you wish to remember her."

"At the end," she said, "there will be much, still. You and I, Alan, will select some things to go here." She pointed at the foil-lined box. "This is for things that no one chooses, but that someone someday will wish that they had chosen."

It made me want to cry. I signed off on Sofie's plan.

What was left after Lauren's sisters took some things would go to the women's shelter and to Goodwill. It was a fine plan. But that was Sofie. She'd been born on another continent as the product of others' passion, misadventure, and serendipity, yet she'd arrived in my life as an intuitive expert on helping me plan my next chapter, whatever it turned out to be.

Sofie found an envelope in the inside pocket of Lauren's only peacoat.

The peacoat was Sofie's choice during round one. Sofie told me that her birth mother had been wearing the coat the time they met as adults. She named a canal in Amsterdam as the spot where they first saw each other.

The memory that the coat kindled for me was necessarily different from the joyful memory that it created for Sofie. My memories included the fact that Lauren had returned from that trip to the Netherlands partially paralyzed from an MS exacerbation. The exacerbation had occurred while she was in the arms — literally or figuratively I never knew only because I never asked — of Sofie's birth father, Joost, in Hilversum. The rendezvous with Joost had been Lauren's way of checking, up close and personal, to see if the flame still burned from the days of Sofie's conception. My wife's remorseful eyes had told me that for her, it did.

Lauren's paralysis meant that the chore of unpacking her things upon her return to Boulder became mine. The peacoat was among the things that I found folded in her luggage. I would be happy to see the coat out of the house, back to Holland.

Sofie read the name written on the outside of the envelope. "Elliot?" she asked me, placing the accent on the final syllable: *elly-OTT.* "Do you know Elliot?"

I nodded. My tongue was knotted. I was trying to find a good descriptor for Elliot. Lauren's friend? Her boss? Her adversary?

My adversary? I ruled out friend. I said, "She worked with him."

She handed me the envelope. "For him?" she asked.

"I guess," I said. "I will pass it on."

I tossed the sealed envelope on top of the box of Lauren's office things that her assistant, Andrew, had dropped by after I brought Lauren home from the hospital. Since the handwriting on the Elliot envelope appeared to be Andrew's, the general vicinity of the box from her office seemed like a fine place to let it age.

The envelope became part of the written record of Lauren's life that I knew I would need to tackle and digest at some point. I was becoming complacent at kicking that point in time further and further into the future. Her desk was cluttered with her written records. With mail, opened and not, and paperwork of all kinds. Personal, work, receipts, statements. Bills. The list went on and on. That piece of furniture — hell, that whole side of that anteroom — was an expanding repository of things that would require my clearheaded attention sooner rather than later.

The thought of diving in to that morass and sorting out what parts were germane to the conclusion of Lauren's life overwhelmed me. Of all the things I had to do to cope, I devoted most of my procrastination energy to that desk. Anything that involved paper and ink that could be put off, whether for a day, or for a month, or until tax season rolled around, went onto that desk. Or in its vicinity.

There I hoped it would spoil, or age, or even mature into irrelevance.

The elly-ott envelope became part of the list of potentially noxious things that I hoped would disintegrate into unimportance without my intervention.

I had always told my kids that procrastination has consequences.

The elly-ott envelope would prove me right.

11

Jonas and Gracie and I drove Sofie to DIA on the eve of New Year's Eve. Her flight was tucked between a big Boxing Day snowstorm and a more gentle snowfall that would arrive hours after she was in the air. She would fly nonstop to Reykjavík on Icelandair and connect from there for the final leg to her home not far from Amsterdam. She was excited to see Iceland in the middle of winter.

The kids and I spent the drive back to Boulder making plans to make plans to go to the Netherlands to visit Sofie. I made it clear that if I was paying, and I would be, I didn't think the trip would take place in the middle of winter.

Gracie began to lobby. She wanted to see polar bears *and* windmills *and* tulips. And the Northern Lights. And canals. And she wanted to have *rijsttafel* again with Sofie and with Sofie's other parents. All of them. She really, really liked Joost.

So, I thought, *did Lauren.* And oddly enough, so did I. Joost, it turned out, was a good man.

We were minutes from home in Spanish Hills when my cell rang. I answered it without taking my eyes from the road to check caller ID. I said, "Hello."

A female voice replied, "It's Izza Kane. Remember me?"

Oh yeah, I do. One of my other loose ends.

"I'm in the car. I don't like to talk and drive. Can I call you back in five minutes?"

"Will you? Really?" she asked.

"Yes."

"You've lied to me before."

I said, "That is true. Not this time. I will get back to you." She hung up.

Gracie asked, "Who was that?"

"Someone Daddy knows who wants to talk about your mom."

All honest. Though not at all forthcoming. Where adult things were concerned, Gracie usually didn't require forthcoming. Jonas, on the other hand, had learned the hard way about the territory and conventions of adult grief. He had lost more parents than most of us ever have to lose. He looked up from the game he was playing on his phone long enough to say to his sister, "Get used to it. Goes on and on. Phone's going to ring for months. Don't answer, ever — they'll talk to you, too, like they know you. They'll talk to anybody who picks up."

Sofie was as transparent a teenager as I'd ever met. Grace was an open book to me. Jonas? I searched for clues about his identity wherever I could find them. And I treasured every scrap he left lying around. Since Lauren's death, as far as I could tell, Jonas had been listening mostly to early Feist, live stuff I didn't even know was out there. The songs made me cry. Even the ones that weren't sad made me cry.

After his birth mother, Adrienne, died, he'd listened to a steady diet of Girlyman. I was trying to make sense of what the musical evolution meant for him. I couldn't.

I dropped the kids at home. I began to walk out the lane. Could I use my cell to call Izza or was it — my tracker — really bugged? What about the landline in the house?

What if her call was a setup? *Shit.* I returned to the house and told Jonas to watch his sister while I ran an errand. He gave me no indication he had heard me. But he didn't argue with me. I decided to believe that he had heard me, despite the earbuds in his ears, and that he would watch his sister.

I got back in the car and drove out South Boulder Road until I got to my favorite pay phone outside a convenience store on the outskirts of Louisville, the nearest town to Boulder's east. Some of my not-so-healthy paranoia also informed me that having a favorite pay phone probably wasn't a good thing from a security point of view. I made a mental note to find a new pay phone. Or two.

I dropped coins. I dialed with the tip of a key as I tried to keep from imagining what the crusty yellow shit between the buttons of the pay phone might be. "Hi," I said. "It's me, as promised."

"New number," Izza said.

"Different number. Landline."

"It wasn't five minutes."

"I underestimated. I am sorry."

"From my end, it's hard to tell the difference between underestimating and lying."

Her words, I thought, though accusatory, lacked zeal. I had prepared myself for Izza's wrath — I had earned Izza's wrath — but all I was getting was a matter-of-fact recounting of the fact that I'd dissembled. The paucity of zeal left me off balance.

"Guilty," I said. "I did mislead you." I allowed her an opportunity to respond. She didn't. I asked, "How is your father, Izza? I recall that he was ill."

Five seconds passed before she said, "He died last fall, Alan." Those words were spoken with no lack of zeal; they were sharpened to a fine edge.

"I am so sorry for your loss," I said.

"How did you know he was sick? My father?"

"You told me. That first day at the ranch? The day you walked me through the cottage. You were explaining to me that your father and Big Elias didn't get along well. That's when you explained that your dad was in and out of the hospital."

"I don't remember that part." She grew quiet. "I remember other parts better. The parts when you were deceiving me."

My clear disadvantage unnerved me. I didn't know what to say.

She said, "Did I mention anything else about them? My father? Or Elias Contopo?"

Izza's questions sounded sincere, not like the questions of someone setting a trap. I remained cautious; I knew I could be misreading her. I was adept at misreading women.

Lauren, not Izza, had told me that Big Elias had been blackmailing Izza's Irish father about his immigration status. Izza had never revealed that during my visits to the cottage. I reminded myself that I had to be careful with Izza — she had seen the drawing that Elias Tres Contopo had made the night that Sam had visited Frederick to commit murder.

"I think you said that they had been friends at one time. But no longer, that there was some tension between them." I suspected that Izza's father died unaware that his wife — raped by his ex-friend — was actually the mother of Big Elias's son, Segundo.

Izza had learned that part of her family history. But Izza did not know that I knew. That information, too, had come my way via Lauren.

"Yes," Izza said, as though my words had kindled a memory. "But I don't think I mentioned anything to you about Elias Contopo and his grandson, Elias Tres."

I was perplexed. Lauren had told me about Big Elias's abusive behavior toward his grandson, but I didn't recall that Izza had ever mentioned it to me. I was wondering if it was important. I considered the possibility that Izza had begun testing me.

"You spoke a little about Elias Tres. I got the sense that you are fond of him. Smart kid? But, no, you didn't talk about him and

113

his grandfather." I almost said "not to me." I didn't. *Whew.*

I was eager to believe that the purpose of this call was uncomplicated, that Izza was trying to clarify some things in her mind about our earlier meetings. I was trying to convince myself that I was fine with that motivation.

Then Izza said, "I saw your daughter dancing at your wife's funeral."

YouTube. Damn YouTube. My working hypothesis about the purpose of the call required some fine-tuning. Izza had learned I was married. And she knew that Lauren, my wife, was dead.

I fell back on the safe ground of apology. I wasn't sure what else I had to offer. "I am sorry, Izza. For misleading you about that."

"Why did you do it? Why did you come out here that day? Why did you lie to me? Why have you continued to lie to me?"

I couldn't tell her that I had to familiarize myself with the circumstances of the place where my friend had murdered her father's tenant. So I said nothing.

"It would help me to know. Please."

Her plea sounded sincere. And a little heartbreaking. I reminded myself that her grief for her father was as fresh as mine was for my wife.

Izza said, "I knew her, you know. Your wife."

The words had the slightest hint of *I gotcha* in them.

Yes, I thought. *I do know that you knew her.*

12

I had dreaded the possibility that I might someday arrive at that specific juncture in a conversation with Izza. It was one of many reasons I hoped never to speak with her again. The reality that she wanted to talk with me about her only meeting with Lauren meant I had reached a huge choice point. *Do I tell Izza more lies? Do I offer some edited version of the truth? Or do I hang up, and hope that she leaves me alone?*

Lauren had revealed to me that she'd met with Izza immediately before she came to my office the morning the Dome Fire started in Boulder Canyon. The same morning she was shot. But Izza had no way to know that I knew about her meeting with Lauren.

Revealing the truth to Izza would be absurd.

At the time that Izza met with Lauren, Izza didn't know that Lauren knew me. Let alone that she and I were married. It wasn't until Lauren and I spoke in my office later that morning that I told my wife about my involvement in the murder in Izza's cottage. The timing meant that Izza could not have learned anything about my role from Lauren.

Lauren had led me to believe that her conversation with Izza that morning concerned Elias Tres — and his drawing and his memories — from the night of the murder. It was Lauren, not Izza, who had recognized pertinent details revealed in the drawing and the memories, and it was Lauren who reached the — correct — conclusion that her car had been used in the crime, and that the driver of that car had been Sam Purdy.

Lauren was always circumspect when talking about her work. She never would have revealed to Izza, a potential witness, what the facts she had just learned might make clear about the old murder in the cottage.

Lauren came to my office immediately after her meeting with Izza to warn me that she had reason to have Sam arrested. She told no one else before she told me.

How was I so sure of that? Because if Lauren had told any of her colleagues what she had learned, Sam would have been arrested later that very day.

Where did that leave me? It left me certain — well, almost certain — that Izza and Lauren never spoke about my possible involvement in the death in the cottage on Izza's family ranch in Frederick. In Izza's mind, my crime was deception. Not homicide.

But the damn YouTube video meant that Izza had learned I had a personal connection to the Boulder County prosecutor who had been coordinating the investigation of the Frederick murder with the Weld County prosecutor.

That, I decided, was what her call to me was about. My deception. Had to be.

Telling Izza the truth about my subterfuge during my initial visit to her cottage was out of the question. I began juggling the nature of the pretense I might adopt when —

Unless — Christ. There's another possibility.

What if someone in the DA's office, like Lauren's assistant, Andrew, or Lauren's boss, Elliot Bellhaven, had subsequently informed Izza that Lauren visited me that morning after Izza's meeting with her? Or what if Izza had worked out the logistics herself from reading news reports? It was possible that sufficient facts were online for anyone assiduous enough, and motivated enough, to piece them together.

What if Izza already knew that I had met with Lauren right after the meeting when she had turned over Elias Tres's drawing that morning?

Was Izza trying to see if I would lie to her yet again?

My paranoia upshifted. What if Izza was working with the Weld County DA — or, God forbid, with Elliot — to try to discover exactly what Lauren and I had spoken about that morning before Lauren was shot?

What if the phone call I was having that very moment was bugged not from my end, but from Izza's end?

My pay phone subterfuge in Louisville? It would be laughable.

I had a headache from juggling the consequences of the permutations.

"No comment?" Izza said. "Really? I thought you would find that curious. That I knew your wife."

No more lies from me. "I know that Lauren had been out to Frederick. Did you meet her on one of those visits?"

"Briefly," Izza said. "But that wasn't the only time."

I said, "I still have a difficult time talking about her." No lie there. Not too much truth, either. No important truth. Not for Izza.

"Would you like to know about the other time?"

"Sure." I was thinking that if she tells me about the meeting the morning Lauren was shot, then I don't have to lie and tell her I don't know about the meeting.

"I took Tres to meet her. He told her some stories, about his memories."

I waited. After about ten seconds, she said, "This is when you ask me about those stories. Tres's stories about the night the tenant died. In the cottage."

"I was thinking that you would tell me if you wanted me to know. It sounds like you would like to tell me, Izza. If that's true, I would like to hear. Very much."

She laughed an unkind laugh. "Ohhh, that's right — you're a shrink. I forgot that for a second. But that was something else you neglected to tell me at the beginning." She paused. "Sins of omission, and sins of commission."

"Those stories?" I asked. "From Tres?"

"Maybe another time," she said. "He saw a lot that night. The night the woman died in the cottage. He saw the car. The man. But he was such a little boy. He may have seen too much. Maybe I'll tell you another time."

I felt like I could drown in the vulnerability I was feeling. I said, "Are your new tenants working out well? The couple from Wyoming? I hope so."

She laughed again. "Do you really think I called to chat? You think I want to be your friend? You really don't want to tell me, do you?"

"Tell you what?" *God.*

"The reason you came to the ranch pretending to be interested in renting the cottage? That. Tell me that. Or the reason you were so interested in the previous tenant who committed suicide in the living room? That, too.

"Or we could talk about the reason I drove to Boulder with Tres to talk to the Boulder County deputy district attorney. Who just happened to be your *wife*? How about any of that? Alan Gregory. *Doctor* Alan Gregory."

Good list. Not comprehensive. But a fine start. "I will listen to whatever you have to say, Izza. You have my complete attention."

"That's it? I have your *attention*?"

Izza had a sarcastic gene. I said, "Yes."

"Has it crossed your mind that this isn't about you, you . . . stupid fool? That it

121

might help *me* to know what the hell was going on that night? That it might help me to know what that little boy has gone through? That maybe you're not the only one who is hurting? Who has lost? Who *is* lost? That maybe you're not the only one who has a child to worry about? Have you considered that?" She hung up.

. . . not the only one who has a child to worry about?

The truth was that I had not. Considered those things.

With Izza, from the moment I first made her acquaintance, I had been using almost all of my energy considering ways to cover my ass.

13

I knocked on the door of Ophelia's double-wide. Sam's Cherokee was outside. It had not been there when I drove away in search of my favorite pay phone.

Ophelia answered the door. I tried not to let my eyes drift south to her almost-always almost-exposed breasts. Experience told me that if her boobs were covered, they were hardly covered. I succeeded in not shifting my eyes in their direction.

Pretty much.

"You looking for my koala?" she asked. She had a variety of endearing names for Sam. Most were variations on the bear theme.

The first time I heard Ophelia employ a bear endearment I found it quasi-cute. But as the range of bears morphed — Sam could be a koala, a teddy, a polar, a grizzly, or a panda — my tolerance diminished. Only someone in love with Sam, sweet romantic love — the kind that distorts senses and judgment — could mistake the man for a koala.

If Sam were a bear, he was the freckled northern pale bear.

"I am, Ophelia. I'm sorry to intrude without calling." With dismay I realized that Ophelia looked and smelled of sex. She was being gracious even though I had just busted up a nooner. "I, uh, I won't keep him for long. I promise."

"Oh don't be sorry. No matter," she said, opening her eyes wide as she broadened the smile on her face. "We can just start up again, you know, from scratch. Sometimes that's better." Her eyes sparkled to emphasize her sincerity. "People get weird about mulligan sex, but I don't know why. Who the hell is keeping score?"

"I couldn't agree more," I said, even though I could hardly have agreed less. I was busy shooing away unsavory visual images involving the role that Sam's naked ass might play in the mulligan erotics. It was possible that for the rest of my life I might suffer unwelcome confabulated images of Sam as an ursine furrie.

A moment later he came to the door in boxers. If I had seen his naked abdomen before, I'd suppressed it. Barring the blessing of fresh traumatic repression I would no doubt recall the present opportunity with unfortunate clarity. Sam had no dearth of body hair — the hue was gray-orange, basically the color palette of a moldy pumpkin — and the sheer size of his belly had me thinking marine mammal thoughts. As earlier, with Ophelia's bosom, I endeavored to keep my eyes from drifting farther south to whatever bits Sam might have left inadvertently overexposed.

Once again, I succeeded. Pretty much.

"Sorry about the timing," I said. "Can we talk? Elsewhere? It's important. Otherwise, I wouldn't —"

He held up two fingers and closed the door. I couldn't tell if Sam had flashed me a peace sign or a two-minute warning. Probably not a peace sign.

He was dressed when he rejoined me on the deck. He slammed the doublewide's door behind him. It didn't *thunk.* Not even close. "You want to get a coat?" he asked me.

I hadn't realized I was underdressed. "I'm not cold," I said. With the exception of a paltry few storms our winter had been barely recognizable. More days in the fifties and sixties than the twenties and thirties.

"Suit yourself. But at some point soon you

will be." He pointed northwest.

The coming storm loomed. The wind was starting to whip in gusts. We walked out the lane. Sam was right; I should have been colder than I was. I said, "I was surprised to see your car here today. I thought you had Simon this whole week."

"Sherry asked to flip with me. Simon got picked up for shoplifting two days ago. Second time. She's trying to exert some control. He's resisting her. Epic struggle time. It's been brewing for a while. Kid is tough to handle. Something might be going on."

"I am sorry. He got picked up both times while he was with his mom?"

"She's making noises that she can't handle him at the same time she's trying to prove to him, and me, and herself, that she can. I'm getting worried she might be right."

"About which?"

"Not being able to handle him. He's . . . sullen. Withdrawn. Pissy. Like you, now that I think about it."

"You haven't had any trouble?"

"He's mouthy. But that's it, or at least I think that's it. I may just not have caught him doing whatever else he might be up to. Simon has a temper. You know that."

"He may feel safer with you. More secure

with the boundaries you provide."

"That's shrink talk? Right?" He smiled at me. "Or he just holds his breath while he's with me. Lets her have it when he's with her. I have made my share of mistakes, Alan. But when it's my turn with Simon I think that I am a pretty damn okay father. It's possible that Simon may be better off with me. Might cramp my style with O, but so be it. I got a kid who needs me."

"I'm sorry, Sam. I didn't know. I've been so consumed with my own problems. Maybe I can help. I know a little something about teenagers acting out."

He shook his head. "Ophelia says you don't knock on her door very often."

"We just drove Sofie to the airport."

Sam took two slow steps before he said, "She's a great kid." Sam took two more steps before he said, "But you didn't knock on O's door to tell me about driving your daughter to the airport."

I really liked thinking about Sofie as my daughter. She was a gift I'd had nothing to do with creating and one that I did not deserve. I could have told Sam about my feelings about her but I didn't think he would appreciate either the sentiment or the timing of my digression. "On the way back here Izza Kane called me."

"Well, shit," he said.

"She saw the YouTube thing. Saw me standing next to Grace at Lauren's funeral. She put all the family connections together. My cover is kind of blown."

"I bet she saw you dance, too. That could be an even bigger tragedy." I saw his grin. "You ever want some lessons, I'm your guy." I managed a smile that was only mildly patronizing. "That damn video? The whole viral thing on the Internet? Amazing. I have the clip in my favorites. I admit that I've shown it to some people."

"Sam? Izza?"

"Can you be more specific? What does she think she knows?"

I shook my head. "She connected me to Lauren, and then to the morning that she met with Lauren, and to the shooting in my office. I don't think she knows that Lauren told me anything or that she gave me the drawing that I gave you. She may suspect it, though. Still, that's a lot of dot connecting. I'm concerned that Izza's making reasonable assumptions about why I pretended to be interested in renting the cottage on her father's ranch."

"Reasonable assumptions, or accurate assumptions?"

"Could be both. She wasn't explicit, but

128

she left the impression that she thinks my intrusion into her life has something to do with the suicide by the tenant who lived in the cottage. Her word, by the way. 'Suicide.' She didn't say 'homicide' or 'murder.' "

Sam stopped walking. "You never should have done that — gone to Frederick, saw the cottage, met Izza. It got you nowhere. Earned you nothing. I told you at the time —"

"Don't. I'm using all my energy not to succumb to regret. If I start I'm going to drown. We've both made some mistakes."

Sam put his big hands on my biceps. "It's been years since the shooting. I haven't been arrested. You haven't been arrested. We may be thinking they know more than they know. We have to stay cool about this. Not act guilty."

"Even though we are?"

"Even though we are."

"The surveillance?"

"They may be fishing. They may be blowing smoke. It may be an illusion."

I could tell he didn't believe that. I made eye contact with him, holding it for a few seconds before I asked, "Are there any developments in Frederick I should know about that might have motivated Izza to reach out? With Big Elias? Or with the Weld

129

County DA? Are they interested in us? Are you hearing anything?"

Sam had contacts in Weld County, mostly through the Greeley police department. He considered them good contacts, but not great contacts.

"Nothing. But I'm being cautious about not seeming too interested."

"Big Elias? Has he been making any noise?"

"You sure you're not cold? I'm wearing a jacket and I'm cold."

I was getting cold but I shook my head.

Sam said, "The old asshole is mine. You made it clear that I could handle things in Frederick my way, Alan. I think that was a wise plan. Let's stick with it. I will continue to take care of Frederick. And Big Elias."

Sam let go of my arms and we continued walking out the lane.

"Now tell me what you told Ms. Izza."

"I did okay, I think. I was suspicious from the get-go. I'm getting to be so paranoid that I acted as though she was in bed with the Weld County prosecutor. That the call could be a setup of some kind. I didn't tell her anything. I didn't admit anything. She ended up getting frustrated. She hung up."

"Good."

"Is it? If she is working with Weld County

law enforcement, frustrating her may be in my self-interest. But if she's not? What then? Is pissing her off going to help? I'll be pushing her straight into Elliot Bellhaven's arms, won't I? We have to remember that she took that drawing to the Boulder County DA, not to the Weld County DA. At any point, she could pick up the phone and ask Elliot what's up with the drawing."

Sam said, "I still can't figure out why she chose Lauren. Why she didn't take it to Weld County. I don't like things that don't figure. I hate things that don't figure."

"My take? She is distrustful of Weld County law enforcement. She might think they're on Big Elias's side. She met Lauren once at the ranch, liked her. It's simple."

"Izza told you that?"

"No. A deduction."

Sam made an exasperated noise. "Leave the deductions to the professionals."

I asked, "If I meet with Izza, is there a way I could tell that she's wearing a wire?"

"Surveillance wires have gotten pretty tiny. Good ones anyway."

"How could I tell if she had one on her body?"

Sam smirked. "I think you know the answer to that."

"Well, that's not going to happen."

Sam let his smirk become a laugh at my expense.

"You know you look like shit, Alan. You need to get out, see some grown-ups. We're going to a party on New Year's Eve. Want to join us?"

"I don't have much interest in being social, Sam."

He tried again. "Then what do you say you and the kids eat with me and O for a while? At least dinner when I'm up here. She likes to cook. She likes to take care of people. You know me, I'm a social animal."

I laughed at that thought just before I heard a scream from behind us, back toward the house.

It was Gracie.

14

Instantly my blood had ice crystals in it.

"Dad, Emily's coming!" She'd screamed it with the same intensity she would use if she were being attacked by a raptor. And a saber-toothed tiger. At the same time.

I knew that Gracie's screams lacked nuance. She would have used an identical scream if she had grown intolerant of being teased by her brother. But those days knowing that to be true never did me any good.

The big black Bouvier was upon us in seconds.

"I almost had a heart attack just then when she screamed. I'm a little on edge," I said to Sam.

"Understandable," he said. "The kid screams like she has a future in horror flicks. Maybe you should meet with Izza in person. See if it can soothe your soul a little. Are you up for that?"

"But what if she's, you know, wired?

Would they use a wire?"

Sam scratched the side of his head. "Probably not. Depends how suspicious they are. How badly they want us."

"How badly do they want us?"

"For Elliot? Pinning Frederick on us would be a major coup. Could be his ticket to front pages outside Boulder County. It could certainly help him begin to posture for statewide office. Maybe get some blog and cable attention out of it. The national pundits love Hickenlooper, so why not Elliot, too?"

"Elliot's no Hickenlooper, Sam. Elliot has disadvantages. He steps up to the plate with two strikes. Elliot's gay. And he's from Boulder. Most of the state still thinks Boulder is a foreign country. Like San Marino."

"Where's San Marino?" he asked. I shook my head, regretting the allusion. Sam went on. "You just don't like Elliot. Gay is in. People love to hate Boulder, but even the haters know Boulder is always in. Look at Jared Polis. He's gay. He got elected to Congress here and then he got reelected. Elliot's much smoother than Polis. Polis is taller, though, there's that. Hickenlooper and Polis are both tall. But look at Perlmutter. He's a shrimp, and he keeps getting elected, too."

Sam had pulled out his smartphone. He was Googling San Marino.

"Perlmutter's not gay," I said. "And he's not from Boulder." Sam's criteria for judging local politicians baffled me, yet I was arguing with him as though they were sensible. Or relevant. The problem, I knew, was mine.

"Elliot has aspirations," Sam said. "He may think this is his time."

"Jared Polis only had to convince his congressional district — mostly Boulder — that being gay didn't matter. Elliot has to convince the whole state. That means the plains. The mountains. The Western Slope. Even El Paso County, for God's sake. That's some conservative country out there, Sam."

"Those are my peeps. Trust me, gay is in," Sam repeated, as though it was his new mantra. "There's no time like the present to be a gay politician in Boulder. If not now for Elliot, when? The tide will turn back. Always does, look at history. Gay people never stay in favor for long. The Greeks? The Romans? Gays were in, and then — *bammo* — here come the Dark Ages. See what I'm saying?"

I did not have the psychic resources to discuss homosexuality and the Dark Ages with Sam Purdy. Fortunately it didn't matter. He was ready to move on — maybe to the Enlightenment. I crossed my fingers.

"I got no bars out here. Damn. Anyway, my point? If Elliot were to bust one of us it might help his national profile."

One of us? Why not both of us? I said, "Jesus. You've thought about this."

"You had other things to pay attention to, but Lauren's death was big news. Not just here, everywhere. Big-stage everywhere. National everywhere. If her grieving widower is suddenly arrested — by her boss, no less — for another local homicide? With the YouTube dancinggravegirl thing on top of it? Wow. I could see Nancy Grace moving her tour bus outside our courthouse. Maybe she buys a condo here. Adopts babies here."

I wondered if Nancy Grace had a tour bus. "Why arrest me, Sam? Not you?" Understood, I hoped, was *since you're the one who fucking shot somebody.*

"I've never really understood the animosity Elliot had for Lauren, and for you. Is there something there I don't know?"

Sam knocked me off balance with that question. By getting me lost in the Dark Ages and Hickenlooper's height and Nancy Grace's future in Boulder, he'd lulled me into forgetting what a skilled interviewer he was. I stuttered before I said, "It started as a professional rivalry for Elliot and Lauren. Then? I'm not sure. Things just deteriorated. I got dragged in. There may have been something I don't know about." I was suddenly freezing cold.

"We need to assume that Elliot wants us. Badly. Two reasons. It's the only safe assumption. And I think it might be true."

"Why 'us'? Why not you?"

"Lately? I'm thinking it's more you than me. Maybe even more you than us."

Oh God. "Why?"

"Exactly. Why? All I know for certain is what I was told by the friend who gave me the initial heads-up about the surveillance. It means we — you — are on their radar, and not in a good way."

"Me? I thought the surveillance was on us."

"I told you about the surveillance, Alan."

"You said it was on us, Sam."

He was examining the dirt on the lane. "Turns out it's more you."

"How long have you known that?"

"Does that matter? It's the latest information I have."

I fought a rush of vertigo. *Why is Elliot targeting me, and not Sam? Why would Sam not make that clear to me the moment he*

137

knew it?

I felt the ground shift. "Why me? What's the upside of that for the DA?" What was implied, but what I didn't say to Sam, was *since you're the one who committed murder in Frederick, not me.*

He said, "Can't say. Lauren gave you that kid's drawing. Maybe Elliot knows about it. Maybe he's seen it. Or maybe it's not the only drawing. He could have others."

"Lauren didn't mention any other drawings, Sam. Just the one."

"It's possible there are more. Absence of a mention isn't mention of an absence."

"Is that a real aphorism? Or did you make it up?"

Sam ignored my question. "Or maybe Lauren told her assistant about the one she gave you before she went to your office. Or she scanned it and emailed it to everybody in the damn county before she walked over to see you."

"But that drawing implicates you, Sam, not me."

"Does it?" Sam said. "It's a picture of a specific car, Alan. Not my car."

He was reminding me that the car in the drawing was mine, not his. Sam had borrowed the car, without permission, to commit the crime. But Elliot didn't know that.

To Elliot, the vehicle in the drawing would appear to be my car. Not Sam's.

By giving that drawing to Sam, had I left the DA with no real suspects but me? I had a sudden uncomfortable insight into why Sam wasn't as upset about the change in investigatory focus as I was.

He was relieved that they weren't looking at him. Sam feared more drawings because he feared they might refocus the DA's attention on him.

The implications of Sam's concerns, for me, could be life changing.

15

I dared the storm to stay north while I remained outside to do physical chores — mostly having to do with removing dried brush and weeds. Wildfire abatement meant clearing growth away from structures. I was doing my part, though I did refrain from gathering the tumbleweeds that were closest to Ophelia's doublewide.

Even from a distance I could tell that she and Sam were fornicating vociferously. I wasn't in the mood to eavesdrop on that. Nor did I know what odd mood I might need to be in to wish to eavesdrop on that.

I spotted a car dropping around the far curve on the dirt and gravel lane. At first I thought it was a limo. But as the vehicle drew closer I could see that the front end was that of a brooding Chrysler 300, the paint as shiny as a gorilla's coat. If there was a fingerprint, or a water drop, or a streak on the finish of the sedan, I was missing it.

The fine Colorado dust the slow-moving car was stirring up would soon settle on the black paint with the certainty of a plague.

I hadn't been expecting a visitor. I hoped the car was heading to Ophelia's. She and Sam could take another sex mulligan.

I introduced him to the kids as Carl Luppo. He corrected me. He said, "Franco Carelli." He winked at me and tapped at an imaginary breast pocket. "Remember the paper? When I asked for the paper I got my name back, too. I'm Frank."

In my head I added his real name to the street handle he'd earned when he was an active enforcer for one of the prominent crime families in the Northeast during the flaming sunset of the old-time mob. He had once admitted to me in therapy that in the social club where his crew gathered he was known as "Jaws." In his heyday, when he was the stuff of other people's nightmares, he would have been Frank "Jaws" Carelli.

"Like the shark in the movie?" I'd asked him.

"No, I was before the movie. I was the guy who don't let go. That kind of jaws."

Carl Luppo was his WITSEC name. The

141

paper that he was referring to was his official release from the Witness Security Program of the U.S. Marshals Service, WITSEC, what most of us know as the Witness Protection Program. I met him when he was a protected witness, and I was doing a brief gig as a WITSEC mental health consultant. At that time, Carl Luppo was considered "hot." The *hot* designation meant that if his enemies found him he would be a dead man. During my WITSEC briefing I was told that he had numerous enemies, primarily his ex-compatriots, but also a few of his remaining ex-antagonists. Given what he'd done — not only the crimes he'd committed to earn his passport into the realm of WITSEC, but also the testimony he'd offered in court to keep the government happy after he went underground — it was hard for me to imagine that all had been forgiven between Carl, his onetime crime family, and that family's natural enemies. In Carl's world, revenge had a long, long fuse.

Yet here he was, driving himself to my door as though nobody was dying to put a bullet in his head.

The kids treated Carl like he was a garrulous grandfather. He had wrapped Italian candies in his pockets ready for them.

I hoped I saw Carl for what he was, an affable wiseguy, a self-described "gorilla." But I told the kids that Mr. Luppo was an old friend from work and explained that Anvil, the miniature poodle they loved and knew so well, had originally belonged to him.

Anvil died of liver cancer, Carl explained to me after the kids grew bored. Neither of them liked the candies; they'd both moved on. "Last year. Had to put him down."

"I'm sorry," I said. I felt a wave of sadness. "He was a good dog."

Carl shrugged. Loss wasn't his thing. Causing it, or experiencing it. Grief rolled off his back like a Colorado monsoon would stream off the hood of his Chrysler.

"I always thought the little guy was kind of fey." He was talking about Anvil, and dismissing his demise. "I'm out doing a grand tour," he explained. "A few years back I got the leukemia," he said. "The AML. Acute myo . . . log-ness leukemia." He mangled the second word. He knew he'd given it a good try and he knew he mangled it. "I call it the killing-you-softly kind of leukemia. Takes its fucking time. They knocked it down with chemo. Now, to keep me going? They give me other people's blood? Irony? You bet.

"My grandkids tell me that the transfu-

143

sions make me a vampire. They call me 'Vamp Gramp.' Fucking kids." He laughed.

I felt a need to redirect the conversation. "How are you holding up?"

"Good. They keep telling me someday soon I won't be so good. But one doctor — a young girl, too young to be a doctor, but I like her — she thinks my lungs will kill me before the AML does." He shrugged. "If I was a betting man — what the hell, I am a betting man — I would lay ten grand even-up on a bullet or a blade." He laughed.

"But until something or somebody does me in I get to pretend I got nothing to lose. After the life I've lived I'm playing on house money. Before the last days tick by, whenever that is, I got some old acquaintances to see. You. You're one of those."

I think he wanted me to thank him. I didn't.

"Like my car?" he asked.

"Love your car," I said. "It's you. Classic, but with a . . . sneer to it." I meant it as a compliment. He took it that way. I put my open hand on my heart. "It's good to see you, Carl."

"I've been checking you on the Bing," he said. "My daughter gave me one of those iPads. Old dog, new trick? I never got good with the computers. The booting, the rebooting, the left clicking, the right clicking. But the iPad? It's okay. My fingers are fat. Every day comes a point I want to fling the thing out the window like a Frisbee because my fingers are fat, but mostly I like it. I like the Bing a lot. My daughter showed me how it can help me remember stuff. That's not my best thing no more. The Bing remembers for me. I don't know how it does that, but I don't fucking care, either. I tell it, like, I want to know about you going forward, into the future. It does that, then it tells me when something comes around.

"The Bing told me about your recent troubles."

Carl examined my face for a tell. I didn't think he saw anything. I sucked at poker — playing the odds wasn't my strength — but I was okay at poker faces.

"Anyway. On the tube part, the Bing tube? The one that plays the home movies? Crazy shit. Cats? So many cats. And the Koreans? Don't get me started on the Koreans. Anyway, that's where I saw your little girl dancing. Broke my heart, I tell ya. Sorry for your loss."

He recited those last words as though they were a prayer from someone else's religion. Along the way Carl had learned that loss touched others.

In movies, and in life, people often mix up the traits of sociopaths and psychopaths. In my mind, the simplest distinction is that the sociopath doesn't care. The psychopath doesn't even know.

Carl knew. I weighed the likelihood that Carl was actually sorry for my loss. If it were true that Frank was currently living somewhere north of absolute sociopathy and south of rank psychopathy, then it was possible that I was the best psychotherapist in the world. Unlikely, but whatever. I chose to be touched by Carl's sentiment. Or his pretended sentiment. Which was true in the moment didn't matter. I thanked him.

"But," he said, "if you had to dance to eat you'd be one skinny dead man. Just saying. Case you had any illusions about your abilities."

I laughed.

"She was pregnant last time I was here," he reminded me. "The dead wife. With the little dancing girl? It was that long ago?"

The dead wife. Carl's words made me shudder. They were a stark reminder about his comfort with the states of being and not being. I would never forget the details of the life he'd lived, how he'd dug his first grave — dug his first literal grave and then dug his second — before he had attended his First Communion. How he had killed a man with his own hands months before the day he stood for his confirmation.

That first confession must have been something to hear. Carl had lived a life that, were I to deign to offer judgment, I would need to judge from way beyond a horizon. It was that far out of my experience.

I didn't judge him. I feared him. "Yes, with the girl. It was that long ago."

"Back then I told you I owed you one." He shrugged. "A favor. I'm at a place in my life where I'm eager to settle the debt. It will help me die in peace if I don't leave markers behind. You know what I'm saying?"

He looked around. It was reflex for him to be certain we were alone.

That I knew what he was saying gave me gooseflesh in places I didn't know I could get gooseflesh. During therapy with Carl I had learned that nuance wasn't a helpful strategy. When I wanted to be sure he heard me, simple declarative sentences worked best. I said, "You don't owe me, Carl."

He said, "I be the judge of that." He leaned forward a little, which made him small and hard, like a fighter coiling up to absorb a few quick shots, or like a cannonball atop a pile of other cannonballs, all potential energy. The cannonball in front of me had a lot more ear and nostril hair than I recalled.

"Tell me about the shoot," he said. "What happened, 'zactly."

I assumed he was talking about the shoot he read about online. On the Bing. I told him about Diane shooting Lauren without having to mince words, or protect anyone's feelings — Carl knew none of the players.

"Your friend then? The shooter? She lost it?"

"Yeah. It seems."

"Seems? No payback with her?"

I shook my head. "She snapped, Carl. I can only live with what happened if I believe that to be true."

"You're choosing what to believe? That's different from knowing. I seen people die believing like that. Not knowing, but believing."

"I guess I am choosing to believe. Can you relate to that?"

"Never seen it work, not a single time." He rolled his neck this way and that. I heard cracks. "In case you're wondering, the favor I owe doesn't expire until I do." He laughed. "If you change your mind, if things develop in ways that cause you to adjust your beliefs, make you less certain about your friend's motives. And maybe less confident about justice because justice is a capricious fucking bitch." Frank's pronunciation of *capricious* was closer to *capiche-ee-us* — an intentional amalgamation of the Italian-American and the highfalutin two-bit English.

"There are always things that can be done. People can be influenced. Solutions found. That was my specialty back when. Solutions." He popped his chest forward with confidence as he spoke of his previous life. Carl's solutions meant threats would be made. Or knives would be plunged. Triggers would be pulled. Garrotes tautened.

Jaws would be clamped. He tapped his watch. It was a fat gold Rolex. Real? Fake? Either was possible with Carl Luppo.

The only thing that wasn't possible was that he had paid retail.

16

I walked him to his car. "You need a place to spend the night? You're welcome here. I have a guest room."

I felt obligated to make the offer, but I had no idea what I would do if Carl accepted. I would probably put the kids on a late flight to go see their sister in Holland. Charter a Gulfstream to get them out of town fast if I had to.

Carl's past choices meant he went through life with a target painted on his chest. Fate and guile and cruelty, all his, dictated that he'd survived.

Plus some luck. Carl's eyes, I thought, were as cold as facts. He said, "Truth?" The word came out more like *troot.* "I bring danger with me. Not fair to your family. I'll be in Denver tonight at the Four Seasons. I like the Four Seasons. Stay with them whenever I can. They treat me like I'm important."

"You'll be there for the holiday?"

"Who knows? I may itch for the road again tomorrow. New Year's Eve used to mean family early, hookers late. Now? Can always find a hooker. The Bing."

Okay. "Four Seasons means you must have some money."

"God gives. I pray that God forgives, too. The Lotto? The Powerball? I play. Used to be the numbers. Always I play. Even inside I played. Match three all the time. Like, regular, more than my share. Have me a knack. Few times, four. Then a year or so back? When there was that big jackpot. Remember? The gazillion dollar one? I matched all five regular numbers, but not the fucking Powerball. I missed that fuck by a mile. I hate the fucking Powerball.

"Still, five matches on a big jackpot was a lot of dough for a guy with a short calendar. A guy like me with the AML." He lowered his voice. "Split it with my kids and grand-kids. Left me with one hundred sixty-two large after taxes. Used some to get me the car." He laughed. "I'm leasing it, bettin' I never make that last payment? Suckers.

"I've always wanted to take a long road trip. One I wasn't forced to take. Never had that freedom. I'm seeing me a lot of Four Seasons."

151

"Can I get in? See your car?"

"Be my guest. She's gorgeous."

Through the windshield I saw Sam standing with his hands in his pockets on the cedar deck of Ophelia's doublewide. He was staring at the big nose of the Chrysler.

Carl saw Sam, too. Carl's nose twitched like he was a predator and Sam was a veal chop. Carl said, "Your neighbor's a cop."

He had certain instincts. I said, "He's okay. He's a friend."

Carl stared at Sam the way I eye coyotes that pause across the canyon. Warily.

"The one from that night? The big fight? He came late to the party."

"Yes. But he's forgiven. He wasn't invited to that party."

"I remember."

Changing the subject seemed prudent. "Your daughter gave you the iPad. You gave the kids the gift of some serious money. So you must be talking with your children again?" Carl had long been estranged from his family. I said, "That's a good thing?"

He smiled as he put a closed fist on his heart. "A blessing." He glanced in the mirrors reflexively. Rearview, then sideview. Then the other sideview. Even in the wilds of Boulder County at the butt end of a dirt road on a promontory with a view of a hundred miles, while expressing love for his family, Carl couldn't feel safe.

He checked the mirrors again. Some bruises don't heal.

The quiet between us extended for a while.

I didn't know it, but jeopardy, different for each of us, and gravity, the same for each of us, were conspiring to pull us the same way as our quiet filled the car.

He busted the silence. He said, "Huh. I can tell I'm not even asking you about the right problem."

It wasn't a question. Nor was it something that Carl could have learned on the Bing. Carl knew I had another problem because the man could smell trepidation like he could smell a fruit seller's fresh peaches from a half block away on a quaint *via* in Naples in July.

"There's this guy named Michael McClelland," I said.

For me it was watching Carl check the mirrors, and check them again, and then again, that had moved me to speak about my problem with McClelland. Watching Carl's paranoia showed me my future if I didn't find a way to stop McClelland.

I was close to acknowledging that I was too exhausted to face that future. Too careless a guy for the vigilance it would require to protect my flanks, and my kids. I knew I didn't have Carl's memory for faces. I didn't have his heart for the long game.

I didn't have his immunity against the virus of loss. Not at all.

"So how can I be of help?" Carl said.

He laughed. I laughed, too. As his therapist, I'd once said the same words to him. He'd remembered my opening line from our first session: *How can I be of help?*

"Well played," I said.

"Without a good memory I'm a dead man twenty years ago. Thirty maybe." He laughed. "Forty."

It took me ten minutes to tell him the highlights of the story of Michael McClelland.

When I was done, he said, "Couple things? Your ethics? Got you into this mess. Forget them. This Mike guy? You got yourself a whatchamacallit, a . . . a nemesis."

"I do. And I don't know how to stop him. He's got reach. He's determined. He's patient. He's brilliant. Smarter than me. Smarter than anybody I know."

"Smart has limits," Carl said. "Never met a guy smarter than a bullet."

Or a shiv. I had dreams, literal dreams, that Michael's end would involve a shiv.

I said, "For the longest time I thought he wanted to kill me, that he spent his waking hours planning how he would do it. Now? I think what he wants is to ruin my life, make me sorry every day that I'm still breathing."

Carl powered down his window and spit into the dirt. It was an editorial expectoration. He brought the window back up. "We never worked that way. Might kill somebody one day, take care of his family the next. You know, make sure they got an envelope. If they knew what happened, they might have cursed, thrown it back in our face. But after we left, they'd pick it up. Move on.

"What we did in those days was about business, not about causing suffering." He considered his words. "Not for the family anyway."

Carl caused a little suffering on the edges. He was okay with that.

"He's in prison," I said. "McClelland."

"In the pen?" I nodded. "Federal or state? Which one?" I told him.

"Can be more complicated, but I got some reach, too," Carl said. Carl had done hard time. He knew all about reaching over the walls and through the bars.

"Yeah? Not hard to do?"

"Not too hard," he said with the kind of offhanded confidence that a cold-blooded killer brings to the type of conversation we were having.

"My guy is easy to find," I said. "Looking on the bright side of his incarceration."

Carl laughed. "Sometimes, so you know, reaching inside from outside is a little more complicated than reaching outside from inside."

I said, "What we're discussing? No decision has been made. That has to be clear, too. To you." He nodded. "I mean it. We talk again. Before?"

"Yes."

"Promise me."

"You got my word, Doc."

"Thank you. I trust your word."

He touched his heart with his fist again. I decided it was an affirmation of something good. Or, given whom I was talking with, at least something I could live with.

"Are you visiting Kirsten while you're in town?" I asked. Kirsten Lord had been another of my WITSEC patients. A protected prosecutor. Carl had figured that fact out without too much effort. He had tried to befriend her. And more.

He tried not to smile at my question about Kirsten. He failed. The mention of her name put a glow in his eyes that even a hardened wiseguy couldn't disguise.

A little gorilla in his tone, he asked, "What makes you think that?"

Because you fell in love with her, I thought. Stopping by to see a woman like her is the kind of reminiscing an old man does when he has a fancy new car, ample free time, a wallet full of Powerball Benjamins, a suite at the Four Seasons, and, especially, when the AML roulette wheel has his number and he's just hanging out waiting for the day the thing stops spinning.

"Have you spoken with her already?" I asked.

"We'll see. She's on my list. Old friends. Like I said."

"Did she send you here? Did she tell you I needed your help?"

"Don't know anything about that," he said. "Nothin'."

I grinned at him. "Your memory? It's not suddenly failing you, is it?"

Carl thrust his jaw my way. He didn't want to lie to my face. Me and Carl? We had a history. He said, "I'm an old man. The only parts that aren't failing me are the parts that have already failed me." He pointed at his dick.

The gesture was funny. But my self-preservation instincts kicked in. I didn't laugh.

He explained, "These days I need to see Alice if I want to enjoy myself."

"Alice? You have a girlfriend?"

"Alice?" Carl laughed. "Nah-nah, *da* Cialis, the pill."

I got out of the Chrysler. Before he drove away he lowered his window, reached into his pocket, and pulled something out. He held it out to me, whatever it was invisible in his meaty hand.

I thought he was giving me a candy. Or one of his Cialis. I was wrong.

"Powerball. A ten-pack. I try to spread the luck, you know? Keep an eye out for the drawing. Good fortune. Yeah?"

I faced north until the dust he stirred up as he drove away completely settled.

I felt heavy. I had just arranged to — maybe — arrange a hit with a hit man.

I felt bad that I didn't feel worse.

The first snowflakes began to fall.

17

As the flurries mingled with the dust from the lane behind Carl's departing car I wondered if the timing of his visit had been coincidence, or if it had been precipitated by a conversation he had with Kirsten. My gut was insisting that Carl had phoned Kirsten with an update as he was driving away.

When I turned to walk back to the house, Sam was approaching from Ophelia's.

He said, "Do I know him? Your visitor? In the black car."

"That one? Just now?" I said, as though there had been a parade of black cars carrying visitors down the lane and Sam and I needed to select one from the fleet.

I didn't want to get into it with Sam. I was confident that he'd recognized the visitor as the protected witness with the WITSEC name of Carl Luppo with whom Sam once crossed paths. Sam's cop memory for faces was at least as good as Carl's criminal memory for faces. I told myself that Sam's curiosity wasn't complicated; he was just being a detective. But I was suspicious anyway. Because I had grown suspicious of Sam.

He said, "Yes, that one."

"He's a guy. I know him from work." I stressed the word *work.*

Sam nodded but I could see disappointment in his eyes. He recognized that I'd played the confidentiality trump card — *work,* between us, was my shorthand for privileged information — and he knew from long experience with me that once I chose to play that trump I would play it stubbornly.

"That's it? A retired wiseguy shows up on your doorstop out of nowhere and you're going to blow smoke up my ass that he's a guy from work?"

It was a challenge. Meek on the Sam-challenge meter, but a challenge nonetheless. "What?" I said, playing dumb, or comfortably wearing the costume of someone playing dumb. My short-term goal was the distraction value. Sam, I hoped, would be left to wonder which was true about me. Dumb? Playing dumb?

He would believe either. Sam wasn't

happy about my stance but he had no good options. He dropped the inquiry about Carl. He asked, "You're doing okay?"

I had an old impulse: to invite him in, to offer him a beer.

I ignored it.

I said, "Good. You?"

Ten minutes later I was winnowing a list of potential therapists in my head. It was time.

SAM AND LUCY

Sam's car was in the shop. Again. Lucy picked him up at the doublewide to get them both to Thirty-Fifth Street to start their shift. The recent string of mid-January days felt stubby and gray. Stock Show weather.

Sam was disappointed she hadn't stopped to get him coffee first.

"Ophelia made you coffee, Sam. Didn't she?" Lucy said.

"Yeah? So."

"Breakfast, too?" He nodded. She said, "I wasted all my time driving up here to get your butt. You can buy me coffee. How's that?"

Sam slumped down a little bit in his seat. He said, "That's reasonable."

"I found time to look at Prado, discreetly. Couple things you should know."

"Give me the short version. Don't want to

still be talking about this when we get to Starbucks to buy your super-duper extra-whatever foamy soy vanilla latte thing."

Lucy glared at him. "Hazelnut, not vanilla. I have the high ground here, Sam."

He knew she was right.

She said, "Doctor Doctor's roommate was due home late the afternoon of 9/11 but he got caught by the airports shutting down. Didn't get back for days. The next Saturday to be precise." Sam grunted to let her know he was listening. "And, get this, Elliot Bell-haven's name is in the damn file."

Sam sat up straight. "I don't remember that. He was the deputy DA who worked Prado after Lauren?"

"No. He's on a list of contacts of the deceased put together by Mendelson — remember him? — from an address book and a later interview with the roommate."

"Mendelson did that? Really? Hopeless detective. Worst I ever knew. Any follow-up calls or interviews made to the names on the list?"

"No notes about that in the file," Lucy said.

"Course not. Mendelson? If he hadn't moved to Texas he would have gotten the Prado 911 call that we got. Fate's a bitch. So Bellhaven was living in Boulder when the towers got hit?"

"I knew that already. Didn't need Mendelson to tell me that."

"Was he out of the closet?" Sam said. "He wasn't when he first got here, was he?"

"That matters? You're asking because Ophelia said the roommates were gay."

"I don't know what matters. I don't like handguns on bungee cords in fireplaces. Until I understand that piece, everything matters."

"The DA doesn't know all of what we know, Sam. I was careful."

"The fact we found the gun is in the file. And the bungee. Bellhaven knows all that."

"You're buying me one of those breakfast sandwich things, too."

"Yeah yeah," Sam said. "I might get one, too. O may be trimming my calories."

"You think maybe you should get a new car, Sam? Yours is a little unreliable."

"I missed the end-of-the-year sales. Maybe during the summer closeouts."

"Most of the sales go till the end of January. You have a few days yet."

"I can't afford a new car. I spend too much of my money buying my partner coffee and breakfast sammies." He laughed at the word *sammies.*

19

DOCTOR LILA

Alan had canceled the previous week's appointment. Despite how monumental our last session had seemed to me — and maybe because of how monumental it had seemed to him — he'd left no explanation for the cancellation in his voicemail.

It was as though he didn't owe me one.

He sat down. He looked at me. He asked, "Do you know Diane Estevez?"

That was how he chose to begin our third session. How our February began.

He didn't mention the cancellation. I didn't confront him about it. I had intended to. I knew I should. I told myself I would, later on. But I wouldn't. Later on.

If he were another patient I might have asked him whether it was important if I knew Diane Estevez. But not Alan Gregory; I had already decided to be specific with him about those kinds of facts. Not that I felt I had much choice.

I was still believing he should have chosen another therapist. Someone who had treated another therapist before. Like, ever. Someone with some gravitas. And some balls. He needed someone with balls. Gender didn't matter. Balls mattered.

I said, "I met Diane. Once at a conference in Denver a couple of years ago. That was just an introduction. And once at a party at her house up Lee Hill. A big party, an open-house type thing. She and I have never had a conversation that went beyond pleasantries."

I wondered if Alan recalled that he'd been there, too, at that party. That he and I had met that evening. I had probably introduced myself as Lila Travis, not Delilah. Maybe he did recall, and that's why he called me Lila. Or perhaps I had made so tiny an impression on him that he had forgotten the two or three minutes we talked at the foot of the stairs, me up on the first tread so that I wouldn't have to look up at him literally as well as figuratively.

He had probably forgotten. He called me Lila because some colleague of ours did.

"You and Diane are not friends?" he asked.

"Not at all. No professional contact, either. If you're concerned about that."

"Her husband, Raoul?"

"I met him at the same party. Spoke with him for less than a minute. He was charming." *Raoul was flirty. You weren't, Alan.*

I wondered if I had been flirty. I'm not always aware.

He stared at my face for at least ten seconds. I thought he was deciding whether he could trust my answers. Or weighing whether my encounters with his friends were too frequent or too intimate. I had thrown in the part about Raoul being charming so that he would trust that answer. I couldn't imagine that my tangential contact with his friends would disqualify me. I asked, "Are you wondering if you can count on what I say?"

"Yes," he said. "The stakes are kind of high."

"They are," I acknowledged. I didn't care about the stakes. I did not like not being trusted.

He shook his head. "Not the way you might think. Higher than you can imagine."

I remembered. *Survival. Culpability. Freedom.* I felt that chill all over again.

"Why would I break your confidence?" I asked.

"I don't care why, Lila. Therapists get misguided. Careless. Foolish. Grandiose. Therapists lose sight of their roles. Get cavalier. Misunderstand their responsibilities. Lots of reasons."

"Have you?" I asked him. "Done those things?"

He looked at me. I suddenly understood the true meaning of the word *glower.*

"Do you know what's going on with Diane now? Or do I have to tell you?"

"You have to tell me," I said. Insisting that he tell me felt mean. *Jesus.* But I couldn't pretend I knew what he needed me to know. I knew the rumors, but I wasn't that cool therapist who heard all the good rumors. I also knew what was in the news, but I didn't read the *Camera,* so I probably did not even know all that was in the news.

"You know we were close? Diane and I."

"Only from context. Your long association with her. In town, people — other therapists — refer to you as 'Alan and Diane,' 'Diane and Alan.' You're linked, like a couple that's been together forever. You must know that."

He nodded. "We were friends. Good friends. Partners. We share an office. Shared. Own it together. Still. So close. For years. It would be hard to exaggerate the depth of our friendship." I didn't respond. He went

168

on. "The last time I saw Diane she was on a gurney in Community Hospital on the way to get a CT scan to check for a subdural bleed. She had banged her head — hard — when I tackled her to get a gun out of her hand. She wasn't thinking well. But she hadn't been thinking clearly even before she hit her head."

"People are saying she was pregnant, but they did a CT?" I regretted my words the instant they left my mouth. I had spoken as if to a friend, not to a patient.

He looked at me perplexed. I had not only interrupted him, but I had also questioned his reality. I'd screwed up.

He said, "Let's assume they shielded her abdomen. May I go on?"

I had questions about other facts, too. The gun. Particularly where it might have been pointed while Diane held it. I decided to wait to see if he got there on his own.

"What kind of not thinking well? Decompensating?" I asked.

"Possibly. She was tangential. Her grasp on reality was tenuous. I didn't do a mental status exam. But she might have done poorly. Would have."

"Earlier that day she had shot your wife in the back." I felt a need to keep that fact in the room. One of us had to say it.

169

"Before I knocked her down she had been cradling her shoes like they were precious. I'd thought she had told me they were Jimmy Choos, but a nurse in the hospital told me that the shoes Diane wouldn't give up were a pair of Christian something. Christian . . . Louboutins." Alan Gregory shrugged. "Expensive, I guess. Doesn't matter. She was more concerned about the damn shoes than she was about the pistol."

Or about your wife, I was thinking. *Your dying wife.* I was breathless while I listened. He wasn't breathless. To me that said we hadn't yet approached the ripe part. I knew his rhythm by then. There had to be a ripe part.

"The shoes had red soles," he said.

I heard the words as *red souls* and began to ponder shoes with tinted souls, allowing myself to become distracted by the notion that doing psychotherapy with Alan Gregory was turning out to involve a whole mess of metaphor.

"They all have red soles," he continued, "regardless of the color of the shoe. It's distinctive to the designer, or brand, or . . ."

I didn't know fancy shoes. So not my thing. My most expensive shoes were ski boots. After that? Rock climbing shoes. In my brain I changed all previous references from *red souls* to *red soles.*

"Diane didn't have a bleed," Alan said. "But the scan showed she had a lesion."

I knew that from the rumors. It was part of the harmonies of "Did you hear?" and "Can you believe it?" that ricocheted around town in the days right after. The harmonies led to the chorus everyone was soon singing: "Diane might actually get off."

Diane hadn't yet been arrested. I was one of many people who didn't understand why not. All the public facts pointed toward Diane as the only suspect.

The harmonies about Diane getting away with it did fade with time. The scope of the tragedy became so great after Alan's wife's death that decorum drowned out the allure of good gossip. The little girl dancing at her mother's funeral had a lot to do with that. That poignant dance changed the conversation in town, for sure.

"The lesion was a few centimeters. An anaplastic astrocytoma," Alan said. He looked at me. I wasn't trying to disguise my ignorance. "Brain lesions aren't good. Grade III gliomas are particularly not good."

I'd heard that Diane had a lesion, but I knew nothing about brain tumors. The words *glioma* and *astrocytoma* did not

171

sound good. They also sounded more like cosmology than medicine.

"I don't know if this part is out there, but Diane is at Mayo Clinic. The one in Arizona, not in Minnesota. The court approved it. Her leaving the state, going there. A mutual friend told me that there was a complication with her initial treatment in Denver." He shrugged. "I don't believe it. I think that Raoul and her lawyer — he was a friend of mine, too — wanted her out of town for strategic reasons. The lawyer is Cozier Maitlin." He narrowed his eyes. "Do you know him?"

I shook my head. I had never heard of him.

"They, Raoul and Cozy Maitlin, wanted her out of Colorado. She could have been treated here. Radiation? Surgery? Both? I don't know what they're doing. The doctors and hospitals here could do it, whatever she needed. I think it's all part of a legal strategy to postpone her prosecution." Suddenly less assured, he said, "If you hear anything about that, would you tell me?"

"I'm not comfortable saying I would," I replied. "I have to give it some thought." *This is therapy,* was what I was thinking, *not Reuters,* but I didn't say that. Thank God.

He said, "Although I might ask you for things that are not part of a typical psychotherapy, Lila, I won't ask you for things that are not important."

"I will consider each request you make," I told him. "But I have to trust my instincts. If you insist I set those aside, we should stop this now. You should find someone else to treat you." I felt proud saying that. I also felt a little mean. I did a dipstick check of my countertransference. *Do I feel proud because I was a little mean?* I couldn't decide. My friends tell me I can get mean. But in therapy? Not good.

"Justice is a funny thing. You know Diane hasn't been arrested? For shooting my wife in the back? No arrest. Lauren used to tell me to be patient with the system. Time. That these things take time. Prosecutions take time. Cases get built an interview at a time. A report at a time. A motion at a time. A witness at a time. A deposition at a time. Time.

"I have a friend who is a Boulder police detective. He says that the fact that Diane is in treatment for a brain tumor removes any time pressure the DA might feel to arrest her. That's crap. He's stalling."

"You are unhappy at the progress? The lack of progress."

"Damn right," he said.

"Those things you said about time? Those

are things you feel that Lauren would be saying if she were still alive," I said to him. I was determined to keep her death in the room. "If your once-dear friend hadn't shot her."

That mass of silence settled on us, as though it had been hovering awaiting a tug that would cause it to blanket us again. My words provided the tug. I said, "I would prefer to make it through this session without asking you this kind of question, but I can't see a way around it. How do you feel about the glioma, the astrocytoma? About Diane still being free, about her being in Arizona for care at Mayo? You are angry. What else?"

He slid his lower jaw from side to side. His eyes were quiet, focused on something that registered as nothing. An unadorned wall behind me, to the right.

"I don't think the glioma had anything to do with it."

"With what?"

"With anything. That morning. That night. The shooting. The murder. Diane's decompensation. The fact she's still free." He opened his mouth, closed it. He said, "The red soles. The little Kahr. Mary-Louise Parker."

"The actress?" *What?* "How is she part of this?"

He shook his head. "Sorry. Not important."

"Diane was driving a little car? I don't know about that either."

"No, no car. I'm sorry. *Kahr* with a *K. K-a-h-r.* It's the gun Diane had that night. She called it her 'little Kahr.' "

Almost from the first moment I'd felt that he should provide me with a glossary for this therapy. A cheat sheet. I said, "That's the pistol you took from her?" He nodded. I said, "Go on." I almost asked him what he did with the Kahr. I should have asked him that. He would have asked his patient that. I made a mental note to go back to it.

"The lesion is too convenient," he said. His tone of voice told me that he was aware that his conclusion about the lesion, too, was convenient. "Cozy, her lawyer, will blame everything on the glioma. But it's ancillary. It's not what this was about."

"How do you know? What was it about?" I asked. He took a deep breath and I actually convinced myself he was about to tell me. I was wrong, of course.

"I'm not sure," he said. "I had a patient who was injured in a car wreck. They did an MRI of her spine while she was in the

ED. Small fracture of a vertebra. But the MRI also revealed a mass on her ovary. The ovarian cyst didn't cause the car wreck. And the car wreck didn't cause the ovarian cyst. Nor did the fractured vertebra cause the cyst."

I assumed he had a point. I said, "Okay." I was hoping to discover his point.

Alan shook his head in a way that left me feeling dismissed. My *okay* wasn't okay with him. At another moment, if he were another patient, I would have confronted him about our process. It wasn't another moment. He wasn't another patient. With him, I would come back to it. That list grew and grew.

He said, "The car wreck was caused by her distraction because she was screaming at her husband on her cell about an affair he was having. No one knew that part but me."

One of my known flaws as a therapist? I tend to debate inconsequential facts. I said, "Her husband had to know. Right? She was screaming at him." I think I wanted to say something unassailable to Alan. Something correct.

Alan laughed an ironic laugh. "No. Her husband had already hung up on her. He thought the accident was his fault because he had upset her by hanging up on her."

Shit. Got that wrong, too. But I thought I saw his point. I said, "They found Diane's glioma because they were looking for a sub-dural caused by the fact that you knocked her down to get the gun from her. The Kahr. It doesn't mean the glioma caused the behavior that led to the subdural in the first place."

He exhaled audibly. I read it to mean *close enough.* "The day of the Dome Fire? I saw another patient that morning. Before everything got crazy. She was a companion."

I frowned the frown of someone continuously on the periphery of comprehension. I said, "For an elderly person? Disabled? That kind of companion?"

He smiled in a way that was either patronizing or ironic. I felt it was patronizing, but I chose to go with ironic.

He said, "No. Think escort, but longer term."

"Oh. Okay. Sex?"

"Sex, yes," he said. "But not just sex."

Of course not. Probably acrobatics, too. And trapezes. Like Cirque du Soleil.

"There's more," Alan said.

"I am trying to keep up," I said. I was sure that sounded snarky because I was beginning to feel snarky. I was also thinking that Alan Gregory's caseload was much more interesting than mine. By, like, a factor of ten. Until he became my patient.

My caseload was much more interesting with him in it.

"The woman, the companion I was treating, resembled Lauren, especially from behind. Hair. Body type. Right after it happened, after she was shot, I thought there might have been some confusion that morning. For Diane, I mean.

"The woman, the companion, had just left my office when Lauren came to see me. I thought Diane might have somehow known the companion was there, but had not seen her leave. And had not seen Lauren arrive."

I leaned forward into the neutral zone between us. "Are you suggesting that Diane wanted to shoot one of your patients? The companion? She thought she was shooting that patient, but she ended up shooting your wife by mistake?"

"Perhaps, but it's irrelevant."

What? "How can that be irrelevant?"

"The woman mattered. That she was my patient? That didn't matter. Diane didn't care. But later at the hospital? When I was trying to make sense of it? That's what I was thinking — that Diane had confused my patient for my wife, or my wife for my patient."

"Can I ask why Diane might have wanted to shoot your patient?"

"Diane thought the woman was her husband's companion. Was jeopardizing their marriage."

"Raoul? Your patient was Raoul's companion?"

"Yes. She was Raoul's paid mistress, his . . . concubine. Who happened to be my patient. But I didn't know those details that morning."

"*Happened* to be your patient? That feels like a coincidence to you?" I allowed incredulity to give heft to my confrontation. How much? Too much. Were my incredulity water, I'd used an amount sufficient to float an aircraft carrier out of dry dock.

"I know. The chicken and the egg problem is murky," he said.

Murky? "But to you it feels irrelevant?"

"It's easy to get distracted by the pieces. This situation has alluring parts, things that sparkle. Don't get transfixed by them."

Are you kidding me? "But now? Now that you've thought about it, you are no longer sure that Diane intended to shoot the companion? Is that correct?"

He said, "No, not a hundred percent certain. But I know things now I didn't know then. Raoul was going broke, fast. Bad

179

bets in his business. They, Diane and Raoul, had been wealthy for as long as I'd known them. Diane may have snapped from stress. Long-term stress. PTSD. And acute stress, too, the companion/mistress thing. The going-broke thing. And the pregnancy and STD thing."

"What? I don't think I know about the STD thing."

"You'd heard rumors about the pregnancy. Well, she had an STD to boot."

My mouth was hanging open. I closed it. Volitionally. There *were* lots of sparkly things. I was tempted to get lost in the details and, if I did, I would completely trample any psychological momentum of our work. I said, "I may come back to the glitter later. But now? I need a clarification. When you say you think Diane snapped, do you mean psychotic-snapped?"

"Hard to say," he said. "That's where Mary-Louise Parker came in. Along with the Louboutins and . . . Did you know Diane was wearing a cocktail dress that night? For no reason. Purple organza."

Is organza a fabric people wear to the Oscars? Or to the prom? I did not know how to respond. The little car with a *K* handgun and a cocktail dress and a glioma and STDs and Mary-Louise Parker all showing up together in my office tied my tongue into a complete twist.

Oh my God.

He is displaying the sparkly stuff so that I don't notice something else.

Alan is part of it. Oh my dear bleeding God. He did have motive.

This is about him. That's what he's telling me.

He knew damn well I'd need supervision about this.

That's why he told me I couldn't get it.

20

ALAN

My practice continued to wither. For a psychotherapist all publicity isn't good publicity.

My first new patient of the new year — my only referral in over three months — was scheduled for the morning of Valentine's Day. She would be my sole patient that day.

The red light indicating my intake's arrival came on ten minutes early. I didn't see a reason to delay. I walked out to the waiting room.

"Alan," he said.

I closed my eyes and cursed silently. "Elliot," I said. My mind jumped back to my contentious conversation with Sam over New Year's, and his revelation that the maybe-surveillance that was maybe focused on me maybe came from Elliot's office.

Elliot Bellhaven, the Boulder County district attorney, was probably thinking, *Got you. Finally.* Elliot's phone calls since the shooting? I had not kept count. At least five, maybe ten. Half with voicemails in their wake. Three or four during January alone.

Initially, *I am so sorry. Thinking about your family. Anything at all I can do.*

The messages evolved as I ignored them. *Maybe we can meet for coffee. Or a drink. I would love to buy you dinner. Catch up. See how you're doing.*

The most recent voicemail, only a week back, was pointed: *A work thing has come up. We should talk. Soon. Kind of urgent. Call me, please.*

I didn't like Elliot Bellhaven. I didn't trust Elliot Bellhaven. That was why I hadn't returned any of his calls, or replied to any of his invitations. My refusal to respond was undoubtedly why he was camping out in my office waiting room determined to catch me between patients.

Shit, I thought. I was unprepared. He was prepared. Advantage: Elliot.

Elliot and I weren't buddies, though there had been a time when I thought we were heading that way. He became a colleague of Lauren's when they were both young deputies in the Boulder DA's office. Lauren was more experienced, more skilled, and more

183

polished in those days, but Elliot had a better pedigree. He was a Harvard grad with a degree in finance who then went on to Harvard Law — Lauren had called his educational background "Harvard squared."

She was a better prosecutor, but Elliot was always a measure or two more ambitious than she. Had Lauren not been handicapped — her word, and she meant it literally; when Elliot came to town she was recently diagnosed with multiple sclerosis — it would have been a fine fight. But her conclusion as she was coming to terms with her life with chronic illness was that a protracted alpha dog battle with Elliot was not a battle she could afford to engage, or to win. With the unpredictability of MS, and her inexperience dealing with the vagaries of her illness, she lacked both the confidence and the endurance necessary to protect any office turf she might gain with battle victories over Elliot.

Knowing she would never wake another morning, not one, without the threat of her illness complicating her life, she capitulated to Elliot early. The tension between them never did seem to let up, though. I never knew what to make of that.

Elliot and I both rode bicycles for recreation. Initially, I thought that might be our pivot toward friendship. But conflicting agendas, his and mine, and his and his, seemed to interfere with our relationship. One of Elliot's agendas had to do with office politics. Lauren believed that Elliot never trusted her abdication in the workplacc and that he continued to protect his status in the office at almost any price. She thought his aggressiveness had to do with his other agenda — his longer-term goal of getting elected DA of Boulder County, or maybe even attorney general of Colorado.

The last bicycle ride Elliot and I took together was up the challenging incline of Flagstaff Mountain, above Chautauqua, on the way toward Gross Reservoir. The climb wasn't steep. Steep, for me, stopped at half that angle. The Flagstaff Mountain climb was silly. Punishing. Ridiculous. The roster of people who had passed me on the way to the top of the cruel Flagstaff ascent wasn't a small one.

Elliot rode with average speed on the flats — most days I could beat him on open roads. But on hills? The man had thighs of pewter, and lungs transplanted from zoo animals. Large zoo animals. He could climb a mountain like Jack could mount a beanstalk. That day Elliot beat me to the top of Flagstaff by over two minutes.

His tenacity and power were good traits for a politician. Over the ensuing years, Elliot would demonstrate political chops that played well along with other skills that I hadn't recognized early on. The misjudgment was mine. His focus on the next electoral prize was unwavering. The fact that he could appear at times to take his eyes from that prize was mere illusion. Over the years I had occasionally fallen for Elliot's misdirection, as well as for the accompanying insincerity that he packaged so well as sincerity.

I had learned two enduring lessons about Elliot. One, that I wasn't good at reading him.

The second was that I should never trust him.

I shook his hand in the waiting room. I did not invite him back to my office.

I was aware he had probably been in my office without me that morning. In October. Or the day after. To see the crime scene. To see the place where his deputy DA was shot in the back. Or to leave his scent for my nose to detect. I detested that Elliot had been in my office without my permission. He would know that about me.

We stood awkwardly as we covered the

territory that convention required. *I am so sorry. We all miss her so much. How are the kids? That YouTube thing? Everybody is talking about it. Anything I can do?*

In my recent experience of running into acquaintances, the conventions of grief, mostly mine, and expressions of concern, largely theirs, had replaced pro forma questions about the warm, dry winter we were having, or if the mountains had sufficient snowpack to fill the reservoirs.

"Do you mind if we sit?" he asked. "Perhaps your office?"

I was six inches taller than Elliot. That was why he wished to sit. It was why I was reluctant to sit. I was hesitant to yield any advantage; my height was one of the few I had. "I have only a minute," I said. "I am expecting my next appointment." I didn't budge.

Elliot puffed himself up, as though he could inflate and fill the space.

"That day? Before Lauren came here," he said as introduction. He didn't wait for a reply. "Lauren had an unscheduled meeting with a young woman about a case. The woman had a boy with her."

Lauren had been a prosecuting attorney. A healthy chunk of her work life involved meeting with people about cases. That allowed me to play dumb with Elliot. *Be cool,* I told myself. *Be cool.* I shrugged, offering Elliot no hint that I knew about the meeting Lauren had with Izza Kane and with her nephew, Elias Tres Contopo.

Elliot went on. "Did she mention anything to you that morning about that case? Or that earlier meeting? Or anything else work related?"

"Is this an official visit, Elliot?" I asked.

"No," he said. "I am just reminiscing with you."

I could smell the bullshit. I said, "Just to clarify? You mean before Diane Estevez shot Lauren in the back?" I said. "Right down that hall?" I gestured down that hall. I did not want Elliot to allow himself any illusions about that morning. Or about the unresolved investigation he was shepherding.

I reminded myself to be careful with Elliot, to calibrate my words so that they fell in the gray zone between defensiveness and aggression. I waited to see if he was taken aback by what I said, or whether he displayed relief that I was freeing us both from having to tiptoe around in a candy land of decorum.

"Yes," he said, "before Lauren was shot. In your office. Before all of that happened

Lauren had a meeting as my deputy. I am asking if she discussed that meeting, or any other work matters, with you."

I wanted to say, "Cut the bullshit." But I stopped myself.

Elliot had chosen not to mention the shooter. I decided to remedy that omission.

"Lauren was shot by Diane Estevez, who has not been charged by your office with, what, anything? Did I miss an indictment? Illegal discharge of a firearm? Theft of that firearm? Perhaps the grand jury has the case? I would love an update."

Elliot seemed prepared to parry. "You know I can't discuss the prosecution, Alan. Or grand jury matters, if there are any. Anything involving Dr. Estevez is complicated by the circumstances of her medical condition. Please respect the office, even if you don't agree with the conduct of our investigation. Lauren would say the same thing to you."

"You are evoking Lauren's memory to sway me, Elliot? Wow. Using the memory of the murder victim to rationalize your stalled investigation? That takes chutzpah and a half. Bravo." I faux clapped. I knew I'd lost my cool.

"I was hoping our first meeting could be cordial," he said.

First meeting? That phrase gave me a chill. I immediately felt wary about the second meeting. I said, "Are we still reminiscing?"

"The Dome Fire was exploding blocks away in Boulder Canyon, yet Lauren took the time to come over here for a visit and —"

"A visit?"

"She took time out of her day to —"

"Maybe she wanted to see her husband."

"Her assistant told me her workday visits here were rare."

I didn't like that Elliot knew that fact about my marriage. *What else does he know that I wouldn't like?*

"I think she came here that morning because she had something to discuss with you. About her work."

"I don't recall what Lauren and I talked about," I said. "That whole day has become kind of a blur. A guess? I imagine we were discussing personal things. Husband and wife things. Family things. Our kids. Maybe Dome Fire things. Friends we might need to help evacuate. All of that, *before.* Before Diane burst in. Before I saw that damn little gun. And heard the shots. And saw the blood."

Elliot wasn't about to get sidetracked. "The woman Lauren met with at the Justice

Center told me that she gave Lauren a piece of paper that morning. The paper had a drawing on it. Thing is, we can't locate that paper. It is not in Lauren's office. It was not in her shoulder bag, or in her purse." He paused at that, for effect. The intended effect was to allow him to make a subtle insinuation about me. "At least by the time her things were taken into evidence. Here, in your office."

" 'Here' meaning the crime scene?" I said. "I assume my office was under police control minutes after the shooting."

"Yes." Elliot paused. "Minutes after. That's accurate. Those 'minutes' are of some concern to the investigation."

"Are we still reminiscing?" I asked. He nodded. "What woman did Lauren meet?" I knew. The woman who brought the drawing was Isabel Kane. Izza. I was testing Elliot to see what he would reveal.

He said, "Her identity is not germane."

"You're sure? This crime scene? My attorney said it was secured and then sealed until Detective Sengupta supervised a search early the next day. My attorney was present as a witness and to protect my privileged patient files from illegal access."

"Yes," he said. "Accurate again, except for those first minutes. We didn't locate that paper prior to securing the office. Or later during the search."

"Were you here that morning, Elliot?" I asked. "Personally?"

"What?"

"Did you enter my office under the auspices of the search warrant?"

I knew he had. I sensed his spoor. When he hesitated I wanted to hit him.

Finally he said, "In my supervisory capacity. One of my deputies had been shot."

Asshole. He had come to mark my space. "To confirm? This is not an official visit, Elliot? We're still shooting the shit?"

"I will tell you when I am making an official visit, Alan. This is a social call."

I said, "Perhaps the woman who spoke with Lauren at the Justice Center was mistaken about the drawing. It was just one drawing, Elliot?"

"She is adamant about the nature of the meeting, and she confirmed handing over the drawing. A second witness corroborates it. Those facts seem beyond dispute."

Elliot hadn't confirmed the number of drawings. That worried me. Lauren had showed me only one. Had she left others behind at her office? I didn't know.

I thought that the second witness Elliot mentioned would be Elias Tres, the boy who made the drawing when he was only five years old. But the second witness could also have been Lauren's assistant, Andrew. Or someone else at the Justice Center. I had no way to know who had witnessed the moment when Izza handed Lauren the drawing. Or drawings. More disadvantage for me.

I edged closer to Elliot. "Is there an accusation hiding in there, Elliot? Are you suggesting something about my behavior the day my wife was shot in front of me?"

He waited, allowing the delay to make his point for him. "Most of Lauren's things were taken into evidence. Here, after we got a warrant. At the hospital. A few things back at the office." I waited. He went on. "Her shoes weren't collected, though; they were never located. If she was wearing hose that day — we don't know for certain that she was — we don't have them. We do not have a bra, either."

I found news of the disappearance of her bra curious, but not surprising. She had been shot in the back. For all I knew there was a bullet hole or two in the undergarment. During her surgery it would have definitely been an afterthought.

I was confident she had not been wearing stockings. She hated panty hose, and the day had been too warm for tights. Lauren's shoes? They weren't missing. They had been mixed in with my personal belongings in a plastic bag in the emergency department. I had been given the bag later that night. I had her bloody shoes.

"It was chaotic after she was shot," I said. "I was trying to keep pressure on her wounds while I called 911. The ambulance came almost instantly, the EMTs took over, started an IV, tried to control the bleeding. They got us both right into the ambulance. We were separated in the ED. Before I knew it she was on the way to the operating room."

"Right into the ambulance?" he said. "You had been shot, too?" Elliot said.

"Yes. I was shot, Elliot. In the calf." *You know that, you ass.*

"Recovering well?"

I heard no concern in his query. I felt a trap being set. "Yes. A flesh wound. Through and through. I was lucky, I guess."

21

Elliot smiled. It wasn't a kind smile.

"Lucky? Let's see . . . a major wildfire threatening downtown, your wife shot mortally in the back, you shot in the leg. I honestly don't know too many people who would call themselves 'lucky' in those circumstances." My mind went blank. "I may need to extend an invitation for you to join the Optimists with me. It's a good group."

I reached for a shovel to dig myself out of the hole I had dug. I knew the damage had been done. "I have three terrific kids, Elliot. A lot to be hopeful about."

He wasn't done coming at me. "When did you realize you were shot? Here? Later? At the hospital? There's confusion in the chart. About your injury."

Elliot has been reading the record. Lauren had always cautioned me not to speak with law enforcement without an attorney present. Regardless of the apparent stakes. The question that Elliot had just asked me was a fine example of her rationale. *"When did you realize you were shot, Alan?"* appeared to be a simple question. But I knew it was not. I tried to calculate Elliot's motivation. I couldn't come up with an explanation that worked. That worried me. I fell back on my assumption that he was setting a trap.

"It was a crazy morning. The adrenaline. I don't remember, Elliot. I'm sorry."

"You'll think about it, though? For me?"

For a while, I thought, *I doubt I will think about anything else. But not for you.*

The drawing Elliot wanted had made it to the emergency department, where it was later stuffed along with my bloody clothes, and some of Lauren's things, into the plastic bag that contained our personal belongings. Early the next morning, as my vigil waiting for Lauren to die was in its earliest hours, I handed that solitary drawing — the drawing that I felt so clearly damned him — to Sam Purdy.

I did not know what happened to it after that. Though I could guess. I certainly wasn't about to share that guess with Elliot Bellhaven.

Elliot had not mentioned Sam Purdy. I

wondered if that was tactical, or if it was possible he had not recognized Sam's connection to the death in Frederick. The murder in Frederick. It was possible that Elliot remained in the dark about what had happened the night the woman was shot in that cottage in Frederick. Especially about Sam's role.

"Back to the drawing if you don't mind," Elliot said. "The one we can't locate. The police set up a perimeter shortly after . . . ?" he asked. "That's your recollection?"

I said, "My recollection is vague. I couldn't pinpoint when the police arrived. It was after the ambulance I think, but I'm not sure. I may have already been in the ambulance when the first officers showed up. It's a blur. A perimeter? Can't help you. Maybe one of the first responders knows. I don't recall seeing any yellow tape."

Elliot came very close to a smirk. "That's right, you *weren't* here. You were whisked away without a word to the officers. Was correct procedure followed?" I didn't bite. He went on. "A perimeter was put in place only moments after the ambulance departed with our witnesses inside. The forensic team discovered no drawing here. Or among the things that Lauren left behind at her office. Not on her desk or in her files. And there was nothing in pockets of the clothing she was wearing. Nothing in the emergency department, nor in the ambulance that took her there. Not in the operating room, where they cut off your wife's remaining clothing prior to surgery."

He was hitting me hard with memories that felt like body blows. I had to assume that compromising my balance was his intent. I said, "I couldn't say."

"No, I guess you couldn't say. Who knows, maybe wouldn't say."

I wanted to knock his head off. But I wore my trusty therapist mask instead. I wore it like it was Halloween and I wanted to win the best-costume prize.

Elliot had a reason for the visit. I forced myself to figure out what it was.

He said, "The fact that the police didn't discover the drawing doesn't necessarily mean that she did not bring it here with her. One possibility — in my mind — is that she brought it here specifically to show it to you."

I was tempted to point out to Elliot that he hadn't asked me a question. I didn't. I said, "Why would she bring work product here? It doesn't sound like her. I can't think of a single previous time that she had done that."

He made a puzzled face. "Exactly. Why did she do that? What was so important about that drawing?"

Elliot was displaying a quick mind. But I knew that about him already.

I said, "I can't help you with your theory, Elliot."

"Did you see the drawing, Alan? A solitary sheet of paper. With a picture on it."

Elliot could be a provocative little shit. But I knew that about him already, too.

"A drawing of . . . what? Can you jog my memory? Maybe that will help."

"So you do have a memory?"

"Have I misled you? I didn't mean to suggest I have amnesia."

I could hear Lauren's admonition. *Don't talk. Call a lawyer.*

We were standing so close together that Elliot was forced to tilt his head back to maintain eye contact with me. Not an ideal posture for a power player. Elliot Bellhaven most definitely considered himself a power player. "Let us just say the piece of paper, the drawing, is evidence," he said. "In an old case. Does that help with your memory?"

Elliot was appearing to be careless, slowly leaking information he wasn't required to divulge. It made me wary that he was appearing to be careless. "Doesn't sound like my wife. Carrying important evidence out of the building? Showing it to me?"

Elliot said, "You're right, it doesn't sound like her. She and I had our differences, but I never questioned her integrity. I can think of only two reasons for her to bring that drawing here. One, she thought you might have some professional expertise that might guide her investigation in some way." He narrowed his eyes. "No, probably not. She would choose someone with forensic expertise for that."

I thought, *Asshole.* I didn't say it.

"Or, two, perhaps she had concluded that the drawing concerned you in some way. She was, for want of a better word, confronting you with it. It's one of the things that we prosecutors do in our work. We confront people with evidence about crimes."

"Really? That's your speculation?" My wife's voice said, *Shut up. Shut up.*

"Was that a big enough clue for you, Alan? Does that jog your memory?"

I was distracted by the physical and psychic energy it was taking me to keep from instigating physical violence. "What?"

"I asked you a question."

"Sorry," I said. "No, it did not help my memory. I'm hopeless, I guess."

200

Elliot sensed advantage. "You don't know where the drawing is?"

I said, "No." I was prepared to lie to Elliot — it would have been but a small fresh turd on my mountain of criminal deception — but his careless phrasing meant that I wasn't required to lie. Not then. I was cognizant that I might be missing something. The years since the murder had convinced me that I was not nearly as clever as I liked to believe.

"Did Lauren mention a case she was working on in Frederick?"

Many times, I thought. *Too many to count.* "The town?" I said.

Frederick, Colorado, is not the kind of town that comes up in Boulder conversations with any reliable frequency. I had gone years in my Boulder County life without hearing any mention of the Weld County town of Frederick in a conversation with anyone. Until Sam Purdy went there to kill a woman.

And again, a few years later, when Lauren became interested in what had happened there the night that Sam went there to kill a woman.

"Yes, the town," Elliot responded.

"Isn't that Weld County, not Boulder County? Kind of outside your realm."

201

"My *realm*?"

I was pleased that he felt stung by my regal allusion. I said, "Realm of responsibility. Of course."

He put the tip of his tongue between his teeth. Then he said, "Jurisdiction isn't all dark lines. You should know that by now."

"You would be surprised at my ignorance about the law, Elliot. I still am. When Lauren talked about cases with me she was circumspect. She removed identifying details, like names or locations. Frederick, for instance. She spoke in generalities."

"You didn't discuss Frederick with her?"

Here come the lies. I chose my words carefully. Something else that Lauren had taught me over the years was that although accessory to a crime like murder might be hard to prove, perjury was not so hard to prove. "I don't specifically recall it coming up in a discussion, but again it's the type of detail she would exclude. What was the case about? It might help me remember."

Elliot took a step back so he could drop his chin a centimeter. He snorted, pianissimo, just a microburst through his nose. *Derision?* Maybe. I remained worried that Elliot had an advantage I wasn't spotting.

"I should get ready for my next appointment," I said, glancing at my watch. I flipped off the wall switch that Elliot had flipped on when he'd arrived.

The need to prepare for my next appointment wasn't a lie. I had a new patient, my first since Lauren's death. I wanted to be clearheaded. "Thank you for all your concern, Elliot. About Lauren. And us, the family. It means so much," I said. "Your office has been most understanding through everything."

Elliot's capacity for believable disingenuousness was revelatory; if Elliot wasn't so busy being a prosecutor and a politician, he could be a repertory lead in a community theater. He said, "Whatever we can do. You must know that." He stepped back toward the door, stopping when he placed his hand on the knob. "You know," he said, "perhaps I am guilty of an assumption. Perhaps what Lauren brought here to show you was something else. Not the drawing but some notes?" He was watching my face intently.

I shrugged. But he had my attention. *Notes?*

"No? If you hear from me again in the near future — see my name in caller ID, or maybe spot *ellbell* in your email inbox — it's probably about this thing in Frederick. And the missing drawing. Or maybe that

203

other thing she discussed with you. Those notes.

"I suggest you take that call. Respond to that email. Or at least notify your attorney that I've reached out." He smiled with no warmth in his eyes. "If there is a next time it will not be a social contact. You may indeed wish to have an attorney present."

"For the record? This was just a social visit?"

"For the record? I have a detailed log of all the times I've tried to express my concerns and condolences in the past months. This will go down as the day I succeeded in expressing those thoughts to you."

I laughed.

"Take the next call, Alan."

Elliot had to pause before he walked back out the front door in order to allow my new patient to enter. She'd arrived outside at the same instant he had begun to pull open the door from inside.

My gut clenched — it felt as though it folded over on itself — as they passed within inches. I felt as though I were watching two cars slide on ice, certain they would collide.

"Excuse me," he said, stepping back.

"Thank you," she said, as she came inside.

To her I said, "Hello, I am Doctor Gregory, please come on back." I held out my left arm to guide her. I gazed back over my shoulder as I shut the door between the waiting room and the hallway.

Elliot had almost reached the sidewalk on Walnut Street. He was already speaking into his phone.

Lauren had told me she often did the same thing after a meeting. An immediate call back to the office provided a retrievable time stamp for the conclusion of an interview.

22

My new Valentine's Day patient wasn't a new patient after all.

It was Izza Kane, God help me.

In my mind I replayed the little dance that she and Elliot did at the front door as they passed. I was certain they had not recognized each other. That meant — it had to mean — they did not know each other. That they had not met before. *Huh.* Or it meant that this was all part of a rehearsed ruse, an elaborate choreography.

They had intended to run into each other in my office. *Jesus.*

I suggested Izza sit. She did.

Her first words to me were, "Obviously, in order to get this chance to speak with you I deceived you about who I really was." She made a face that I couldn't interpret. "That was rude of me. Who does something like that, right?"

The name she'd used on the phone when

she'd made the appointment with me was Clara. She didn't offer a last name in her voicemail. After I called back and we identified a mutually agreeable time for an initial visit, I asked for her surname. She replied, "It's Tea, like the drink." That was how she put it.

Existing patient names went into my appointment book as initials only. But first-time patients were entered into my appointment book as first name followed by last initial. I had written Izza in for eleven A.M. as "Clara T." *Clarity. God, I'm an imbecile.*

What goes around comes around. I had pretended to be a prospective tenant when I first met Izza Kane, who was the de facto landlord of the Frederick cottage where Sam Purdy had murdered his ex-girlfriend. I had bicycled to Frederick that day because I was curious to see how the crime happened. In the back of my mind I knew I had been trying to ascertain if Sam had been honest with me about the events of that night.

I had encouraged Izza Kane to show me the entire cottage. Each room. I let her flirt with me a little bit, too. Perhaps I even flirted back a little. Izza sitting in my office was payback for my earlier ruse. Not undeserved.

She said, "I would have preferred not to do this. If you had been more forthcoming on the phone when I called, I wouldn't have had to do this. I gave you a chance. I gave you over a month to call me back and tell me the truth. You didn't."

I was silent. It wasn't a therapeutic silence. I was accepting my morning of disadvantage.

"Is this where it happened?" Izza asked, making a show of looking around. There wasn't that much to see. "Is that where you were sitting? Exactly?"

I'd said something similar to her in the cottage. About the violent death of her tenant. When I didn't reply she nodded to herself and stood. She walked to the south-facing window, spun, and examined the room from that perspective. Then she took a few small steps back toward the door. She said, "Your partner — Diane Estevez, is that right? She's ill. A brain tumor. I Googled her. She must have been standing *here.*" She raised her left foot and tapped the pine floor with the toe of her boot. For some reason I thought of Clever Hans doing arithmetic. "When she came in that day. With the gun. Yes, I can see how it happened." She nodded again. "She shot right into the back of the chair? From this spot?

Three times? Exactly. Yes. Good."

She sat back down across from me. She rocked side to side on the cushion, tugging at her skirt.

I was feeling anger. I was feeling sadness. And I was feeling so fatigued that I wanted to curl up on the sofa and sleep for a week. I had tears in my eyes from a hard fresh wave of cold grief as she forced me to reexperience that morning.

I suddenly smelled blood. But not just blood. The aroma in my sinuses was a blend of blood mixed with the harsh burn of gunpowder. I had been suppressing that part of that morning — the unique metallic aroma of the cocktail of warm iron and hot cordite.

I swallowed to keep from puking into my mouth. I wiped tears from my eyes.

She was unmoved by my distress. She squeezed the armrests with her long fingers. She said, "Well, you got a new chair. Had to. Or is this just fresh upholstery? I can't imagine that's the same rug. Nice touch, replacing it with another old rug. Something new would stand out — kind of advertise what happened. Don't you think? Whatever, I approve."

I wiped more tears. I said, "You're being cruel, Izza."

"Am I?" Her eyes were defiant. But they were glistening with tears, too. "Is that you being therapeutic? Because I am not feeling any better so far. At all."

What had Sam said when I asked him if there was a way I could tell if Izza was wearing a wire? He'd said I knew the answer to that. I'd said that was never going to happen. And yet here we were. Izza and I, with me wondering about a wire.

"I get it. You're not here as my patient. Just as I wasn't there as your prospective tenant. Can we move on?"

Back when Izza and I met I had pegged her as an interesting, ambitious woman. I also reached a conclusion that she fought her weight, assuming that stress — school, family, money, relationships — caused her to consume impulse calories.

I'd been wrong. Her recent stresses — her father's death, the revelations about her mother, Big Elias, Elias Tres — had diminished her appetite, not exacerbated it. Izza was at least fifteen pounds lighter than the last time I had seen her.

She was wearing what appeared to be new clothes. The top was a scoop-neck thing that fit her snugly. Her skirt was on the short side but appropriate for her age. Her boots were cowboy boots I'd seen before, battered to perfection. The patina on that leather wasn't for sale; Izza had earned the character on those boots the hard way.

I said, "Before we go on, would you please put your bag out in the hall?"

"What?" She looked offended. "Why?"

I took a deep breath. It wasn't for show — though if I hadn't needed the breath for fortification I would have taken the deep breath for show. I said, "I could make something up. I do with other people so I don't have to explain my anxiety. But I will tell you the truth. I have —"

"Is this an amend?" she said. She didn't say it kindly. "You being honest?"

"Sure," I said. "If you want, it's an amend. Since the shooting I have post-traumatic stress. I can't relax here wondering what people have with them. I become distracted. I don't attend well. I find I can be present here" — *present* was a perfect Boulder word to complement my ruse — "only if I ask that coats and bags go out in the hall. I am sorry. It's all my . . . stuff."

She stood, picked up her bag, and stepped toward the door.

As she leaned over for her bag I examined her back. My eyes traced the outlines of the straps of her bra as the loops disappeared over her shoulders, and they traced the wider strap of her bra across her back and under her arms. I saw nothing there that shouldn't be there. No nonstructural wires. No mics. Nor did I spot any lines or lumps below her skirt on her hips or butt that were out of place or unexpected.

She returned to the office from the hall. In an instant when I felt her eyes averted from mine I examined her upper body. Her chest was smooth where it should be smooth. Round where it should be round. Her bra left the kinds of outlines and bulges that bras tend to leave.

If Izza were wearing a wire it was taped between her legs or tucked into a boot. I knew nothing about the acoustic properties of the microphones used for surveillance, but neither location seemed to me like an ideal spot to secrete a mic.

"Better?" she said.

"Thank you," I said.

Izza said, "Did you know the tenant? You didn't seem upset about her death. I don't know what to make of that. For a while I thought she might have been an old lover of yours. But now I don't think so."

Izza and I were back in the cottage together. We were talking about J. Winter Brown. *Currie* to Sam Purdy. Currie was the woman Sam killed. The homicide that he'd made to look like suicide. Izza was in my office to talk about *that* murder. Not Lauren's.

"I did not know her," I said. It hadn't crossed my mind to lie. That surprised me.

"Why did you visit? If it wasn't about her, then it had to be about her death."

Yes, I thought. *It was about her dying, and about what it would have meant if she were living.* I got lost in the thought. I wanted to say, "She was going to kill my kids." I felt that Izza would have understood that. I didn't. I couldn't risk it.

Izza said, "Later? I thought you were just a creep. Somebody who visited crime scenes. That's what I had decided until I saw you on YouTube. With your daughter dancing. At that funeral. At your wife's funeral."

I didn't have a lie ready for Izza about that. That was novel for me; I seemed to always have a lie on deck for Izza.

23

The drawing Elliot wanted from me, the one that Lauren made a special trip to show me that last morning in my office, was done in crayon by Elias Tres Contopo, the then five-year-old eyewitness to the prelude of the murder across the country lane from his home.

The woman was planning to kill children. Lauren's and mine. Sam's.

The threat to the kids was imminent. And it was real.

On the night Tres became the unwitting witness to Sam's arrival in Frederick to commit homicide, he was a not-quite six-year-old boy who was waiting impatiently for his recently deceased father — Elias Jr., whom everyone called "Segundo" — to return from battle in Afghanistan. Elias Tres was sitting upstairs in his grandfather Elias's house looking for his dad when he saw a white station wagon park on the street not

214

far from his window.

The murder in the cottage had gone off according to Sam's plan, well out of the young boy's sight and hearing. The body wasn't discovered for a few days. The authorities ultimately made a determination that the death had been the result of suicide — a gunshot wound to the head — exactly as the killer, Sam Purdy, had planned.

I eventually became Sam's unknowing and reluctant, but willing, accomplice in the homicide. If he had asked me to assist him with the planning or commission of the actual act, I would have. Our kids' lives were at risk.

But Sam had not asked for my help with the murder in advance. In fact, with his choice of timing for the homicide — I was in New Mexico with Jonas — and the secrecy with which he carried it out, Sam made certain that I had an excellent alibi for the night of the crime.

But my personal reality, and my legal reality, was that I was as responsible as Sam was for Justine Brown's death. Even though I was ignorant, I was willing. Even though I never had to fire a bullet or lift a gun, I was willing. Even though I had an alibi, I was present.

Legally, I shared culpability with Sam Purdy.

In my mind, I was guilty. Guilty as in not innocent.

But guilty as in remorseful? Not for a day since. Replay the circumstances, and I would again sign on as accessory after the fact. Or I would load and fire the gun myself.

Initially I spent some time worrying about what that said about me as a person. But even that narrow version of remorse had diminished over the three years plus since the murder.

By then the five-year-old witness had grown into an almost nine-year-old boy.

The drawing he had made years before was artistically immature. The kid might have been a mensch, as people who knew him maintained, even a savant, as some boasted, but he was no Leonardo-in-waiting. His lack of artistic talent didn't diminish the impact of his drawing. Alongside his story of what he saw that night, the picture he made of our car was a damning piece of evidence.

I was hyperaware of an odd piece of eyewitness reality recorded in that drawing. That twist was that the drawing itself implicated me — it was my car — more than it implicated Sam. The drawing became damning to Sam only when it was combined with the story the boy related to Lauren the morning she was given the drawing. Only together did the drawing and the boy's recollections implicate Sam Purdy.

By itself, though, the drawing pointed at me.

Lauren was sharp. Despite her ignorance about the details of the murder, she saw immediately what the drawing and the boy's memories said about culpability for the crime. She concluded, accurately, that Sam Purdy was in Frederick that night. And that I wasn't.

Lauren came to my office to offer me advance notice that Sam would be picked up for investigation of the murder in Frederick. But she came to see me unaware that I knew details she didn't know. I knew Sam's motive. Lauren didn't know that. I knew Sam had an accomplice after the fact. Me. Lauren did not know that.

While a wildfire was storming to life only blocks from my office in parallel canyons that spilled smack into Boulder, I shared those damning facts with my wife.

I described Sam's motive — the risk to our children — and I admitted my role and my culpability. My confession to her was,

217

almost, the last thing Lauren and I ever discussed. The very last thing we discussed? It was trust. Trust between parents. Between lovers. Between husbands and wives.

She was defiant that I had erred. "You should have trusted me," she scolded.

She was arguing to me that trust — between us — demanded that I should have revealed to her what Sam and I had done back when we had done it.

I admitted that I had failed to do that. I also shared my rationalization with her, explaining that if things went south — as they were heading due south that very day — one of our children's parents, either Lauren or me, needed to have clean hands about the crime. Deniability about the crime.

Simply, one of us had to be able to stay out of prison to raise our children.

Once I became Sam's accomplice it was too late for me to keep my hands clean, so by default I had chosen Lauren for the clean-hands role. To keep her hands clean, I explained, I couldn't tell her what I knew about the murder that night in Frederick.

Trusting her with my truth, and with Sam's, would have soiled her hands. And that would have endangered our children's future.

Not a day had gone by since that morning that I had failed to think about Lauren's admonishment about my failure to trust. And about the continuing necessity of having someone being around to take care of our children.

Someone with clean hands.

The irony that weighed so heavily on me in the wake of Elliot's visit, and of Izza Kane's fake intake, was that the drawing — in the absence of Elias Tres's memories — implicated me, not Sam, in that old murder in Frederick.

Elliot had walked away from my office that morning without revealing even a hint of an innuendo that he was aware of my friend Sam Purdy's involvement in the events in Frederick. I could conjure only two possibilities to explain that.

One, Elliot was holding his cards close to his chest. That was the simplest and most likely explanation. Or two? Elliot hadn't heard, or didn't recognize, the subtle clues in Elias Tres's memory that led directly to Sam Purdy, and that exonerated me.

Over the years since the murder I had been worried that Sam would get caught, somehow, and I would eventually be fingered as his accessory after the fact.

Suddenly — and not because of his knowledge of what was in the drawing, but rather because of his ignorance about the contents of Elias Tres's memory — it seemed possible that Elliot Bellhaven was looking at me as the principal offender for the crime.

That meant that Sam Purdy might end up being the one with the clean hands.

Our plan all along was that, worst case, only one of us would go down for the crime.

I had always felt that the clean hands should, and would, be mine.

Sam had, after all, pulled the trigger.

I was foolish enough to believe that should count for something.

24

The session with Izza ended in a predictable stalemate. She wanted information from me that I wouldn't provide. She left my office angry. She didn't try to disguise it. I didn't see another way it could have ended.

My next move was impulsive. I made a call to Kirsten Lord.

"You're home? I thought I'd get your voicemail."

"I come home for lunch when I can."

"May I stop by? Briefly." More impulse.

"Uh yeah, I guess. Now?"

"Now would be great." My ego had left my body. I was all id. And all in.

"Is this personal or legal, Alan?"

What? I suddenly recalled that it was Valentine's Day. *Shit.* "I haven't — I don't — I need to see you, Kirsten. It's important. Urgent even."

I had no doubt that she could hear the

anxiety in my voice. The pressure. In the wake of Lauren's death, people were still granting me latitude for my lability.

"I don't have much time. I have a thing right after lunch. Keep it short?"

"It won't take long," I said. Considering that I had no idea what I planned to talk with Kirsten about, I offered that assurance with remarkable confidence.

Kirsten Lord. How to start? We met around the same time I'd met Carl Luppo. She, like he, had been my patient while I was doing my consultant gig for the Witness Security Program of the U.S. Marshals Service, WITSEC. Kirsten was a newly enrolled protectee of the marshals, a prosecutor from New Orleans, who had been relocated by WITSEC along with her daughter to try to safeguard them from organized crime thugs who were dedicated to ending their lives. By the time WITSEC whisked her and her daughter away from southern Louisiana to the anonymous safety of Boulder County, Kirsten's enemies had already gunned down and killed her husband.

I continued to wonder if she had heard from Carl Luppo when he was in town over New Year's. I knew their contact wouldn't have been cordial. Kirsten would never invite Carl into her home. If they met face-to-face in Boulder, perhaps they re-created their first-time meeting across a table at the Dushanbe Teahouse.

Did I believe Kirsten would enlist Carl's help on my behalf?

No, I did not. But things I never believed could happen were coming true in my life with troubling frequency.

Years before, Kirsten had transitioned from initial hatred of Carl Luppo to having conflicted feelings about him, but she never displayed any conflicted feelings about what he had done with his life. To Kirsten he was, and he always would be, an amoral killer no better than the one who had shot her husband to death on the sidewalk outside Galatoire's in the French Quarter in New Orleans.

To Kirsten, Carl's choice to live that life had been an unforgivable sin.

My clinical treatment of Kirsten back then was uncomplicated. She was suffering from a completely understandable reactive disorder. The treatment was also truncated; it ended in a chaotic night of mayhem, with me trapped beneath the rubble of the entryway of my collapsed house as assassins closed in on her and on my family. I had somehow ended up saving lives that night, including hers, with one ever-so-fortunate eyes-closed shot of a silenced .22 handgun.

In the ensuing months Kirsten had voluntarily exited WITSEC and had become friends with my wife. They had a lot in common as prosecutors. But that friendship ended abruptly after about a year. Kirsten's choice.

Kirsten admitted to me years later the reason the friendship ended. She had, she explained, fallen in love with her therapist. Me. From the day she made that admission — years had passed in the interim — she and I hadn't spoken much. She eventually returned to practicing law.

On the short walk to her house from my office, my id decided that sufficient time had passed that I could ethically seek her help. Was it true? Probably. Was I rationalizing? Of course. My id, like everyone else's, specialized in the black side of black-and-white constructs. It had no flair for ambiguity.

She lived on Fourth Street in one of the city's earliest residential areas in a Lilliputian old stone cottage that she'd renovated with modern comforts. The warren of small lots from Boulder's pioneer past that included hers was nestled in a rise of gentle hills just north and west of the heart of Pearl

Street below the sharp vault of the foothills of the Rockies.

I had been to her house once before — on the day she revealed her love for me.

After Lauren was shot, Kirsten was one of many who reached out with condolences and offers of help. Hers was one of the familiar faces I recalled seeing that day at the cemetery, which meant that she was one of the witnesses to Grace's dance performance. We spoke only briefly at the memorial service — "I'm so sorry," she'd said, "that we have something new, and awful, in common."

The new thing we shared was that we'd both witnessed a spouse's murder.

When she opened the door, I said, "I am sorry about intruding."

"Not at all," she replied, but her greeting was restrained. I suspected she was wary of a completely inappropriate Saint Valentine's Day ambush from me. We shook hands — the handshake felt odd — before she led me toward the same small sofa we'd sat on the day she confided she loved me. She had kissed me then. It had not been a passionate kiss, nor was it chaste. It was a kiss about what might have been but wasn't, and wouldn't.

I sat opposite the fireplace. She chose a nearby chair. She tapped her watch. "I have ten minutes, Alan. No more. I wish I could stay but —"

"I understand. This was inconsiderate of me. I shouldn't have come."

"Talk. Don't apologize."

I felt innuendo. I couldn't afford to be distracted, so I ignored the innuendo. I took a deep breath before I opened my mouth but I couldn't find a second word. The first word — *I* — I repeated twice more. I exhaled, emptying my lungs, hoping to get past the pronoun.

Kirsten leaned forward far enough that she could place three fingertips on my wrist. "Slow," she said. Then she smiled and added, "But not too slow."

"I need your advice."

She gave me a second or two to continue. Then she said, "Not my favorite headline. Additional details might make me feel better. Or not."

Her accompanying smile felt kind. I said, "What's going on could cost me everything I haven't already lost."

Her shoulders slumped slightly. "Personal mess? Legal mess?"

"Yes. Both."

"Pick one to start. But start." She glanced

again at her watch.

I hesitated. I said, "Legal first."

She frowned as though I'd picked the wrong one. She said, "I was under the impression that Casey Sparrow was representing you."

Casey was a criminal defense attorney I'd known forever. I said, "Casey helped me with issues around the search of my office. That morning."

"Are you looking for someone with expertise beyond Casey's? I'm not sure who that would be. She's good, Alan."

"Between you and me? Casey's up for a district court appointment. She's being vetted. This wouldn't be a good time to involve her with my problems."

"That explains things." She made a go-on, go-on motion with her hand.

"Elliot Bellhaven cornered me in my waiting room this morning. The conversation we had was complicated, but he was insinuating that I might be the target of an investigation into possible evidence tampering he thinks took place the morning of Lauren's shooting. In my office."

The tip of her tongue found a small opening between her upper and lower teeth. "Mr. Bellhaven was alone?"

"Yes."

"He arrived without an appointment?"

"He came under the guise of a social call, but it felt to me like an ambush. He has been trying to reach me. He'd called about Lauren. Condolences. I didn't take his calls. Didn't return any of the messages. You know some of my history with Elliot. There is not much affection or trust between us."

"Today? He presented himself as . . . ?"

"He said repeatedly that the visit was social. But it felt prosecutorial."

"He didn't suggest to you that you might wish to have an attorney present?"

"As he was leaving he mentioned that he thought I should consider including my lawyer the next time I hear from him. He implied there would be a next time."

"He said those words?"

"I'm not quoting. But yes."

She rolled her eyes. "No Miranda?"

"No."

"No witness to the meeting?"

"I don't have a receptionist." She'd been my patient. She knew that.

"The alleged evidence tampering? It was something that took place in your office the morning Lauren was shot?"

"Yes."

"By you? Is that a safe assumption?"

"That was his insinuation."

I could see her weighing my answer in her head. She looked at her watch. She dug into her purse before she attached a device the size of a big sugar cube to the top of her mobile phone. "Do you have a credit card with you? Personal? Not business." I handed her a card from my wallet. She slid it through the device and pecked at the screen.

"You just gave me a small deposit on a legal retainer. I have a digital record for the transaction."

"Please don't take this the wrong way, but I don't want you to be my lawyer. I need a friend. Some guidance. Maybe some reassurance."

"Please don't take *this* the wrong way, but I don't want to be your lawyer. But if I am going to be able to avoid becoming part of whatever problem you're having, I need to hear the story about what happened between you and Mr. Bellhaven in confidence.

"I don't wish to be compelled to testify in the future about this discussion. You and I have a choice to make about how to maintain privilege. I can think of only two options. Either you become my client — thus the retainer — or I become your patient. Do you have a preference?"

That was a no-brainer. "Retainer it is."

"I'm pleased. I promised myself I would

never go back into therapy."

I began to speak. She held up a hand, interrupting me while she completed a call. The call was short; she requested that a taxi come to her house.

"That buys me a few minutes. I was going to walk to the Justice Center for a pretrial conference. The taxi will save time."

I spoke nonstop for the next two minutes.

"Couple of things," Kirsten said when I reached a place to pause. "We both know you're not being forthcoming. Yes?" I nodded as I opened my mouth to explain my reticence. She stopped me. "I am making an assumption that what you're not telling me leaves you even more vulnerable than what you are telling me." Again, I began to respond. That time she stopped me with a traffic cop's raised hand. "Assure me that what you have told me so far is true."

"It is."

"Elliot may well think that you're hiding or withholding evidence — evidence that you have not specified — about what happened the morning Lauren was shot. The fact that Elliot is suggesting that, even obliquely, concerns you enough that it brought you to my door in a bit of a panic."

"Pretty much. But the evidence Elliot was confronting me about wasn't evidence about what happened the day Lauren was shot. The evidence Elliot was alluding to is about an old case, a different shooting. Elliot thinks I'm withholding evidence about that one. In a different jurisdiction. A death."

"What kind of death? A homicide? Where?"

I shook my head as I nodded. "Weld County. Manner of death is suicide, though that determination may be under review. It could be homicide by now."

"You know what you know . . . how?"

There wasn't time to explain. I said, "From Lauren."

"That morning? She told you then?"

"Moments before she was shot."

"Did her shooting have anything to do with what she told you?"

"No."

"You're sure?"

"Yes."

"Elliot knows all this, too?"

"I'm not clear what Elliot knows. He does not know what Lauren and I discussed that morning. Elliot doesn't have all the facts."

"But you — you personally — do know the things that Lauren learned in her meeting earlier the morning she was shot? Is that correct?"

"I may not know everything. But I do know things that I am confident that Elliot does not know."

"How can you be sure of that?"

"Because if Elliot knew what I knew, I would be in custody awaiting trial for that other death. And I would not be the only one arrested."

She composed her eyes and mouth into a portrait of calm. "Answer this next question cautiously, please. Do you understand what I am saying?" I nodded. "Do you have any personal knowledge that might lead you to a conclusion about which manner of death determination — suicide or homicide — would be closest to the truth for that earlier serious crime?" We both reacted to the sound of a car horn in front of her house. "That's my taxi." She stood.

I stood, too. I said, "I do, Kirsten." She nodded a solemn acknowledgment.

She hugged me in a way that brought our bodies into contact from thighs to cheek. She eased me out the front door. "We'll continue this later," she said. "I will be in touch with a time. In the meantime you speak with no one about this. You know how it goes — if you hear another word from anyone in Elliot's office, even if it's further condolences or a butt dial, I want to know immediately." She locked the door behind us.

I said, "I'm sorry, one more thing. Quickly, I promise. Lauren left an envelope addressed to Elliot. My first reaction after he left today was to open it. Bad idea?"

"Maybe. If it's addressed to him, but was in her possession when she died? Don't open it. We'll talk. I have one more thing I want to say, too. A suggestion?"

"Okay."

"Have you thought about therapy? It helped me a lot during my dark times."

I didn't know if I was supposed to thank her for that compliment. I didn't feel complimented; I felt criticized. I said, "I'm in therapy. Gone a couple of times. Three."

"Is it helping?"

"I don't think I'm a very good patient."

She smiled. "Give it a fair try. Who knows, you might find someone special, like I did."

We descended the walk. I put my hand on her arm as we neared the taxi. "Have you heard from Carl Luppo?"

She made a face that I couldn't interpret. She said, "I have to run."

I thanked her before she jumped into the cab. The car made it no more than fifty feet before it came to a sudden stop. Kirsten ran on her toes back to where I was standing in front of her house. She stood close to me, all of her attention on my eyes. I couldn't tell if she saw what she was hoping to see.

"So you know," she said, finally — she was more breathless than the short jog should have left her — "I am seeing someone." She squeezed my hand and turned.

I held on to her hand to keep her from running. "Are you happy?" I asked.

"Getting there, Alan. Dry ice, you know."

I know all about dry ice, I thought. Sublimation. *I'm getting to know it all over again.*

I went back to my office. I could barely keep my eyes open. I took a throw pillow from the sofa and I fell asleep on the floor.

For some reason I could sleep where Lauren was shot, even though I couldn't sleep at home, where we had lived together, and where she had died. The last thought that rumbled around in my consciousness before I found sleep wasn't about Lauren or Izza or Kirsten.

It was about Elliot's latest maneuver and how it could complicate things for me with Sam Purdy.

I was beginning to get an uneasy sense that Sam had begun to think of himself as the one of us with clean hands.

Oh boy.

25

Sam and I didn't speak for the next two weeks. We exchanged waves across the lane. Each day of silence increased my anxiety about the state of our friendship.

Our next contact did nothing to allay my concerns.

Sam answered the pay phone after the first ring. He'd already called me three times, hanging up the first two. He left a coded voicemail with the third.

"My heart is pounding. What's wrong?" I asked. We had agreed to the cumbersome emergency contact system back when Lauren was still in the hospital. We'd also agreed to use it only if something felt urgent. This was the first time either of us had used it.

"Just news," Sam said. "Took you long enough to call me back. I walked over to Community Hospital for the pay phone. Place feels like it's teeming with SARS and MRSA and Legionnaires'. I'm glad they'll be knocking most of this place down soon."

Legionnaires'? "How bad is the news?" I asked. The silence on my end of the line was the kind that crackled with fragments of other people in other places. I heard a woman's voice say the phrase "probably the best that we can do."

"Why does it have to be bad?" Sam asked. "Doesn't matter, I need some context about one of our adversaries. This an okay time?"

Our adversaries. That meant either Michael McClelland, or . . . *Huh.* Maybe it was Big Elias, Elias Tres's grandfather. Or the Weld County district attorney. He was always a potential member of our adversaries club. After the encounter I'd had with Elliot a couple of weeks before he was definitely on my enemy roster, but I didn't see any reason he would be on Sam's. I said, "I have a few minutes."

"Tell me something, was our DA out of the closet in 2001?"

I'd been waiting on a Michael McClelland fastball. The Elliot slider tied me up, blew right by me. The anonymous conversation echoing elsewhere on the line filled the void. A woman said, "That one, really?" I found her comment to be ominous.

I had not told Sam about Elliot's visit to my office. Why would he count Elliot Bellhaven among our adversaries? My suspicions about Sam, already on the rise, accelerated ominously. I finally said, "Elliot? Isn't he my adversary? Not yours?"

"The enemy of my friend is my enemy."

Bull. Shit. "Is that how that saying goes? Or did you just make that up?"

"Was Elliot out of the closet in 2001?"

"How is that relevant to anything? Whenever he went public with the fact that he was gay has to be old news. Decade-old news."

"Humor me."

"I don't know. He wasn't out when he first came to town. It's Boulder, Sam. I don't think he threw a party. People found out gradually. And they probably yawned. I don't recall much controversy about it. People just began to accept that he was gay."

"There were cops who thought it was a big deal."

"Great. Maybe they can tell you when he came out of the closet."

Sam said, "Listen, I've come a long way about this. From 'queer' — not too long ago I used to say 'queer' — to here, where I am today, is a long friggin' way. Give me some credit for the ground I've covered about this thing."

"It's true, Sam," I said. "But this is one of

those races where you get the ribbon only when you cross the finish line."

He said, "That's probably true. Shit. Back to my question. Do you have a way to figure out when Elliot came out of the closet? Within a few months, plus or minus."

"I could waste some time and try to piece it together. Why is this important?"

"Our mutual interest. That's all I can say. And this, too: Why did Elliot come to Boulder County anyway? He was a hotshot, right? Ivy League, if I remember. Princeton? People like that don't come here to be baby deputy DAs."

"Elliot was Harvard, not Princeton. Princeton doesn't have a law school. Lauren used to wonder why he chose Boulder, too, thought it might have something to do with how well he did or didn't do in school. Or because he had political aspirations. But he never told her the reason."

"Explain," Sam said. "Pretend I don't get it."

"In Lauren's frame of reference, Elliot either chose to come here for some career plan, or he ended up here because it was the best he could do because he screwed up in law school in some way."

Sam said, "I'm interested. What did she decide?"

"I think she decided he thought he could raise a political tent in this environment faster than he could in some big city on the coasts. It worked. Elliot is a rising star."

Sam harrumphed, acknowledging Elliot's star without endorsing its ascension.

I said, "Look at Obama. He was president of the Law Review at Harvard. But when he left law school he turned down plum jobs to become a community organizer. He was playing the long game. He had his eyes on a bigger prize. Local power base to state politics to Congress to . . . It all worked out okay for him. Why not Elliot?"

Sam harrumphed again. "Can we not talk about Obama?"

"Yes, Sam, we can not talk about Obama." As a general rule it was prudent for Sam and me not to talk about Obama. But it was also wise for us not to talk about gays and coming out. We were already in dangerous territory.

"Thanks. Wise of you to acquiesce. Will you check? Find out if Lauren's speculation was accurate?"

"I don't even know how I would do that."

"It's important. Could you try?"

"You still haven't told me why it's important."

"I am not sure it is — yet. In my business

I walk into dead ends all the time. This may be one. But depending on what the facts are, it may give us some leverage."

Leverage? I was tempted to ask, but I feared revealing something if I did. "What's your supposition, Sam? Something got you thinking about this."

"It has to do with a case. A long story I can't tell you."

"I left the kids alone to make this call. I have to get back home."

Sam said, "You should get a burner."

"Do you have a burner?"

"I'm between burners at the moment. Soon I will have a new burner. That's how burners work."

26

The next morning broke bright and too warm for the first Wednesday in March. All the snow was gone from a rapid storm that had dumped six inches the weekend before. I got on my bike and rode east. I had a destination. And a task. Both were unusual for me those days.

During the time after the shooting but before Lauren succumbed to her injuries, I had ridden my bicycle a lot. I had convinced myself it would help me cope.

It didn't. But it helped pass the time. On one ride I had dared to go near Frederick.

Frederick borders the east side of Interstate 25, north of Boulder County. The city of Boulder is far to the west of I-25. I didn't cross under the highway on that ride. I stayed on the west side, the safe side, allowing the huge concrete edifice to protect me.

It was on the earlier ride, on a ranch near the road that could have taken me under the interstate into Frederick, that I saw the missing Tyvek for the first time. The jump-suit was adorning a scarecrow in the midst of a circle of raised garden beds near a house on a farm. The crop growing in the fields, I thought then, was young winter wheat.

Until that day, Sam's Tyvek jumpsuit — the one he had worn while he had killed the woman in the cottage in Frederick — had been a loose end about the crime. He had never told me the details about how he'd gotten rid of it, but he'd admitted that he'd disposed of it in a way that left him feeling vulnerable.

I was riding back to that farm to determine if the scarecrow was still wearing Sam's Tyvek jumpsuit.

It was not. The scarecrow was still there, but it was dressed in camo, not Tyvek. The big sentry gripped a toy rifle in its upraised hand. I wondered if Sam had reclaimed his Tyvek. Or if the farmer had just moved on to a new seasonal look for his scarecrow.

I also wondered if Izza had seen the Tyvek at the farm and recognized the costume of the espíritu her nephew had immortalized in his memory during his meeting with Lauren. With every breath I took I was wondering if I could trust Sam Purdy.

My phone chirped while I straddled my bike on the shoulder of the road opposite the camo-clad scarecrow. Caller ID was from an unfamiliar area code. I said, "Hello."

"It's me. No need to say my name."

The accent told me everything that caller ID failed to communicate about the person on the other end. I said nothing. Carl Luppo had that effect on me. I did the math. He had driven down my lane just prior to New Year's. Almost nine weeks had passed.

"Your guy? The one who is not a friend?"

"Yes."

"Found him. He's not where you thought he was anymore. He's gone, but good gone. Turns out he had a stroke." Carl tried to swallow a cough. "You didn't know?"

My heart added an extra beat. Or two. "A stroke? No, I did not know." Then I asked, "Wait, is that a euphemism? The stroke?"

Carl Luppo responded with a rheumy laugh that degenerated into a coughing fit that sounded serious. "Happens. Not a small stroke. Word is he's a sick guy. Got moved to a hospital in Grand . . . Junction. I got that right? Saint somethin'."

"St. Mary's," I said.

"Yeah. Thought you could take some

243

comfort that maybe he now knows what it's like to wish he was dead."

"God."

"The finish? It's easy, now. Hospital security? Amateur hour. You want to wake up with the nightmare over, you need to give me a sign."

I was furious at the implication. Then I felt a surge of relief at the opportunity.

Just like that, I wasn't furious anymore. I looked at the sky as though I expected to see God chastising me. Nothing. God didn't seem to give a shit.

"Natural causes?" I said. "The stroke?"

"What else? Damn prison food, probably. Or karma. My daughter would say karma. She's a Buddhist now. Not sure how I feel about that. We been Catholics" — it came out of his mouth as *Cat-licks* — "forever."

"We had an understanding, Carl. You and I."

"We still do. Remember, St. Mary's is cake. I'm always good with the saints. You take care of that little dancing girl."

"How's the trip going? Are you calling from your favorite hotel?"

"Let's just say I have sand between my old man toes 'cause I'm walking on the beach." He laughed until he coughed again. "Of the fucking Pacific Ocean."

244

Carl Luppo, Frank Carelli, killed the call. He was offering to kill my nemesis.

I took off my bicycle helmet and ran my fingers through my hair. I thought, *Does that little gorilla know how to cause someone to have a stroke?*

Did I do this?

27

The conversation with Carl got me thinking about Kirsten. I would always link them. As she promised she would, she had stayed in touch with me by email after my Valentine's Day visit to her home. She checked in a couple of times to be certain I had not heard again from Elliot. Another email concerned her ongoing efforts to locate a colleague who could assist me if and when Elliot made his next legal, or extralegal, move.

Elliot had not yet made another move. I was beginning to allow myself the luxury of believing that my earlier anxiety about his intentions had been unwarranted.

On the ride home to Boulder I almost persuaded myself to reach out to Kirsten again. I had not come up with a good excuse to make that call when a voicemail on my office phone line altered my plans.

During my ride from Frederick, Amanda

Bobbie had left me a message wi h an invitation that sounded more like a prelude to a booty call.

Was I suspicious about agreeing to meet an ex-patient in a bar? Yes. That particular ex-patient? God, yes. Amanda had been Raoul's self-described companion — she was the paid mistress of the husband of the woman who shot my wife in the back.

If I didn't go to meet her I would be left wondering what she wanted. And, given all that was unsettled for me, I feared that ignorance would fester and I would feel worse.

Choosing among bad options seemed to define my current lot.

Amanda had picked a restaurant close to my office. That was either considerate of her or provocative of her. Or irrelevant to her. I didn't know which. For me, not knowing things about Amanda was par for the course.

Amanda was waiting at the bar at Riffs. I hadn't seen her since the night after Lauren was shot. I didn't see her turn her head my way, but she must have sensed my arrival — she lifted her purse off the stool beside her as I approached. The purse looked expensive. Amanda looked expensive. The bag was not only holding a place for me but also served to caution strangers to stay away. Amanda was the type of woman — confident, composed, pretty but not gorgeous — who attracted people, welcome or unwelcome, male or female, eager to fill an empty stool beside a stranger at a bar.

If Amanda had been sitting in profile to the door as I entered I might have been able to make a judgment from her silhouette about the state of her pregnancy. I guessed that was why she was sitting sideways on her stool.

"I wasn't sure you would come," she said in greeting. "I can't imagine you're eager to see me." She did not look at me as she spoke.

I considered making an unkind reference to the booty call tenor of the summons. I refrained. I said, "Please don't make me regret it." Though I tried to say those words with some neutrality, I feared they came out closer to the tone of a warning.

She tapped a few fingers on the bar as though she were on a keyboard playing a one-handed rhythm from a slow song. "Well, it's good to see you, Alan," she said. "You helped me. I'm grateful for that. I still think of you fondly."

She said it as though she meant it. But

her psychotherapy had already demonstrated to me that Amanda was capable of getting me to believe things that weren't true. That she was happy to see me in the bar of a nice restaurant on the Pearl Street Mall? Way too easy for her. Convincing vulnerable men, like me, about her intentions — whether honest intentions or bought-and-paid-for intentions — was about as much of a reach for her as polishing her nails while she watched the latest episode of *Mad Men.*

Amanda was either happy to see me. Or she wasn't. Her assertion that one option was true and the other not true was nothing I could trust.

The fingertips of her left hand were touching a glass of water. "Something else to drink?" I asked. I was curious if she would drink alcohol. She didn't answer me.

If we were going to have an interaction of mutual distrust — initial evidence indicated we were — I did not have the energy for it. Despite any and all vigilance I could muster, the agenda, and all advantage about that agenda, would be Amanda's.

I considered walking back out the door onto the Mall.

Amanda had not turned toward me since I walked in. Her gaze remained fixed straight ahead. I knew she had smiled when I pulled out the stool only because of her reflection in a mirror behind the bar. The smile I saw had been the lopsided one I knew so well from our previous time together as doctor and patient.

That smile had tugged at me with its poignancy while I was her psychotherapist. It was a smile of honest pathos that cut through her defenses and provided an open window into her youth, a smile that illuminated the life she lived before the complications of living it had robbed her of her innocence.

But by that night at the bar in Riffs I was allowing that the smile might have been nothing more than another one of Amanda's manufactured illusions. I could no longer afford the luxury of trusting Amanda, so I cautioned myself to believe little. To assume less. To watch for anything. The extent of my beliefs? We were sitting at a bar and she wanted something from me. That was it. To presume that Amanda didn't manage her allure the way a hedge fund managed its risk was a luxury I simply couldn't afford.

"I am so sorry," she said, interrupting my train of thought. "About everything you have been through. Your wife? Dear Lord. And that night — on the other end of Pearl

Street, in that awful condo, after that terrible day when she was . . . shot — was so difficult. I fear I made that day even harder for you. I am sorry. There is no excuse for my behavior. I never expressed my gratitude for your help, or my sorrow at . . ." Her words drifted away. The ensuing silence was filled by a dozen other conversations taking place elsewhere in the room. The strangers' words made no sense in my brain.

I was drifting, recalling the many days I'd spent in Riffs' predecessor in the Pearl Street space, the long hours I'd wasted gleefully with a book inside or out of the old café.

"Alan? Alan? Did I lose you?"

She had not. I was hearing Amanda's words but they hadn't caused me to feel any imperative to respond. I had no need to reflect on my "terrible day" with her. The difficult night that Amanda alluded to had been my first opportunity to see her in the same room with Raoul. Her customer? Her lover? What did she consider him?

During the therapy Amanda had lied to me about her feelings for the man she'd called the Buffer. The man I later learned was Raoul. I did not know where Amanda's lies ended and where her truth began. From her, I expected continued deception.

I felt a renewed urge to exit. I lowered one foot to the floor in preparation. I said, "If that was the reason for this invitation — your condolences — thank you, I guess. Are we done? The reality is that I shouldn't be here at all. Professional distance, you know?"

I placed my hands on the edge of the bar to push my stool back.

"No," she said with the confidence of someone who expects deference. "Do tell me about your need for professional distance."

I didn't bite. I said, "How about this as an alternative? I accept your condolences. I don't doubt your sincerity, Amanda, but —"

"Of course you doubt my sincerity. This weirdness between us since you walked in has everything to do with questioning my sincerity. Doubting my motives. Doubting anything and everything I've told you since we met probably."

I ignored the accusation. Ignoring it was more convenient than parsing out the things I did doubt from the things I rejected out of hand. I continued where I left off. "*But* condolences aren't worth the risk we are taking. I shouldn't be here with you. And for what it's worth, vice versa. You shouldn't be here with me. It's too soon after the termination of our . . . work together."

Amanda smiled a rueful smile. She said, "I suspect you are not being kind. I may deserve that from you. But don't leave. Not yet. I saw your daughter dance." I paused. She looked away from me. "Your daughter? It was so precious and so sad. It tore at me. To see her loss, to see her express it like that. I envied her ability to put herself out there. To be so at peace with her feelings. I never had that kind of outlet for my grief.

"She moved me. I saw the father you are. The woman her mother was."

"Don't, Amanda. Do not talk about my wife."

"I didn't mean to offend. I said what I had to say."

God. "YouTube," I muttered in exasperated dismay.

"The dance is on YouTube?" she asked.

"You didn't know?"

"I didn't know. I was at the cemetery. You should have seen the look on your face when she started to dance."

The expression on my face when Grace started to dance wasn't on the YouTube clip. The camera didn't find Grace for the first ten seconds or so. If my initial expression had been recorded my Twitter hashtag would be #stunnedgravedad.

I realized, with surprise, that I believed Amanda had been there. She had been present for almost every step of my decline. For all the anticipation. For all the complications. For all the tragedies that ensued. Why not at the funeral, too?

Amanda Bobbie — if that was her real name — was the raven-haired patient who was the last visitor to my office before Lauren arrived the morning of the Dome Fire. Amanda was the professional companion that Raoul was paying for her time, her affection, and as she put it to me during her psychotherapy, "her accommodation."

Amanda knew many of the secrets I was choosing to keep to myself about Raoul and Diane and her. That she knew my secrets made her dangerous. That she was dangerous meant I had to treat her with caution. That she was dangerous also meant that I couldn't ignore her or walk away, even if my instincts told me to do just that.

I didn't have to be nice. I said, "Going to the cemetery? Was it a *Harold and Maude* thing? Or a simple perverse need to see my wife's body buried?"

"Ouch, I think," she said. I didn't respond. She lifted her glass. Sipped some water. "You made that movie reference not to be clever, or interesting, but because you

254

expected I wouldn't recognize it and you wanted to feel some advantage over me. Is that why you're here? To be petty?" I doubted she expected me to respond. "This minute? You don't want to be with me. I get that. But I don't run from death. You should know that about me by now. I adore Ruth Gordon. I love *Harold and Maude.* Someday I plan to be exactly that kind of feisty old lady."

Amanda looked at my reflection in the mirror. "I wish I could say that I was there to support you. To honor your gifts to me. I can't. I was there to see Raoul."

"The Buffer?" I said. "You lied to me about him."

"I misled you." It was apparent she considered it a venial sin. "I didn't anticipate that you would need to know. I was wrong. Shoot me."

"George?" I asked. Her other client was named George. "Did you lie about him?"

She shrugged. "I like George. I don't love George."

"Present tense?"

"I like George. Can we move on? I went to the funeral to look in Raoul's eyes one more time. To find some hope. Or to feel some closure, something that would allow me to walk away without yearning to know

255

if his eyes were on me.

"I was there for selfish reasons, not compassionate ones. You deserved better from me. You did your best to help me. I remain grateful to you. I am sorry." Her eyes were imploring me to understand something. "I am not sugarcoating any of this. I don't want you to have to wonder about my motives for wanting to see you tonight."

I am still trying to discern your motives. Once I do that, I certainly intend to distrust them. "In therapy? You flipped them for me? Your feelings for Raoul were the ones you ascribed to George. And vice versa?"

She mouthed a *yes.* "I didn't want to tip my hand. Again, I didn't think it would matter."

I said, "Hoping to see Raoul at the services — was that the final act of the smitten kitten?" I wanted her to recognize the reference to a touching part of her therapy. I wanted her to feel something from my intentional dig. Pain was my preference.

"Ouch." She winced. "Maybe I deserve that, or maybe you're being cruel. We each have our vulnerabilities. We've each endured losses. Do you want to keep this up?"

It wasn't really a question. "Raoul wasn't there, at the cemetery," I said. "I checked. He wasn't at the memorial service earlier.

He never sent a card. Or flowers. He never called. Not one of the covered dishes left at our door was from him" — I went ironic with that thought — "too bad, because the man makes a remarkable cassoulet."

Amanda said, "I've had his cassoulet," making the dish sound like a sexual act. She said, "He was your friend. I'm sorry. We share that loss."

"If you knew that Raoul was my friend you shouldn't have chosen to see me for therapy." I tried to keep the accusation out of my voice.

"Really? You came here tonight so you could slap my hand about choosing you, and not someone else, for therapy? No. That's not why you're here."

I said, "Maybe I came because I was curious what was so important that you would risk being seen with me. You barely made it away that night." I had urged Amanda out the door of the dreadful condo before the ambulance arrived to take Diane to the hospital. Long before the first cops showed up.

Amanda shrugged an old-history shrug. "The police know I was there, Alan. I've been interviewed. They didn't seem to know I'd had a session with you that morning. I didn't tell them." She tilted her head. "I bet you didn't, either. I didn't commit any crimes. Well, not that day, and none that they're interested in prosecuting me for."

"Are you pregnant?" I asked.

She reached over and took my hand off the bar as though she was anticipating the question. She held my hand in hers for a moment longer than was necessary before she guided it to her abdomen. Her belly was as flat as my singing voice. If I were inclined, I could have felt the definition of her muscles with my fingertips. She placed my hand back where it had been on the bar. She left hers on mine a moment longer than was necessary.

She reached into her purse and pulled out a business card. She slid it until it partially disappeared beneath my palm. "I wanted to see you because I know that, face-to-face, I am a difficult person to refuse." She waited until I blinked before she smiled kindly. "Give me ten minutes. Have a drink. Try the meatballs. Oh, you probably don't eat meat. It's a short walk to the address on the back of the card. We do need to talk. There are things that I must say that we shouldn't discuss in a public lounge."

She swiveled away from me and slid off the stool. She turned in profile as she exited. No baby bump. Not even a little.

Had the pregnancy been a lie? Had it been intended as a provocation to Diane all along? Or perhaps as some leverage with Raoul? If it had been real, had it ended with a miscarriage, or with an abortion?

Did Raoul get a vote? Would he have wanted one? Did he give a damn?

"Cocktail?" the bartender said.

"I think I will pass." I put twenty bucks on the bar before I stepped out onto the Pearl Street sidewalk. Amanda was approaching Broadway. Every time I'd tried to accommodate her in the past it had turned out to be the wrong decision for me. I couldn't convince myself this time would be any different. I turned toward my office, away from her, away from the address on the card. I told myself that it was not only the wise thing to do, but it was also the ethical choice for me.

For most of my professional career I had been making decisions based on underlying ethics. Was my current choice rationalization? Self-deceit? Naïveté?

I chose naïveté. I also chose the route back to my office via the pedestrian alley that runs between Pearl and Walnut. I was just opposite the dining room of Ten Ten when I heard the *tip-tip-tip-tip* of high heels clicking on the concrete behind me. One of Boulder's legions of lithe spiked-heeled twenty-somethings was on her way somewhere for something that felt worthy of a quick step.

I felt a gentle hand on my shoulder. I didn't need to turn to be certain who it was; I could detect Amanda's scent. I held my breath. In a low voice, she said, "I know things I would want to know were I in your shoes, Alan. This isn't about me. This is about you."

I rotated to reply — I hadn't formulated the reply; I was hoping something would come to me — but Amanda was retracing her steps in the direction of Pearl Street. She turned her head, "Please? Go to the address. We need to talk."

I didn't know why I was looking for a fight. Let alone one with Amanda, but I found it absurd, even insulting, that Amanda thought that she had some affinity for my current life. I said, "What shoes are those, Amanda? That you think I'm in?"

Amanda stopped but she didn't turn back my way. With a dancer's grace, she extended an arm for balance as she bent her left leg at the knee. She lifted her foot until her knee was at ninety degrees and the sole of her fashionable high heel was perpendicular to the ground.

The sole was red. A shade of red I recognized as clearly as the violet hue of my wife's eyes. *Those are just like Diane's red soles. The Christian Louboutins.*

Amanda was reminding me that she had been there the night after Lauren was shot, the night that Diane was clutching the stylish heels to her chest as though the shoes were a favorite stuffed animal. But why was she reminding me?

Damn. She wanted me to meet her at the address on the card. And she had just given me a reason to do so.

28

I allowed Amanda a short lead before I followed her in the general direction of the address on the card. I stayed on the Mall until Thirteenth. I passed the Boulderado and continued to Pine Street.

The address that Amanda had given me was assigned to a unit of a fourplex crammed onto a lot on the north side of Pine. Two of the units were in a subdivided plain-Jane Victorian that had graced the front side of the property since the late nineteenth century. That house had been alone on the land until the restrictions of Boulder's growth controls — love 'em or hate 'em — motivated the owner to squeeze more revenue out of the investment by erecting a utilitarian addition behind the original home.

The unit I was looking for was D. Upper rear. Amanda had left the door cracked open. I paused at the sidewalk to shut off the power to my smartphone, my "tracker." As I climbed the stairs toward the apartment I realized that the alley between Pine and Mapleton provided an alternative entrance to the rear apartments. That meant an alternative exit, one I might need if it turned out I was being lured into a trap. The nature of Amanda's trap? If it occurred, I had a suspicion that it would involve Raoul.

Amanda was standing in the kitchen. Expensive flowers arranged into a too-large bouquet were beginning to die in a cheap crystal vase on the laminate bar. Beside them were a stack of red plastic Solo cups, a half-consumed jug of cheap vodka, a bottle of good red wine, and a glass candy dish full of condoms.

She had called them "covers" during her therapy with me.

The apartment's bones were utilitarian. I felt certain that Amanda didn't live there. "Yours?" I said, wondering if she would lie to me.

"God no." She shivered dramatically. "I'll explain. Close the door, please."

In layout and construction the flat was a basic rental. Living room and kitchen in front, a bath with doors to both the hallway and to a solitary bedroom in back. Builder finishes. Laminated counters and flooring. Hollow doors, cheap carpets. Mini-blinds. White appliances. Not a place where Amanda Bobbie would go home at the end of the day to kick off her Christian Louboutins.

"I borrowed this so that we could have a quiet place to talk. It's a friend's. A colleague's. It's private."

Amanda was a grad student at CU, about to get her master's. A colleague could be a fellow student. Amanda was also an adult service provider. An escort. A colleague could be a fellow adult service provider.

Despite its pedestrian construction the apartment was comfortable, even welcoming. It didn't look like a student's abode; the space had a clear sensual vibe. I made a guess I was in an escort's lair. I felt relief that I had turned off my tracker.

I said the obvious. "Your colleague doesn't live here."

"It's set up for work. The previous tenant was a graduate student who was kicked out of school for selling weed on campus. My friend is paying his rent. She and one of her girlfriends use it to see clients. The landlord is in Oklahoma, doesn't know the grad student is gone."

"Clients?" I said. I realized that Amanda

wanted to be certain that she and I talked about her business. During her therapy she had demonstrated an ability to distract me by sharing provocative stories. She was adept at it. I had a proclivity to fall for it. This was shaping up to be one of her provocative stories. I was forewarned.

"Some girls prefer hotel rooms. Most hotels look the other way, but there is always a risk of discovery, and hotels get expensive. A few girls bring guys to their homes. I don't get that — the security issues make my skin crawl. Others get places like this. Or short-term rentals. Month-to-month things. Sublets. Industrial spaces. Or they make kickback deals with landlords who are happy not to notice things.

"By the time neighbors begin to get suspicious the girls are scouting the next place. This one expires at the end of the semester, one way or another."

I had an image of a prostitute/landlord/vice cop game of Whac-A-Mole. I thought, *In Boulder?* I then felt naïve for thinking it. *Why not in Boulder?* I nodded as nonjudgmentally as I could. It was my therapy nod.

"This is an incall," Amanda said. "If you're wondering." I had been wondering. She continued the lesson. "If a girl has the place — flat, hotel room, whatever — and the guy joins her, it's an incall. If she meets the guy where he is — his hotel room, usually, or sometimes where he lives — that is an outcall."

I wasn't sure why I was getting the lesson, why Amanda had invited me to meet in that particular incall, or why she was emphasizing the sex trade she worked in. My history with her told me to redouble my vigilance for prurient distraction.

I said, "I get what here is. That leaves the question of why? Why are we here?"

"It's better that you don't know where I live. I moved after that . . . day. From the place he was renting for me. I don't want the Buffer to know where I live." I didn't know it while I was treating her, but the Buffer was Amanda's nom de guerre for Raoul. I was puzzled why she continued to use it. "I have no more confidentiality with you. What you don't know you can't reveal. This is an impersonal place, and it's private."

Amanda was hiding from Raoul. Not from the cops.

"I will leave town as soon as I graduate in May. Until then? Caution."

I said, "Same plan? Legit job? Atlanta?" She nodded. "What do we need to talk about?"

"I'm getting there," she said. "Back when I used to smoke? This is the moment when I would light up. When I'm anxious. This isn't easy for me."

My empathy for other people, those I didn't love, was nearing an all-time low. I almost tipped my hand by telling Amanda that I didn't care if anything was easy for her. The only reason I didn't say it was because I feared the admission might drag out our ordeal. I wanted to get to the part about the shoes with the red soles.

"Do you work here, too?" I wanted to know if she had gone from being the companion of an überwealthy man to being a worker bee in the world of hourly escorts.

As soon as I spoke, I recognized that Amanda had succeeded in distracting me. My question was provocative, even hostile. And it was certainly inappropriate.

She flipped her hair. "Why? Are you interested, Alan?"

She wasn't flirting. She was letting me know she had taken offense at my question. She was also sending a clear warning that she wasn't planning to take more.

I would have to behave myself. The apology I offered lacked sincerity.

She said, "I neither need nor want your understanding. Your approval? Hardly. I have income to replace. A lot. I intend to land in Atlanta with no debt." She had answered my inappropriate query without admitting a thing. "Would you like to sit?"

The living room offered a choice of a reasonably new futon or a leather sofa from a decade past. Not a recent decade past. The kitchen counter was fronted by two simple wooden stools. "These look fine," I said.

From the counter I could see into one end of the bedroom. A massage table. I assumed the other end had a bed. Or maybe something else. I felt a flash of curiosity. "You wanted to talk, Amanda. I'm here."

She sat beside me and waited until I made eye contact. She said, "We're not doing this well, are we? I'm good at it — at making people, men, feel comfortable. So the awkwardness is on you. You may be unwilling to feel comfortable."

Provocative went both ways. I was tempted to lash out, to cause some damage. I didn't. I said, "Maybe you should just tell me what you think I need to hear."

Amanda checked her perfect posture. She touched the insides of her knees together primly as she tucked her modest skirt into alignment. "I think you should know, you have the right to know," she said, "that Diane Estevez had motive that morning."

"Motive?" I said.

I'd said it as though I didn't know what the word meant.

29

Motive? What?

"This is hard," Amanda said. "Diane had a motive to shoot your wife."

Amanda's words seemed to bounce around the room, not so much an echo but in a syncopated repetition, as though a DJ were spinning the sounds on vinyl. Over and over, fragments of the words kept hitting at my ears. Gaining, then losing amplification.

Motive . . . to shoot your wife. Diane. Motive to shoot your wife. Diane. Motive.

I took a few steps away. I didn't return to the stool until the reverberations stopped. I said, "May I have something to drink? Please."

"Vodka or water?" She didn't look; she knew the choices.

A Solo cup of cheap vodka was unlikely a wise idea. "Water."

She retrieved two bottles of Eldorado Springs water from the refrigerator. I took a long drink.

She said, "You are taking this better than I expected. Did you know?"

I tried to be gracious. "I know some of what Diane was dealing with that day. Thank you for being honest enough to tell me what you think. I was — I have been a jerk tonight. I apologize. I'm not in a good place."

Amanda screwed up her nose and eyes and forehead into an expression of you-know-I-don't-think-so. She said, "Wait. What is it that you think you know? What do you think Diane was dealing with?"

She wasn't challenging me. Her voice was compassionate. She was inviting my reply. That her concern for me was sincere made me more wary, not less. I said, "Last summer? Diane hacked into Raoul's computer. She found out about you and Raoul. She'd read the emails or texts or whatever was there between you and him. The pregnancy? Your arrangements, the finances? She knew all of it, I think. She was already fragile over some other things."

She said, "Go on."

I thought I was making perfect sense. "My guess? Your relationship with Raoul overwhelmed her. But I think it was Raoul's financial setbacks that pushed her too far.

The shooting, that morning? She wanted you to suffer. Like she was suffering."

Amanda's shoulders slumped. She said, "Oh no." She momentarily puffed out her cheeks and lifted her hand to her mouth. "No. No, no. You have it so wrong. I'm sorry."

I shook my head. "I've known Diane a long time. I'm right about this, Amanda."

She leaned toward me. She reached out to touch my cheek. I pulled away. She reached out farther. I allowed her touch. "No, Alan. You are wrong."

In a nanosecond I went from *I'm not wrong* to *I don't want to be wrong* to *I could be wrong*. To *holy shit. Holy shit.* My pulse jumped. It skipped the canter. It went into full gallop.

Amanda said, "I'm not telling you that Diane had a motive to shoot *me*. No."

"What then?" I asked. In the moment I was already feeling the truth as a stab into my flesh. I knew that Amanda lacked any explanation that might comfort me. In any way.

The stool I was on suddenly felt as though it lacked the requisite number of legs.

She said, "Have you been thinking that Diane confused Lauren and me that day? Physically confused us? Like shot the wrong

272

one? No, baby, no." She bit her bottom lip and she shook her head. "I wish it were true, but that didn't happen."

My mouth hung open. *Of course I've been thinking that. I was there. That's exactly what happened.* But in that instant I began to accept that I was missing something crucial. I managed to blurt, "It didn't happen that way?"

"No, baby, it didn't happen that way." Amanda's phone buzzed. She ignored it.

I was growing more uncomfortable by the second. My ignorance about why I was in that incall and my confusion with whatever Amanda was trying to tell me were coalescing to leave me feeling completely off balance. My instinct was to run like hell.

Her phone buzzed again. I said, "No one else is coming here?"

She used a soothing tone. "If the door is closed, men knock. My friend knows I am here. This is a one-girl-at-a-time place. No one is coming here tonight."

She reached out and touched my hand. She knew she was doing this operation without anesthesia. Her fingertips carried the heat of midday sand at the beach.

I returned to my confusion. I said, "Your hair was dark. The day of the fire. You'd colored it recently. Cut it short." *Lauren's raven hair was short that day, too.*

"Yes. He asked me to." *He* was Raoul, the one who would not be named. "He liked things to be certain ways at certain times. Clothing. Hair. Makeup even. I'd been blond for a while. For him. I'd gone back to my natural color. For him. He wanted me to let my hair grow. Then he asked me to go as black as I could. He wanted it short again. I did all that. For him."

Amanda had told me in therapy that the most important part of her job as a companion was accommodation, not sex. She was describing that accommodation.

"George didn't care?" She had been a paid companion to two men. Raoul was one. The other was George.

"George cared about a lot of things." She laughed. "But not about that."

I did not know what to do with the information about her hair. I tried to put it in the pile marked "coincidence" but it kept jumping away as though it had the wrong polarity to remain in that vicinity. I made my case: "You had just left my office, Amanda. After our session? Lauren came to visit. Then Diane burst in. She fired the gun. Your hair was black. Lauren's hair was black. She could see the hair from the door. She confused Lauren with you."

Amanda shook her head, her eyes soft. She was not only disagreeing with my statement of facts, she was also sad that she was about to hurt me. I could see the hurt coming, but I wasn't prescient enough to anticipate the nature of the pain.

I tried to postpone the agony by expressing some desperate certainty. It was all I had left. "Diane thought it was you. In my chair. She was shooting *you.*" *That explanation fits. It's an explanation I've proven I can choke down and digest without vomiting.* I didn't ask for much those days. But I did require an explanation for that morning that didn't make me gag and that didn't make me puke.

"No, baby," Amanda said. "That's not what happened. I am sorry. God."

"What are you saying? About Diane? And Lauren? What did happen? If that didn't happen — Wait. Were you still there? Did you stay around after your session?"

"I left when we were done. Out the back door like you asked. Over to the spa at the St. Julien. A mani-pedi? I left when you thought I left."

"That's right," I said. Those facts supported my version. I felt some hope that we would come back around to Diane's confusion about identity. Nothing else fit my facts. "You weren't there. What can you know?"

The words sounded more persuasive in my head than when I said them aloud. Aloud they sounded like something defiant Grace would say with her hands on her childish hips.

"It's what I know to be true, Alan. That's all."

"Then tell me, damn it. Please."

Amanda sipped water. "I so hoped you already knew this." She winced. "I thought you knew this. So here it is: they were having a thing."

A thing. What?

She said, "This shouldn't be up to me. One of them should have . . . They —"

"What kind of thing? You're nuts." Her words weren't registering. *A thing?*

"You know I'm not nuts," Amanda said. "Nor am I wrong about this."

Her craziness — she wasn't — was irrelevant. But I could hardly have been more certain that Amanda was wrong. Diane and Lauren had never been that close. If it hadn't been for me, I didn't think they would have mounted the pretense to be friends.

Lovers? Absurd. A thing? A sexual thing? My wife and my friend? The two most important women in my life? Involved with each other? *Involved involved?*

"Are you okay, Alan? I am . . . sorry."

I was shocked to discover a small part of me willing to believe that Amanda had it right. I knew in my heart that Lauren didn't view fidelity like I did. But I said, "No way. Diane and Lauren? No."

Amanda's eyes went wide and she shook her head in a fast, tight arc as her hand flew up to her open mouth. Her eyes implored me to take a big step back. She said, "Oh, no. Oh God. I am so blowing this. Diane and Lauren didn't have anything going on. Not them. I am being so careful with you that I am not being clear."

Reality was returning to a dimension I recognized. The moment I felt that relief, I felt another blow was coming. "Then what? Tell me! Just fucking tell me, Amanda."

She pulled away. She said, "Okay." She touched the top of my hand again. I felt her heat, again. My hands were cold, bloodless.

"Raoul and Lauren were having an affair."

Before my brain had a chance to attach meaning to her words, someone turned the knob on the front door. The door was locked. A second later, the person knocked. A male voice said, "Sasha? Sasha?"

The same sequence — something earth-shattering said, someone intruding — had occurred the morning Diane shot Lauren. I felt the new fright as that old terror, along with some indescribable new overlay of anguish and dread.

Amanda witnessed my temporary catatonia, but she wisely chose not to rely on it. She put her hand over my mouth. She shook her head slowly as she raised a finger to her lips. I reached up to pull her hand away. I mouthed, *Are you Sasha?*

Amanda shook her head. The knob rattled again.

I mouthed, *Raoul and Lauren? Yes?*

She nodded. The voice outside said, "Sasha? You in there? I see the lights."

I mouthed the word *shit.*

I intended for the profanity to cover a wide range of territory.

30

I was forced to sit with my agony as the man outside the door phoned Sasha.

Amanda mouthed a prolonged barely audible *shhhhh.*

"Hey, it's me. Paul. I'm here. It's locked." Pause. "What do you mean? . . . Yeah, I know you always confirm. I tried, but you didn't answer so I figured you had a phone problem." Pause. "What do you mean that's not how it works?" Pause. "Of course you don't answer when you're not working. But you are working. Last week, we —" Pause. "Really? Tomorrow? Are you sure? Crap. I'm in Tucson tomorrow." Footfalls going down the steps. "Fuck," Paul said. "I can't do tomorrow."

Amanda waited. Paul was not light on his feet. We knew when he made it down the stairs. Finally, I said, "That's how it goes down?"

"Not usually. Mostly it just happens. It's

comfortable. People want to have a good time. Do people understand the work you do, Alan? Your business?"

"Hardly."

"Same for this business. People don't understand the work we do."

With Paul gone, my interest in Sasha dissolved. I didn't care.

"Raoul and Lauren," I said. "You are sure? Completely sure?"

I hadn't rejected the pairing out of hand, the way I had with Lauren and Diane. I already knew about Lauren and Joost, Sofie's father. I felt myself chiseling this new pairing into stone in the part of my memory that stored things in granite. I was nearing the kind of certainty that would have required Amanda to talk me out of believing it.

"I am sure," she said. "That night in the condo? I thought you knew, and then I was afraid you didn't. If you didn't know, I felt someone needed to tell you." Her eyes were wet. "It should have been Lauren. Or him. Not me."

I felt defeat. Despair. All the grief I'd felt since the shooting evaporated. My loss felt new. Raw. I knew I would need to start grieving again from the beginning. The grief would be different the second time. The rage quotient would be so much higher.

Amanda said, "Raoul is —With the situation with Diane, all the legal problems, her health. His financial issues. He can't be your friend. Mostly because of what he did. But you know all that. Now."

Amanda still loved him. She wanted to excuse him.

I said, "Apparently Raoul hasn't been my friend for a while."

She said, "You were good to me." I saw a fat tear forming in her left eye.

"I understand," I said. "I do." I had an inclination to add the words *thank you.* But the sentiment seemed wildly inappropriate to the circumstances. I asked, "The damn building Raoul was developing downtown? On Pearl Street. Is this why Lauren was so determined for us to move there? To be near him, his home?"

Amanda nodded. "That was their plan. His office would have been there, too."

God. "I should go," I said. I got up. The second I stood I had more questions. "How long have they been . . ." I tried on the word *fucking.* It seemed to fit. But — perhaps because of the bizarre circumstances, or the Louboutin-clad messenger, or the peculiar location, or because of Sasha and Paul's failed tryst — I chose a different word.

281

". . . involved. How long?"

"A while," Amanda said. "Before me. I didn't know about her at first. Later, when I figured out that he was involved with a friend of Diane's, I thought that I was supposed to be a solution to that problem. That it was my job to give Raoul a reason to . . ."

Her thought drifted away. Or drifted into a place she didn't want to expose to me.

"I get it," I said. "You were supposed to break them up?"

"No. Yes," Amanda said. "I was to fulfill him. To complete . . . him."

"Diane knew?"

"She did."

I thought my friend's gradual psychological decline had been precipitated by Las Vegas. Her kidnapping. Her trauma. Later, by her anxiety about all the damn wildfires. By Raoul's money problems. The irony of the truth was that, of all my friends, Diane was the one who considered me the most naïve sexually. It turned out she had been an expert on the topic: she had known more about that naïveté than anyone. Save for Raoul. And Lauren.

I asked, "Do you know when she knew? Diane?"

"A while."

"What while? A long while?" I struggled

with the time frame. *A while* meant it hadn't been an indiscretion. A moment of weakness. A mistake. *A while* meant it was an affair — a part of their lives that provided a piece missing from some other part of their lives. The other part of their lives was their marriages. *My marriage.* A piece of that.

"Yes, a while," Amanda said. "Years."

"Diane knew about you and Raoul? All along?"

"I don't know when she knew. Raoul had outside interests. Always. I wasn't the first. Lauren wasn't the first. Diane knew that."

I felt so wounded that I was surprised I wasn't bleeding.

31

Amanda locked the door to the apartment. She told me to wait as she disappeared behind the staircase to stash the key. I didn't wait. I mumbled something about needing to get home to the kids.

I walked away from Amanda and away from the Pine Street incall in a dull daze, heading in the direction of Pearl. I remembered to power up my phone after I crossed Pine. Anyone paying attention to my digital footprint would find that my signal reappeared on the grid while I was opposite the entrance to the Boulderado Hotel.

Reboot complete, my phone pinged. I had a text waiting from Kirsten.

Check your email.

The night had turned cold as though some meteorological switch had been thrown. I stood outside the old courthouse while I clicked through to the email. Kirsten had written it on her professional account, not her personal account. She had arranged for me to be represented by a prominent Denver defense attorney. She used two unnecessary sentences to sing the lawyer's praises. She had determined, she said, that it was preferable for me to go outside Boulder for representation. The local defense bar was "incestuous." The attorney was, Kirsten said, expecting my call.

My new lawyer's name doubled the chill I was feeling. The roster of famous and infamous defendants represented in the recent past by the attorney rolled through my vision like credits at the end of a movie. I never thought I would see the day when I would have anything important in common with Colorado's more infamous criminal defendants. But that day had come.

I pecked the keys that would move the attorney's information into my contact list.

It was the first step to calling him and making him my lawyer.

That, I knew, would be the last step I would take while Sam and I both still had clean hands.

I had only one patient scheduled the next day, a woman I'd seen on and off for almost five years. She lived her life in blissful oblivion. She was the only one of my remaining few patients who had never mentioned seeing my name in the news, despite the reality that my name had become a staple in the local news.

I had been treating her, in part, for her isolation. That day I almost envied it.

She left my office at three forty-five. I sat in the quiet room with my old grief, my new grief, and my growing entropy.

I felt paralyzed trying to decide how to respond to Kirsten's email from the previous evening, and about whether I should call my new lawyer. I started composing a reply to Kirsten five times. I deleted my efforts five times.

I was rescued from my ambivalence by my cell phone buzzing with an incoming call. Caller ID showed an unfamiliar 818 number. Although my inclination was to allow it to go to voicemail, I picked up. Grace was visiting the home of a school friend whose parents I didn't know well. It was possible one of them carried a Los Angeles area cell phone.

I said, "Hello." A woman said, "Hey there. Remember me?"

I didn't but I did. Her voice generated the neural signals I get from a familiar smell — a food, a perfume. Something pleasant. Once gratifying, now elusive. I could have

286

picked the woman's name from a multiple-choice list on a test, but I could not have filled in a blank.

She bailed me out. "It's Amy. Amy Wise? Cara's friend."

"Amy," I said. To prove to both of us that I had it, I added, "LA Amy."

My animal brain attached an aroma, something slightly sweet, a blend of fresh sweat and subtle florals, warm flesh after a sunny day. That led to the bonus of a specific location — the crook of her neck, right at her hairline. My nose had been there, exactly there. That narrowed the list of possible women considerably.

"LA Amy," she said. "That'll work. I'm glad you remember."

I remember most of the girls I almost slept with. After I'd confessed my complicated feelings regarding Amy to Sam Purdy — he and I had been in California at the same time years earlier when I met her — he'd started referring to her as the "fucking beguiler." She was that.

I leaned back on my desk chair, curious where the phone call was coming from, literally and figuratively, and where it was heading. My laptop pinged with an email. I glanced at it to assure myself I could ignore it.

I could not. The new email was from ell-bell — Elliot Bellhaven, written from Elliot's personal email account, addressed to my personal account.

I tried not to read it.

I said, "How could I not remember you, Amy? We had the kind of unfortunate adventure that is hard to forget." I wasn't talking about her seduction. I was talking about some nonvolitional time we spent with a madman — a very mad man — in the Southern California desert *after* the attempted seduction.

She said, "I don't talk about that. This isn't about that. Clear?"

I considered myself warned. "Gotcha." I wasn't eager to go there, either.

I read Elliot's email.

Alan, Elias Contopo was crushed to death last night by a horse inside his horse trailer on North County Road 23. Trailer had a flat. Something went wrong with the tire change, I guess. No need to send this to your attorney. Just a friendly FYI. Unless it isn't news to you. Then you might want to call your attorney. Joke. Hope you had a good evening last night whatever you ended up doing.

EB

Amy was still talking. I had not been listening. I forced myself away from Elliot.

"— if you would be happy to hear from me, given what happened. But I'm in your neighborhood, thought you might enjoy seeing an old friend."

I locked on to a fragment I could respond to. I said, "Boulder?" Cara, Amy's friend, had lived in town.

"I'm in Leadville — you know where that is? Sure you do. Still in the business. I'm second AD on a studio feature. I have a small crew doing exteriors up here. It'll probably take a couple more days, though that's up to the weather gods."

I was trying not to think about Elliot and a dead Elias Contopo. I managed to say, "Leadville? A feature? Big deal for you?" Leadville is a boom-and-bust mining town high in the Rockies. Not a big magnet, or a little magnet, for movie companies.

Amy said, "The shoot is in Vancouver. I got the AD gig — assistant director — on that indie film I told you about. That led to another. I scraped together financing for a short, which got a tiny bit of festival attention in Toronto. DreamWorks noticed. And then, and then . . . This is my first gig as second AD on a studio film."

"Congratulations. Would I recognize the

movie?"

"Do you live on IMDb?" I admitted I didn't. She laughed.

My feelings about Amy retained some of the earlier complexity. The trill of her laugh retained its allure. I recalled the tender way she had ministered to a friend who was deteriorating before her eyes. I also remembered her naked breasts on my naked back as she gently spooned, prodding me out of a dream.

Elias Contopo is dead. Jesus. But Elliot's wrong; I had never met any of the Elias Contopos. I knew of him. People in Frederick called him Big Elias. Is Elliot suggesting a murder? Shit. I haven't called my new defense attorney.

I mentally moved the task to the top slot on my to-do list.

"Are we breaking up? Alan? Hello. You there? Can you hear me?"

Amy. "Better now," I said. "I got you again. Is this clear?"

"I was wondering how you are, Alan," she said. I went quiet. She cooed, "Did I lose you again, or are you deciding whether to lie to me? In real time? You *are.*"

I laughed. I said, "I am. Deciding that."

"I appreciate your honesty about your dishonesty. I saw the YouTube video. I doubt that I would be calling today if I hadn't. I am truly sorry for your loss. And the circumstances? Heartbreaking."

"Thank you."

"The hurt on your face in that clip? Given what you've been through, I . . ."

Given? Given how large the Contopo clan loomed in my life, it's ironic that I never met any of the Contopo boys, all of whom were named Elias. Not Elias Contopo Senior, Big Elias. Not his Marine son, known to almost all as Segundo, who died in Afghanistan. Nor Segundo's son, Elias Tres.

". . . pretty shitty? If you said otherwise, I wouldn't believe you."

YouTube? Amy is talking about YouTube. "God. That video follows me everywhere."

Amy said, "I had no idea how badly you danced. I would absolutely not have crawled into bed with you if I did. Had to say that. You know, for my reputation."

I laughed. I stopped laughing abruptly when I realized that the person Elliot was thinking, or hoping, had killed Big Elias was me.

I tuned back in as Amy said, "I am also happy for you that the whole adored thing worked out so well. You remember that? The nutty adored thing you told me about."

"I do," I said. I hadn't considered it so

291

nutty. In trying to explain to Amy why, and how, I'd resisted the opportunity to hook up with her that night in LA, I told her that I wanted to wake up adoring the person beside me, and I wanted to go to bed feeling adored by the person I was kissing good night. I'd told Amy that having sex with her — as enticing as the prospect was — was certain to interfere with the adored thing ever happening with Lauren and me.

"And?" she prompted.

I was quiet. My mind drifted to Lauren and Raoul. Then back to Big Elias. The odd trio comprised a major impediment to my ability to recollect the specifics of the whole adored thing.

"You're doing it again. Deciding whether to lie to me. No need to get all twisted — I was talking about your daughter's adoration. That little dancing girl adores her daddy. And her daddy, despite his dancing, adores his little girl."

"All true," I said.

"I have an offer for you," she said.

Oh God. I thought of Amy's prior offer, overtly erotic. "Go on."

"Don't go reaching for your running shoes. I know you can get skittish. If you would like to spend a little time with someone who remembers you fondly, I could stop in Boulder on my way to the Denver airport. I'll buy you a drink, or even an entire meal." Before I had a chance to speak, Amy added, "I promise to keep my clothes on."

"Well," I said, "then the answer is a definite no."

Am I flirting? Big Elias was barely cold. Elliot was on my tail. I was flirting.

I blamed it on Lauren and Raoul.

Amy said, "I'm an old friend saying hi. Do you believe that?"

"Sure." Amy might believe what she was saying. I also knew from years doing psychotherapy that believing something like that is different from something like that being true. I said, "I'm not in a great place. Can I think about it? Get back to you."

"You'll blow me off. Worst that happens is that we have an awkward drink someplace. That's not the end of the world. Say yes."

I needed to deal with Elliot's email. I said, "Okay, let's do it, Amy. Old friends."

"Perfect. I'll text you with a Leadville update, let you know when I'll be heading to Denver. It could be as early as the weekend. Could be midweek next. It all depends on how the clouds behave over the Divide. The AD wants some moon and stars. The celestial kind."

"I thought you said you were the AD."

"I'm second. The first AD is my boss. Big difference."

"Thank you for getting in touch, Amy."

"Adi, Alan."

Ah, that good-bye. *Adi,* as in *adios.* I never knew whether the aloha-ish parting was an LA thing, a Cali thing, or merely a peculiar Amy thing. Maybe I would ask her about it once she was done chasing stars in Leadville.

What was more likely, I knew, was that I would cancel the rendezvous.

I had once managed to walk away from a beautiful naked woman offering me lust and comfort.

Faced with a similar opportunity Lauren had not. Walked away. I felt a flare of burning rage. Like the white-hot chemical flames that engulf the sulfur on the end of a match.

Is that my soul on fire?

Why not, Lauren? Why did you not walk away?

I reread the ellbell email.

I used my laptop to locate North County Road 23 in Weld County. It wasn't there. I checked Boulder County. Nope. The logic of the state's system of county road numbering — if there was a system — had always

294

eluded me. I tried Google.

Google found North County Road 23 for me, but much farther north and west than I expected, in Larimer County in a rural location near the spot where the northernmost Front Range foothills melded with the high prairie, not far south of the Wyoming border. The closest major burg to that stretch of county road was Fort Collins.

I had no familiarity with the terrain, but I assumed from what I was seeing on the map that Big Elias had been driving a rural route not too far from the road that traced the route of the Cache La Poudre River out of the Rocky Mountains.

The *ellbell* email was specific about neither manner nor cause of death. Cause had to be a variant of trauma; when hooves meet human flesh and human bone, hooves tend to prevail. But Elliot was vague; he left open the possibility that the manner of Big Elias's death could have been just about anything. The crushing could have been the result of carelessness or accident. It could have been the result of an MI or a stroke. Or it could have been a death by another's hand.

Big Elias Contopo had been in the horse business. I did not consider it a wayward leap to conclude that he had been in rural Larimer County pulling a horse trailer because he was doing some literal horse-trading. Nor did I have a reason to question the facile assumption that Big Elias, after years in the horse business, knew the ins and outs of horses and horse trailers the way I knew the ins and outs of my road bicycle and my derailleur. That simple conclusion left me no room to quibble with Elliot's assessment that something had to have gone wrong for Elias Contopo to end up trampled to death by his own animal inside his own horse trailer on the side of a county road on the edge of nowhere in Larimer County.

I checked the online edition of *The Coloradoan,* the local Fort Collins newspaper, hoping for details. The only article was brief. The truck and trailer had been parked along the shoulder of Tatonka Trail just beyond the intersection of North County Road 23E, not North County Road 23. *The Coloradoan* reported that the death appeared to have been "accidental," and that the horses — plural, not singular — were uninjured and in the temporary care of a large animal vet at his nearby ranch.

I slammed my laptop closed.

I cursed Lauren, again, for fucking my friend.

I cursed Elliot for tormenting me.

I cursed Sam for killing a monster.

My rage was unfocused.

That fact didn't alarm me as much as it should have.

32

SAM AND LUCY

Sam was driving. Lucy was giving directions. It wasn't going well.

"We've had a productive day, Luce. Don't you think?"

"Yeah. I didn't expect to close either of those cases so quickly. That's it on the left, the blue house." The last stop of their shift was to pick up a forty-three-year-old man for questioning about stealing tens of thousands of dollars from his ex-mother-in-law.

Sam pulled to a stop across the street from the house. He started to get out.

Lucy said, "He's not home yet. Let's talk Prado. You're not going to take my advice, are you? About walking away from it?"

Sam squirmed. "Can we discuss Prado after we roust this guy? He's going to lawyer up. After he does we can talk till dawn. How can you tell he's not here?"

"Did you say 'roust'? He's an accountant,

not a gangbanger. Detect, Sam. That's an Amazon box at his door. A new Kindle. No way he leaves it out there if he's home."

"Did you just tell me to 'detect'? Maybe he's so distracted by all his larceny he didn't notice the box. Anyway, it's ill-gotten gains. All the money he stole from his mother-in-law? DA will confiscate his damn Kindle."

"His ex-wife told us he has an OCD streak. He probably had UPS email him when they delivered it. It's bugging him that it's sitting there."

Sam started the engine. "Okay, then we'll go someplace I can pee, come back in a while, maybe interrupt him playing with his new Kindle. That'll be satisfying."

Lucy removed the key from the ignition. "If you won't agree to walk away from Prado, we are going to figure this thing out. Prado's a puzzle. Puzzles have solutions."

"Right now? You think we're going to solve it sitting here?" Sam knew he was being an ass. That didn't bother him. That it wasn't having the desired effect with Lucy? That bothered him.

"Yeah. Right here, right now. Why not?"

"I really do have to pee. I wasn't kidding."

"I really don't care. What was your plan? You were going to ask to use the guy's john? Splash urine all over his bathroom floor before you read him his rights?"

Sam released the latch on his seat so he could extend his legs to remove pressure on his bladder. The car was parked on an incline. Sam was slightly overweight. The seat flew back on its rails as though it was rocket powered.

Lucy laughed. "Don't be a jerk, Sam. Let's get this done. We have to figure out the bungee."

"That's the part of the puzzle I like least."

"That's why we're going to use a decision tree."

He groaned. "I hate your decision trees." Sam tried to put his elbows on the armrests, but with the seat all the way back he couldn't reach them without sitting forward, which defeated the purpose of having his seat all the way back. He tried resting his arms on his gut but he felt conspicuously Buddha-ish in that posture, and it didn't quite offer the comfort he was seeking.

"You hate most things. If you avoided all of them you'd never get out of bed except to eat and have sex. Maybe watch hockey. Here's how I see it: First branch? A, the gun that Jumble Guy found is the gun that killed Doctor Doctor, or B, the gun that killed Doctor Doctor is some unknown handgun of the same caliber. Pick."

"You said this is about the way you see it. If I pick, it becomes the way I see it."

"Why are you being such an assbite?"

" 'Cause I feel like a hostage. What neighborhood is this? Is this still Boulder?" They were east of the Flatirons golf course. Sam knew it was Boulder. "This is probably a good neighborhood for trick-or-treating. Pricey houses, but not too far apart. Maybe our guy gives out full-size candy bars. Are thieving accountants generous or cheap? Probably cheap."

"This nice neighborhood is called Sombrero Ranch. Pick a branch, damn it."

Sam said, "The chimney gun killed him."

"Good. Our next branch has two options. Vic's manner of death? Suicide or homicide?"

"Vic has a name, it's —"

"Yeah yeah. Did Doctor Doctor kill himself or did someone else kill him? Are your hemorrhoids bothering you again?"

"The problem is my bladder, not my butt. Doctor killed himself. The damn bungee broke his index finger after he fired the gun."

"A fine choice. Next? Who did Doctor think was going to find his body?"

"Whom. And . . . *what*? Find his body? I don't get that part."

"Don't correct my grammar. You know I can't stand that. This is when the decision tree gets tricky — this branch has four options: His roommate. Somebody else he was expecting to come over. Law enforcement. Or a random stranger."

"Why are those my choices?"

"That's what I came up with. You're free to add your own. That's why we're discussing this together. It's called collaborating. It involves two or more people —"

"Oh, I get it. To make sense of the bungee we have to have an idea *whom* — whom whom — Doctor intended to deceive with the disappearing pistol. That's good thinking, Luce. I like it. That's why I picked you for my partner. Because you're smart."

Lucy wasn't about to get distracted by the compliment. "To us? That day was 9/11. But when Doctor Doctor pulled the trigger he didn't know it was 9/11. To him, it was Tuesday. He died never knowing we were attacked by Al Qaeda."

"That's nice for him," Sam said. He liked pondering the 9/10 world much more than he liked pondering the 9/11 world.

Lucy said, "Take 9/11 and Osama bin Laden out of the equation and tell me the next person who should have walked into the house on Prado. That's who-*oom* Doctor expected to discover his body. And to be perplexed by the absence of a suicide weapon."

"I see where you're going. The ME says time of death was late on September tenth or early on the eleventh. The roommate was due home — what did you tell me — later that day?"

"His flight was due into DIA five thirty-ish. Had to get his luggage and grab the shuttle to Boulder. Say he was due home about seven thirty. So Doctor could have been planning for his roommate to discover the body then. If the flight wasn't grounded."

"No," Sam said. "Doesn't compute. Doctor does this complicated setup with a bungee and a vanishing gun. Took planning. He's meticulous. We have to assume he knew exactly what time his roommate was due back. Would Doctor allow for such a large window of time between his suicide and someone finding his body? No. It introduces unnecessary variance. Doctor wasn't an unnecessary-variance kind of guy."

Lucy said, "I'll buy that — he wasn't and he wouldn't. So Doctor wasn't expecting the roommate to find his body. We can rule him out. See, we're making progress."

Sam was getting into it. "And I don't want to hear any serendipitous random stranger bullshit," Sam said. "Same issue. Doctor planned this well. He wanted someone specific to find his body. And to not find the gun. Someone he was certain would come by —"

"The morning of 9/11," Lucy said. "On schedule. Shortly after Doctor killed himself."

Sam agreed. "Yes, yes. And definitely before the raccoons. But that person didn't show up like Doctor expected. Or? Maybe that person came by but didn't call 911. Why? Twice."

Lucy said, "The same *why* works twice. The person didn't come by on the eleventh because the towers had been hit. And the Pentagon had been hit. And Shanksville had happened. Or the person came by on the eleventh but didn't call it in because the towers had been hit. And the Pentagon had been hit. And Shanksville had happened. And that had changed things."

"If 9/11 explains everything," Sam said, "it may explain nothing."

Lucy said, "Then we go back to the decision tree. Either the person Doctor expected didn't come by or the person came by but didn't call 911. Pick."

"I have a new twig for that branch," Sam said. "Try this: the person came by on 9/11 like Doctor expected, but didn't call it in until the fourteenth."

"That doesn't make any sense," Lucy said. "Who would see a dead body on Tuesday and wait to call it in until Friday? Popeye?"

Sam laughed. "Good one. But you're thinking of Wimpy. Tuesday was the eleventh," Sam said. "You said so yourself."

"Mimicry? That's all you got?"

"Somebody called it in on the fourteenth, Lucy. We know Doctor didn't plan it that way. Either somebody he expected on 9/11 showed up later in the week. Or somebody, random or not, showed up on the fourteenth."

"That's it? Those are my choices, Sammy?"

"The decision-tree bullshit wasn't my idea. But feel free to make additions. The possibilities about who showed up on that Friday are unlimited. Remember, the 911 call on the fourteenth was anonymous."

"You've said that before. But why?" Lucy said. "Why do it anonymously?"

Sam said, "Do decision trees have whys? Is that allowed?"

"I gave you a why earlier. I get a why, too. Look," Lucy said.

The OCD accountant was pulling into his driveway.

"Ha, an Acura," Sam said. "How did I know he'd drive an Acura? Turns out I'm pretty good at this detecting shit."

Lucy gave him about ten seconds to be pleased with himself before she said, "On the way over here I told you he drove an Acura. I even told you it was silver."

Sam laughed.

He tried but couldn't manage to get his seat to slide forward.

Lucy laughed.

She told him he could go home after they had the accountant in custody. She'd process him and hang around until his lawyer showed up.

33

ALAN

I wasn't in a good place.

My smoldering rage at Lauren's betrayal was refueled by the ellbell email. In the heat of my anger I convinced myself that going unannounced to Sam Purdy's house to confront him about the events on Tatonka Trail was a fine idea.

The three-minute drive didn't give me much time to reconsider the wisdom of the visit. The fact that his Cherokee wasn't in its usual spot at the curb did. But Sam not being home didn't dissuade me. I parked at the end of the block. I turned on the radio, took a deep breath, and tried to find a calm place while I waited for him to get home.

I didn't find the calm place. Instead I began to feel trapped by unwelcome erotic images of Lauren and Raoul, by echoes of the infuriating, barely couched accusations in the ellbell email, and by the vision-compromising ground fog that was already accompanying LA Amy's return into my life.

When I finally succeeded in corralling those intrusive meanderings, I discovered that all I had left in my head were ugly thoughts about Big Elias Contopo and Sam Purdy together in a horse trailer on Tatonka Trail.

Before I knew about any of them, the three Elias Contopos lived in a distinctive, multi-gabled home on a compact ranch on the eastern edge of Frederick. That's where Big Elias had been in the horse business.

The morning she was shot, Lauren traced out the recent branches of the Contopo family tree for me. She offered it as foundation so that I might understand why she was informing me that she was about to have Sam Purdy picked up for investigation of a homicide on the property of one of Elias Contopo's rural neighbors in Frederick.

The enduring Contopo family tragedy extended back many years. The concise version was that the patriarch, Big Elias, was a bully, a rapist, and a child abuser. He was likely also a blackmailer and an extortionist. Everything else was consequence.

The first Elias Contopo was the ill wind that proved the proverb by blowing no one any good.

During Izza's visit to Lauren the morning of the Dome Fire, Izza had made clear that she was desperate to rescue her nephew — her half brother Segundo's son — from his grandfather's home and to raise him herself. Lauren told me all that before she was shot.

Eighteen hours after Lauren was shot, at the conclusion of a brief negotiation that took place in the middle of the night, I had handed Sam Purdy the drawing that young Elias Tres had made the night Sam had killed Justine Brown in Frederick. The drawing would help convict Sam if it surfaced, and would help exonerate Sam if it disappeared.

I would have given the drawing to Sam either way. But, in return for the drawing, I asked him to give me his word that he would try to find a way to make Big Elias pay for his numerous previous crimes, and to do what he could to make things right for young Elias Tres. As part of the negotiation, Sam had demanded one concession from me.

He got me to agree that anything he did, he could accomplish his way. Without my interference. Now that Big Elias was dead, I felt compelled to know if Sam had been involved.

Involved as in responsible for his death.

I had almost convinced myself to go home when Sam drove up. He jumped from his old Jeep as though it were on fire and sprinted to his house.

I recognized a man who needed to pee when I saw one.

I pulled forward from the corner and parked across the street before I texted him.
Look out your window.

Sam's home was modest — truly modest, not just modest by Boulder standards — but his neighborhood below North Boulder Park was no longer so modest. Sam's was one of the few remaining Levittown-ish post–World War II bungalows.

Nobody knew when the Great Recession would ease or when Boulder's next housing bubble would ignite, only that it would happen. Once Boulder property values took off I had trouble seeing a real estate future that included the survival of Sam's aging cottage. Most lots in Sam's neighborhood were too small to cram much of a McAnything on, but the location — against the mountains north of Mapleton Hill — was glorious. His house offered easy proximity to downtown, a great nearby park, and a short stroll to the mountain trailheads. Sam's investment strategy was to hang on to his crappy house in its ideal location until somebody offered him too much money to tear it down.

That moment was coming.

Two minutes after I sent the text Sam's head appeared in the diamond-shaped opening cut into his front door. Sam's head was bigger than a normal person's head and bigger than the window in the door. Through the glass I could see no part of either ear, no chin, and only a triangular portion of his too-big forehead. My lip-reading skills were in fine tune. When he spotted me his lips and teeth were mouthing the word *fuck.*

I was curious for an indication about which type of surveillance Sam was most concerned. Would he phone my cell and risk the chance there was a tap on our phones? Would he return my text and risk that there was a trap on my digital accounts? Or would he walk out the front door, march right up to my car, scream at me about my stupidity, and thus make an in-person wager that the DA's investigators didn't have the budget or the legal justification for real live surveillance on my butt?

I had my money on Sam choosing the last option. In-person surveillance was an inefficient use of dollars. The current budget environment in Boulder County had no margin for inefficient use of dollars. As worried as I was about taps, and bugs, and cameras, I didn't waste much of my paranoia looking over my literal shoulders.

While I waited impatiently for Sam to make his next move I began to reset the buttons on the radio. Jonas had changed my available options to an incongruous combination of annoying pop stations, annoying hip-hop stations, and one Spanish language station that played Banda music. Jonas enjoyed neither pop nor hip-hop; he remained entrenched in his Feist-before-she-was-cool phase, the advent of which had predated Lauren's death. There was no radio preset available for coffee-house Feist.

What Jonas did enjoy was screwing around with my radio presets. He would be most disappointed to learn that I was developing a taste for Banda.

Sam made his move. The communication tool he chose was one that I had not considered but one that was relatively surveillance-proof. The living room of his little home had a solitary picture window. I watched the curtains swing open fast, as though someone — Sam — was making a point with the alacrity with which he pulled the cord.

Sam stood in the center of the picture window holding up a fractional sheet of fluorescent green poster board. On it was scrawled, "THE DAMN PARK."

He had the Sharpie he'd used for the scrawl clenched between his front teeth. He was scowling at me as though he wanted to appear to be a particularly mean pirate, or as though the Sharpie tasted poorly. I guessed the latter.

He pulled the board down and flung it. It acted like an airfoil, flying above the plane of the window before drifting back down toward the floor. Sam then held up both hands in my direction, his fingers spread. After allowing me time to count to ten, or to multiply two times five, he reconfigured his hands so that they each featured a solitary middle finger in prominent erection.

I drove away from the curb. I thought the song on the radio was Katy Perry, but I was far from certain. Differentiating the current crop of female pop artists was beyond my capability. I switched stations. The Banda option was playing commercials. My sung Spanish comprehension was so undeveloped I couldn't tell what the ads were selling, only that they were mightily enthusiastic about selling it.

I found myself yearning for a little early Feist.

Sam sat down beside me on a bench near the playground. "Bad friggin' move."

"Couldn't wait."

"Sometimes you need to be patient."

"Sometimes I need to talk."

"You sound like a child. I have one too many of those these days."

People had been treating me with deference since Lauren's death. Sam was the first friend to call bullshit on that. In the abstract it felt good. But I had actually planned the encounter out in a way that relied on Sam granting me a little deference. I was also wishing our friendship were in a place where I could talk to Sam about Lauren's betrayal. I needed that. But we weren't in that place.

My introspection went on too long. Sam said, "What? I'm here. I have better things to do. Much better."

I almost said *like what*? but that would have stoked his meme about my childishness. I said, "I heard McClelland had a stroke. In prison. You know about that?"

"What? Heard from whom? Is the warden a friend of yours?"

314

"Don't be a detective, just answer me."

Sam's eyes went wide. "That WITSEC asshole. The Luppo creep? Jeez. He's a killer, Alan."

"Sam. Please." I was thinking *we're killers* but saying it might have risked an increase in the body count. The latest victim, me.

"I hope it's true. I'll check, I'll check. That's it? Good." Sam stood.

"Tell me about Elias Contopo," I said.

Sam sat back down. He was looking straight ahead. Although I tried, I couldn't see his eyes. His tone of voice unchanged, he said, "Which one? Uno? Dos? Tres?"

It was impossible for me to hear those words without adding a silent *cuatro, cinco, seis.* I somehow managed not to continue to *siete, ocho, nueve* but the effort required concentration that distracted me. I refocused. *Is Sam really going to play ignorant with me about Big Elias?* I said, "Uno," intentionally mispronouncing the word so that it sounded like "you know."

Sam's Spanish wasn't fluent. He'd been known to use the *you-know* pronunciation himself non-ironically, but his reply indicated he considered my intentional use to be mocking. "What about him?" was what Sam shot back. "The fat fuck is my problem, remember? Our agreement about Frederick

315

was don't ask, don't tell. That means you shouldn't be asking and I'm not going to be telling. So Elias Contopo the senior" — he made it sound like the Spanish *señor* — "is my problem." He shifted his weight again as though he was preparing to stand. He held up a hand. "We done here?"

I was getting his drift. I didn't care. I said, "No, as a —"

He said, "Look." I followed his line of sight. A bland gray sedan with tinted windows was parallel parking into a tiny spot along the curb across from our bench. We watched the maneuver develop in painful herky-jerky stop-motion. Sam, I guessed, was suspicious of the sedan because of its blandness and grayness. My impression, on the other hand, was that the driver of the car was not the most accomplished parallel parker in the known universe.

Eventually — it took way too many backs and forths and stops and starts — an elderly couple emerged slowly from the car. They held hands as they entered the perimeter of North Boulder Park. She was relying on him, and on a cane, for support.

They wore matching walking shoes. I found that cute.

"Got to be careful," Sam said.

"Couldn't agree more," I said. "If it wasn't

for the cane, she could be a threat." I paused. "Elias Contopo. Uno. Grande." I emphasized the second syllable of *grande.*

"Does grande mean fat?" Sam asked, mimicking my pronunciation. "Like at Starbucks?"

Sam was smart. But he was smart almost entirely in English. "I think you're thinking of *gordito,* or *gordo.* Like at Taco Bell." He was fluent in fast food. "People in Frederick call the first Elias 'Big' not 'Fat.' They might think he's fat, but since he's such a bully they're afraid of him. What they say out loud is 'big.' That's grande, not gordo."

I was being careful with tense, speaking of Elias in the present, not the past.

Sam didn't quarrel with my impressions, my Spanish, or my tense. He said, "Well, Grande Gordo Elias is my problem, not yours. Like I said earlier, sometimes you need to be patient. It may take time. I don't have a plan, but I have a plan to have a plan."

I shifted on the bench to face him. I needed to see his reaction to my next words. But our side-by-side positioning meant I still couldn't look into his eyes. I stood. I took two steps back. He looked up at me with an expression of unadorned suspicion, as though he feared I was the person —

idiot, from Sam's perspective — about to initiate a flash mob extravaganza he wanted no part of.

I said, "Big Elias is dead."

Ten seconds later — he spent the time cogitating — he said, "What?"

Sam wasn't requesting repetition. His *what* had been a form of "you shittin' me?"

"Big Elias died last night while he was in Larimer County on horse business."

More cogitating. Then, "How?"

"Unclear. It involved horses and a horse trailer. And a flat tire."

Sam's eyes narrowed. "He rolled his truck?"

His tone was barbed. Provocative. I didn't reply. Picking up the barbed provocation just to pick it up felt stupid, like poking a skunk to see if it would spray.

"Ah," he said reaching a conclusion about my intent. *"Homicido."*

Homicido isn't a real word. And even though it was his own made-up word, Sam had managed to mispronounce it. I considered correcting his vocabulary and his pronunciation. It took some self-control but I didn't.

He lowered the volume to conspiratorial levels. "You're wondering if I borrowed your car before I drove to Larimer County to kill

318

off Gordo Elias? Or are you waiting for me to offer you an alibi for the time Big Elias was in Larimer County on his last-ever horse business trip." He opened his eyes wide to emphasize the point he was making. But given the immense size of his forehead they looked no bigger than a couple of grapes on a pale-pink dinner plate.

I didn't reply. I was gathering information. Not providing it. And I was trying not to be provoked. Sam was feeling provoked, and provocative. That was clear.

He stood and walked past me. If I hadn't jumped aside he would have bowled me over. He stopped twenty feet down the path. He looked back over his shoulder with animus in his eyes. "How did you hear about this? Your friend Izza?"

I shook my head. His contempt was putting me in a worse mood than I'd been in when I was parked outside his house listening to commercials on my Banda station. And I had been in a terrible frame of mind when I'd parked outside his house. I considered whether or not I should tell him how I knew about the death. Finally I said, "No. Not Izza. Elliot."

"Elliot?" He snapped the name back at me, disbelieving. He wasn't pleased at Elliot entering the equation. It was as though he

319

had just seen the Elliot question on the final but he knew damn well it hadn't been covered in any of the lectures.

He didn't wait for me to confirm. I thought I heard him mumble a long profanity as he walked away. The sincerity of the profanity was clear, but I wasn't confident about its length. It could have been multiple repetitions of a compact profanity.

Sam stopped, twirled, and took five or six steps back in my direction. I saw spittle flying before I heard the next words, which came in the form of a screaming whisper. "You do not come to my house right after law enforcement gets in your face." He made a completely exasperated face of his own. "Understand what I'm saying? That's when they're watching. First they come at you, they rile you up. Then they see what you do next. It's basic shit, Alan. That's being-a-suspect 101. Action/reaction. Laws of . . . law, and thermodynamics. Human nature. Mostly? It's common friggin' sense. Got any?" He spit. He actually spit. The loogie almost hit his right shoe. "It's just basic damn shit." He tapped his skull twice with his index finger. "Use your head."

I was tempted to defend myself. I didn't. He spun and continued away from me. Into the wind, I think he said, "I do this every day. It's who I am. Leave this to me. God-damn. Jesus. I can't believe you . . ." His voice faded. Another twenty feet down the path, Sam looked over his shoulder again. Loudly, he said, "Elliot?"

"Yeah."

"He called you about this?"

"Emailed me, but yeah."

"Why would he tell you about some old guy who died in Larimer County? What am I missing? How does he connect you to Big Elias Contopo. I don't get it."

I wondered if Sam was being disingenu-ous. Sam had to know why Elliot would connect me to Frederick, and to Big Elias. He had to. *Tres's drawing.* In case I was wrong I said, "I'm thinking Elliot learned why Lauren came to my office that morn-ing."

"Do you know that?" Sam got even more terse. "Or are you guessing?"

"He suspects that Lauren coming to my office had to do with the visit Lauren got from Izza and Tres."

"He can't prove that, can he?"

"Not that I know of. But there are things I don't know."

"You think?" Sam was looking for pieces to complete the puzzle in his head. He wasn't finding them. Insulting me was a way of passing the time while he searched.

I said, "Reading between the lines? I think Elliot thinks, or hopes, I was involved somehow with Big Elias's . . . demise. The only possible connection he might have to connect me to it is Izza and that damn drawing."

Sam shook his head. My explanation wasn't working for him. "That's crazy. If Elliot had seen that drawing one of us would be in jail. Maybe both of us. Did you even know the guy? The old Elias?"

I shook my head. I said, "I heard stories. But I had never met him."

"Stories from whom?"

"My wife. That morning." I was feeling lost. Nothing about Sam's reaction to the news of Big Elias's death was what I'd expected. I was determined to stay silent until the ground steadied. I feared I was making things worse for myself every time I opened my mouth.

His shoulders relaxed a smidge. "Big Elias was crushed? Literally crushed?" I nodded. "How? Under the trailer?"

I couldn't tell whether or not he already knew the answer. I had assumed I would be able to tell from his expression. People in the movies are always supposing that mental health professionals can magically tell when someone is prevaricating. But I couldn't tell what Sam was thinking. *Damn.* I was no better at it than Grace.

Pretending I didn't know the answer to Sam's question was also futile. I knew that if Sam really didn't know he would Google the incident on his phone the second he was out of my sight.

"By a horse or two. Inside the trailer. That part is unclear."

Sam laughed. Then he resumed storming away. Again, he stopped.

"Why does Elliot hate you? What did you do to him?"

"I wonder the same thing. I have no idea."

My instincts were screaming that Sam had figured out a way to solve the Frederick problem I had laid at his feet months before. His solution had been to eliminate Big Elias Contopo. I wondered why. I also wondered if he had accomplished the latest homicido without leaving any evidence or witnesses behind.

I realized I had a third question. *Is Sam Purdy out of control?*

34

On the way back across town to Spanish Hills I detoured to a convenience store where I had never bought gas. I could barely keep my eyes from gazing up at the surveillance camera behind the register.

I bought a prepaid cell phone with cash. A burner.

The first thing I did after killing the engine in my garage was to text Amy from my regular cell phone, my tracker. Contacting her didn't require the subterfuge of a burner; it merely required some sober reconsideration of my self-interest.

Second thoughts. Rain check? It was good to hear from you.

I was grateful that texting convention encouraged brevity. If I had emailed her about my ambivalence, I would have felt an obligation to offer an explanation for bailing. I didn't have an explanation. And I didn't feel like inventing one to be polite.

I wasted the next twenty minutes trying to rationalize away my determination to continue the spelunking project I had barely started into the almost impenetrable cave of Lauren's personal papers, both real and digital. But I failed. I knew I had to get to the bottom of those piles, or at least to make a dent in them.

My fresh motivation for the search, and my fresh resistance to the search, both had to do with learning if what Amanda was alleging about Lauren and Raoul was true.

I asked myself what difference it would make to learn more. I asked myself whether I could live with what I knew already. I decided that I wouldn't know what Amanda's allegations meant until I learned some facts. I had reached a point where not knowing was no longer an option for me.

I sat on the end of our bed and stared at the scope of the project. Daunting.

My only certain conclusion from the mess on Lauren's desk — and the associated messes on the desk chair, on the floor nearby, on the cushion of the club chair that we'd mutually identified as "hers" — was that Lauren had not been anticipating her death.

I liked that. I knew that she woke most days wary of the unpredictability of her illness, but I found comfort that she wasn't waking with a sense of foreboding about her life.

Had she been concerned about her death, I believed I would have seen some evidence of it on her desk. In some re-sorting of her very uncollected papers. Or in some collation of active accounts that might require immediate attention by someone, like me, who was designated to manage her affairs. After her death. Or in some small sweet note to me, or some personal sign, that said, "Start here, babe, here."

My wife had tended to approach journeys of all kinds with a burst of organization. Trips were arranged from detailed lists. Suitcases were judged for appropriate size with practice packings, sometimes repeated practice packings. I found no sign that she had done any preorganizing for this, the most extended of all departures. If there were a journey that required anticipation and planning, this was that one. I saw no evidence of it.

I had previously peeked into the hills of paper. My initial scans had been tenuous and ambivalent; I'd looked around the way I searched for a mouse after spotting droppings. It was an effort to appear serious about looking for a problem and simultaneously being careless enough with my search that I minimized the odds that I would find what I was hoping wasn't there.

On two separate occasions I had dived in to find specific pieces of paper that others — one lawyer, one accountant — told me couldn't wait to be found. Those searches had been unsuccessful; I'd found neither of the essential papers.

The sky didn't fall without the essential papers. I took comfort in that, too.

Lauren's desk was more repository than workspace, always had been. The desk chair was just another surface on which she balanced stuff for later attention. If she had writing to do — MS had robbed her of any pleasure from longhand correspondence — and the writing involved something more drawn out than filling out a check, or scribbling a reminder in one of her Field Notes books, she did the work on her diminutive laptop.

And she did it elsewhere. Most often she carried the laptop to the bed. Or she pulled an odd little chair/high stool thing up to the pool table in the dining room. On relaxed, lazy days she might stretch out on the chaise she loved in the family room.

Lauren was an organized person in the sense that her tendency toward order was greater than her tolerance of disorder. But the organizing inclinations had lacunae. Her bedside table? Impeccably neat. *House Beautiful,* find-things-in-the-dark neat. Her designated cabinetry in the bathroom? Surgical-nurse precision for cosmetics and things. Her car? The front seat was showroom quality. The backseat she abdicated to the kids.

The kitchen? A serious lacuna. At work? I'd been told that her litigation files were works of organizational art.

But my wife's inclination for order had never applied in the domestic paperwork terrain she considered her own. No signs of obsession or compulsion were enforced on her tranche of our home paperwork, regardless of category.

The desk was a conflagration of what I had teasingly called her "piles and files." The mess, I knew, was less random than it appeared. I recalled many instances when I had asked Lauren for some specific something I needed. Lauren could reliably retrieve the requested document within double-digit seconds. She knew the wilderness on top of her desk the way a tracker knows the backcountry. I hoped, as I anticipated diving in, that the terrain appeared to me as wilderness only because I wasn't yet as familiar as Lauren with her peculiar chunk of backcountry.

I had to end my procrastination. I had legal responsibilities to perform. Death notices to send. Accounts to cancel. Taxes to preorganize. Accountants' questions to respond to. A life to begin living.

After my evening with Amanda in her friend's incall, I also had an affair of the heart, and of the flesh, to confirm. To rage at. And to grieve. So I dived into Lauren's piles and files. To the place where I might discover evidence that my wife and my friend were fucking.

That Lauren was dead? My heart still seeped from that wound. That grief would endure until it ended. That she had been having an affair? Since her tryst or almost tryst with Joost, I was not in denial about Lauren's fidelity. In a vacuum I was certain I could have found context for a new betrayal.

But that her love affair was with my friend? That was no vacuum. That hurt me so much it cleaved my already wounded heart in two. The pain from that injury felt impossible to me.

I was suffering a compound fracture of my heart.

■ ■ ■ ■

I began by taking photos. I used my digital camera, with the flash, to record how Lauren had left her home office behind the morning of the Dome Fire. I was thinking that the organization she left behind, such as it was, might prove important later, after my digging around rendered the original disorder impossible to duplicate.

Then I dug in. After an hour and a half of what I knew was but an initial round of sorting and re-sorting, I realized that there was a chance that Lauren's strategy in regard to her papers might have an underlying elegance to it. But I also had the humbling realization that in these circumstances I was neither Lewis nor Clark.

I was incapable of recognizing the specific nature of the underlying elegance.

Each time I thought I'd discovered an organizing principle that might guide me, I quickly found an exception or three or five. Any hope proved fanciful.

The mail addressed to Lauren that had continued to arrive after her death provided me with signage that I could use to mark trailheads for future exploration. I knew that my task would be easier if I could see and read the email that continued to arrive for Lauren after her death, too.

But my digital access was blocked. The BlackBerry she carried had been provided by the DA's office. I never saw it again after she was shot. Whether it was collected into evidence to be used in an eventual prosecution of her murder, or whether it had simply been handed over to her employers by the police to protect work product, I didn't know. I accepted that I might never know.

Whatever guidance Lauren's BlackBerry might provide about intimate correspondence with Raoul would not be available to me. But it might, I knew, be available to Elliot Bellhaven, Lauren's boss. That pissed me off.

Her personal laptop was password protected. That was not a surprise. During a conversation we'd had one date night about marital transparency — her issue more than mine — we had exchanged laptop passwords. I had never used her password and had misremembered or forgotten it. Or she had changed it after she told me what it was.

Or she had lied to me.

Some of that had, apparently, been going on.

The piles and files exhausted me. I took a break to spend an hour with the kids. I made them dinner. I returned to the chore in the sitting room. I got them to bed.

Midnight came and went. At 12:20, I got a text from LA Amy.

Good Night Moon! The light tonight!!! Go look!!

I went and I looked. Fine moon. Not full, but still. I returned to find another text.

Ur 2nd thoughts? Not a date. Don't apologize.

I considered replying. With an apology, or some defiance. I didn't bother.

At 2:37, I gave up trying to solve the office puzzle, flicked off the lights, and collapsed onto the bed in the guest room. I couldn't sleep; my brain was busy pondering the weight of all the potential surprises I was postponing until the next day.

On top of the list of what was keeping me awake? I had located a stash of apparent work material in two discrete locations among her things. One source was in an inch-thick file marked "Pending Resolution, Work" that was in the short file drawer of her desk. The other, parallel collection was contained in an unsealed fat Tyvek envelope — damn Tyvek — that she had marked "Personal, Work." Oxymoron, that.

The envelope was buried among a pile of papers and catalogs.

The file appeared to be neat and organized. The envelope was not organized. Papers of all kinds were stuffed into that Tyvek repository in a haphazard fashion.

By chance, I had tossed the envelope that Sofie had pulled from the pocket of Lauren's peacoat in the week between Christmas and New Year's — the sealed envelope that Sofie said was addressed to "elly-ott" — on top of the stack that included the Tyvek.

I wasn't sure whether I was demonstrating admirable restraint by not reading the work materials, or whether my cowardice about my wife's secrets had become a dominant trait. Regardless, I greeted the unknown on Lauren's desk with trepidation. I had trouble believing there was something there that I wanted to know. I was also doubtful that I would find something that would confirm, or deny, the existence of an affair between Lauren and Raoul. Lauren had hidden her affair successfully. I didn't believe she would have left careless clues for me on her desk at home.

Closure with Lauren would be elusive. Closure with LA Amy? Easier. I got out of bed, returned to the bedroom, and found the texting thread with her. I pecked out:

You were sweet to reach out. Sorry, no. Maybe next time I'm in LA.

I felt some accomplishment as I hit send. I flicked off the light. In the fractional second before the master bedroom went from dark to black, my eyes fell onto the line of left shoes that Sofie had arranged against the long wall opposite my side of the bed.

Specifically, my eyes rested on a left shoe from a familiar pair of heels. The heel was tall. Probably four inches. The shoes were, well, sexy. Lauren, her balance compromised by multiple sclerosis, hadn't been able to safely balance on high heels since early in our relationship. I felt a pang of sadness. I returned to the guest room.

Oh God. I jumped back out of bed. Naked. I ran down the hall and I grabbed that high heel. *No no, not it.* My composure failed me. Not gradually. All at once. I kicked at Sofie's entire neat lineup of left shoes and boots and sandals. I lifted every shoe that had a heel of any height, tossing each in turn over my shoulders. Some left, some right.

No shoe had a red sole. Not one. "Shit. Shit."

My composure fragile, I stepped into the closet. Nearly two dozen shoe boxes were arranged on the highest shelves, out of reach. I grabbed a step stool to examine the identifying labels that Lauren had placed on the shoe boxes so that she could easily locate a precise pair she was seeking. I fought an impulse to yank all of the boxes to the floor so I could sort through the resulting mess with the total lack of discrimination of a tornado.

Instead I took a deep breath, read each label, and I chose a single box from among the many. It was an earth-tone box, a medium brown. The designer's name on the top was in an ostentatious script. The word *Paris* was in a more restrained font in one corner of the lid.

The box was empty. The other boxes all contained a single shoe, a right shoe. The matching left shoe from each pair should have been among the ones that Sofie had lined along the wall in the bedroom. But both shoes were absent from the brown box.

Diane? I began thinking of the shoes she'd cradled that night in that condo. Did she have Lauren's shoes? *How,* I thought, *could she have? Did Diane really come into my house and steal my wife's shoes?*

Then I thought, *No. Not Diane. Oh my God.* I began to yank all the remaining shoe boxes from the shelves, ripping off the lids. I kicked maniacally at all the right shoes, at all the sandals, at all the pumps, at all the sneakers, at all the mules, and at all the heels.

I talked to them. I yelled at a few. I cursed more than once. As my insane tantrum neared a conclusion — I was running out of footwear to abuse — I looked up to see Jonas standing in the doorway to the closet.

He said, "Dad, are you okay?"

It was, I knew, a reasonable query.

Observing ego is the capacity to look in a figurative mirror and see one's self and one's behavior with negligible psychological distortion.

How was I doing in that moment? In my figurative mirror it was the middle of the night and I was a naked guy cursing at his dead wife's footwear while tossing her saved shoe boxes and right shoes around the walk-in closet, then drop-kicking and examining the soles of the shoes before tossing them over my shoulders.

The expression on Jonas's face made clear how I appeared to him. My closet shoe-fit must have looked like one of the crazy GIFs he liked to create from bursts of anime melded with brief clips of Oprah. The similarity only underscored the extent of my crazy.

I recognized the evidence of my acute

decline. Which meant that my observing ego was reasonably intact. I tried to take comfort in that.

The remainder of my psychological makeup? That would require serious work.

It took me a while to convince Jonas I was okay. The discussion started with me pulling on some sweatpants.

It ended with me coaxing him back downstairs to bed.

I didn't have to wonder whether I had convinced him I was all right.

He told me he wasn't convinced I was all right.

I told him I completely understood.

35

I checked on Jonas — the light was off in his bedroom — before I returned to the guest room bed. I was glad it had been he, and not Gracie, who witnessed my tantrum.

I sat, leaning against the headboard in the dark, pondering whether a more observant husband would have noticed the day that the nondescript brown shoe box arrived in the closet.

Or would that have been a more controlling, paranoid husband?

I knew it wasn't whatever kind of husband I had been.

I broke in my new burner by phoning Amanda. Since it was the middle of the night I assumed the call would wake her. I heard five rings before she answered.

In a sleepy voice she said, "Wrong number," before she hung up. She hadn't recognized my new burner number on her caller ID. How could she?

I was elated by the anonymity. I phoned again. One ring only. She answered. I said, "Amanda. It's —"

She wasn't listening. She spoke when I spoke. "Stop calling." She hung up again.

I hit REDIAL. Before I even detected a ring, she said, "Alan?" She'd heard me say her name before her last hang up.

"Yes."

"Jesus. It's three o'clock in the morning. What's wrong?" It was apparent that she was trying to engage with me without actually waking up. I didn't think that would end up working out for her.

"Almost four. It's starting to snow. I have a question. It can't wait."

"What?" The *what* didn't reflect any curiosity about my weather update, or about my question; it reflected her incredulity that I would intrude at that hour.

I asked, "Did Raoul give you the shoes with the red soles?"

"You woke me to ask me that? Yes. He gave them to me. He has a shoe thing."

I wanted to know all about Raoul's shoe thing. And I didn't. I was a coward about self-inflicted wounds. Begging for details of Raoul's shoe thing with my wife would have been the psychological equivalent of taking a blade to my own flesh.

From Amanda's mouth, in the context of her red-soled shoes, *thing* meant fetish. I so much didn't want confirmation about the role of Lauren's spike-heeled feet in Raoul's fetish. But then, of course, I did. I had to. *Didn't I?*

That was why I'd called. I said, "Your shoes? They are Christian Louboutin?" The French from the brown box rolled off my tongue as though I'd practiced it. I had, of course, practiced it. I had no choice. I couldn't get the damn name out of my head.

"Yes." Amanda was wide-awake. "I'm impressed you know women's shoes."

"My education is recent and reluctant. I apologize for waking you. Good night."

"Wait," she said. "I get it. I think I see. You found some? Lauren has a pair too. Are hers Louboutins or Kurt Geigers? They're Louboutins, of course. Red soles?"

"Yes." I didn't know what the hell Kurt Geigers were.

After a pause of five seconds, Amanda purred, "He used to call the Geigers 'his consolation prize.' Any chance Lauren's shoes are eights? If the toes are open — Raoul loves women's toes — I can wear seven and a half. Are you attached to them?"

I hung up.

I needed to know if my wife's Louboutins

exposed her toes for Raoul's pleasure. Though why I needed to know that was not at all clear to me.

I shut down my burner and went back to my tracker. The phone juggling thing was going to take some practice.

It was nearly midday in Holland. Sofie responded to my text almost immediately. After some back-and-forth to explain why I was up so late — I told her the broadest outlines of the truth, that I was busy working on cleaning up Lauren's papers:

The things you took to remember your mother? Did they include shoes?

Sofie: **One pair. Ok?**

Absolutely. Heels?

Sofie: **Ja. My vader, dad, is not pleased. 2 hi. 2 sexy 2. So tall! I must save them for later. Do u want them back?**

Not at all. Would you please take some photos? Including the soles?

Sofie: **Soles?? WTW?**

WTW was Sofie's English texting shorthand for *what's the word*.

Bottoms of the shoes? The red part?

Sofie: **On me?**

Always want pics of you. But this time just the shoes. I am trying to match them with an empty box. When your vader says the time is right, enjoy the

341

shoes. Then please send a photo of you all dressed up in them. I miss you so much.

The shoe photos arrived from Sofie in the next few minutes. The JPEGs loaded slowly, like in the old days of the Internet. Pixel by pixel, line by line. The pace of the reveal felt agonizing. After two minutes I had three photos of the Louboutin heels.

I had never seen the shoes before. Lauren had never shown them to me. Modeled them for me. Worn them out with me. Or worn them in with me.

I would have remembered. The shoes were sexy. Mostly black, with open toes. No, I scolded myself, not *open* toes. I heard my wife's voice. *"Not open toes, these are peep toes,"* Lauren had teased me when I'd described a pedestrian pair of shoes she was wearing to work as having "open toes."

Peep toes, then.

The Louboutins had a geometric pattern of crystals on one side, and a delicate strap above the ankle. And those red, red soles.

After a few minutes passed — minutes I spent mentally filling in blanks I so much didn't want to fill — Sofie texted me one more time.

She never wore them. They are like new. That's sad. Makes me cry.

I typed: **Me too.**

Any residual disbelief I was clinging to about Raoul and Lauren and the Louboutins crumbled in the face of the tsunami of sadness that bowled me over. Despite my earlier efforts to ward them off, I was drowning in images about what had transpired and what the damn shoes confirmed. *She wore them, Sofie. She just didn't walk in them.*

I cried for a long while.

I was hoping Jonas was asleep.

36

The next morning, Friday, came on schedule. The snow that fell overnight was like powdered sugar on a crepe. It would be gone before the sun blinked twice.

The world hadn't stopped. I registered some surprise at that. And a small sliver of disappointment. At breakfast Jonas never mentioned my naked meltdown in the middle of the night. He did tell me he wasn't feeling well.

I drank coffee as I checked *The Coloradoan* online for an update on Big Elias's demise. A follow-up story indicated that a witness had come forward and provided a statement to the Larimer County sheriff's investigator.

The witness was driving home on North County Road 23E the evening before Elias Contopo's body was discovered. He thought that he drove past the horse trailer and pickup on the west shoulder of Tatonka Trail a little bit after eight o'clock. He reported two things of note to me. First, when he drove past the horse trailer there was a second vehicle parked along the road, but on the opposite shoulder. He had assumed the second driver had stopped to offer help. If he hadn't spotted the second vehicle, the witness told the reporter, he would have offered assistance.

The other thing the witness reported was that a man was standing in the back of the open door of the horse trailer wearing white coveralls. The man's back was turned; he couldn't see his face. The witness didn't recall any details about the second vehicle other than that it was a sedan. The headlights were on; the glare was in his eyes. His attention had been on the truck with the horse trailer with the open door, and on the man in the coveralls.

I stopped breathing halfway through my read. Sam Purdy, I knew, was smart enough not to use his own vehicle on his homicidal errands. He had proved that in Frederick. The white coveralls? I thought, *Tyvek*. The man standing in the door of the horse trailer wasn't wearing coveralls. He was wearing a disposable jumpsuit. The Tyvek coverall was becoming a reliable enough presence that I considered it to be Sam's MO. A *modus op-*

erandi. A way of operating.

If that was Sam on Tatonka Trail he was batting 1.000 with his choice of homicidal haberdashery. If that was Sam on Tatonka Trail he had worn Tyvek jumpsuits for each of the murders he'd committed.

At least the ones I knew about.

I Googled Tyvek jumpsuits. They were cheap and easy to procure. *Shit.*

I also checked the online price for a pair of Louboutin spike heels.

The cost of a pair of fancy heels much less ornate than the ones that Sofie's *vader* rightly thought were too sexy for his daughter started below a thousand dollars. A pair with crystal details not too unlike Lauren's came in at just south of three thousand.

Dollars. Before the crash in 2007, chump change for Raoul.

I checked Kurt Geiger, too. More women's shoes, but at a fraction of the cost of the Louboutins. All of Raoul's women didn't wear Louboutins.

Apparently only the special ones did.

Lauren had affixed a label on the ends of each of the shoe boxes in her top shelf collection. Each label had a shorthand description — "green pumps, 2 in." "sky blue espadrilles" — along with an acquisition date written in a month/year convention. The date for the Louboutins was just shy of two years before the day that Lauren was shot.

Two years. Did the affair begin with the gifted pair of Louboutins? No, that would be too forward, even for someone with Raoul's confidence. *So not two years.* More. Their relationship started earlier. The gift of the Louboutins marked a transition of some kind between them. A day had arrived when Raoul didn't have to say what they meant. A day had arrived when she didn't have to admit she couldn't walk in them.

The gift came at a time when things could go unsaid. Sexual things.

What kind of transition did the Louboutins mark? I could imagine the answer to that question with relative ease. Absolutely no comfort, but remarkable ease.

Lauren's label on the box identified the shoes as "CL peeps letts." The *letts* puzzled me. The solution to the puzzle came to me in the shower. *Letts* was for *stilettos.*

Christian Louboutin. Peep toes. Stilettos.

The image of my wife on the first day or night the erotic event played out, Lauren in her peep toe stilettos and Raoul in, well, nothing, became etched with acid on my brain.

Raoul had been screwing my wife for years. How blind was I? So blind that Lauren didn't even bother to hide the shoes from me. They had been sitting in plain sight on the same shelf on her side of the closet from the day she received them from her lover.

I made a halfhearted effort to explain the shoes in another way. The act was like trying on clothing in the wrong size pretending it would fit. For me, the definition of futility.

The Louboutins explained so much, so well. So painfully well. All that was necessary was a simple truth: Raoul's special women wore Christian Louboutins.

How inadequate was I as a husband? Apparently quite.

I couldn't find rage. Not for my dead wife. Not for my onetime friend.

God, that troubled me.

37

Kirsten sent me a text as I was getting dressed for the day. I was getting dressed for the day because I had a rescheduled therapy appointment to attend.

The kind with me as the patient.

I had forwarded the ellbell email to Kirsten shortly after I read it the day before. She'd emailed a reply right back, indicating that she read Elliot's missive the same way I did. She also echoed her earlier urgency that I retain good legal representation immediately.

The new text was a follow-up.

You make that call yet? Say yes.

I considered hedging but realized she might already know that I had not.

On my to do list. Promise. I have a lot going on.

My words were true, but they wouldn't sway Kirsten, who was becoming a reluctant expert on my procrastination.

My hands felt tied. By revealing to her, or to the Denver attorney, the truth of what happened that night in Frederick, or the details of the clean-hands negotiation that took place between Sam and me, I would abrogate the arrangement I had with Sam. From that moment on it would be every man for himself. Clean hands be damned.

The consequences of that? Completely unpredictable.

I wasn't willing to do that to my children. Or to Sam's son. Sam and I had to work this out. Somehow. Before I saw that attorney in Denver.

How would we come to terms? I did not know. I actually thought that if Sam were arrested for killing Elias Contopo on the Tatonka Trail, the clean-hands decision would be made for me. I hated that I thought that.

But I thought it. Another text arrived from Kirsten:

Be honest. Please. How about now? Call NOW.

Promise was what I began to type. But before I had a chance to send the text I heard Sam calling my name from outside the front door. I joined him on the porch.

I felt no inclination to invite him into my

home. My lack of hospitality would seem odd to Sam, though Sam would use the Iron Range word *goofy,* which was a fine descriptor for the circumstances between us. He asked, "You're doing okay?"

We hadn't talked since he stormed away from me in North Boulder Park. I wasn't sure what he was asking with his inquiry about my well-being. My feelings about the argument we'd had? My general welfare? My assessment of the likelihood of my imminent arrest for the Frederick murder? Or of Sam for the Tatonka Trail?

Sam's question was not a banal social inquiry. I had to keep the big picture in mind. The fear I had was that Sam was setting me up to be identified as the shooter in Frederick, or that he was willing to let the momentum of fate settle out toward that end. As long as that fear simmered I couldn't afford to let anything be banal with Sam Purdy.

I was sad. I was angry. I was disappointed. I was lonely. Mostly, right then, I was wary. I wore my therapist face to disguise as much as I could. I could not identify a non-sports topic that I was eager to initiate with Sam so I said, "Yeah, sure. You?"

My distrust left me with a vague sense of peril. It was like walking into the house thinking that maybe, possibly, I smelled mercaptan, the telltale perfume in natural gas.

Each time I saw Sam I was thinking I smelled mercaptan. How sure was I? Not quite certain. I was opening windows and doors for ventilation but I wasn't ready to call for help.

"Are the kids home from school?" he said. "I thought I saw them."

"They both have that bug that's going around. Monday is a teacher training day. I thought I'd give them four days to get over it. They're around somewhere."

"Walk with me," he said.

"Can this wait?" He shook his head. I checked the time.

I thought, *Oh God,* as I followed him out the lane.

When he reached a spot that he decided was far enough away, his hands went into his pockets. His eyes found my eyes. I looked away. He waited until we connected again. He said, "You ever figure out the answer to that thing I asked you about our DA?"

What? Sam's question was so unexpected it distracted me almost as much as it irritated me. We had walked out the damn lane to talk about the closet our DA hadn't been in for a decade? I said, "Elliot coming out? That question?"

Without any apology in his tone he said, "That's it."

"Why did we come out here? The kids know Elliot's gay. They don't care. Nobody cares."

He allowed me my rant. He said, "Well? Got an answer?"

"I haven't given it a moment's thought. It's ancient history. I've been distracted by other things. I didn't realize Elliot's exit from the closet was that urgent."

"Your life? I don't know what to say. I feel so much sorrow for you. For the kids. But other things don't stop because you keep getting beat up. Our other problems — you know what I'm talking about — don't go away because you're bruised and bleeding. I'm your friend. I'm the one who needs to remind you that no matter how much you hurt, it's always possible that you could be hurting more. I'd like to prevent that. So, yes, the question is important."

"What are you saying? What do you know, Sam?"

"Please get me the information. If I'm right we can talk about what it means."

"About what are you trying to be right?"

He pondered the question for a moment.

"Gay rights and the role of homosexuality in contemporary society."

The sarcasm felt too obtuse for Sam; his typical flavor arrived with less nuance. I was half serious when I asked, "Was that your master's thesis?"

He laughed. "At St. Cloud State? Hardly."

We grew silent. I wasn't any more comfortable with the silence than I had been with our conversation. "We done, Sam?" I asked. I spun to head back toward the house.

"Wait. Fucking . . . wait."

I could no longer disguise the fire in my eyes as I turned to face him. His eyes seemed full of sadness. That tempered my fire.

A good thing. I still smelled mercaptan.

He said, "At my house, at the park? Were you thinking — are you thinking — that I had something to do with killing that old man in his horse trailer? Do you think I somehow arranged to off the old fuck? Or did it myself?"

I had anticipated that accusation. I said, "I wanted to know what you'd heard about it. That's all. If you were keeping something from me."

"Bullshit. Why would I keep that from you?"

"Clean hands," I said.

He stared at me while he processed variables. "No, that's not it. Elliot put you on notice about the old man's death with the damn email. You turned right around and did the same to me. Elliot thinks you did it, or had a hand in it. But you didn't. So you came to my house and did to me what Elliot did to you. You think I killed him, or had a hand in it."

I finally understood why we'd left the house to have this conversation.

Sam went on. "You think my solution to Tres's problems in Frederick was to murder his grandfather? Is that what you think of me? That I'm some kind of cold-blooded killer? That my solution to every problem in life is to find someone to whack?"

I was aware that I had a recent conversation with Carl Luppo not too many steps away from where Sam and I stood about applying exactly that kind of solution to a very similar problem. I was also thinking that Sam's accusation was in the vicinity of accurate.

I had no defense ready, no reply handy. I said, "I have to go." I took two steps toward the house.

Sam's voice carried menace. "Don't walk away. What about you? Why would Elliot

Bellhaven think you might have a reason to kill Big Elias? You're missing something. Part of Elliot's message. Or you're not seeing something. Or you see something that you won't trust me to help you with."

I felt my disadvantage. My distrust of Sam was based on my belief that he was too comfortable with having me on law enforcement radar for the murder in Frederick. Was he playing me in some new way? I did not know.

Sam asked, "Does Elliot have something on you? About Frederick? Is he pushing on you about that woman's death?" Sam's ex-girlfriend — the murder victim in Frederick — had become "that woman." *Wow. Chutzpah.* "Does Elliot have leverage that I don't know about? Alan? Tell me. We are in this together. Don't forget that."

We are in this together. Maybe Sam was being my friend. Or maybe he was using our friendship to compromise me further or to minimize his own vulnerability for the Frederick murder. I couldn't tell which was true.

Sam asked, "The drawing of the car? The one the kid did, the one you gave me that night in the ICU. The one that probably kept me out of prison?"

Sam was acknowledging that I'd had his

356

back when having his back was most crucial. "Yeah?" I said into the breeze, wondering where he was going. I could see no remaining evidence of the previous night's flurries.

Sam asked, "Did Lauren show the drawing to Elliot before she came to your office the day she was shot? Has Elliot seen that drawing?"

It was a good question. Elias Tres's drawing only tied Sam to the murder if it was combined with the child's story about the man he saw getting out of a car below his bedroom window. A man wearing a Twins cap and carrying an Avalanche duffel.

Sam was the Twins fan, the Avs fan. Lauren and I knew Sam's sports teams. Elliot probably did not. Without that knowledge? Elias Tres's drawing implicated me, not Sam, because the car pictured in the child's drawing belonged to Lauren and me.

I said, "If Elliot saw the drawing, one of us would probably be in jail awaiting trial. The other one of us? Clean hands."

"Is that what this is about?" he said. "Is that what you're waiting for? Does Elliot have that evidence? Am I already fucked and I just don't know it?"

I said, "Or I am the one who is fucked, Sam, and I just don't know it?"

"What does that mean?" He rushed up to

me, stopping inches away. "You don't think I have your back, do you? You don't trust me? What did I do, Alan?"

I walked away. Sam followed me for a half-dozen steps. His voice more modulated, he said, "Do you have something on Elliot that you're not telling me? Who's blackmailing whom here? Are you setting me up with him?"

I said, "I have an appointment in town, Sam. I need to go."

I was continuing to smell mercaptan.

I was a few steps away from him when Sam said, "Your hitman friend was right, Alan. McClelland did have a stroke. I checked. Left side." I stopped, but I didn't turn around to face Sam. "It was a big stroke. He can't talk."

The news about Michael McClelland was good news. But I felt no elation. I had forgotten how to feel when I heard good news.

I walked to the house with great care. I didn't want to generate any sparks.

I didn't recall reaching a decision not to tell my therapist about Lauren and Raoul and her Louboutins. Or about not trusting my best friend.

Or about the good news that my nemesis

had been neutered.

But as I drove to town to see Lila I knew I wouldn't tell her any of it.

38

DOCTOR LILA

Alan Gregory's regular appointment had been set for the first day of March, the in-like-a-lion day. At his request, we had rescheduled it for the afternoon of the fourth.

The rescheduling came on the heels of his cancellation of the previous visit. I was keeping score. That made three misses out of eight appointments. Plus two reschedules. Not a good ratio.

The rescheduled in-like-a-lion session started in silence. Two entire minutes of it.

I thought Alan looked defeated. I anticipated that he had absorbed some new esoteric blow. Like the psychological equivalent of being blinded by dust from a comet. I waited to learn what it was. I prepared myself to be surprised.

I prepared myself to be more off balance than he was.

The extended silence began getting to me. I was trying to find the courage to query him about the cancellation. But he spoke before I found the mettle.

"Lila, I am not sure this is working," was what he said after the two minutes.

Those are not words that any young therapist wishes to hear. I get anxious when I hear them, or their like, from a patient. I keep some stock responses rehearsed and handy to mask the anxiety I inevitably experience when it sounds to me like I'm about to be fired.

I pulled one of those lines off the shelf. "You haven't been keeping your appointments. That might be a reason this feels like it's not working."

He didn't look at me. He said, "Symptom. Not cause. You know that."

I didn't know that. Neither did he. But from my limited experience with Alan Gregory I knew that when he got parsimonious, I got nowhere.

"Well," I said, "maybe, maybe not. Why don't we take a clean look at your goals? That can help sometimes."

He laughed. It wasn't obvious ridicule. It was a kind enough laugh, given the circumstances. But he did laugh. *At me?* Close enough.

"My goals?" he said. His eyes were wide. "Really?"

"I was thinking . . . what you hope to gain from psychotherapy." I was on my heels. I knew it. He knew it.

He shifted his weight on the chair. "What are your goals?" he asked. "For me?"

In an admirably even voice I said, "That is not my role here." *And you know damn well it's not my role. Do not be cruel to me. You are making me uncomfortable right now because you can. I am trying to be helpful to you.*

"I'll go first," he said. He moistened his lips with the tip of his tongue. He took a deep breath.

I felt some trepidation. I did not like the fear I was feeling.

"My goals?" he said. "I want my life back, my wife back, my work back, my friends back. I want to stop writing big checks to big-time lawyers."

He had adopted a cadence for his speech that he'd never used before with me. The pace was rapid and breathless. Almost hostile in its crispness. The thought that exploded in my brain? *This feels like an old lover suddenly trying out a new, unwelcome move.*

That I had *that* thought with him troubled

362

me. A lot. I tried not to let it show. His aggression felt so palpable it distracted me. *Listen,* I told myself. *Listen to him.*

He went on. "I would like to sleep for more than two hours. To have an appetite that lasts for more than two bites. I would like to trust somebody. To enjoy the company of someone older than my children.

"To work. To be wanted at work. To want to work. To be able to work.

"I want to smell my wife's perfume. To have my wife want me to smell her perfume. I want to feel her flesh against my flesh. To kiss her. To be kissed by her. To love. To be loved. I want romance.

"I want to be . . . beloved.

"I want to feel not toxic. Or fragile. Or lost. Or vengeful.

"I want others to treat me as not toxic. Or fragile. Or lost. Or vengeful.

"I want to stop feeling that I must create new victims so that I don't have to feel like one myself.

"I want to move on. And I don't.

"I want to start a simple task and finish it. One. Wash the car. Scrub the floor. Clean out my wife's closet. Organize the papers on her desk. Go from A to Z. Once.

"I want to have a single day without harassment from near and from far. I want to look into the future and see beyond the end of my fucking nose.

"What do I want? One sunny day. And then another after it."

He sat back. I swallowed. He said, "So how are those goals? Are we getting close? What does your list for me look like?"

I had recoiled from the intensity of his pain, from the rawness of his longing. I knew I had to recover. My next words had to connect with him.

"Harassment?" I said. "That's . . . a new one." I hoped it was new. In the moment I wasn't sure. I almost chose "creating victims" from his list but I didn't know what he meant with that.

He slid his lower jaw sideways. He tilted his head, too. "The harassment is legal. High up. The top. I need to find a way to stop it. Not for a day. Or a month. Permanently. Stop it."

The rhythm of his speech had returned to the familiar, but his vagueness was driving me no less mad. His aggression seemed to have dissipated, like smoke in a breeze after an explosion. I said, "That's not much information for me to work with, Alan."

"You are correct, Lila. It's not. Clean hands?"

Clean hands. He always kept that card up

his sleeve.

I had to undermine his despair. "If? If we resolved the trust issues between us, you could — you would — feel assurance that my hands and your hands were the same. Then we could talk openly. Then you could let me help you with those goals."

I knew I was sounding like a supplicant. I hated that I sounded like a supplicant.

Alan's next words were not a reply to mine. I felt no assurance he'd even heard me. He said, "The only solution I see is to take him down before he takes me down."

"Down?" I asked.

Alan winced. He said, "I can't live like this. With this constant sense of jeopardy. The accusations. The threats. The implied risks to my kids. I can't."

"Down?" I repeated.

"Him before me. Yes. I have to find a way. Therapy can't help with that."

"What can help with that?" I said. *Don't tell me,* I thought.

Alan chose silence. Three entire minutes. I timed it. Digitally.

He broke the silence. He said, "If I can't be open with you, this process won't work."

Exactly. Finally. Yes.

Progress! Progress.

"I can't," Alan said. "Be open, Lila. With

you. I've tried. It's not working."

Wait. What?

"I will get back in touch if I begin to feel differently." He stood.

I stood. "Our time isn't up," I said.

"It is," Alan Gregory said.

ALAN

Kirsten phoned me later. She said, "I thought I'd get a reply to my last text."

"Sam came over. I got distracted. Sorry." I left out the part about the time I had used up quitting psychotherapy. I didn't think Kirsten would be a fan of that decision.

Adrienne or Diane, I thought. Oh how I missed them. I would have loved to talk with either of them about quitting therapy. Diane would have given me shit. Adrienne would have applauded.

Kirsten was silent for a moment, as though she was allowing me time to reminisce and to mourn. I did realize it was far more likely that she was deciding whether or not to believe my distraction excuse.

She asked, "Alan, are you seeing patients Monday morning?"

The odds were that I wasn't but I did a mental review of the empty spaces in my calendar. "I might have one. I will need to check, get back to you."

"In the interim I will take that as a no."

"Safe enough bet. My referrals have dried up. I am kind of unemployed."

"Can you be at your office at ten? We need to talk."

"I can come to your office, Kirsten. You don't have to —"

"Humor me, please. Your office Monday at ten."

"You don't trust me to be at your office? I promise, Kirsten. I'll be there."

"Monday. Ten. Your office. We'll talk."

I asked, "Is this about the email from Elliot?" She hung up.

Winter continued to be a stone skipping on water. It came, it went, it came back, mostly mocking the calendar. That first weekend of March was bitter cold, straight from the January playbook. But Monday morning arrived with a sneak preview of the May that was on the horizon. To me that meant a bike ride.

I rode downtown for my appointment with Kirsten. The day was not merely comfortable, it was truly warm; I hoped a little sweat wouldn't offend her. After our meeting I planned to do a real ride: to climb

Flagstaff up to Gross Reservoir. From there I would detour down Coal Creek Canyon to return to Spanish Hills.

My thighs and my lungs hated the ride up Flagstaff, but my spirit loved the ride along the high peaks, through the backcountry below Miramonte and Mirabelle, and then the steep downhill along Coal Creek to 93. I hadn't quite decided to do the trip, though I wasn't ambivalent about the ride or the route. I was concerned whether what I needed to carry with me would make the trip impractical.

The face-to-face meeting with Kirsten would allow me to show her the papers I'd found on Lauren's desk — the "Personal, Work" file and the "Pending Resolution" envelope that were full of material that Lauren had brought home from the DA's office. Kirsten was an ex-prosecutor from New Orleans. She would recognize the importance of the documents that Lauren, another prosecutor, had collected. Kirsten would be able to identify their genus, and she would have an opinion about what I should do with them.

The problem was that to get them downtown on my bicycle I would need to stuff them in a messenger bag and wear the thing on my back as I rode, not a problem for a commute, but not an ideal thing for a mountain climb. I finally decided that I could lock the bag in my office after I met with Kirsten. That would free me to make the grueling part of the ride unencumbered by the extra weight and aerodynamic inefficiency.

I arrived downtown an hour early. I pulled my bike into my office. I allowed the extra time so I could take a stab at draining the fountain in the waiting room. The acquisition of the ornate thing had been a unilateral decision of Diane's during a renovation project. Maintenance had been her responsibility. But without the benefit of Diane's preventive ministrations the water in the fountain was developing the unwelcome aroma of a neglected aquarium. My plan was to drain the installation and mothball it. The draining part went well; the artist on the llama ranch in Niwot who had designed and built the thing for Diane had installed a plug in the bottom of the reservoir.

Stench abatement was going to require the application of some bleach. I hesitated with the bleach because the fountain had a series of phallic copper tubes that transported gushing water in choppy cascades toward the bottom pool. I had no idea whether chlorine and copper got along. I would need to check Google. Or the Bing.

I heard a knock — too vociferous I thought — a couple of minutes before ten. I realized I had neglected to unlock the door to the waiting room for Kirsten. The animation in the pounding suggested that she was not pleased at my oversight.

The me that greeted Kirsten was wearing riding Lycra, bright yellow rubber gloves, and Diane's take-care-of-the-fountain apron, a less-than-flattering thing that attempted the onerous task of relating the entire history of the teapot on a small expanse of fabric embellished with scalloped edges and a completely unnecessary touch of lace.

I hadn't checked a mirror but I doubted that the ensemble worked. As ridiculous as I appeared I thought Kirsten's expression carried way too much alarm. I said, "I'm dealing with some mold in the fountain. Chlorine? The apron is Diane's. I apologize about the locked door. Time got away from me. Sorry."

"You don't know?"

Since the Dome Fire my adrenals were recalibrated to a hair trigger. Any natural gradation in hormonal release that was designed into the human body's alert system was absent from mine. When my adrenals received a neural order to engage, the adrenaline release that followed was ejaculatory, not measured.

Kirsten's "You don't know?" triggered the neural order. My adrenals erupted like a sliced artery, my bloodstream instantly flush with liquefied fight-or-flight impulses. Out of the gate, fight had a good three or four bike-length lead on flight.

My dukes, such as they were, were ready for my enemies. Unfortunately I hadn't identified my enemies. "I don't know what?" I said as alarm seeped into every cell in my body, including my larynx. The words exited my mouth in an unflattering squeak.

She said, "The search? The cops outside?"

"What search? What cops?" I was nearing panic.

"No one gave you a warrant." It was a statement, not a question.

"No one gave me anything. What cops?"

She took my hand and yanked me out the front door onto the porch. The first person I spotted was Detective Amal Sengupta, the Boulder police detective who had investigated Lauren's shooting. He was standing in profile out near the Walnut Street sidewalk, checking some papers on an old-fashioned clipboard. Sengupta had a gently protruding, rounded belly. Although he was a slender man, his gut silhouette was that of an early second-trimester pregnancy. I had not noticed that before.

Sengupta had interviewed me the day after the shooting. He was serene, composed, and respectful that morning. I had answered his questions under my previous attorney's guidance. The questions I had feared from him — the ones about Frederick and about the child's drawing that Lauren had given me — were never asked. I had assumed that meant that Sengupta didn't know that history. At the time I had also assumed that Elliot's office didn't know that history.

Until recently I had lived with the luxury that all that law enforcement ignorance was a good thing for me. But in the moment, in the teapot apron, I was rethinking all those assumptions.

I had seen Sengupta only once since that first interview. He had attended Lauren's interment. I had no illusions about his presence that day. He wasn't there as a mourner; he was there as an investigator. He wanted to see who showed up for the service.

He had been present to watch my daughter dance at her mother's open grave.

Kirsten released my arm and marched to

within two feet of Sengupta. She was in a feisty mood with him, kind of mother-bearish in her intensity. I had never seen her in advocate action before. It was revelatory.

She said, "Detective?" When Sengupta didn't look up from his papers, she moved even closer. She was inches from his clipboard. "Hey. I'm talking to you."

Sengupta placed a finger on the spot he was reading. He lifted his head slowly, as though he was wary about allowing it to achieve any momentum. He said, "I assumed that. Addressing me as 'detective' was my clue. The 'hey' was unnecessary. Counselor." His tone was modulated; he might have used the same voice to remind his young child about recapping the toothpaste tube.

Kirsten's irritation level was aggravated by Sengupta's composure, which may have been the detective's intent. In any good cop/bad cop duo, Sengupta was the natural good cop. She said, "You told me that no one was inside."

"Actually, Ms. Lord, I said no one responded to my knock. A difference. The knock was a courtesy. Courtesy, I find, goes a long way for us. So much of what we do in criminal justice is contentious. Don't you think? Courtesy is like a salve."

Kirsten returned to my side. She whispered, "Did you hear a knock?"

I whispered back, "I was in the back looking for bleach. I wouldn't have heard a knock. What's going on?" I was trying to remove the apron but I had managed to knot it behind me.

Kirsten said, "I'm not sure. I haven't seen the warrant."

I didn't know what to make of the fact that one of the cops on the driveway was carrying a device that looked like a metal detector.

"What kind of warrant?" I said. I tried to think of warrants other than those that indicated probable cause for a search. I wasn't wearing handcuffs, so it wasn't an arrest warrant.

Sengupta meandered up the walk toward us. *Ambled* was probably a better word than *meandered.* The detective didn't have a lot of hurry in him. However this situation developed in the next few minutes, we were not going to see Sengupta sweat.

Kirsten said, "I am Dr. Gregory's attorney. May I see the warrant, Detective?"

His expression became one of disappointment, as though he'd recognized that his opponent wasn't as skilled a chess player as he had hoped.

Kirsten had no patience for Sengupta's process. Her reservoir of courtesy exhausted, she said, "Please?" in an impolite way. Her hand was out, palm up.

Absent any attitude Sengupta said, "There is no warrant. Nor is one necessary." He faced me. "Dr. Gregory, the co-owner of your property provided permission for a search of the building and the grounds. One owner's permission is sufficient. Today's search is limited to the exterior of the property."

Kirsten said, "Speak to me please, not to my client."

"What co-owner? Dr. Estevez?" I asked. I didn't care a tittle who spoke to whom.

Sengupta was delighted to defy Kirsten. He said, "No. Dr. Estevez's husband."

I said, "He is not an owner of the property. Check the deed."

Sengupta pulled a solitary page from the papers in his hand. I could see the sheet was notarized. "Mr. Raoul Estevez is Dr. Diane Estevez's attorney-in-fact. He authorized the search in her stead."

I mouthed, *Fuck me.* "Raoul's idea? Or yours?" I asked.

Kirsten said, "Shut up, Alan." She stepped in front of me.

376

Even without the teapot apron I realized I wasn't being an ideal client. Over my attorney's shoulder I demanded, "Tell me, Detective."

Kirsten glared at me. To Sengupta she said, "You contend that you have permission to search what exactly? And to look for what exactly?"

"Since no warrant was needed, no probable cause is required. I have no obligation to share any details with Dr. Gregory, or with his designated legal representative, Ms. Lord." He smiled a flat smile at her. He was thrilled that he didn't need to tell her, well, shit.

"Investigation of what?" Kirsten asked.

Sengupta looked at me. "I don't see your personal vehicle on the driveway or on the street, Dr. Gregory. Where is your car parked?"

Kirsten whispered, "Don't reply." To Sengupta, she said, "Direct your questions to me. Why is that important, Detective? Neither Raoul nor Diane Estevez co-owns his vehicles."

Sengupta pulled a folded document from the clipboard. "Judge Bunuelos has determined we have probable cause for a vehicle search. Actually, two vehicle searches." He handed the papers to Kirsten. She examined them for mere seconds. She was not happy with what she read.

I said, "Bunuelos and Lauren had a history. Problems."

She whispered in my ear. "Old news. Nobody cares. Where is your car?"

"Home. I rode my bike here." I was thinking that the fact that I was wearing Lycra clothing should have been a clue to everybody. She rolled her eyes at my Lycra.

Sengupta's assertion that Diane had granted Raoul power of attorney didn't feel kosher. I put my lips to within an inch of my lawyer's ear. "Can you challenge the POA? Diane may lack competence. Her concussion? The brain lesion? She's being treated for an astrocytoma. Maybe surgery or radiation. She also has serious PTSD." I had convinced myself. "Competent to sign a power of attorney? I don't think so."

"Good arguments," she said. "But it won't help. Not here, with Sengupta."

She stepped away to join the detective. She was no longer posturing with him. She made the case about Diane's lack of competence. Sengupta was attentive but I could tell he was being polite. Open-minded? No. A judge would sort out legal issues related to Diane's competence later. Sengupta's job was to collect the evidence he was tasked with collecting. The judge would determine what to do with the evidence.

The search of the property proceeded. My phone beeped. A text. Amy.

Got gr8 rushes! That moon! I have 2 days rnr in Aspen. Is the Jerome good? Come up? Deets to follow.

God. The phone rang before I had a chance to put it away. I checked the screen again, expecting it was Amy with the promised deets. I was wrong. It was the home landline. That meant the kids.

"I have to take this," I said aloud to no one. I turned my back. Into the phone, I said, "It's me. What's up?"

40

I could never decide which kid slept more soundly in the mornings.

That morning it was Jonas, apparently. Gracie was the child on the phone. Her voice was packed with drama, but Gracie went through life with *Peter and the Wolf* issues; her voice was often packed with drama. She said, "Daddy, Daddy! The police are here! At the door. They want you!"

Gracie was not a child who lied to get my attention. She sounded more exhilarated than frightened. But that was my daughter.

I felt a bolus of fresh adrenaline roar into my bloodstream. Gracie had said "police." I immediately translated that to mean *sheriff*. We lived in rural Boulder County, not Boulder proper. Uniformed officers pounding on my door were likely to be sheriff's deputies, not police. Or maybe officers accompanied by deputies.

"What do they want?" I asked.

"The police want *you*, Daddy. Now!"

I said, "Shit." Because of all the friggin' adrenaline in my friggin' bloodstream I had transitioned from a silent *damn* to an aloud *shit.*

Gracie said, "That's a buck in the cuss bucket. Come home, hurry! I have to pee. They're at the door. They have a paper. I have to pee."

A paper? A warrant? "Wake your brother before you pee, Grace."

"Do I have to?" I could hear her growl as though she were standing in front of me.

"Yes, you have to. Tell him I'm coming right home. And, Gracie, are the dogs around?" If the dogs were home, one or both of them would be nearby her, or in her face. Most likely Fiji. Emily would be at the door, threatening to consume flesh from the officer with the warrant. Emily's instincts were to protect the castle and its occupants.

"Um, no," she said. She had just recognized she was dogless.

"Have you seen Clare? Is she out walking the dogs?"

"I don't see her. I guess she is."

Clare was babysitting. An underemployed recent graduate of CU — her primary gig was at the counter of the new Snarfburger on Arapahoe — Clare was my crutch since Sofie returned to Holland. Jonas didn't require a sitter, but Grace did. Clare's presence meant that the dogs were cared for and that Jonas wasn't tied down. Clare gave me peace of mind. I hoped she also gave Jonas, adolescent in most ways, a bit of a fantasy life.

"When she gets back, tell her I'm on my way and to be careful with Emily. Emily isn't always nice to strangers. Stay on the line while you wake your brother."

Sengupta and Kirsten continued their tête-à-tête. I ran down the stairs of the porch and forced myself between them. My tone was neither cordial nor respectful. I said, "You're searching my home, Detective? Simultaneously?" The question came out of my mouth as an accusation. I blamed it on the adrenaline overdose.

Kirsten grabbed my arm. She said, "Alan, please, let me —"

"Answer me," I barked at the serene detective. I didn't yell, but I came close.

Sengupta hesitated. That convinced me that my worst fear was true. Authorities — I didn't yet know which ones — were mounting simultaneous searches on my home, my office, and my vehicles.

Kirsten pulled me aside so forcefully I

found myself surprised at her strength. I told her what Grace had told me. I asked if there was any way to stop the police from searching my home until I could be with the kids. To protect the kids from more trauma. I must have said, "They are too vulnerable for this," three different times.

She thought for a few seconds before she said, "Maybe I can slow things down here. At your house? If they have a warrant? No. Your vehicles, no. I'm sorry, Alan. I am so sorry. This is escalating, I'm afraid. We feared this."

"They woke my daughter. The cops *woke* my daughter. My son is still asleep. They've been through so much already. This can't happen to them. Not like this. Please. Do something. Get them to wait. Just until I get home. Please."

I was begging. Grace came back on the line. "Jonas won't get up. He doesn't believe me about the police. I have to pee." She hung up.

God. I searched for Clare's cell number. I had to get her back to the house with the dogs. I said, "Fifteen minutes, Kirsten? We can be there in fifteen minutes. They can wait that long, right? I'll cooperate. Please, please. I need to protect my kids."

Kirsten found a number she wanted in

her contact list before I found Clare's. She lifted her phone to her ear. I heard her say, "Kirsten Lord for Elliot Bellhaven. Urgently." Pause. "He knows what it's about." Pause. "Interrupt him." Pause. "I don't care."

I was hanging up with Clare as Kirsten lowered her phone. She moved so near that I could taste her breath. She said, "Some good news." Nothing I could see in her eyes suggested actual good news on the horizon. The good news would be relative. At best it would be a slight tempering of otherwise very bad news.

"Yes," I said.

"Elliot gave us fifteen minutes to get to your house before they execute the warrants. He expects full cooperation from you. I do, too. Understood?"

"Yes." Kirsten assumed that my commitment would guarantee my cooperation. Not a bad assumption, but it had a flaw. An unless. *Unless* Elliot did something to my kids.

My assumption about the relativity of the good news proved correct. Elliot permitting me fifteen minutes to get home wasn't good news — it was an abeyance that allowed awful news, the search, to be briefly postponed.

"Thank you," I said, trying to sound grateful to Kirsten. "There's bad news, too? Something else? Isn't there?"

Of course there was. I tried to imagine how things could get worse. The kids were unhurt. The house wasn't — yet — on fire. I was certain that the fact I couldn't presage the precise bad news was an indication that my imagination was failing me.

My attorney's bright eyes welled with tears. She took both my hands. She said, "You are being investigated for murdering your wife, Alan."

41

I said, "What?"

I said it calmly, the way an innocent man might say it.

I didn't kill my wife. Diane did. I saw it all happen with my own eyes.

Those eyes didn't leave Kirsten's. I waited for her to retract her words. She didn't. She said, "Elliot Bellhaven just informed me that you are a target, a principal, in the homicide investigation of Lauren's death."

A target? I'd been feeling like a target. Just not that kind.

Again I said, "What?"

I said it less calmly the second time.

On the way to Spanish Hills in Kirsten's car, the timer on my fifteen-minute probation ticking, I asked her why she'd wanted to meet with me that morning. I was making conversation because it felt like a human thing to do. The only alternatives would have been tense silence or reviewing my current reality. The latter would have crumbled my defenses. My kids were waiting for me. They needed me to be as uncompromised a parent as was possible in the circumstances.

"My plan this morning? I was going to drive you to Denver to introduce you to your new defense attorney. I didn't trust you would go on your own."

She spoke without irony. The implications of all my previous procrastination filled the interior of her car like a noxious odor. I had managed to force my friend into the exact professional situation she had been determined to avoid.

"And now look what I've done," I said.

She said, "Yeah." Her *yeah* was nothing like, "That's okay, I understand." It was the acknowledgment of the acidity of life's capriciousness from a woman who had learned the hard way that whim often arrived alongside evil, but absent whimsy.

"Get your thoughts together for that meeting with your new attorney. Any reasons that you are on Elliot's radar for Lauren's death will be prime topics of discussion."

We neared Fifty-Fifth Street, heading east, not far from the turn to Spanish Hills. I asked, "Will Elliot be there for the searches?"

She took my hand for a second. I read the gesture as her eagerness to make the transition from attorney to friend. "I doubt it," she said. "Whether he is or he is not, you have to behave."

"Will I be arrested?"

She said, "I don't know. It may depend on what they find. If it comes to that, I hope Elliot allows your new attorney to arrange a surrender."

Surrender. "Did Elliot tell you what they're looking for in my house?"

"He did not. Do you know?"

"I don't."

"Will they find anything problematic? I've been assuming that they won't. Alan?"

That's when I remembered the damn gun. Aloud, I said, "Oh, fuck, the Kahr."

Kirsten blurted, "What car?" Her eyes darted left and right on the road. She tapped the brakes. She checked all her mirrors.

"Not that kind of car," I said. "Not on the road."

She turned toward me, her eyes narrowing with exasperation. The car started to drift toward an oncoming delivery truck. In a calm voice I said, "Truck. *That* kind of truck."

She corrected back into her lane with a jerk of the wheel. The last half hour had depleted my adrenaline. I felt no new alarm at the almost collision with the truck.

I said, "I need to find someone to take care of the kids. God." As soon as I said it I realized I was excluding Sam from the list of potential caretakers.

So much for the whole *clean hands* solution.

Kirsten switched into the right lane, preparing to turn into Spanish Hills. "What's the car thing? Are they going to find evidence in your vehicles? Is there something we need to talk about before we get there?"

I hadn't explained the difference between *Kahr* and *car* to Kirsten.

I decided that I would save the distinction for my next attorney.

The middle of the night after Lauren was shot, Diane, Amanda, Raoul, and Kevin — Kevin was Diane's real estate agent with, dear God, benefits — and I had all ended up in an expensive, tacky condo near the east end of the Mall on one of the teen numbered streets not far from Frasca. Diane had arrived late to that impromptu gathering wearing the apparently de rigueur Christian Louboutins — Diane's were silver metallic pumps — along with a throwback strappy purple organza cocktail dress.

In those halcyon days I'd been blissfully ignorant about women's fashion footwear. On that night I had mistaken Diane's Louboutins for Jimmy Choos.

The most unusual accessory to Diane's outfit wasn't her shoes, it was the compact Kahr semiautomatic that she had used to shoot my wife in the back. The gun fit Diane's palm as though it had been custom forged for her glove size.

The middle of the night denouement began with Diane's real estate friend, Kevin — adhesive allergies had left his face looking like an unflattering cross between Homer Simpson's mug and a baboon's butt — firing a double-barrel shotgun in the general direction of the condo's unfortunately tiled ceiling. Tile shards and buckshot rained down, Diane suffered a closed head injury, and I ended up pocketing the Kahr.

I took possession of the gun to keep it away from Diane and from anyone else in the room that night. By then my trust for everyone in attendance was nearly zero.

We all left the condo before the police arrived, most of us headed toward the hospital. I drove with Raoul, who was going to the emergency department at Community to check on Diane, who was the first to be rushed away, by ambulance.

My solitary goal was to resume my vigil at Lauren's bedside in the ICU.

I may have made a conscious decision to hold on to the Kahr. But I don't remember it. I may have intended to hand it to the first cop I saw. I don't recall that. I do recall a lucid moment of appreciation about its dense mass against my lower back — some sense that the square block of steel might provide odd security on a night that I felt a pressing need for odd security.

My appreciation for the weapon was transitory. Once I was back by Lauren's bedside in the ICU, my need for whatever ephemeral security the Kahr represented vanished. Before the kids arrived to see their mother, I stuffed the pistol into the bottom of a plastic bag full of bloody clothing that had been collected earlier in the ER.

And then I forgot about it. Sometime the next day, or the day after, I re-remembered the Kahr and went through a series of rationalizations about what I should do with it. My problem solving was neither rigorous nor consistent. I went back and forth between convincing myself having the gun didn't matter and convincing myself that having it might matter too much.

That multiple days had passed since Diane shot Lauren with the Kahr was, I knew, becoming a real problem. But it was one of a few real problems. Lauren was near death. The kids were freaking out. I didn't know which way was up. I recalled that I considered giving the weapon to Sam, as police detective. Then I considered giving it to Sam, as friend. I rejected both options.

I later considered discarding it, throwing it away. I became fixated on Gross Reservoir as a good place to toss a gun. The errand almost became a plan. But some crisis ensued, and by the end of one of the first of many exquisitely stressful days after that morning, the Kahr became one more thing that was too much for me to deal with.

By the time that hours passed and became days that piled up to equal a week, and then two, the Kahr simply became too complicated a puzzle for me to solve. I must have decided that I could no longer turn the pistol in to the police. I must also have recognized that admitting that I had been in the possession of a murder weapon for most of the time since Lauren's shooting might be misinterpreted. And not necessarily in my favor.

I could not provide a good rationale as to why I'd held on to the gun for so long. Kirsten wouldn't believe my story. Sengupta wouldn't believe my story. I did console myself that the gun would prove superfluous to his investigation, that once the detectives were done dotting i's and crossing t's — whenever that was — Diane would be arrested for shooting Lauren.

My rationalizing logic was compelling. After all, I was a great eyewitness. I had seen it all. For the police, that was the sundae. Having the murder weapon would be a mere cherry on top.

Sometime around Lauren's death — blame it on stress, I did — I stopped thinking about the Kahr. To hide it from the kids, I hid the handgun in the master bedroom beside Lauren's Glock in a peculiar hollow on top of an old wardrobe, a crevice always covered by a lacy quilt from Lauren's grandmother.

Lauren had a carry permit for her Glock. I didn't have one for the Kahr.

Sitting in Kirsten's front seat on the way to my home, I began to suspect that sometime shortly after the search warrant was executed Elliot would be delighted to stress the importance of that last fact to me.

■ ■ ■ ■

"Maybe," I said to Kirsten.

The interlude of silence between us had extended too long. She said, "Maybe they'll find something? Or maybe there's something we need to talk about?"

"Yes," I said. "Yes. Both." I wasn't trying to be coy. My brain was overloaded with the potential consequences of my earlier rationalizing, my earlier procrastinating, and my earlier idiocy. I was acutely aware of the distinction between being innocent — I was that — and being not guilty.

Having the Kahr in my possession would cause me to appear to be not not-guilty.

"Alan?" Kirsten could tell that my mental acuity was becoming an issue.

I was having trouble breathing. The consequences I was imagining were weighing me down like winter clothes in icy water.

"There could be a problem," I said. "With the search."

"What kind of problem?" Her words were mild, but they were the kind of mild that parents learn how to force into their words to keep from spreading alarm to their offspring. I knew the trick. I could hear what was in the fissures that fell between the sounds Kirsten was using to form the mild words.

In those fissures she was saying, *Oh shit oh shit oh shit oh shit.*

"I screwed up. I didn't shoot Lauren. Later, though, I screwed up. The police might find something that I never thought anyone would find."

"Do you want to tell me what it is?"

I thought she had figured it out. "Something I shouldn't have."

"Do you want to tell me what it is?"

She asked the question more slowly the second time. She wanted me to understand her words, not merely respond to them. I said, "Should I? Want to tell you?"

She didn't answer. I took that to be a *no.*

"Do you have someone in mind? To watch your kids?"

That was not a reassuring question to hear from my defense attorney. I would have preferred something along the lines of *Don't worry. We have legal options for this kind of situation.*

"I had a plan," I said. I did not have time to walk Kirsten through the whole clean-hands progression. "But I don't think it's going to work out."

"Okay." Her attempts to make her voice reassuring weren't having a salutary impact.

I kept hearing the *oh shit oh shit oh shit oh shit* tucked into the fissures between her words. "Do you have a . . . plan B?"

"Not really."

She passed our mailbox as she made the final turn onto the dirt lane. I had less than a minute to conjure some magic. But I couldn't see beyond the kids, and what my past actions to protect them would do to jeopardize their futures.

Kirsten asked me how therapy was going.

I almost laughed. Instead I lied. I said it was good.

Getting the lie out of my mouth proved a huge chore. My failure as a parent was threatening to paralyze me.

42

Rage solved the short-term paralysis problem.

To an observer my behavior must have appeared wildly unfocused, a conflagration of all the anger I hadn't allowed myself to feel since the morning of the Dome Fire. The precipitant? From a hundred yards down the lane I could see my screaming, struggling son — he was all head and arms and legs — being half pushed, half carried to the open backseat of a Boulder sheriff's SUV.

Jonas was barefoot. He was wearing the worn plaid cotton pajama bottoms that he slept in. He was wearing no shirt. My kid was scrawnier than twine. He was all sinew and taut muscle like his birth father. His hands were cuffed behind his back.

He was screaming. Mostly "Let me go! Let me go!" But I also heard "You fuckers!"

a couple of times. He had a lot of Adrienne in him.

His rage became mine. It focused me. I became trigger and bullet. Bow and arrow. I wanted to kill. I hadn't chosen a victim. The target would be instinctive. Absent Elliot, or Raoul, or Diane, I would go after somebody in blue manhandling my innocent but profane son.

I screamed out the window of the car, "Jonas! Jonas! I'm here."

I heard, "Daaaaaaaaad! Help meeeeee!"

Kirsten said, "No! Alan!"

"Goddamn it!" I pounded the dash of Kirsten's car. "Hurry."

"You promised to behave."

Yeah well. Unless. "And Elliot promised to wait. The fucker. Hurry."

Kirsten touched my leg. "Alan, this is awful. Don't make it worse."

The front door of my house was wide-open. I could see people — cop people — walking into my home. Strangers. In my house. Going through my things.

I couldn't see Grace. Or Clare. Or the dogs. I saw my terrified, struggling son. The violation of my home. A future without my family. My kids without their parents.

At that moment, I also felt a clarifying rage at my dead wife.

I thought, *This is your fault. Yours. Fuck . . .
you . . . Lauren.*
Fuck you.

43

I jumped out of Kirsten's car before she pulled to a stop. In the process I learned that the long list of things in life at which I did not excel included exiting a moving vehicle with anything resembling aplomb.

I remained vertical for less than a complete second. I then rolled heels-over-head twice before I popped back up on my feet with agility I usually lacked. My hands were balled into fists. I was prepared to take on the cops. Though I was facing the wrong direction. And bleeding profusely from one elbow.

The next couple of minutes weren't pretty. I did a lot of screaming. I made multiple threats while I was restrained on my knees by two deputies.

Kirsten was playing defense, dancing to stay between me and everybody else. She was also simultaneously on her cell phone with someone while she examined the warrants that authorized the searches. At some level I think I recognized that she was doing her damned best to try to keep me out of custody. I knew I wasn't helping.

I was so focused on Jonas's plight — he was confined in the backseat of the SUV, his hands cuffed behind his back — that I didn't see Sam Purdy's Cherokee coming down the lane. I didn't see him get out of his car and run toward me.

I did hear him hiss, "Quiet shut the fuck up you goddamn asshole," into my ear as he wrapped me in a bear hug from behind, pinning my arms to my sides. To everyone else nearby he said, in a clear voice, "Detective Sam Purdy. Boulder Police. I got this one, I got him."

He had me. He'd lifted me off the ground as though I were a child the size of my daughter. He then carried me across the lane to the cedar deck that was attached to Ophelia's doublewide. I heard Emily barking fiercely from inside.

He tossed me onto one of the flimsy plastic chairs and he twisted my body until my posture resembled that of a sitting person. He straddled my legs with his own. Each of his legs was the size of both of mine. His weren't wrapped in skin-tight Lycra.

He said, "Shut up. Stop fighting me." He leaned forward and locked one of his big hands on each of the chair's armrests, imprisoning me.

"Let me go, Sam. Let me go." I recognized the futility of my protest.

"What? You got a plan?" In a stern tone absent any vitriol he said, "Don't make this worse. You can still make it worse. Those cops are dying for an excuse to throw you around. You understand me?"

"They have Jonas in the back of —"

"I'm on that. You stay here, shut up. I will take care of Jonas. You need to —"

"I have to —"

"No. You do not need to do whatever it is you think you need to do. Stay the fuck here, Alan. Don't go back over there. Don't make this worse. They have a warrant. The search is going to happen whether you're in custody or you're in this chair pouting. If you give them a reason to choose, they'll choose custody. Got it?" I stared at him. "Answer me."

I nodded.

"Now look at me. Look at me! I cannot go back over there to help your son until you calm the fuck down. Are you going to let me go over there and help your kid?"

From inside the trailer I heard a crying

402

voice. "Daddy, Daddy. The police took Jonas. They took him!" *Gracie.*

To Sam I said, "Yes, Sam. Please. Go help him."

Sam didn't move his arms. He lowered his voice and leaned his big head forward so it was almost touching my normal size head. "First? I don't know why you had it or where that damn German gun is now, but I am almost a hundred percent certain it isn't in your house. Do you understand what I'm saying?"

I said, "What? No. I don't know what you're talking about."

"Don't fuck with me. The gun? You know what I'm talking about, right?"

Jesus. "Yes."

"They are looking for that gun. They are not going to find that gun during their search of your home, Alan. Just tell me you understand . . . what I'm saying."

I did not get it. But I said, "Yes."

"Is it in one of the cars?"

Sam's question sounded like a line in a children's book. *Is the Kahr in the cars?* As did my answer, "No, there are no guns in the cars."

I was pretty sure that was what Sam wanted to hear. I needed Sam to help Jonas. Toward that end, I would have told him that

403

there were no Kahrs on the planet, and that the Second Amendment had been repealed by the Intergalactic Council.

He said, "I am going to go get Jonas. You will stay right here. You're not going to yell. Or even speak. You can mutter. But that's it. Are we good?"

I was not good. But I nodded my head. I was prepared to wash his freckled feet with my tongue if he would go save my kid. "Please go help Jonas." Sam jogged away. He was one of those people who was much more graceful on the move than he ever looked while he was still.

"The German gun?" Does Sam know about the damn Kahr? How the hell does he know where it is? Or where it isn't?

44

The kids stayed with Ophelia while I began to return the house to some semblance of order.

I didn't know where Sam had gone. He'd kept his promise about rescuing Jonas from the back of the sheriff's vehicle. He delivered Jonas to Ophelia before he'd returned to monitor the search from the front seat of his Jeep. Shortly after the search was completed, he drove away without another word to me.

I never got to ask him about the Kahr, what he knew, and how he knew it. I wasn't enamored of any of the suppositions I was making on my own.

Before she left Spanish Hills to return to her life — a life that was much less complicated when I wasn't in it — Kirsten told me that the search was limited to firearms, work product from the DA's office, and certain children's drawings. She asked me to put together a list of what might have been removed from the house so she could compare it with the not very specific inventory of seized items she would eventually be provided.

I was still feeling a tad contentious. I explained to her that seeing what was missing from a familiar tableau was not one of my native perceptual abilities. For some reason, in the moment, it actually seemed important that she know that about me.

She wasn't at all interested in my perceptual deficit, which served to ground me a bit. "I understand," was what she said. But I could tell she was prepared to stop me if I displayed an inclination to explain myself further. She added, "One of the items listed on the warrant is a .32 caliber semiautomatic pistol." She had the warrant. She put her index finger on that line. "The judge authorized them to search for and remove a .32 semiautomatic from your home."

The voice she used was pointedly matter-of-fact. She could have said a "nine-inch cast-iron skillet." But we both knew the .32 wasn't a matter-of-fact anything.

I was thinking, *The .32 is the Kahr, the German gun that Sam said they wouldn't find.* "Did they find one?" I asked. "During the search? A .32 pistol."

"So there is a pistol," she said.

In my head I replayed our earlier discussion about the handgun. Although I had gotten close to an explanation during the drive to Spanish Hills, Kirsten and I had not edged around to discussing the Kahr. If she was about to hand me off to a new defense attorney — and it was abundantly clear she was determined to do so at her first opportunity — I thought it might be better to leave things ambiguous with her about the missing Kahr.

I said, "Lauren has a Glock, a 9mm. It was inside. Before the search. Maybe someone was confused about the caliber of the gun they were after." I gestured toward the inventory Kirsten was holding. "Did the investigators find the pistol they were looking for during the search?"

"We'll see." She narrowed her eyes. "You don't know guns, do you? A 9mm is not a .32. And vice versa. Different-different, not same-same."

"Okay," I said. I was being tested, and I knew it.

"Lauren was shot with a .32, Alan. The police are looking for that weapon."

She didn't use the cast-iron-skillet voice for that declaration. "Yes," I said.

I was, too, I thought. *I was shot with a .32.*

Through and through. And it's possible the same damn .32 will bring me down a second time. No flesh wound the second time.

I walked her to her car. I thanked her profusely for her help. I apologized profusely for dragging her into my mess. She told me to stop apologizing. I gave her a hug. She allowed it, but she didn't return it.

She lowered the window after she settled onto the driver's seat. She looked at me with a mix of disdain and something else.

Oh, pity.

Her pity almost floored me.

The first thing I did once I had the house to myself was to go to the highboy in the master bedroom and look for the two handguns that had been hidden in the hollow on top. All the items that I'd left in place to disguise the hiding place had been removed — I saw those items on the floor — but the guns weren't where they had been.

I didn't know whether or not the searchers had found the guns. Sam had promised me that the Kahr wouldn't be there. But the Glock? Sam had not mentioned the Glock.

I was facing a multihour job of trying to undo the mess the searchers had left behind. They had not been careful as they rifled through our stuff. Neither had they been wanton. The chaos they'd created was middling. The damage? Minor.

They had chosen to pile a lot of our stuff on Lauren's pool table. Seeing how the heavier items had crushed the felt on the table would have caused her to go ballistic.

My sympathy was absent.

"Don't worry, Dad," Jonas said, startling me. I assumed he had sneaked away from Ophelia. Jonas could be sneaky. In life he was often not where I expected him to be, or doing what I expected him to be doing. I blamed it on Adrienne's genes.

"Hey," I said, taking him in my arms. "I didn't want you to have to see this. I didn't want you to have to go through . . . this. I am so sorry for today. You must have been so scared when the —"

"Don't worry, Dad." *Shut up, Dad.*

"Okay," I said, trying to be the grown-up so that he did not have to be. "You and your sister have been through too much already. I do worry, you know that."

He wriggled away from me. "Don't *worry,*" he said again, his eyes wide, a measure of unfamiliar determination in his voice.

I finally heard that he wasn't trying to assuage me; he was trying to tell me something. I said, "Why shouldn't I worry, Jonas?"

"Because I have the . . ." He lowered his voice. "I have the guns. Both of them. The police didn't find them."

A fresh adrenaline ejaculation shot through my circulatory system. How unnecessary was the bolus of hormone? If a bear walked into the house right then, I would have tried to wrestle it to the floor. I reminded myself that I was with my adolescent son. I had responsibilities — I couldn't get lost in hormone-induced reveries about wrestling matches with bears. Instead I had to deal with the reality that just about everybody I was speaking with seemed to have an opinion about the guns that I thought were so masterfully hidden in the highboy.

I cleared my head. The only thought left was *what the fuck?* I almost said, "What guns?" to Jonas but I realized that any latitude I had for prevarication with my son had already been squandered. What I said to Jonas was, "You have the guns?"

"I do."

"The ones from the bedroom? In that little hollowed-out section sort of below the crown trim on top of the highboy?"

He nodded. I nodded back. "Don't be

mad," Jonas said.

"I'm not mad." Technically that was true. I wasn't mad. Though I had moved beyond any desire to wrestle, I found myself stifling an urge to slaughter a wild animal.

I was also willing to argue that was different from mad.

Jonas wasn't so sanguine about my mood. He said, "You don't look not mad."

His appraisal was reasonable. *Not not-mad* just about covered my affective state. I made a conscious decision to go back in time to the cast-iron-skillet voice. "So, you have the guns. Can you tell me how that happened?"

"You haven't been in a good place lately," my son said, his voice somehow not betraying the extent of his understatement. "I took the guns for safekeeping."

I could see no margin in mounting a protest against Jonas's assessment of my recent mental state. I said, "It has been a tough period for me."

Jonas nodded enthusiastically, relieved that we were on the same page. "After that night you woke me up? The night that you were naked and tearing apart shoe boxes and throwing Mom's shoes around, I didn't think I could trust you around them any longer. At least for a while."

Jonas had interrupted the cyclonic tantrum I'd had in the master closet with Lauren's boxed right shoes. But my face must have continued to betray some of my general befuddlement about what he'd done with the guns.

He explained, "I mean trust you around the guns. Not the shoes."

Jonas was too young to understand how the shoes felt as destructive to me as the guns. Or maybe he wasn't. I wondered then if he knew about his mom and Raoul. God, I hoped not.

"You knew the guns were there?" I had thought Lauren's contrived handgun-cubby hiding place — one I'd inherited from her — was genius.

"I knew Mom's was there. The other gun surprised me."

"How did you know about Mom's gun?"

"She showed me."

"She showed you?"

"After she started leaving me here alone with Grace she taught me how to shoot her Glock. She thought I should know how to use it. You know, just in case. We went to the firing range sometimes when you were at work. I can clean it, too."

She taught you how to shoot her Glock. I had just identified another important parenting conversation I would never get a chance to have with Lauren. I was thinking that I would need to begin a list of those.

"I was not supposed to tell you about it. She didn't think you would . . ."

Jonas stalled. I suggested, "Approve?" He nodded. "Are you a good shot?" I said.

"Better than her. My mother was a surgeon. My father was a woodcarver. I have steady hands." He held them out for me to see.

He did. "You're right. You have steady hands. Guns are a big responsibility. Knowing how to shoot one is different from knowing when to shoot one."

He rolled his eyes. The eye roll was intended to inform me that the present moment was not prime time for a sincere parenting interlude. Jonas's instincts about such things were reliable.

I said, "Where are the guns now?"

"Can I show you? It would be easier."

"Sounds like a plan."

I followed him from the room. "They're outside," he said. I guessed in his father's old workshop someplace. He added, "I didn't think anyone would search a police detective's girlfriend's place for them."

"Ophelia has the guns?"

"No. I hid them above one of the axles on the doublewide. There is too much metal

413

there for a metal detector to pick up a couple of guns."

He showed me where he had removed a section of skirting from around the trailer. We crawled in near the front axle. He pointed to the guns. He told me they weren't loaded; the chambers were empty and the clips were in the drawer in the base of his father Peter's joiner in the old barn.

We agreed to leave the guns where they were below the doublewide.

Jonas helped me get the house back together. I was grateful for his assistance, and for his company.

45

Amanda and I met at Locale late the next afternoon. I had requested the rendezvous because I needed to see her face as I spoke with her.

I used my burner to set up the meeting. I was beginning to like my burner.

Amanda initially suggested we use the in-call again. As we talked she texted me instructions to find the hiding place of the key. I hadn't recovered from almost having the opportunity to meet Paul and Sasha the first time I'd been at the incall, so I asked her to suggest an alternative location. Locale was her fallback option.

Amanda had staked out the two seats where the sinewy bar of the pizzeria abutted the big rolling window adjacent to the Pearl Street sidewalk. Boulder's interlude of springtime weather was continuing. Despite the late hour the window behind the bar was open. We ordered drinks. Hers was an icy cocktail made with prosecco and an orange-hued aperitif I didn't recognize. Mine wasn't.

"I feel badly about how I ended up telling you about them," she said.

"Them" wasn't the Louboutins. "Them" was the erotic threesome: Raoul, Lauren, and the Louboutins.

"I needed to know," I said. "I'm grateful." I felt no need for social pleasantries. I was terse but I was trying not to be impolite. My sense was that Amanda understood.

I waited for the bartender to move away. He did, parking himself within arm's reach of a young woman who was slicing cured pork on a gorgeous machine that looked completely over-engineered for the task. Cutting prosciutto with that apparatus was like using a smartphone to make a local telephone call.

It didn't take a genius to recognize that the bartender was much more interested in the young woman than he was in the sliced meat. I was grateful that he was distracted.

I lowered my voice to a whisper as I said, "Diane intended to shoot Lauren?"

Amanda's eyes grew wide for a second. She said, "Oooh. Just like that? No foreplay? You walk in all hard and ready?"

The crudeness was unlike her. I had been

getting her attention by being blunt. She was getting mine the same way. "I did buy you a drink first," I said.

She laughed. She said, "I need to eat something."

"Please," I said, sliding the menu her way.

"Want to share?" she asked. I declined. I had left my appetite somewhere in the previous calendar year.

The young woman departed toward the kitchen with her sliced prosciutto. The bartender took Amanda's order for a pizza topped with fresh arugula. I didn't consider it an epiphany that Amanda and I didn't have the same taste in pizza toppings.

Using the almost whisper I'd used earlier, I returned to the original question. "That morning? Diane intended to shoot Lauren? That was her plan all along?"

Amanda rotated ninety degrees to face me. Her kneecaps came to rest against my thigh. I decided that the contact was happenstance. It distracted me, but it didn't distract her at all. She said, "You're not convinced? About Raoul and your wife? Are the Louboutins not enough?" When I hesitated, she added, "There are shoes that women like, that other women think are cute, and there are shoes that men like, that they like to see women wear. Sometimes they're similar. Sometimes not."

"I will keep that in mind." I wasn't trying to be a jerk, but I was aware that it was taking more effort than it should.

"Women know the difference. Raoul does, too." She looked away as she sipped her drink. "He's good at choosing shoes in the sweet spot."

I fortified myself to go on. I wasn't eager to learn any more of Raoul's strengths with women. I said, "The work I do? The life I had with my wife? I have a resistance to believing certain things. Maybe it's denial; I don't want to believe things that I don't wish to be true. Anyway, I'm ninety-nine percent convinced about the shoes. Is that enough?"

"If you choose to chase that doubt away? Raoul has some Bogart in him. Among your wife's things there will also be stockings, likely real silk. The ones for him will have back seams. She'll have garter belts for them, too. One of those will be black."

"That's not Lauren's style."

She rolled her lips inward before she said, "It's his style. Raoul's."

I so much don't need to know that.

Amanda could tell she had wounded me. She also knew I was the one insisting that she twist the knife. The roles we were playing were probably not unfamiliar to her. She said, "Your question? About whether Diane intended to shoot your wife? That answer is yes."

"You know that?"

"I do."

"How? I have to know. Without a doubt."

"You do know. Find the back-seam stockings. Your doubt will go away."

I didn't believe that the last drop of doubt would ever evaporate. "Not you? Diane didn't think it was you in the chair that morning? There was no mistaken identity? No confusion?"

I was challenging Amanda but nothing in her voice betrayed any animus in return. Her reply was as tender as she could make it. "For Diane, I was a solution. For Diane, Lauren was a problem. Lauren threatened everything that was important to Diane. I didn't. Diane knew exactly whom she was shooting that day. It was not a case of mistaken identity."

"Diane wasn't crazy?" I said. "That morning?"

"You're asking me? I think you're mixing up our professions."

"Did Diane have a clear enough head to know what she was doing?"

"I'd like to allow you the comfort that

might come with believing that she did not." She shook her head. "Diane chose a solution that felt rational to her. Sure, the solution was mad. Does that make her crazy? That's for you to ponder, not for me.

"Raoul had been telling me that he thought she was 'off.' Was that day worse than others? I don't know. That new fire in Boulder Canyon? Wildfires were hard for Diane. Their money problems were bad. Raoul couldn't win for losing that summer. The financial calamity they were facing was much harder for her than it was for him. Raoul knew he would make more money. It might take him a year. Or three. But he would be wealthy again.

"But the money was Diane's security. As Raoul spent more time away, at work, with me, and with Lauren, she became more unstable. The less she could count on him the more she relied on the money. When the investments began to fail? It was too much for her, I think." She waited for me to disagree. I didn't. Amanda threw out a theory. "Was it possible that Diane being 'off' was tactical? The fact that you even ask whether she was crazy says that she succeeded in making you wonder."

All I could do was nod. My tongue and lips felt disconnected from my brain.

"Later that night? At that condo? Her cocktail dress? The nutty makeup? That STD speech? The whole Mary-Louise Parker thing? I never understood what that part was about. Diane thinks they're sisters? Are they sisters? Either she was crazy or she wanted us all to believe she was. Which would make her anything but crazy. Yes?"

"Do you think Diane had any concern about getting away with it?" I asked.

"I don't know. I'm not saying it wasn't impulsive. Or that it was. I don't know. All I'm saying is that she had a reason."

"When did Diane learn about Raoul and Lauren?"

"Raoul suspected she'd known for a long while."

"She was reading his email," I said. "Diane is smart." I was recalling all the things she had done in the months leading up to the shooting that had left me questioning her mental state. I had taken each of them at face value. I never once thought I was being played. Let alone set up.

Amanda was looking at me with kind eyes. I tried to cast aside any remaining doubts about her sincerity. I almost succeeded. "The brain lesion?" I asked.

She shook her head. "They didn't know about it."

"You're sure?"

"I am. Diane had been getting headaches. They both thought it was stress. Raoul was losing patience with her. The pressure to sell the house. Her not working much. But they didn't know about the tumor. If you wish to believe the tumor caused Diane's instability, it may make you feel better. But it won't make it true. I guess you get to pick."

Amanda's pizza arrived. She draped her napkin onto her lap.

"Do you still love him?" I asked. I was gauging her allegiance.

She took a long pull on her drink. "No. I don't. Could I be re-smitten? Yes. Raoul is one of those guys. I am glad I'm leaving town. It's better that I get away. Out of Colorado. Away from him."

"This is you burning bridges? Telling me what you've just told me creates a huge chasm between you and Raoul."

"That's my plan. There are other women for him. Less complicated women than me. For men like Raoul there are always other women." She smiled wryly.

"What was that? That smile?"

Her eyes grew moist. "Each of the new women will have a moment when she is convinced that she has become special to him. That is one of his gifts." She duplicated the earlier smile. I watched a tear form in one eye.

Her words were piercing me. In my heart I knew that Raoul had made Lauren feel special. The inadequacy I felt as a spouse in that moment had actual mass in my heart, as though a ventricle or two had been filled with a heavy metal. "Go on," I said. "Please."

"An occasional woman will be right. For a while a girl might be special to him. Then some will get Geigers, some Louboutins. But in the end, they will all be wrong."

I still didn't understand. "Tell me about Lauren." *Was Lauren still special to him when she died?*

"Raoul is special to Raoul. Diane is special to Raoul. The rest of us? We're mirrors. Raoul is addicted to the reflection of his charms. His attractiveness, his seductiveness, his brilliance, his success, his power. When that reflection gets distorted, he moves on. Any distortion is intolerable to him. Diane knows that. It's how they've lasted this long. It's why he's so attached to her. She never allows his reflection to remain distorted."

Amanda lifted her knife and fork.

"Lauren?" I said. "What about her?"

The wry smile returned. "She was special. Would it have endured? No. He didn't have to deal with her limitations. Their relationship existed in his head. And in his bed."

I felt primal anguish. Her words burned at my flesh. I used every bit of my consciousness to mask it. I drank water until the glass was empty.

I said, "Are you aware that Raoul is trying to blame me for shooting Lauren?"

"No." Her word was defiant. She put the silverware back on the plate. She shook her head. "No. He wouldn't. Raoul is not vindictive."

Amanda was being instinctively protective of her ex-lover's reflection. *Old habits.*

I said, "I don't know that he's being vindictive, but I'm not wrong. He may be defending Diane. Or protecting that view he has of himself. But he is setting me up, Amanda, with the DA. I know that for certain."

She carved a slice of pizza. She dabbed at the corner of her mouth with her napkin though she hadn't yet taken a bite. "Makes no sense. What motive does he ascribe to you for killing your wife? How does Raoul explain that to the police?"

I was not unaware of the irony.

I said, "For certain? I don't know. But I

424

imagine he told the police that my wife was having an affair. Apparently the homicide I committed was a crime of passion."

She folded a small wedge of pizza that she'd cut from the whole, the bitter rocket a leafy filling in a petite Neapolitan sandwich, a wire of cheese connecting the slice to the pie. She left the food hanging in the air halfway between the plate and her lips.

Her face looked sad.

I said, "Will you be leaving town soon? Is that still the plan?"

"New job. New town. New life. All set. This phase was . . . good. I'm glad I did it. But I'm going back to the business world. The next phase will be good, too."

She was a survivor. I knew that about her. "I wish you well, Amanda." I stood. I put too much money on the bar. "Thank you," I said.

"Thank you," she said.

I heard her call my name as I passed by the machine that sliced pork thinner than paper. I didn't look back. I kept walking.

46

I phoned Kirsten from my car. Her greeting was understandably wary.

"You're not in custody?" she said.

I hoped she was being ironic, but I wasn't sure. "I should know more after my first meeting with the new lawyer tomorrow. He's been in touch with Elliot's office. The reason I'm calling is that I left my shoulder bag in your car the day of the search. I put it on the floor in the backseat when we were on the way to my house. I'm downtown right now — is it possible that I could stop by to get it? I need some papers for the consultation in the morning."

Kirsten hesitated. I assumed not only that my intrusion might have been inconvenient for her, but also that she would be disinclined to see me after all the difficulties I had caused her. I was prepared for her to instruct me to collect the bag from her office receptionist the next morning.

I said, "If you leave it outside your door, I can retrieve it without disturbing you."

"Fifteen minutes?" she said. "Knock."

"Thank you," I said.

I used the fifteen minutes to get noodles and baos for the kids and Clare at Zoe Ma Ma, plus a couple of extra veggie baos in case one of them had turned vegetarian while I wasn't looking. In Boulder it was always a distinct possibility that someone had gone vegetarian or vegan or pescatarian since I'd last checked in. Gracie changed her dietary preferences with the seasons. Jonas was less mercurial than Grace.

But then mercury was less mercurial than Grace.

As a peace offering I ordered food for Kirsten.

While the order was being prepped I checked *The Coloradoan* for updates about the death of Big Elias. The paper reported that the Larimer County district attorney was investigating the death as suspicious. *Huh.* No new details. I wondered what they knew.

My personal Clean Hands Scoreboard wasn't at all where I needed it to be. I was a principal suspect in my wife's homicide. Elliot Bellhaven, the Boulder DA, also thought, or at least hoped, that I was somehow involved in Big Elias's death, a suspicion I had no doubt he had already shared with his counterpart in Larimer County.

If anyone surfaced who had seen Elias Tres's drawing before my last meeting with my wife, I knew I could also become a suspect in the old murder in Frederick. My vulnerability — only one of the many charges had to stick to annihilate my life as I knew it — left me numb as I drove to Kirsten's cottage.

She was standing in the open front door as I climbed the stairs, bag in hand. "Comfort food," I said. "A mea culpa. I am so sorry about what happened. About dragging you into my mess."

She sniffed the air. Her expression was suspicious — either of my motives, or of my choice of comfort food — as she eyed the bag. She said, "From where?"

"Zoe Ma Ma."

Eyebrows up. "What do you have?"

"Beef noodles. Vegetable bao. Covering my bases."

Her accent and her tone changed latitudes. "New Orleans girls don't tend to lean vegan." She wrinkled her nose. "Any potstickers?"

"I never leave without potstickers."

"If I were a troll at a footbridge," she said, "you would have just solved my riddle." She stepped aside. "You may cross with your potstickers, sir."

"If you were a troll I would spend more time crossing footbridges."

She didn't smile at that. "Come in. I made tea. But I didn't know about the potstickers when I made the tea. I have some beer someone left here."

The guy she is seeing. "A beer sounds great."

She returned from the kitchen with plates and with two cans of lager from a little brewery on Lee Hill not far from where Raoul and Diane lived. "One of my current favorites," I said. I assumed that the guy Kirsten was seeing was an Upslope fan, too.

"I'm told they're good," she said, shrugging indifferently about the beer. I asked her if she'd looked at the contents of the messenger bag.

She explained she'd glanced at the contents of the file marked "Pending Resolution" and leafed through the contents of the Tyvek envelope labeled "Home, Work," just to see what was there. "It is mostly stuff that Lauren should not have had at the house. A few of the documents date back ten years, some of it should not have been away from the office at all. Certainly not where a civilian could see them."

"I be the civilian?" I said.

"Yes. You be the civilian. What was she up to?" Kirsten asked. "Do you know?"

I shook my head. "I was hoping you could tell me."

"If I read them carefully I might be able to figure it out, but I'm not sure I should. I would need time to do that." She smiled a rueful smile to let me know it was time she was not planning to invest. "Have you looked at them?"

"No. I've been ambivalent about going through Lauren's papers. Any of them. Every time I dive in I end up discovering things I would rather not know. These? I didn't want to have to admit to someone later — or lie to someone later, especially under oath — that I'd been reading work product from the DA's office. Remaining ignorant not only seemed self-protective, it's also consistent with my current emotional inclination.

"Where Lauren's life intersected with —" I stopped the thought. "Let's just say that denial and avoidance have become dear to my heart." Kirsten's expression was quizzical. I added, "Until very recently."

"Yeah? What changed?"

"Elliot. I will take any leverage I can find to thwart Elliot. Maybe I can earn some goodwill by turning those papers over to him. Or maybe there is something inflammatory in there I can use against him. If you have any advice, I'd love it. You know that."

She dug into the Sichuan noodles. I could tell from her closed eyes that the comfort food was providing comfort. She asked, "Why me? And why now?"

"You mean why not my new lawyer? And tomorrow?"

She nodded. I placed my chopsticks between my teeth — probably not a good look — and reached into the messenger bag. I grabbed the sealed envelope, the one from Lauren's peacoat, the one addressed to ellyott. After removing the chopsticks from my mouth I said, "The day Elliot cornered me at my office? I came by here? This is the envelope I asked if I should open." I provided a capsule history of Sofie's discovery of the envelope in the peacoat.

"Valentine's Day," she mused. "You came here on Valentine's Day. That's how it looked when you found the envelope?" she asked.

"When Sofie found it. I assumed that Lauren stuck it in her pocket with the intent of delivering it to Elliot. But that never happened."

"What makes you think that she intended it for Elliot?"

"It was in her coat pocket. It seemed logical that she put it there at home in anticipation of wearing the coat to work because she planned to give it to him," I said.

"Why her coat pocket and not her satchel?" I didn't have an answer. "The alternative makes sense," Kirsten said. "Someone could have given the envelope *to* Lauren. She could have put it in her pocket after receiving it. Or maybe your theory is right, but she had a change of heart. Or she forgot about it. Or she left it in her coat intentionally with plans to hand it to someone else. Not Elliot. Or not at work."

Those were all possibilities.

She asked, "Is that her handwriting?"

"I think it's Andrew's. Her assistant."

"Is it okay if I make a copy of the contents? You can take the originals with you for your meeting. I'll go over the copies if I get a chance. If I see anything that provides you with leverage I will let you know. Best I can do."

She left for a few minutes. When she returned she stuffed a freshly sealed envelope back into my messenger bag. "I copied the contents. I put the originals into a fresh envelope along with the original envelope. I've signed and dated along the seal. You can explain all that tomorrow. At your meeting." She leaned back on the deep chair, her feet beneath her, a beer in hand. She said, "So what did you find among Lauren's things that you didn't wish to find? Something that hurt?"

I swallowed a potsticker before I said, "Yes."

"Want to tell me about it?"

"As my lawyer?"

"I will be your lawyer only until tomorrow morning. I hope to be your friend longer than that. You get to decide whether you want to talk to me about things that cause pain."

I was not a hero in my story. It was a tale of being cuckolded in a grand way. Kirsten sensed my ambivalence about telling it. "Not sure?"

I said, "Do you know anything about Christian Louboutins?"

I could tell that my words hit her ears as non sequitur, not as segue. She said, "They are shoes I can't afford. Fortunately they are shoes I can't afford that I don't run across where I shop." She smiled at me with her eyes. "When I covet — which isn't usually, not my thing — I am more inclined toward purses I can't afford than shoes I can't afford. Bags are my weakness."

"Good to know," I said.

"Did you find some pricey pumps? Were designer shoes Lauren's weakness?"

I put down the food. I put down the beer. I sat back. "She did have a weakness. And I did find some Louboutins. Stilettos."

Kirsten leaned toward me. "You didn't know she had a shoe thing? You discovered what — how much they cost?"

I said, "Lauren's weakness wasn't for expensive shoes. It was . . ."

She sighed. "I'm not following. Sorry. If you don't want to talk —"

"Lauren couldn't walk in stilettos. She had balance issues from MS. The shoes were a gift to her from a man who didn't care that she couldn't walk in them."

Kirsten frowned. I felt a small stab of ironic comfort that at least one other person in my universe was as sexually naïve as me.

"Oh," she said suddenly as she got it, her eyes wide. "I am so sorry."

I told her about the "CL peeps letts." And about Raoul. And about Diane's Christian Louboutins. I didn't tell her about Amanda's Louboutins. At some point I had to protect my patient's confidentiality. Along with my professional credibility, or whatever crumbs remained of it.

Kirsten moved from her chair to sit beside me. The chair was plenty big for both of us. She said the right things. I felt a temptation to settle in. I didn't.

"I have to get home," I said. "The kids are starving. I have their dinner in the car." I stood. "Thank you. It helped to say that out loud."

"Before you go," she said. "This is me putting on my lawyer hat." She got up while she pantomimed putting on her lawyer hat. "The triangle — you and Lauren and . . . Raoul — gives you motive. From Elliot's perspective Lauren's murder becomes a crime of passion. Juries understand crimes of passion. They don't always understand crazy people who think they are movie stars' older sisters suddenly shooting people for no apparent reason. But a husband in a jealous rage? Juries get that."

I said, "I didn't know about the triangle back then."

"And you think you can convince a jury of that? Good luck."

"I know. God. I know I'm being set up. I assume Raoul told Cozy about his affair with Lauren as a way of protecting Diane, specifically as a way to provide an alternate theory to Elliot about why the shooting happened. Diane becomes witness instead of perpetrator. When Cozy suggested to Elliot that he consider widening the pool of potential suspects to include me, I imagine Elliot could not have been happier to oblige."

"Because you've been married to a prosecutor I am going to lay this out like I would to another lawyer. That morning?" The fact that Kirsten used my coded phrase for that awful day caused my diaphragm to seize. "Elliot's minions will argue you had motive and opportunity. The searches that were just done at your house? He was trying to lock down means, as well, by trying to find that gun in your possession."

"He didn't find the gun."

She shrugged. "They'll make a case you had it. And that you ditched it. If they come up with a good narrative it can be almost as effective."

"MOM?" *Means, Opportunity, Motive.*

"Yes, Alan. MOM." She sighed. "They say there's a storm coming. Tomorrow night."

"When the weather is as nice as it's been? It seems we always pay."

Kirsten gave me a hug at the door. I could feel her spread the fingers of each of her hands as she pressed them against my back.

She turned her head sideways, leaning her body into mine. I could smell her hair.

You're seeing someone, I thought.

My car smelled of potstickers. I lost Kirsten's scent in that scent before I crossed Pearl.

47

The kids felt abandoned. The dogs wanted a walk. Clare was late to meet her boyfriend to go to a club I didn't know existed — some speakeasy-conceit in the basement of a nondescript storefront on Broadway that grown-ups like me were unlikely to notice. I was beginning to feel old in Boulder. That could not be a good thing.

I pondered the myriad ways my kids would take advantage of it going forward.

Mostly Grace. It wouldn't be pretty.

Clare drove away with my gratitude, a vegetarian bao, and a bonus twenty in her pocket. I set out food for the kids. I was tempted to sit back and watch Grace's chopstick performance — she'd been practicing her skills on dry cereal — but the dogs needed out.

Before I got Fiji's leash, and despite a caution to myself not to be looking for trouble, I detoured to the tables in the master bedroom where Sofie had sorted Lauren's clothing. Other than my hissy fit with the shoe boxes, I had not disturbed Sofie's work.

I felt compelled to prove Amanda right or to prove Amanda wrong. I was on the prowl for silk stockings I was determined not to find.

Lauren's underwear was neatly folded and placed in a large rectangular plastic bin. Right next to a surprisingly varied selection of panties was a small pile of tights and stockings. Next to them, beneath Lauren's bras, I found two garter belts.

I stared at the garter belts as though they didn't belong. *Huh.* I would remember my wife wearing a garter belt. I did not remember ever seeing one on her.

I was aware that I could suddenly hear my own pulse. The thready *pop-pop-pop* was accelerating in my ears.

Most of the tights were familiar. A few caused a twinge of sadness associated with a specific memory. On top of the stack of tights but below two pairs of unopened pantyhose, Sofie had placed a solitary pair of sheer hose. The stockings were dark in tone, but transparent. My pulse continued to race as I unfolded the wispy fabric with a reverence I didn't try to comprehend.

Without conscious volition, my left hand entered one stocking and the tip of my right index finger traced a raised seam all the way to the heel.

I had not seen the back-seam stockings before. Ever. Not on her. Not off her.

"Find the back-seam stockings," Amanda had said. *"Your doubt will go away."*

I felt as though I were in freefall. I had been clutching doubt as though it were the rip cord on a parachute. My only protection against annihilation.

The back-seam stockings obliterated my denial. The reaction I felt holding them was instantaneous and chemical. My doubt had allowed me a modicum of uncertainty. The uncertainty had allowed me hope. Without hope?

My anguish felt gruesome. I was feeling again the incongruous agony that accompanied a compound fracture of my heart.

I had lost Lauren, I knew, long before I had lost her.

Emily and Fiji didn't get the walk they wanted, but they got what they needed. When I returned with the dogs Gracie was dancing in the family room and Jonas had retreated to the basement to write code. The last six times I had asked him to tell me

440

about the code he was writing he'd replied, "It's for a game." I couldn't read code. He may have been being truthful with me but I was unable to kick a nagging suspicion that Jonas was messing around with hacking. I couldn't prove it. I had no doubt he had the skill to hack. I wasn't sure if he had the inclination.

He pulled a bud from his left ear when he sensed that I had walked up behind him. The one ear was all of Jonas's attention that I was going to get. I was grateful for it. The music was the by-then familiar early Feist, but he was listening to a song I'd never heard before that was sad and upbeat all at once. I put my hands on his shoulders and told him how brave he was. How proud I was of him.

And I told him that I hoped he wasn't hacking.

He didn't stop pecking out lines of code to respond to me. But, as I retreated to leave him to what gave him solace, he said, "I didn't know how much handcuffs hurt."

"Ain't that the truth. You okay?" He had long sleeves covering his wrists. I asked to see them.

He didn't show me. He said, "I'm good, Dad. You okay?"

"Yeah." I handed him an envelope from

that day's mail. "My friend? The old Italian guy you met? He sent some more Powerball tickets. Will you check them against the drawing?" Carl had been sending me ten entries a week.

I thought I knew why. Carl had been into amends. The entries into the Powerball lottery were part of his amends. His mea culpa. I suspected Kirsten was getting some, too.

Jonas pulled the small sheet with the numbers from the envelope. He barely glanced at it before he declared, "Sorry. No winners."

"You know the winning numbers?"

Jonas was not a romantic. He said, "No, Dad. I know the odds."

48

I used the landline in my bedroom — it was a blocked number — to call Diane.

Occasionally I felt the urge to call her to learn how she was doing. To reconnect.

That time I called to ask her why. Not to reconnect.

The call went straight to voicemail. I hung up.

Sam was sitting alone on the deck outside the doublewide. He should not have been able to sit comfortably outside on a March evening, but the night was still, the air mild. I thought he might be waiting for me.

The moon was at half, as though it had been sliced along its axis by a celestial chef with knife skills. Lunar light illuminated ribbons of clouds that sunset had left behind, the nearby Flatirons backlit by the spectacle.

"I was hoping for a beer," Sam said as I approached. He'd spied the bottle I was carrying in one hand and the two glasses I had in the other. "Some new local delight you discovered from a brewery that's been open for like a fortnight. Do Boulder's hipster brewers mark time in fortnights? Is that old enough to be new again?"

I said, "Maybe the ones that make mead. No. I think that's a honey moon."

Sam said, "I think a honey moon is a fortnight."

"Yeah?" I said.

Sam made a who-the-fuck-cares sound with his lips. "We're drinking hard stuff?"

"It's been a whiskey kind of day, Sam."

"Good days, bad days, they're all beer days for me. Keeps life simple."

"Your life is simple?"

Sam's laugh came from his belly. The sound waves rippled through the valley in a way that probably interfered with my neighbors' satellite reception. Emily was not pleased. I heard her bark a reply to Sam's guffaw from behind the front door. He asked, "Are we doing shots?"

"This is a civilized sit-down. We're going to sip whiskey neat. And talk."

Sam didn't miss the absurdity. "We're sitting on plastic chairs that Ophelia got on sale at Target on a temporary deck that's at best quasi-attached to a used doublewide

that wasn't nice even when it was brand-
new. But we're going to be proper gentle-
men, drinking civilized-like, sipping whiskey
from real-glass glasses?"

"That's the plan."

"I assume this is top-shelf hooch worthy
of the elevated circumstances."

"It is." I poured. I said, "I want to start
this off with a thank-you. A sincere one." I
raised my glass. "For rescuing my kid."

He graciously touched my glass with the
rim of his. We sipped.

"Next," I said. "That gun? The one you
were sure wasn't in my house? I would like
to hear about that."

My tracker vibrated. The intrusion was
untimely, but mobile phones — at least
mine — rarely wormed their way into my
awareness at opportune moments. In another phase of my life I might have ignored
the buzz. Not in the phase of my life I was
living. Too fraught. It turned out the buzz
was for a text I could ignore.

**My gf met a guy who got us a room @
Little Nell. Too cool!!!!! ☺☺adi**

Sam said, "Important?"

I intended for it to be an evening of
honesty between Sam and me. I said, "Remember the beguiler?"

It took him five seconds. "From LA? The

445

fucking beguiler?"

"She's in Aspen."

"Good town for her. Place is full of fucking beguilers." He looked at me sideways, his eyeballs distorted by the amber in his glass. "Don't, Alan. Do not."

I didn't want Sam's advice about caution with LA Amy. Sam had gone off the relationship reservation more often than anyone I knew. He was not someone to whom I looked for wisdom about erotic restraint.

I did wish I could tell him about the wound that had pierced my heart from Lauren's involvement with Raoul, but my determination to be honest didn't include enough trust to be truthful with Sam about all things. I did not trust him with the back-seam stockings.

I had an agenda. I got back to it. I raised one finger. "The gun? You knew I had it." I raised a second finger. "And you knew it wasn't in the house. How? And how?"

He wasn't surprised by my line of inquiry. He said, "We'll start with number two. I knew where it wasn't because I'd already searched your house. In fact, when I didn't find the gun the first time, I went back and searched a second time. I'm good, by the way. When people — cop people, prosecutor people — are planning a difficult search, they choose me. I got instincts. I knew the gun wasn't in the house because I checked twice.

"Before we go back to number one, you probably also want to know about the why. Why I searched your house. Yes?"

I preferred the illusion that I had some control. I said, "No, first we'll do number one. Then we can come back to the why. But first, you should have my new phone number." I showed Sam my cheap phone and offered him a sticky note with the digits.

"You finally got a burner." He raised his eyebrows. "It's your whiskey. But number one and the why are nearly the same thing."

The door to the trailer opened behind us. Ophelia walked into the evening carrying a ceramic platter so heavy it required both her hands. She said, "Hi, Alan, good to see you. I still adore your children."

It was one of her standard greetings. I said, "It's good to see you, too, Ophelia. I still adore them, too." She placed the platter, deep with crushed ice, on a low table, in the process exposing swell and curve and skin and, yes, pale areolae and soft nipples. I averted my eyes as I would from a solar eclipse.

I wasn't sure why I looked away. Some Catholic reflex. Ophelia was far from shy about displaying her breasts. Sam was getting used to it. Jonas had adjusted. It was my shit. On the list of things I was working on, I had managed to shove it near the bottom.

"A snack," she said. "For you boys."

"Some whiskey, Ophelia?" I said. "It's fine."

"Another time, but thank you. That's a pretty sky tonight. Enjoy."

Sam said, "Thanks, babe." He put a big hand on her ass as she departed. She danced her way through the flimsy door.

The crushed ice was covered with oysters.

"Kumamotos," Sam said.

You could have knocked me off the chair with a strong fart.

49

"Really," I said. Sam had said *Kumamotos*.
I would not have been more surprised had
he asked for my thoughts about escaping
the liquidity trap. I topped off the whiskey
in our glasses to camouflage my befuddlement.

"You eat raw oysters now?" The Sam I
knew didn't eat raw vegetables.

"Ophelia. What can I say? She gets a
bushel delivered by FedEx. Who knew? With
a little champagne vinegar and shallots?
These things are delicious. I could eat 'em
all day. I'm even learning how to shuck. O's
a pro but I'm getting there. Hardly cut
myself at all anymore." Sam smiled as he
displayed a healing wound on his oyster-
holding hand. "I'm becoming a raw bar guy.
I know, I know. Sushi? O thinks I'll come
around. She wants me to take her to Sushi
Zanmai for her birthday."

Sam had just said the word *shallots* in a

sentence without sarcasm. Sam knew how to shuck. He was anticipating eating sushi.

"Know what else we do? O and I?" I braced myself for some unwelcome sexual sharing. "She's a member at the Boedecker. Turns out art films aren't all about French people with their heads up their asses."

I was afraid I might say the wrong thing to him about the Boedecker or the Kumamotos. Ophelia had become Sam's tour guide into an alternate universe that had no neighborhoods that even approximated the ones of his youth on the Iron Range.

I took an oyster to keep my mouth occupied; it was sweet and fruity and the vinegar and shallots cut the brine to a perfect salinity. Sam spooned some vinegar and squeezed some lemon onto two and slurped them down in stereo.

I tried to savor the moment but Sam collapsed my moment-savoring as though he had taken a leaf blower to a house of cards. "Back to number one? The night Lauren was shot I was in the ICU when you came back from your little night-fire errand. You had a semiautomatic in the waistband of the scrubs you were wearing. For future reference? Great way to lose a nut. Two nuts. Hell, a whole damn scrotum.

"But you'd had the bad day to end all bad

days, so I prayed the safety was on and there was nothing in the chamber, and I let it go. Later I watched you bury the gun in the plastic bag with all the bloody stuff from the ER. I figured the bag ended up here and that the gun was someplace in the house that wouldn't be hard to find."

I interrupted. "You knew it was that gun? The one Diane used?"

"Seventy-thirty. Maybe eighty-twenty." He paused. "It was, right?"

"Yeah. Go on. Trying to get a read on your thinking."

"We both know it's better than yours. Do you want to tell me how you ended up with the gun?"

"Probably not a good idea, Sam. Some laws may have been broken. I should have turned it in. I was not at my best."

"You think? Anyway, the why? I'd been hearing drumbeats about a search. I didn't think it would go well for you if Elliot found the weapon that shot Lauren stashed in your house. So I decided to be proactive."

It was a fine time for me to offer some gratitude. I didn't. That Sam had a pristine motive to search my house didn't mean his only motive to search my house was pristine. "You knew a search was coming?" The words left my brain as a question but they

451

exited my mouth as an accusation.

Sam deflected me without rancor. "No. I heard a search *might* be coming. You used to be a good listener, Alan. I could rely on you to recognize nuance."

I opened my mouth to argue. I grabbed an oyster instead. After it raced down my throat I asked, "Why didn't you tell me to get rid of the gun?" I knew the answer before I finished the question. Sam wouldn't trust me to keep his name out of it if a future push brought an interrogatory shove. That trust thing again. I said, "Never mind."

Sam waited for me to catch up with myself. He said, "Look." He lifted his glass to toast the western sky. "The moon is about to disappear exactly into Eldorado Canyon. See how it fits? Amazing."

The moon was sliding into the cleft of Eldorado like a handgun into a holster.

"You know about Ivy Baldwin?" Sam asked. "Eldorado?"

"No. Who is she?" I asked.

"She's a he. A dead he. You really don't know? Back when Eldorado Springs was a big deal resort in the early 1900s, with the trolley from Denver and the hotels and the dance halls and everything — You know about that, right?"

I nodded but my assent was quasi-skeptical. I had heard the Eldorado-Springs-as-Coney-Island tales since I'd first arrived in Boulder. The contemporary Eldorado was a sleepy and quiet not-quite village with an old natural springs–fed pool up near the entrance to a splendid State Park with legendary routes for rock climbers.

The Coney Island of the Rockies? Not exactly. Hell, not even close.

Ivy Baldwin's name didn't ring any bells, but I guessed that Sam was reflecting on that earlier incarnation of Eldorado Springs, the one that purportedly attracted hordes of the trendy for summer holidays, and honeymooners like Ike and Mamie Eisenhower. I was a cynic about the lore. I believed the old Eldorado tales were a quarter apocryphal, a quarter urban legend, and a third true. The balance was a blend of the random variance and statistical noise inevitably associated with things Boulder.

But Sam had a story to tell. His kindness to my son and the Kumamotos and the Boedecker had earned him some slack. I said, "Please. Tell me."

"Ivy Baldwin was a daredevil type who walked a high wire across Eldorado Canyon for the tourists' amazement and amusement."

I looked at the canyon. I looked at Sam.

"Across the canyon? That canyon?" I pointed. "On a tightrope? No way."

"Wire, actually. Less than an inch thick. He crossed for the first time in, like, 1907. Five hundred feet up. Two football fields across. No friggin' net. No safety harness. Wuss factor? Zero. Ivy would sashay out to the middle of the canyon during his performance and he would proceed to stand on his damn head."

"Sam? Really? I'm not drunk yet."

"I kid you not."

If Sam's Ivy Baldwin yarn was true, I was awed. The unpredictable winds in Eldorado Canyon are neither apocryphal nor are they urban legend. But I failed to see where Sam was going. Given the nature of our conversation to that point, I had my ears peeled for both bullshit and an underlying metaphor. I grabbed another oyster.

"On a night like tonight — but back then — Ivy Baldwin might have felt like he could reach out and touch the darn moon from where he was standing on that wire."

Ivy crossed in the dark? The metaphor continued to elude me. The oysters were disappearing at an alarming pace, disproportionately into Sam's mouth. I ate one more. I could either savor the oysters or eat the oysters. Sam's appetite wouldn't permit me to do both.

Sam sensed my skepticism about Ivy Baldwin. He went into the trailer and returned with an old postcard with a photo of Ivy Baldwin crossing Eldorado Springs canyon on the high wire. "Convinced?"

"Yes. Wow. Wow."

"Ivy said that crossing that canyon on a wire was 'the greatest poison in the world. One drop could kill you.'" Sam jirbled out more whiskey. He examined the bottle before he put it down. "Rye? Goes okay with the oysters, which I would not have thought. Liquor with liquor? I will try to remember that."

"Sam? What's the high-wire story about? Is there a metaphor I'm missing?"

He tossed down the last of the oysters before he settled back. The chair had not been designed with Sam's BMI in mind; I was anticipating a disaster involving plastic fatigue before the evening progressed much further. As though Sam was determined to make things even more precarious than they were, he balanced his flip-flopped feet, ankles crossed, on the top rail of the creaky deck. That maneuver shifted his weight to the rear legs of the certainly insufficient chair.

He then scoffed at fate by resting the stout

glass of rye whiskey on the flattest part of his amply rounded abdomen. The flattest part of Sam's belly wasn't flat, exactly. It was the flattest part only when compared with the completely rounded other parts. To raise the danger quotient to alarming levels, Sam lifted his arms and intertwined his fingers behind his head.

I couldn't take my eyes off of the glass. The whiskey was sloshing as it tried to keep up with gravity's dictate that it find and hold a line that mimicked the horizon, something made nigh impossible by the glass leaning this way and that with every movement Sam made and each breath Sam took.

He said, "No metaphor. I have become Ivy Baldwin's biggest fan. I want to make him a star. I want to go to a movie about him at the Boedecker."

I was not convinced about Sam's sincerity. I continued to be distracted by the damn glass.

He said, "I was just about to tell you about the why. Yes?"

I couldn't remember what the why was about. I said, "Yes, Sam. That'd be great."

Waiting for the glass to tumble was kind of like being part of the century-earlier audience craning my neck to watch Ivy

Baldwin's headstand on his wire high in the sky above Eldorado. The only thing more alluring than the spectacle of success was the prospect of failure. The price of admission guaranteed one outcome or the other. For the audience it would be win-win. Same attraction as the one Sam had for his weekend love, NASCAR. If there was a metaphor to be found I was convinced it lurked in there somewhere.

I felt Sam staring at me. His glare felt ferocious. I shifted my gaze to meet his and forced myself to hold it. I felt a little frightened. Maybe more than a little.

"The why? The why is mostly because you've been such a douche," Sam said. "When you're not misleading me lately, you're accusing me of something. But you know all that." He burped. The glass jumped. "But no worries. I forgive you."

50

My reply lacked maturity. I said, "You forgive me? You've been the douche."

"That may be true," he said. "Do you forgive me?"

The Kumamotos and Ivy Baldwin had knocked me off script. It was not an ideal moment for me to withdraw into contemplation. But contemplate I did, starting with a consideration about whether his request for forgiveness was specious.

"That's what I thought," Sam said into the dead air. "Whatever's been going on between us, it's not about either of us not being perfect. We're both guilty of that. What's going on between us is about not being trusted."

The leaning whiskey glass on his belly had to be the single most distracting non-naked thing on the planet. I couldn't not stare at it.

I said, "Do you ever think about the

morality? What we did? How are we different from" — I tried on potential descriptors like I might try on shoes. *Other killers? Other murderers? Other criminals?* I decided to use names instead — "Michael McClelland or Carl Luppo? They killed. We killed."

Sam said, "Late at night. Sometimes. I think about it. Not the morality. I don't go there. I tell myself that a killer was walking down the hall to my son's bedroom with a gun in his hand and a round in the chamber. That I protected my kid. I tell myself I had no choice but to do what I did."

"That's what I tell myself, too," I said. It was taking all of my self-restraint not to grab the glass off Sam's gut. "Does it work for you? Do you believe in those moments that your rationalization is more self-righteous than the ones that a million others have used? You've arrested killers. I imagine most of them must have rationales."

"Mostly yes, sometimes no." Sam was oblivious to the risk of the teetering glass. I did not know how that could be true. He said, "Somebody needs to say this out loud. I will be the one. I trust you, Alan. Do you trust me?"

Sam was asking a big question. I wanted to tell him I trusted him. I also wanted to be truthful. A frank answer would be nuanced. I feared the pace of our conversation, and the impact of the rye on my cognitive skills, meant I would get insufficient time to get the complexities aligned.

I was right. Sam huffed. "Well, that says a ton. Do you think I killed Big Elias?"

The new question took little contemplation. I said, "When I came over here tonight my intent was to be honest. My honest answer is I don't know if you killed him."

"Well, shit." Sam rescued the glass from his belly, drained the contents, dropped his flip-flopped feet to the floor, and put his elbows on his knees.

As relieved as I was about the glass, I was aggrieved that Sam couldn't understand my position. I said, "What? You're saying that if I read the events of that day a certain way, a certain reasonable way, that makes me a douche?"

Sam said, "No. Accusing me of murder makes you a douche. The way you read events? That makes you an amateur. I've been making allowances for you being an amateur since the day we met."

I was surprised at how little offense I took at that. I said, "Have you followed the case? Big Elias's death? In the press?"

"What? No. I have plenty of my own work. Do you know we have criminals in town that you haven't met?" I shrugged. He said, "Do you watch *Dr. Phil*?"

Point. "You don't know what the witness saw that evening?"

"I didn't know there was a witness." He poured himself more whiskey.

I wanted Sam to explain the white jumpsuit. The Tyvek. But I didn't want to be the one to tell him about it. I wanted him to admit he already knew. I wanted him to give me the explanation he'd already worked out, the lie he wanted me to believe.

He pulled out his phone. "Don't want to tell me? Fine. I can look up the damn article right now. Give me a minute. O has good WiFi."

Shit. He wasn't bluffing. I said, "A witness drove by. There was a second person at the horse trailer. The other person was wearing a white, hooded, one-piece jumpsuit."

Sam was no idiot. I would not have to draw him a map to my insinuation. He swallowed a gulp of whiskey. Then he said, "Could be a coincidence. Good Samaritan."

What I swallowed was the word *bullshit.*

Sam's voice took on a storytelling timbre. "Couple of years ago, I'm on the Mall to see somebody about a case and right in front of me a tourist punches a homeless man in the face. I knew the homeless guy.

461

He was an asshole. Antagonistic. Aggressive. Rude. The kind of homeless guy who gives the homeless guys on the Mall their bad rep.

"The tourist was a German who spoke good English, but what he kept saying to explain why he hit the homeless man was that the guy had 'earned it.' I was telling him that you're not allowed to hit somebody in America because he earned it. We went back and forth a couple of times. He finally resorts to German to make his point — he says something-something then *'backpfeifengesicht.'* "

Sam spelled out the word for me as though the correct spelling would make all the difference in the world. It didn't. "Which means?" I asked.

"Exactly." He made a whiskey face. "I'm getting there. His girlfriend — sweet thing — translated. Her English was like your daughter Sofie's. Perfect. She said that the homeless guy had insulted her and made crude sexual advances and then acted belligerent when her boyfriend stood up for her. And then she explained that the word — *backpfeifengesicht* — translated, very roughly, as 'his face was in need of a fist.' She scrunched her hand up into a cute little fist and showed it to me. You know, to help me understand.

"See? That's Big Elias. Backpfeifengesicht. An asshole going through life with a face in need of a fist. Am I sorry that it was a hoof instead of a fist? Not really."

As calmly as if he were checking hockey scores, Sam pulled up an article from *The Coloradoan* on his phone. He had to mount his reading glasses onto his nose to read the story. "You're exactly right," Sam said as he finished reading. "That's what the witness said. White hooded jumpsuit."

"And?"

"And you should drop this, Alan. Find a new hobby. Detecting doesn't suit you."

Sam's dismissive attitude wasn't unfamiliar. I usually succumbed to its pull, gave him what he wanted. Not that time. I forced the issue. "Did you?" I said. "Kill him?"

"Fuck you," Sam said. He spoke the words under his breath, not as though he didn't mean them, but as though it hurt him to say them. "Big Elias was an abusive prick who used people like he traded horses — his eye on nothing but the bottom line and what suited him best. He went through life without consequence. Horse, kid, family, neighbor. Didn't matter. The more I learned about him, the more I came to despise the old fuck. I stayed up late nights wondering how to get that child out of his house."

"Elias Tres?"

"Child protective services had given the old guy a lifetime pass. Why?" He shrugged. "Law enforcement had given the old shit a lifetime pass. Why? I was too much of an outsider to learn how or why he got so much deference in that town but I know it happens. I assume that half the skeletons in the asshole's closet were other people's skeletons. You know what I'm saying? There are jerks like him in Boulder who get away with all kinds of crap, too. It's almost always because they possess a stash of someone else's Kryptonite."

"I suspect you have a theory about the dirt he had."

"I do not. But I bet it's good. Unless Elias Contopo robbed the local bank at gunpoint on Friday afternoon while in drag, no one was going to do anything to him. That was a fact. The truth? Here's some truth for you: I am glad the man is dead."

"You're basically admitting that you had a motive to kill him, Sam."

"Motive? Nah. I had a rationale for wanting him dead. But a lot of people did. You talk to ten people who knew him, ten more who did business with him, you'll find nineteen didn't like him and five or six minimum who would load a gun if someone else would pull the trigger.

"What happened in the horse trailer that night? As far as I'm concerned that was someone else pulling the trigger. That's all."

The whiskey insisted I say what I was thinking. "You know what, Sam? I don't give a shit whether or not you have a rationale, I care that you have an alibi."

Sam laughed. His laugh was bitter and was supercharged by his blood alcohol level. Just like earlier I heard Emily bark her response to him.

"I don't owe you an alibi," Sam said.

"I beg to differ. Without that drawing I gave you in the ICU? I think your life would feel less contented right now." I was thinking the absence of oysters and Ophelia. The presence of lawyers and prison.

"You 'beg to differ'? That's hilarious. What, you want it back?"

I said, "You still have it? Really?" I assumed Tres's drawing was ashes.

Sam didn't answer. He had no reason to give the drawing back to me. He said, "The night the horses killed the old asshole, I was in a meeting here in town that lasted until seven thirty. Is that a good enough alibi for you?"

He drained his drink. He poured us each

another inch.

I did the arithmetic. Shy of a waiting helicopter there was no way that Sam could have gone from Boulder to north of Fort Collins in time to arrange a flat on Big Elias's horse trailer and then somehow prod the horses into crushing the old man to death. If Sam was in Boulder at seven thirty he didn't squeeze into that Tyvek jumpsuit on Tatonka Trail to kill Big Elias. The logistics didn't work.

I wondered if I had the dates wrong. Or if Sam did. But the real question was whether Sam was telling me the truth about his meeting in Boulder.

"With whom" — the correct grammar felt odd on my whiskeyed lips — "were you meeting?" I asked. My wandering mind immediately began to consider the most reasonable possibility — that Sam's "meeting" was a euphemism for him having an affair. Yet another affair. From my point of view, one more in a string of unlikely trysts. Women loved Sam. Sam lacked compunction. Over the years, I'd felt occasional envy about it all. I also felt a lot of bewilderment.

If it were true that Sam was straying again, what I was feeling in the moment was acute empathy for Ophelia. If it were true, then my best friend and my dead wife had a lot in common. Which meant that Ophelia and I had a lot in common.

I did not wish to have that in common with her.

"The meeting was with someone you know," Sam said. "Let's leave it there."

The words burned like he'd thrown his rye into my eyes. His casual admission forced me to imagine something — *ugh* — I really didn't want to be imagining: that the person Sam was *shtupping* was someone I knew, perhaps well.

Kirsten's repeated insistences that "I am seeing someone" seeped into my brain like floodwater coming in under the door. Along with the memory of the Upslope she had in her refrigerator . . . *Sam likes Upslope. Shit. No. Would you, Sam? Really?*

"No," I said. "Tell me who the meeting was with."

"No. You need to trust me," Sam said. "How about that?"

I belched. The burp was a digestive artifact of bao and beer and oysters and rye and was completely noneditorial in nature.

Sam's words were echoing in my head. *Trust me . . . trust me . . . trust me.*

I was feeling the same complicated feelings about trust that I'd had with Lauren in our final minutes together the morning before she was shot. The only unfamiliar part of the dialogue with Sam was that I was playing Lauren's role while Sam was playing mine.

Sam was not easily offended by the out-putting of bodily gases. But my belch had apparently crossed a line. He said, "That was gross." He waved his hand in front of his face. "Your situation these last few months? Jesus alive. Losing Lauren like that. Doing everything — everything — I've watched you do to hold on to those kids. To keep them afloat. To keep them together. To help them survive all this. It has . . . informed me, Alan." He put his huge hand on his chest with his fingers spread.

I was thinking, *You don't know half of it. And your sudden empathy isn't going to make me trust you.* I said, "I don't know what that means, Sam." My words were true, but mostly I was buying time while I plotted my escape so that I could be gone before he got to the part where he admitted the detail about him and Kirsten hooking up while Big Elias was being trampled to death by equines. *Jesus.*

"It means that, through observing your life, how you were living, I saw that I was at risk. That I could lose it all. In a second. I could lose real love. I am talking Ophelia.

Simon. *God.*" Probably due to the rye I couldn't tell whether the *God* was indicative of Sam's fear that he was losing his deity, or whether it was a simple invocation, or even an instance of him taking his Lord's name in vain. "I came to the conclusion that it was time to clean up my act. To stop being stupid. To stop seeing what I could get away with. To stop fucking around with what's important in my life.

"I needed to stop being a good man only when my good woman was looking, to stop being a good father only on those days that my son was under my roof. It was time for me to earn — *earn, damn it* — a reliable spot in the hearts of the people I treasure. And to find a way to go to bed each night confident in my heart that I had earned that spot in their hearts again that very day.

"I had to cherish what I had — what I loved — enough not to fuck it up."

Speaking seemed stupid. I wasn't being smart, but I wasn't quite stupid. I could also feel the element that was trust worming its way back onto my personal periodic table.

During his soliloquy Sam had been looking in the direction of the start-of-night silhouette of the Front Range, the jagged ragged form of intersecting purple ridges backlit by the lingering light of the half-moon that had already disappeared into tomorrow.

He turned his head to look at me. "The meeting I was at that night? The night Gordo Elias died? I was with my therapist, Alan. My goddamn psycho" — pause — "therapist."

I opened my mouth. He said, "Don't. I'm not done." I closed my mouth.

"I am in psychotherapy trying to learn how to be trustworthy. I am in psychotherapy trying to learn how not to screw things up with Ophelia. I am trying to learn how to not screw things up with my son. And his mother. I am trying to learn how to not screw things with my partner. And, no, not that kind of partner.

"I am trying to learn how to not screw things up with my friend.

"I don't want to screw up ever again in a way that might lead me to fear prison. I am in therapy to make sure I stay out of prison *this* time." He blinked. "That's where I was the night Big Elias died. I was at a friggin' psychotherapy appointment. Happy?" Sam slammed back his drink and poured another.

We were quiet for a good while. I wasn't confident that the interlude was about Sam offering me permission or opportunity to respond. I didn't respond.

I thought the evening might end where it was.

But Sam said, "I am trying to learn how not to be a self-interested prick like Big Elias Contopo. I don't want to die being crushed to death by horses. If you know what I mean." I didn't. "And I don't want to die thinking that most of the people who knew me well would be saying 'good riddance.'"

"You're nothing like Big Elias. You are —"

My phone began to vibrate before I completed the sentence. I bet it was Amy; it felt like her knack for timing. But it could have been one of the kids. I had to look. I checked the screen. Sam had guessed already. He said, "The fucking beguiler?"

"Yep. The fucking beguiler," I said.

I held out the phone so he could see the text. It was a seconds-old photo of Amy and another woman beside an outdoor fire at the Little Nell. Small table. Big smiles. A few empties.

Sam said, "She's a damn ten. I don't remember her being that hot the last time I saw her."

I could have reminded Sam that Amy was unconscious the last time he saw her. Most

471

of us yield an involuntary point or two on the ten-scale during unconsciousness.

"Did you sleep with her?" he asked me. "That night in Tarzana?"

It wasn't a prurient query. Well, not only a prurient query. I knew why he was asking. My mind was busy making connections the way my mind does. Sam had just called Amy a ten. I recalled that he'd once described Raoul as a ten. I couldn't remember anyone else of either gender that had ever earned that designation from my friend. Wait. Maybe Gibbs Storey, an ex-patient of mine. Sam had most definitely been infatuated with her.

I said, "She crawled into my bed. Naked. I came *this* close." I pinched the tip of my index finger and the pad of my thumb together. "But I did not sleep with her."

Sam lowered his voice. He made it so low that even through the tin walls of the cheap doublewide an eavesdropping Ophelia could not have heard his whisper. He said, "That night in the Valley?" He took a deep breath before he went on, his eyes on the photo on my phone. "If *that* woman had crawled into my bed naked? The honest-to-God truth? I would have said 'fuck it.' And then I would have." He sighed. "Fucked it.

"And that is why I am in therapy, Alan. I

472

can't be that guy anymore. I can't be the guy that people can't know when to trust."

"... *when to trust.*"

When to trust. Oh my God, I thought. *Oh my God.*

I didn't recall getting to my feet.

I didn't recall stepping from the deck, or walking, or running, toward my house.

But I was far from the doublewide, literally as well as figuratively, when I heard Sam call out, "Alan, are you okay? Alan? Alan? Are you sick?"

51

I had been remembering that morning incorrectly.

Incompletely would be more accurate.

The ego defense at work? Suppression. Or denial. Maybe denial and suppression in consort. Or perhaps it wasn't an ego defense at all. Maybe I just forgot what Lauren said. That can happen, too. During times of acute stress especially.

That morning had been a time of acute stress. Especially.

That morning, after she heard my belated admission that I had neither informed her that Sam had murdered the woman in Frederick nor that I had been involved after the fact, I had heard Lauren say, "You should have trusted me."

Those words — *you should have trusted me* — admonished me. They hurt me. I had replayed the memory a hundred or a thousand times. Not once had I not felt the sting of her cryptic appraisal of my failure to trust her.

But that was not the entirety of what she said in that sentence. It was only the part that I had been able to remember. Sam's words — *when to trust* — triggered my recall of the remainder.

Lauren had also included a preface to her rebuke, a contextual phrase. A *limiting* phrase. A phrase that, for me, changed almost everything.

The complete sentence she uttered that morning was, "About this, you should have trusted me." *About this . . .*

When Sam said *I can't be the guy that people can't know when to trust* I finally remembered Lauren's qualifying phrase. Standing alone on the lane, in the dark, I recast the entire moment in my memory. Lauren's *about this* had been obscured. But remembering it allowed the totality of what Lauren was telling me that morning to become as clear as the purple in her luminous eyes.

Drunk and bewildered, vertiginous from alcohol and unsettling truth, I replayed the recovered moment and I replayed it and I replayed it. Testing it for accuracy. But not a frame changed, not a syllable was altered with the replays. My memory was clear. I could see the moment in its entirety. My eyes had been on Lauren's face, on her lips, as they formed the two words that changed everything.

Lauren had said, "*About this,* you should have trusted me."

From that morning until the instant on Ophelia's deck — after the spicy rye, the icy Kumamotos, the white Tyvek on Tatonka Trail, the death-defying legends of Ivy Baldwin, and after Sam's admission about what he needed to do in psychotherapy — I had been living in the fog of Lauren's reproach. I had been blinded by her admonishment about not trusting her. In my world I had been hearing the echoes of Lauren's nearly final words as her last measure of her disappointment in me.

By the end — of her life, of our marriage — I was predisposed to hear her words as admonishments. I knew that was mostly on me, not on her. But that morning, I'd heard her tell me that the failure to trust — *you should have trusted me* — had been mine. I'd survived that morning's trauma believing that our failure as a couple was about my failure to trust her.

Since the original sin had been mine, the secondary sin had to be mine, too. Venial mine. Mortal mine. The sins of our marriage, all mine.

But with the refreshed memory and the two new words I realized that my wife wasn't only expressing her disappointment that I had not trusted her, she was also making a clear admission to me that she had not been deserving of my trust about something else.

With the fresh memory I felt myself on a knife's edge, aware of a certain yin/yang synchronicity that was — finally — a balancing of what had always felt unbalanced. For us.

Us.

52

Lauren and I had not been a couple certain we would marry.

We embraced the certainty of our uncertainty. It made everything more tender for us as we approached "I do."

I didn't recognize it then — it didn't come into focus until after her death — but our mutual reticence about marrying was a marriage of our individual reticences.

I never considered that our reticence was due to a lack of love. I didn't doubt her love. I would find it hard to believe she doubted mine. So what was the doubt?

Lauren was reticent about us — the future married *us* — because she didn't feel she was good enough for me. *Her childhood? Her divorce? Her illness?* I never understood the genesis. But her self-doubt dined with us at almost every meal, slept with us almost every night, and joined us for occasional threesomes in the marital bed.

I too was reticent about us — the future married *us* — because I feared that I wasn't good enough for her. *Was that because of the secrets I'd kept? Or the hidden damage from keeping them?* My doubts double-dated with Lauren's doubts long before we said our "I do's" and long after.

Together, though? We moved forward. Sometimes well. Sometimes not. We proceeded as though our reticences balanced us. That crazy yin/yang thing.

Amid all the shared reticence, though, I felt there existed a persistent verity about how we perceived our personal failings in the marriage.

About this . . . you should have trusted me. My suppression of the *about this* from my memory of that last morning illuminated that stubborn truth about our respective character differences in a way that permitted me to see something I had not previously been able to recognize.

My half-drunken insight was this: Lauren had spent our marriage trying to prove that her thesis — that she wasn't good enough for me — was *right.* That is what Joost — her echo tryst in Holland — had been about. That is what Raoul — and the Louboutins and the back-seam silk stockings — was about.

My goal had always been different. I woke each morning of our marriage determined to prove that my thesis — that I wasn't good enough for her — was *wrong.* I was intent on proving the antithetical hypothesis that I was good enough for her.

That is what my restraint with Amy, the fucking beguiler, had been about. And the same for a woman named Ottavia who'd offered me a holiday from my vows. And that is what my resistance to the temptations of Sawyer — a prodigal ex — had been about.

Was Lauren's affair with Raoul chicken, or was it egg? Was it Lauren's failing, or was it her response to her perception of my failing? I didn't know. Perhaps if I had paid more attention to our reticence at the beginning, and in the middle, I would have been able to muster more clarity about our foggy end.

The irony that slapped at me in the dark, on the lane? Lauren and I had each always wanted to be right. And that morning, the morning of the beginning of our end, we were somehow both right.

My original fear — that I wasn't good enough for her — was proven correct. I had failed her in myriad ways. In the many days since that morning I had come to believe that she needed and wanted me to fail her.

How was Lauren right? Her original fear — that she wasn't good enough for me — was proven correct, too. I tried to convince myself that the reason she ended up not good enough was because of her weakness. I wanted to believe that Joost, and Raoul, and maybe unknown and unnumbered other men who might have shared her bed, were all evidence she was accumulating so that she could prosecute her own failings.

I was even tempted to seek craven comfort by wrapping myself in the horsehair of that conclusion. But I knew any comfort would be illusory. Or just bullshit.

Why was that true? Because I wasn't a better spouse than Lauren. She wasn't a worse spouse than I was. We had entered into the marital equation with different proofs to solve. As a couple we never confronted those differences. We didn't let our doubts bring us together. The doubts divided us before they split us.

In the end we failed together.

One of the stray facts rattling in my brain from Sam's telling of the legend of Ivy Baldwin was that Ivy had called his act on the high wire the "greatest poison in the world. One drop could kill you."

That felt right to me. That was the balance of the unbalanced. That had been my marriage.

Sam's voice intruded. He wanted to know if I was all right. I spotted headlights from the north. A car coming. I held my breath, waiting for the shape of the vehicle to emerge from the dark. I was thinking Carl Luppo.

The approaching headlights blinded me and focused me.

Lauren? That I can rationalize why you've hurt me and betrayed me doesn't change a thing. So fuck you anyway.

I looked over my shoulder at Sam.

I want to believe you about not killing Big Elias. And about being in therapy. But I don't. Wishing won't make that true.

I turned away from him.

I didn't tell Sam I was okay.

The night I had planned was, after all, about the truth.

53

The car was Kirsten's. I waited on the steps of the front porch as she killed the engine. To my right, up the lane, Sam stood on the deck of the doublewide, his arms folded across his chest the way big men cross their arms. Not quite all the way.

Were I in Sam's position on Ophelia's deck observing Kirsten's arrival — were I cognizant, as Sam was, of the texts from the fucking beguiler in Aspen — I might have been sorting prurient assumptions about late-night booty calls and alcohol-impaired judgment.

In fact, if my earlier suppositions about the object of Sam's affections were true, Sam might also have been wondering what the hell his current secondary squeeze was doing within steps of his primary squeeze's insubstantial front door so late at night.

Sam appeared to be wavering — as in going back and forth in a horizontal plane in my less-than-rock-solid vision — but I was nearly certain that if Sam thought Kirsten's arrival had carnal implications, at least for me, he was in error. Hers was no booty call.

The right conclusion? I would discover that soon enough.

She exited her car without even a cursory glance toward Sam. He retrieved the platter with the oyster shells and carried it inside the doublewide.

Kirsten sat next to me on the cedar stoop. "You're up," she said. Pause. "And you've been drinking."

"Does a man good on occasion."

"This was one of those occasions?"

"Had a heart-to-heart with a friend. Did some thinking, too."

"Boy friend or girl friend?"

I thought that an interesting question. "Boy."

"Thinking was about Lauren?"

"How did you know?"

"I've been there, Alan. I was widowed the way you were widowed. I know what it's like, after. I know about the reruns. The over and over and overs. That's what my daughter used to call my ruminations. My what-ifs. The over and over and overs."

"Yeah," I said. "I was doing some of that."

"I knew Lauren, too," Kirsten said. "Don't

pretend. You knew she was unhappy. Not just with you. You can't go back and change that."

It wasn't a question. I said, "Yeah."

"Your over and over and over is what? That Lauren was unhappy with you?"

"She was."

"Maybe. Even assuredly. But that wasn't all. Lauren was unhappy with her life. That she'd failed to maximize her opportunities. By her illness, by fate, by choices she made. You couldn't fix that."

I didn't know what to say. I felt like I should argue the point. To defend a woman for whom I felt fury. And love. But my heart wasn't in the debate.

In that moment I needed Lauren to stay buried. So that my rage could stay buried, too.

"She may have wanted you to fix all that. But she knew you couldn't. And" — Kirsten leaned forward until I looked at her eyes — "she knew she wouldn't let you try."

"I did try."

She touched my knee. "That's marriage," Kirsten said. "That's love."

"She let other men try, too."

"She let other men comfort her. Distract her."

Pleasure her. I sighed.

I hoped Kirsten was upwind; my sigh tasted of bivalves and whiskey.

Kirsten said, "That was Sam over there by that trailer?"

"He's become attached to the woman who bought the property after the house fire. It's temporary, I think. The trailer, not their relationship." I watched Kirsten's eyes for shimmers of dismay at the news of Sam's attachment. I saw nothing. She either had a therapist face — one that could go all–Mount Rushmore in reaction to surprising news — or I had rye-impaired vision. Or the fact that Sam had a girlfriend wasn't news to her.

Or meant nothing to her. I was sober enough to recognize that I was drunk enough not to be at my discerning best.

She said, "I didn't want to have this conversation on the phone. Nor did I think it prudent to wait." She paused. "Since you have your meeting in Denver tomorrow. I'm in a position to save you and your new lawyer some important hours and days."

"I understand." I didn't understand but indicating that we were on the same page seemed an agreeable thing to do. I had to come to terms with the rage. It felt raw. I would need to spend a few sleepless nights with the anger to see if I could tame it.

Kirsten asked, "You haven't read the contents of the Elliot envelope?"

Oh, that's what this is about. "No. I remain reluctant."

She leaned forward again. She pulled my chin toward her so that our eyes met. I guessed she was assessing my sobriety. She said, "I did read the pages."

My brain was soft from the whiskey and distracted by the view of my marriage I had in my rearview mirror, but I had enough mental wattage to perceive that Kirsten was sketching out new dots for me to connect.

"I figured that's why you came." I hadn't figured that but it seemed like another agreeable thing to say. "The pages? You deemed them worthy" — I found *deemed them worthy* quite difficult to enunciate — "of a drive across town late at night?"

"I did." She glanced in the direction of the doublewide. "Can we go in?"

We went in. The dogs did their greeting thing before I led Kirsten to the bar stools at the kitchen counter. "No," she said. She took my hand and tugged me toward the sofa that was perched in just the right location in the family room so that it seemed to float above the twinkling carpet of Boulder Valley like an infinity pool. From prior drunk experience I knew that if I put my bare feet on the coffee table in just the right spot I could divide up the urban street grid with my toes.

I considered sharing that fact with Kirsten, but recognized that another time would be better. In that consideration and that decision I saw evidence that I was more inebriated than I thought and that I was less inebriated than I thought.

I sat first. She sat beside me, one knee pulled up so that she could face me. She said, "Lauren was collecting information about Elliot. Had been for years. She seemed interested in why he planted his flag in Boulder. Do you know what that was about?"

I nodded. "She and I had discussed that forever," I said. "The question of why he came to Boulder was a parlor game for us. Why did Elliot — a guy who was Harvard squared — choose the Boulder DA's office?"

"Harvard squared?"

"Harvard Harvard. Undergrad and law? Harvard Square? Harvard squared?"

She didn't get it. She asked me if it was important. I kind of thought it was, but I said it wasn't. I was still being agreeable.

"Lauren was thorough. She found some of his old Harvard Law academic records.

Had spoken with a few of his classmates. She even had a copy of the application materials he sent to the firm he summered with when he was a 2L."

I admitted that I didn't know what the last part meant.

Kirsten shook her head. "Elliot was a top student at Harvard Law. Top ten percent easy, maybe top five. He made Law Review. Didn't try for the editorial board. He summered at a Vault top-five firm in New York City after his second year. He had a clear shot at a clerkship with a feeder judge in the Ninth Circuit Court of Appeals, but he took a lesser clerkship in the First Circuit instead. Did she ever say why he passed on clerking for a feeder judge? It's not in her notes."

Lauren had taught me how to identify the rungs of the legal ladder that ambitious law students have to climb. Elliot Bellhaven had scampered up near the very top of the ladder. Feeder judges are the ones whose clerks have a chance to end up working at the Supreme Court.

"She didn't," I said. I was thinking, *I need to tell Sam all this. He's been wondering.*

It was not until I thought about telling Sam about Elliot's legal heritage that I recognized that whatever Sam wanted to know about Elliot, and why he wanted to know it, might have something to do with whatever Lauren had been investigating about Elliot, and why she wanted to know it. The Venn diagram of our mutual interests had some overlap. Were I sober I would have had a reasonable chance of making sense of that overlap. Having consumed all that rye, my chances were a mite lower.

Kirsten's rendition of Lauren's research findings didn't provide an answer to the underlying question my wife and I had puzzled about over the years — why Elliot chose Boulder. Lauren's discoveries only eliminated the possibility that Elliot chose Boulder because he lacked options.

I said, "Elliot was a big deal in law school. Yes?" Kirsten nodded. Without apparent segue I said, "Where's the First Circuit?" I could tell that my question had been off by a few degrees; I'd asked her about the home of the First Circuit in a voice that approximated that of a game-show host announcing that we were starting the final round.

Kirsten smiled. She said, "Kids are asleep, shhh. It's in Boston."

My phone vibrated. Kirsten heard the buzz. "Boston," I said. "Text."

"Sam?" she asked. I thought it an interesting guess. Was she accustomed to late-night texts from Sam?

"Probably," I said. But I was thinking LA Amy.

"You're not going to check?"

"The kids are here. This is more important," I said. "I don't know how much effort Lauren put into her investigation, but what you told me should be in Elliot's CV."

"Lauren was trying to confirm that his CV was accurate. Curriculum vitae should be nonfiction but sometimes they're short stories. She didn't trust his."

"That sounds like her," I said. I recognized the risk I ran getting lost musing about Lauren and trust.

"In the same envelope is evidence that feels unrelated to the history of Elliot's background. Lauren was also looking into the possibility that Elliot had interfered with a criminal investigation soon after he arrived in town. Do you know anything about that?"

It rang no bell. "I don't. She never said anything. I would remember." I recognized that my declarative sentences were getting brusque. I was distracted by my own staccato rhythm.

"Do you know anything about Elliot and 9/11?"

491

"In 2001? I do not. I thought he was living here by then."

"He was. Did she ever say anything about Elliot and a suspicious death in a house near Eldorado Springs?"

"A long time ago, she'd talked about a death in Eldorado. A psychologist, whether I knew him. Elliot's involvement? No."

Did I think it odd that I was having my second conversation of the evening about Eldorado Springs? I did. But my mind was drifting. I was thinking that the flesh on Kirsten's neck was as smooth as corn silk. I was fighting ancillary impulses: To ask Kirsten if she had heard the stories about Ivy Baldwin and his high wire. Or if she enjoyed Kumamotos.

54

"You told me earlier tonight, at my house, that you were hoping for some leverage with Elliot? These papers may be your leverage, Alan."

"The ones in the envelope for Elliot?"

"Perhaps the envelope was *for* Elliot. If it was, it was a peace offering on Lauren's part. A gift, really. I don't think it was for Elliot. The contents are about him, but I think the envelope was intended for someone else. A colleague maybe, or you.

"What's most curious to me is Lauren's long obsession with that suspicious death in Eldorado. She's been looking at it, on and off, for years. She was sure that Elliot knew the man who died. Yet he never came forward with that information."

I said, "You mentioned 9/11. How is that part of this?"

"Are you sober enough for this conversation, Alan?" I was betting that she, too, had recognized that my sentences were getting less complex.

"I'm not as drunk as I might seem."

Kirsten laughed kindly. No drunk person could speak the line I had just spoken with any credibility. And no sober person would say it.

She went to the kitchen. I checked the text on my phone. It was a photo of LA Amy's bed in the Little Nell with the crisp sheets pulled back on both sides in neat triangles. An orange bra was draped across one of the pillows. I did not think the bra had been part of the turndown service. I checked the texting chain to be certain I had already said no to Amy.

I had. I told myself that was good. I told myself that again.

Kirsten returned with two glasses of water. I took a sip. She sat closer to me with both legs folded beneath her on the cushion. She took one of my hands in hers. "You ready for more?"

I was distracted by her hands, and by the orange bra. "I'm ready." I didn't know if I was ready.

"Lauren was assigned to the suspicious death investigation in Eldorado Springs on September fourteenth, 2001, three days after the 9/11 attacks. The victim was that

494

young psychologist — a twenty-nine-year-old male. He had died three days before. His body —"

"Marshall Doctor. He lived on Prado."

I couldn't interpret her expression. She said, "I don't know what Prado is."

"The road to Eldorado? Parallel to it, there are some great homes and lots that are adjacent to the open space? That street is Prado."

She shrugged. Apparently Kirsten wasn't a real-estate slut. She asked me if I had known the psychologist who died.

"He was new in town. We hadn't met."

"His body had been scavenged by animals. Raccoons, maybe even a coyote, entered the property through a doggie door. It was ugly. GSR was equivocal, mostly due to the animals getting at the flesh. The ME listed cause of death as gunshot wound of the head. Although he thought that the wound was self-inflicted, he left manner as undetermined because of the absence of a weapon at the scene."

"Suicide by gunshot, but no gun? Problem."

"Exactly. The ME estimated the time of death as being between six P.M. on September tenth and noon on September eleventh. That's a wide window, by the way. Lauren blamed that on 9/11."

"Where was the gun?"

"Never determined. The most entertaining theory had to do with a well-armed raccoon, but Lauren wasn't a proponent of the raccoon theory. It didn't matter. The morning after she was assigned to the case the chief trial deputy reassigned it to himself."

That got my attention. "The chief deputy put himself on a suspicious suicide involving a raccoon?" I knew well how deputies were assigned what work in the DA's office. "No way. The chief deputy wouldn't take that case. That week? Jesus. It was nuts for Lauren. Everyone was seeing potential terrorists and terrorist targets everywhere. The deputy DAs were running all over the county guiding investigations into this threat or that threat. Trying to get cops to remember due process and civil liberties. It was crazy."

"Lauren felt the same way. She didn't understand why she was reassigned. But like everybody else, she had work up to her ears. I was still prosecuting in New Orleans that week. We saw bogeymen everywhere. I'm sure it was the same here.

"The original detective on the case was Sam Purdy, but he was reassigned, too. Sam thought the evidence at the scene added up to suicide, but the missing gun was a major problem with his theory. When Lauren went back over the file later, she thought Sam missed some crucial facts about the deceased."

"Wait. Why did she go back to the file later? Why did Lauren care?"

"Her notes indicate that Elliot approached her later that fall with questions about the investigation. That got her interested again."

"What did Sam miss?"

She squeezed my hand. "The deceased was gay. And —"

"That's important? That he was gay?"

"Lauren thought so. He wasn't out of the closet. Had only one sexual partner."

"Okay." I wasn't convinced. The increased suicide risk for gay adolescents tends to disappear as they enter adulthood, though closeted gays have a slightly elevated risk. I told myself to recheck that data.

"The second thing Sam missed was that the deceased knew Elliot."

"Knew? Met at a party? Or had sex with?" I said.

Kirsten laughed. "Those are my only two options? Lauren thought Elliot was the one sex partner. In 2007, while she was in Knoxville for a conference, she talked to the roommate of the man who died in Eldorado. He confirmed they all knew one another. He told Lauren about his roommate and Elliot hooking up."

"Is the guy in Knoxville gay, too?"

"Lauren concluded there was a triangle. Romantically, not sexually."

"Lauren considered the roommate reliable? Not a suspect?"

"He'd been visiting family on the Big Island in Hawaii, was traveling back to Boulder on 9/11. He had a morning flight to Oahu, got trapped in Honolulu for days when aviation was shut down. Good alibi. Good detail. Told her a story about his dog being stuck in a kennel for all that time because his roommate didn't like the dog. She couldn't see why he would lie to her about it."

"Was Elliot a suspect in the death?"

"Not at all. Elliot was caught out of town by the eleventh, too. He had been in Boston since the previous Friday, was on his way back to Denver from Logan on an early flight. On a normal Tuesday he would have been landing at DIA shortly after eleven, been back in Boulder after noon.

"But it wasn't a normal day. Elliot's plane was in the air when the towers were hit. The plane landed in Indianapolis. He drove back in a Ryder truck. Got here on the fourteenth. Lauren has airline records. Truck rental receipts."

Kirsten was hoping that I would see a big picture I wasn't seeing. My mind was wandering as it pondered all the gaps in lives that occurred when all those planes landed in all those wrong places. All those interrupted lives. When that many plans are short-circuited all at once there had to have been stunning consequences all over the globe. Then a bell went off. I closed my eyes tightly the way Gracie did after I had prodded her into tasting something unfamiliar that she was certain would prove toxic.

"I got it. Elliot was still in the closet then."

"Lauren's notes say he was, but that's not the relevant piece of the puzzle."

"Damn," I said. I was sure that was it. I wanted that to be it.

"The first thing Elliot did after he got back to Boulder on September fourteenth? Lauren thinks he drove to the house in Eldorado. The very first thing, even before he turned in the damn rental truck and went back to the airport to get his car. She went so far as to track down the time he returned the truck. It wasn't until late that afternoon. Why would Elliot feel such urgency to get to Eldorado?"

I was impressed by my wife's diligence.

"Did she think Elliot knew about the shooting?" I said.

"Lauren's theory was that Elliot and the man who died in Eldorado had talked while Elliot was in Boston. She thought that Elliot knew he was depressed, even suicidal. Angry at Elliot? Possibly. After the planes were diverted, Elliot wasn't able to reach him. Got worried. That's why he went over to check on him as soon as he got back to town."

"Okay. A guy Elliot liked was depressed? He wanted to check on him." It appeared to me to be a circumstance without consequence. "I don't see any crimes."

"Lauren was discovering pieces that didn't make sense to her. It's not a complete story. If she had reached a conclusion she would have dealt with this herself."

"The pieces that didn't make sense?"

"Mostly Elliot's continued interest. One theory was that Elliot was the RP. The original report was an anonymous 911 call from a pay phone at the King Soopers at Broadway and Table Mesa just after two o'clock in the afternoon on the fourteenth. A male."

Either I was getting sober quickly, or I was deceiving myself about my sobriety more effectively. The timeline fit. The supermarket wasn't far from Eldorado, and it was on the only route between Prado and downtown Boulder, where Elliot lived. I said, "King Soopers must have had security tape. What did it show? Who made the 911 call?"

"When Lauren went back to examine the file later that first year, she couldn't find any record that anyone ever asked King Soopers for the security footage."

"Sam's a good cop, Kirsten. He would have asked." *But it was the week of 9/11.*

"Sam was ordered off the investigation almost immediately. He may not have had a chance. We have to remind ourselves what 9/11 was like. Nothing was normal."

"I admit I'm confused. I don't understand why Elliot would call in the dead body anonymously. What was the risk to him? He had the alibi of the century."

He'd had an interrupted life.

"Exactly," she said. "That's what Lauren couldn't get her arms around. People in the office already suspected Elliot was gay. She didn't think that would be an issue. Even if Elliot had been involved with the guy who died, so what? Elliot was unattached. No big deal. She was sure there was another piece to the puzzle."

"Did she think Elliot had anything to do

with removing the weapon before he called 911?"

"Crime scene techs did not think that a human had compromised the scene. Just animals."

"It is a puzzle," I said.

Kirsten leaned into me then as though she was too exhausted to remain vertical. I felt the weight of her head on my shoulder. I smelled her hair.

I said, "Why was Elliot in Boston?"

Kirsten murmured that she didn't know.

I began to smell mercaptan.

I started wondering if Sam had really missed Elliot's involvement in the death in Eldorado. Or if, maybe, he had been complicit in ignoring it.

Or even covering it up.

Does Elliot owe Sam a favor? A big favor? Jesus.

It could turn out that my clean hands were of no consequence after all.

55

Grace woke me the next morning by poking me on my cheek. I opened my eyes to discover that I was on my side on the edge of the sofa facing the family room windows. From a mental-status perspective I was not well oriented. My head hurt. A lot. I had whiskey and oyster breath that had aged overnight in a warm, moist cavern.

There was not a remotely pleasant thing about that.

I felt the pressure of a body behind me. Not in a spoons position, but a butt against my butt. Heels of feet against soles of feet.

Uh-oh. I felt instant trepidation that I couldn't identify everyone on the sofa.

Grace had her hands on her hips and her shoulders were rolled forward. It was a posture that made her look about thirty. In my experience with my daughter that was never a good sign.

I glanced down. I had clothing on. That

was the first good news of the day.

In my woken-up-by-a-poke-in-the-cheek fog, with my head pulsating from the tympanic consequences of my night before, I wasn't sure whom I was going to see behind me. Seared on my corneas was an image of an orange lace bra on a crisp white pillowcase. Candidates? *LA Amy. Kirsten . . .*

I was worried I might be forgetting someone. I glanced over my shoulder.

The person behind me was Kirsten. She was clothed. And the clothing she was wearing was her own. That was all good news.

Kirsten stirred. One second, two. And then, a mumbled, "Oh shit. Oh . . . shit."

I didn't know if she was cursing at the circumstances. Or perhaps she was cursing because this could be a most compromising situation regardless of the circumstances because she was, after all, seeing someone.

Grace wasn't concerned with such grown-up questions. She saw profit to be made. "That's two bucks for the cuss bucket." She stomped her foot once before shuffling away.

I mumbled that I would pay Kirsten's fines. It was the least I could do.

Twenty minutes later Kirsten had been gone for eighteen minutes. I had already reread the texting histories on both my phones to be certain I had been lucid with LA Amy. The photo of the orange bra troubled me. I had no context for that.

I was worried I had missed something.

I showered. I went to the kitchen. The day was starting for my family.

In one hand Grace held a waffle she'd toasted and slathered with peanut butter. In the other hand she held a banana, half peeled, a quarter consumed. She continued to appear to be some multiple of her actual age.

I knew I continued to be at a significant disadvantage.

Grace chose that moment to ask if she could have some coffee. The timing of her request — oft made, always rejected — I had to admit, was excellent.

I told her "No" in the most indulgent tone I could manufacture. She scowled.

I was determined to keep my head down and to avoid confrontation.

Jonas ambled into the kitchen appearing as oblivious as any other morning.

He sat down, poured milk onto his cereal, and surrounded the bowl with both arms as though he were protecting it against an assault from cavalry on his flanks. He began shoveling food as he read a graphic novel.

If I were an involved parent I would have asked him what the novel was. If I were an involved parent, I might even have already read it myself.

Lately I had not been an involved parent. I had faint memories of the night before and Sam's drunken promises about being a better father to his kid.

In between the third and fourth mouthfuls — and well before any measurable chewing had occurred — Jonas looked up, right at me.

I froze.

He said, "So what was last night about?"

I was not actually in a position that I could admonish him about speaking with his mouth full.

56

I got the kids to school.

As I dressed for my Denver meeting I tried to calculate a way I could scrape together a sum of money that might constitute a respectable retainer. *Respectable* being the minimum amount that would transform my new attorney's cursory interest in my legal problems into a level of concern that approximated my interest in my legal problems. I didn't see a way that I would swell the dollars into an enticing five-figure number without either selling some major assets on eBay or convincing one of Lauren's life insurance carriers to write an insurance benefit check sooner than it intended.

No probate judge would permit me to start selling property I owned jointly with Lauren. The life insurance companies? They didn't care what I wanted. The moment they heard the growing whispers that the

DA considered me a potential suspect in my wife's death was the moment their pay-out departments would completely forget how to write checks.

I planned to pick up 36 in Superior to get to Denver, thirty or forty minutes away. I was in sight of the on ramp when my phone rang. A quick glance told me it was my new lawyer. I pulled to the shoulder before I took the call.

It was actually my new lawyer's assistant. The lawyer's sixteen-year-old daughter had just taken a lacrosse ball to her eye socket in her algebra class. I told the assistant I could, unfortunately, see that happening. She laughed and said she could, too. My lawyer was on his way to the emergency department at the Children's Hospital. The assistant was eager for me to convince her that my legal jeopardy would remain sub-acute for the next few hours until she could get back to me about rescheduling.

I said it would, though I had no idea if it would.

I took stock of my circumstances.

I was dressed well. I was heading, roughly, out of town. My calendar was free. I saw a chance to begin to move the needle on the meter that was measuring whether or not I could trust Sam Purdy.

I powered off my phone. The tracker. I booted up my burner. I imagined that on some screen, somewhere, I disappeared from the digital view of someone's prying eyes. The moment felt empowering. I didn't even bother to consider what it said about my paranoia.

That RV had departed the campground.

I phoned Izza Kane from my burner.

"We should talk some more," I said after I identified myself.

"About what?" she said with defiance — or maybe defensiveness — in her voice.

"Espíritu," I said. The connection went silent. I thought the call had dropped. My cheap burner probably wasn't cutting-edge cellular technology. "Izza?"

"I'm here. I don't know what that means. Espíritu."

"I think you do, but if you need some reminding, I will do that for you." I could hear her short breaths. "You pick the place."

"It has to be now?"

"Only if you wish to be the first one to hear what I have to say about espíritu."

"I'm in Frederick." I was relieved that she wasn't in Greeley.

"Frederick is fine. Thirty minutes? The cottage?"

509

"I have new tenants in the cottage. Two women. They are great. My new favorites. Please don't get them killed." I coughed to disguise the choking sound I made. "Come to the house. I live there now."

57

SAM AND LUCY

Sam Purdy didn't look up from his desk. He knew the cadence of Lucy's approaching footsteps like he knew the scent of his mother's bath soap.

Lucy said, "You look like shit."

The clock said seven thirty. "Alan got me drunk last night. Whiskey. I'm in pain. It's too early. Way too early."

Lucy said. "Early? I've been up since three thinking about the bungee. Are you too hungover to talk about it? I keep going back to why Doctor Doctor wanted the gun to disappear. What was he trying to accomplish? I can't make sense of it. After all this time, I still don't get it."

Sam said, "I know. But I don't know. He may have been screwing with us, the cops. Or he may have been hoping to leave doubt that it was suicide so we would point fingers at somebody for killing him. If his intent was to mess with us, it worked. Look at you and me, a decade later, still doing somersaults about the damn disappearing gun. I don't know. The bungee makes me crazy."

Lucy sat. "I finally got that death certificate from Iowa. The woman who owned the gun in the chimney? I've been dueling with a brand-new county clerk who is deplorably ignorant about how the world works. I was thinking about taking a day off to drive to Iowa and threaten to shoot her if she didn't give it to me."

Sam smiled at the image. He said, "I thought we already had that."

"No, we had it verbally. This has been dragging. It's the last document."

Lucy was trying to pull reading glasses out of the tangle of hair she had pinned on top of her head. It became a process. Sam began losing interest. "Anything?"

He waited while Lucy situated the frames near the end of her nose. She missed with the first attempt, as though she didn't know where the end of her nose was. Sam passed on the obvious opportunity for ridicule because he couldn't recall even knowing that his partner wore reading glasses. He hoped the development was recent, that he hadn't missed it for, like, months.

Lucy said, "Cancer, like we thought. And

1993, like we thought. You want to see it?"
She knew he did. He always did. She slid
the paper across his desk.

He glanced at the name on the death
certificate. "Beulah Baxter," he said aloud.
"She of the shoplifted fancy panties, if my
memory serves me well."

Sam spotted the anomaly in the second
line. His eyes went wide.

Lucy had seen the same expression on
Sam's face often enough to know something
important was coming. "What? Does Beulah Baxter suddenly ring a bell for you?"

"Is the gun registration in that file?"

Lucy dug the form from the folder. She
examined it before she handed it to Sam.
"What?" she asked. "You've already seen
this."

"Baxter's her married name. That's what's
on the gun registration. That was our problem."

"Why was it our problem?"

"Look at the maiden name on the death
certificate." Sam handed it to Lucy.

She read. She closed her eyes. She opened
them and read it again. "No. Well. But . . .
so what? Is he even from Iowa?"

"He doesn't have to be from Iowa. He just
had to have a relative named Beulah who
lived in Iowa. He was living in Boulder on

9/11. You already told me that. And you said his name showed up in the case file. I'm remembering all that right?"

"Yes. He was here. He was a new baby deputy." The composition of the DA's office was a slice of civic history she knew well. "And his name is in the case file — he was in the deceased's address book. The old made-out-of-paper kind of address book. This death certificate means his family name is in the case file twice. Twice, Sam."

Sam was allowing his doubts to sprout. "May not mean anything. There are thousands of people out there with that last name."

Lucy and Sam knew their assigned roles when the band started playing devil's-advocate songs. One of Lucy's jobs was to question Sam's nascent doubts. She did. She challenged him, "It's not the most common of names. Don't kid yourself."

Sam sat back on his chair. "Twice in one file? Why?"

"I don't know," Lucy said. "His relative's gun in that chimney? Not a coincidence. His name in the vic's — in Doctor's address book? Not a coincidence. Could Elliot have known the gun was in the chimney all this time?"

"I don't know," Sam said. "But it's feeling

more possible than it did when I woke up wishing I was dead this morning."

"I don't like this. I'm going back to the file, see if I missed anything."

Before she made it to the door, Sam said, "Luce? Go neutral. Don't try to prove anything. Please. Fresh eyes."

"You said 'please,' Sammy." If Sam had looked up, he would have seen a big smile on her face.

He didn't look up. He said, "One more thing. Is there a way to determine who has looked at the Prado file since September 2001 but without leaving a trail that we checked? I don't want anyone who has already looked at the file to know we know they looked at it."

"I will see what I can do," she said.

"No trail, Luce."

"My trademark."

"Since when?"

"Fuck you, Sam."

"You too, Luce. You too. Nice glasses, by the way."

"Four months, Sammy. Four months ago."

Lucy left.

Sam mumbled, "Damn."

58

ALAN

Izza and I were sitting on aging Adirondack chairs on an exposed ten-by-ten concrete slab at the rear of the ranch house, the side that faced the sunrise and the tilled fields. A narrow packed-dirt access road provided a distinct north and south boundary between the backyard and acres of shimmering alfalfa.

I thought it was alfalfa. I really didn't know.

Izza was drinking Diet Coke. She hadn't offered me a beverage. She was not an impolite woman; the slight had been intentional.

"You're not on your bicycle. And you're way overdressed for Frederick," she said. "You hadn't planned to come here. Or you didn't think I'd agree to see you. Or you're doing something after. Or something."

My shirt was pressed, though not by me.

I'd left my tie in the car. My trousers had a crease. My shoes were shined. "One of those," I said. "Maybe two of those are true." I shrugged. "I hear there's a storm coming. Riding out here may not have been wise."

"They say we could get eight inches. We need it," she said. "I'm waiting. What's on your mind, Doctor Alan Gregory?"

Izza was running low on hospitality. I was making up for it by running low on charm. I said, "Four people knew about 'espíritu.' One of them is dead. One of them is a child. We are the other two."

"Espíritu is?"

Izza didn't dissemble comfortably. I liked that about her. I think that was why I answered her question as though she was sincere. "*Espíritu* was Tres's name for the ghostlike figure that he saw near your cottage on that dirt service road right there" — I extended my arm, pointing right at the road — "the night your tenant died. 'Espíritu' is now my shorthand for people with murderous intentions who wear Tyvek jumpsuits. 'Espíritu' is a fine word for that. To me the image has a Day of the Dead feel that is apropos."

Izza's index finger traced the circle around the rim of her soda can again and again as though she were intent on eroding the edge by the conclusion of our meeting. She said, "The dead person on your list? That's your wife?"

"You know it is. She was shot right after you, or Tres, told her about espíritu." I didn't feel like dancing around, so I got to the point. "You know about Tyvek, Izza?"

She continued to trace the circumference of the can. It squeaked. She didn't.

"Did you see it on that scarecrow? On the farm on the other side of I-25? I'm thinking you must have." She didn't reply. I said, "I have a fine alibi for the night Big Elias died. How about you?" I didn't mention that my alibi involved an escort and an incall. Those details might diminish the impact of argument I was presenting.

When Izza spoke again her voice was ice. "There was nothing big about him but his size. He was Elias César Contopo. *Primero* but not *último.*"

First but not last. I waited to see where she would go. Her tone growing more plaintive, she said, "I have applied to adopt him. Tres. My nephew. He is my family."

I shifted my eyes from her face to the fields. As a breeze moved the tops of the grasses in unison, all my questions about Big Elias's death evaporated.

All the intensity I had carried to Frederick about espíritu began to deflate.

Izza was telling me that Big Elias's murder wasn't about vengeance.

It hadn't been about the past at all.

It had been about a family that was threatened by evil. It was about Izza's future.

More important, it had been about Izza guaranteeing Tres's future.

She had been protecting her own — her family included her half brother's son — from a menace that would never go away.

I knew that territory. The protecting-family mantle. I had been wearing that rationalization as a shawl for years. It all felt so familiar to me.

Sam *had* been in psychotherapy in Boulder the night that Elias Contopo died.

Izza was likely the one who had been on Tatonka Trail. Wearing Tyvek.

She knew horses well enough to make it happen.

She knew Big Elias's habits well enough to make it happen.

She could see in my eyes that I knew the difficult truth about what she had done. She asked, "What are you going to do now?"

I stood. "I think nothing. Nothing at all. I wish you and Tres well, Izza. Take good care of him."

"That's it?" Izza said. She stopped circling the rim of the can with her finger.

"I think so," I said. "The more I think about it, the more I believe that the death of Elias Contopo, primero but not último, was an accident."

Her expression was a muddle of relief and of suspicion. Her suspicion remained on life support.

I had another thought. "That morning? In Boulder? During the meeting you had with the assistant district attorney — my wife? You gave her a drawing from Tres. Did Tres draw just the one, or were there others?"

She examined my eyes. She focused first on the left, then on the right. I could watch her suspicion flicker, then diminish. Finally, she said, "More." She swallowed. "Quatro. Tres más."

"Three more. He drew them all the same night?"

"Yes. Yes."

Lauren had given me only one drawing. I had given it to Sam.

I asked, "Did you give my wife the others? Or do you have them?"

Please please don't tell me you gave them to Lauren.

Izza's suspicion flickered again. She narrowed her eyes and parted her lips. She stood.

I thought she was about to tell me it was time for me to go.

Without a word she disappeared into the house. Two minutes later she returned with the other three crayon drawings.

One was of a stick-figure man on the road, walking. The man was as big as a car.

I knew the man was Sam. No one else would know. The drawing meant nothing.

One was of the same man walking in a field, farther away, but now inside the outline of a child's image of a ghost.

Espíritu. *This,* I thought, *is Sam Purdy wearing Tyvek.*

That one meant something. In a prosecutor's hands? It could mean a lot.

The third drawing was of a man pointing a gun at a woman. The gun was half the size of the woman. The man was twice as large as the woman.

Izza touched the paper. "That is me. That is Elias César Contopo pointing his gun at me. Tres was on the stairs. He watched it all."

"Tres did this picture the same night as the others?" I asked. The morning she was shot Lauren had told me the story of Big Elias's drunken provocation with Izza as he

521

awaited the return of his son's body from the war in Afghanistan.

"Yes," Izza said. She spoke the word on the inhale, as though she couldn't wait to spit it out. On the exhale she said, "But other nights, too. He was a . . . mean man."

"I am so sorry," I said. "For Elias Tres. For you." I pointed to the drawings. "Has anyone else seen these?"

"No." She held out the drawing with the ghost. Her voice shook. Her hand didn't. She said, "You may take this one."

I did. I held the drawing to my heart. I said, "Thank you."

She hugged me.

I walked around the house to my car.

I hoped I was leaving Frederick for the last time.

59

SAM AND LUCY

Seventy-five minutes after Lucy gave Sam the death certificate from Iowa she called him from her car. "This is from public records on the Internet. Most of it was free, but I had to pay for one search, which I put on my sister's PayPal account. I did the searches at a computer in the branch library in Gunbarrel while I was wearing those yellow sunglasses and that big hat you hate."

"It's an awful hat."

"Thank you. Elliot grew up in Grosse Pointe, Michigan, with one sister, younger, and one brother, older. His mother was an only child born and raised in Grosse Pointe. His father is a fraternal twin, who met his wife at U of M, and married into his wife's family business, something about railroad maintenance. Train cars? Tracks? I don't know. But that's why Grosse Pointe.

"Elliot's father's side of the family is

military as far back as I looked. Patriotic and conservative to the core. Elliot's grandfather was a two-star general. An honest-to-God hero in Vietnam. I found two different testimonials that he deserved a Medal of Honor for how he handled a surprise assault on his firebase near Cambodia in 1975."

"Did he get the medal?"

"No. The country wasn't in the mood for heroes then, apparently."

Sam sighed.

"Aunt Beulah — the fancy panties lady — was Elliot's father's fraternal twin. She married a farming equipment dealer — the big green ones, what are they called?"

Sam said, "John Deere."

"Them. Rory Baxter sold John Deeres in southern Iowa. He is only recently retired. I couldn't determine how he met Beulah. You are free to create a romantic story that's to your liking. Still following?" Sam said he was. "Rory has been a widower since Beulah died. I pulled her funeral notice from the local paper. Rory apparently called his wife 'BB.' I think that's cute. Rory continues to live in the home that he shared with BB.

"He has an active presence online amongst a certain group of numismatists. He has a reputation as a collector with discerning and expensive tastes in Civil War–era coins. Union only." She paused. "Numismatists are coin collectors, by the way."

"I know that," Sam said.

"Of course you do. I'm pulling up to the building. I will be inside in a minute."

Sam leaned back on his chair when he saw Lucy. The desk chair was almost as old as the driver's seat in his Jeep, and had put in almost identical time cradling his big butt. When he put stress on the chair the hardware moaned like an old man doing a squat.

Sam opened his mouth to speak, closed it. Lucy suggested an interview room. They found an empty. Sam picked up the earlier conversation as though it hadn't been interrupted. He said, "The gun that ended up in the house on Prado was Aunt Beulah's."

Lucy says, "I can see a variety of ways that it gets to Boulder. After Beulah dies the gun ends up in Elliot's hands. Maybe she gave it to him. Maybe he took it. Whatever. Rory's alive; he may know the answer. But somehow Elliot has the gun when he moves to Boulder to join the DA's office. The true mystery is how the hell it ends up on a bungee inside the chimney on Prado." She looked up at Sam. "Right?"

"Could be a red herring," Sam said. "Can

you see if Elliot reported any burglaries, or muggings, or car thefts, or anything else while he's been in town? Especially the first couple of years. I want to see if there is any record of a crime occurring during which someone could have taken the gun from him."

Lucy said, "Would he have reported the gun stolen? Technically it wasn't his."

"He may not have, though there's nothing illegal about possessing your dead aunt's handgun. I don't expect to be able to prove the theft of the gun, only to rule out a reported theft of the gun. If it was reported stolen, or if a crime took place where he can argue it was stolen, we need to look elsewhere for an answer."

"Otherwise what? We proceed as though Elliot had knowledge of the whereabouts of the handgun until it got stuck in the chimney of the house on Prado?"

"A nice dinner says we'll never prove it. Can you think of a way to learn whether Elliot lived alone when he first came to town? Or if he had roommates?"

"You revisiting Ophelia's theory about a lovers' thing at Prado?"

Sam shifted his posture. He did it again. For some things Sam could not find the correct posture. "I am a man with an increasingly open mind. I think."

"You are slowly becoming that man, but it took a village of us years to pry that mind of yours open. At times we've had to resort to controlled demolition."

He put his hand on his heart. "I am grateful to all of you," Sam said. "My gratitude comes in all the colors of the rainbow."

Lucy asked, "Can these new questions wait until tomorrow? I got a meeting."

"I don't see why not. They've been waiting a long time already. Wait — did you find out if anyone else has looked at the file?"

Lucy said, "The records clerk is being a dick. He wants me to make an official request. Getting that information off the record may cost me a blowjob." Sam looked up at that announcement. "How important is it to you, Sam? Is it worth me giving that dweeb a blowjob?"

Sam stared at her. He narrowed his eyes.

Lucy said, "You asshole, you are actually deciding if you want me to do it."

"I was not."

"You were. Hell's bells." She turned to leave the room. "I'll talk to Gary."

"Lucy, I —"

She stopped in the open door with a smile on her face. "Bye, Sam. Gary's not really a dweeb. Get him some Rogaine and some free weights . . ." She poked her tongue into the side of her cheek. "Some manscaping?"

"God, Lucy, you know I hate it when you're crude."

She laughed. "I do know that. We still having lunch?"

"Late breakfast."

"Whatever you want to call your feeding time at the Village trough is fine with me."

60

ALAN

I drove from Frederick to my office as though I had a reason to be there. I didn't know what else to do. I powered up my tracker in case the kids were trying to reach me.

I had all of Lauren's work papers in my messenger bag. My plan was to get them into my new lawyer's hands. As soon as I could. I sat at my desk for a while as I leafed through the contents of the elly-ott envelope to begin the long-postponed process of getting some insight into Lauren's thinking about Elliot's past. Around twelve thirty I locked everything in my file cabinet. I walked over to the Mall as though I'd had a busy morning at work and it was time for lunch.

I was trying to feel normal. The pretense wasn't working.

The day felt like spring but the calendar

insisted it was very much winter. The forecast said winter would win out before night fell.

I crossed Broadway, scoping out places I might have wanted to eat back in the days when I experienced routine hunger. I convinced myself that something at Cured would be good. Some salume and cheese. Some olives, maybe. Just before I reached Fifteenth Street a man brushed into me from behind. He apologized.

He had dropped a few index cards. Three-by-fives. I bent to corral them before a breeze blew them away. I said, "Excuse me, you dropped these." The cards were blank.

"Oh, thank you," he said. He squatted beside me. I recognized his scent before I saw his face. Lauren's assistant, Andrew, said, "Shhhh, please. I'm hoping anyone who might be following you doesn't recognize me. I overheard one of Helliot's loyalists talking yesterday. I think he is coming for you."

That news left my major skeletal support bones feeling as though they were turning to dust. "How did you know I was here?"

"I was on my way to your office. Saw you leaving. Thought this would be better than having someone see me walk into your building. I'm improvising."

We both stood. I handed him the cards he'd dropped. He handed me back a folded sheet of plain paper. He said, "The missing Field Notes — the yellow one she gave me before she went to your office that last morning? When I couldn't decipher Lauren's scribbles I would copy the page I couldn't read and then return the notebook to her. She didn't like to be without them. The next time we talked I'd clear up the confusion with her handwriting or her abbreviations or whatever. The yellow Field Notes book that is missing had a few lines of things I couldn't understand."

I didn't understand what he was telling me. "I don't get why —"

"No time. Lauren's notes about her project were getting more cryptic because she thought Elliot was looking through her things. I could decipher most of what she wrote, but that day's notes were too cryptic for me. I think what's on the paper I just gave you has to do with an old case and her ongoing feud with Helliot. You know about that?"

I feared I didn't, but I said, "The feud, maybe. The old case? I'm not sure."

"The building was evacuated while she was with you. Because of the Dome Fire? When we were ordered out I had already copied the pages but the copier was out of paper. When we got the all-clear to go back in, the yellow Field Notes book was missing from my desk, but the copy I'd made of that page printed as soon as I reloaded the tray with paper. I never got to ask her what these notes meant. I hope you can make some sense of them, and I hope that it helps you. With Helliot. And go through that box of personal things I gave you. Carefully. There might be something there, too."

"Andrew, please. The yellow Field Notes. What were they for? I don't know that. I don't understand."

"She called them her puzzle books. Long-game notes about cases that didn't make sense to her. Stuff she couldn't let go of, some of it involving misconduct and mistakes by cops and other staff. All things she didn't want anyone to know about."

"Old? New?"

"Both." He made a motion that was both nod and shrug. "I need to get back. Good luck, Alan." Andrew walked away. I stuffed the sheet of paper into my pants pocket.

Helliot was Lauren's private diminutive for her adversary, and boss, Elliot Bellhaven. Andrew had just warned me that Helliot was coming after me. I assumed he meant soon. He'd also warned me that it was possible I was being followed. I assumed he meant presently.

I called out, "You missed one." Andrew stopped. I hustled to within a foot of him.

I said, "The child's drawing from Lauren's meeting that morning? Helliot looked for more when he searched my house. Do you know anything about that? Had he seen —"

Andrew looked over my shoulder with wide eyes. He said, "I thought you —" He spun and walked away from me. I looked behind me. I saw nothing alarming.

The look on Andrew's face was further confirmation that he believed Elliot had me in his sights. I felt relief along with fear. I wondered if the surveillance Andrew was warning me about was electronic, keeping tabs on me via my tracker, or if some poor soul on the public payroll was following me around downtown Boulder as I pretended to have a life.

I kept walking down Pearl until I spotted what I hoped was an opportunity to thwart either kind of tail. I went into the hole-in-the-wall café near Frasca. The place was about the size of a restroom at Starbucks. An actual tail would be forced to observe me from outside. Or sit in my lap.

I ordered an espresso and took the only open table, nearest the solitary window. I read Andrew's note, a photocopy of two side-by-side pages from one of Lauren's notebooks. The page on the left had clear references to Marshall Doctor's death on Prado, some of the same information that Kirsten had shared with me from the elly-ott envelope. Below those notes, the number 38 and the word *bungee* were underlined twice and followed by five question marks. She had also written **frac ind fing □ twist??** At the bottom of the page was **FREDERICK I/E** and **A4BCOP** in double-size letters.

On the right-hand page she had written: **ALIBI GOOD. 90801 □ HB&HBL BG □ Tog?? NoE IND. DEAD END??**

Whose alibi was Lauren assessing? The mention of the alibi came right after the Frederick note on the prior pages. Was it my alibi, when I was in New Mexico with Jonas during the murder in Frederick? Or was it Sam's? She and I had talked about the Los Alamos trip that morning. Had she jotted down a reminder about it before our meeting?

What were I/E and A4BCOP? *Internet Explorer? A4B COP? A4BC OP? A4 BCOP? A 4BCOP?* I didn't know. Or the number 90801? The obvious candidates for the number were a zip code or a date. Possibly an address. I focused on the right-hand page. *HB?* My gut said that Andrew was correct — HB would be Lauren's sardonic initials for Helliot. The good alibi might have been Elliot's. I knew I was reaching. Why would Elliot need an alibi?

I muttered, "Who the heck are HBL and BG? What are Tog and NoE?"

The man next to me — our tables were ten inches apart — was reading something on his iPad. He raised his index finger from the screen. He said, "Just a second." Then, "I thought I had something for you, but . . . nothing. Want me to Google any of it?"

"No. Thank you," I said. *Boulder,* I thought.

Boulder. *Boulder. BCOP. Could BCOP be Boulder cop?* I knew that Lauren had her investigative eye on Sam before our meeting that morning. If BCOP was Sam, what was A4? *Our car is an A4.* Lauren had scribbled these notes after seeing Izza and Elias Tres, but before coming to my office. *A4BCOP* could have been her shorthand notation for Sam using our car in Frederick. *I/E?* That had to be Izza and Elias Tres. Or did it?

Okay, did the *B* in *BG* stand for *Boulder,* too? *Boulder G . . . ? Boulder G . . . ?* I had no idea.

I shut down my tracker. I immediately wondered if doing that was a mistake because my tail, if I had one, would witness my digital disappearing act in real time on his smartphone. I assumed there was an app for following trackers like mine. If my tail had that app, then my tail had just learned that I was attempting to confuse my surveillance. Perhaps. Or not.

Was attempting to thwart surveillance something that an observer would perceive as a good thing, or a bad thing? I couldn't decide. I wasn't cut out for this. Countertransference was my thing. Counterespionage? Not a demonstrated skill.

I had to get in touch with my new lawyer, but I couldn't decide whether to use my burner or my tracker for the call. Plan C was a pay phone. *Oh hell.* I used my burner. My lawyer's assistant said he was at the hospital with his daughter, who was in surgery for an orbital fracture. I expressed my sympathies. The assistant and I spoke about our kids, and all their odd injuries. For thirty seconds I forgot I was a fugitive.

Then I remembered I was a fugitive. I explained to my defense attorney's assistant that my jeopardy seemed to be growing more acute by the minute. I asked about my lawyer's partners' availability. "They are both in trial all day," she said. She promised to talk to someone soon and get back to me with guidance.

I phoned Kirsten. Voicemail. I explained about the orbital fracture and the canceled appointment and the shit that seemed to be hitting the fan from Elliot's office. I asked her to text me back any guidance at the number she had just captured.

I didn't tell her it was a burner. I didn't want her to think I was paranoid or something.

61

SAM AND LUCY

Sam hadn't read the menu at the Village since sometime in the eighties.

He and Lucy scored a table on the wall opposite the griddle. Sam told Donna he wanted the usual. Then he told her to bring him a short stack, too. Donna reminded him that his usual had included a short stack since the day Obama was inaugurated.

"Really?" he said.

"Yeah, babe," she said with a hand on his shoulder, "it's come to that. You've been drowning those sorrows in syrup for that long." She smiled at Lucy. She said, "I got you, hon. Breakfast or lunch?" Lucy said she wanted breakfast.

Sam told Donna to hold their order for a few minutes. He whispered, "Cop business."

Donna laughed. "Five?" she asked. Sam had overtipped her about a hundred times in his life. She probably would have sent

538

somebody out to wash his car if he asked nicely. He told her five minutes would be plenty.

Lucy whispered, "Are we really going to talk cop business now? Here? Around the public?" She sat back. "You are such a flirt." Sam considered it a compliment. "Ever notice how Donna treats every man in here like he's an ex-husband she doesn't hate?"

Sam said he could see that. "Did Gary give you the history of the Prado file?"

"Hold your horses. Jeez. The file has been pulled for the usual periodic open-case reviews. And it was part of the 9/11 look-back the department did in 2003."

"That man-hour thing the chief wanted? God, that was no fun," Sam said.

Lucy poured more hot water into her mug. Redunked her tea bag. "My advice hasn't changed. Let this go, Sam. It was a despicable week. I'll write up the new stuff, add it to the file. Bellhaven will see it when he pulls the record next year. We move on."

Sam leaned across the table. "Remember the OCD guy with the Acura? Waiting for his Kindle in Serape Ridge? Our decision tree conversation?"

Lucy said, "Sombrero Ranch. Full-size candy bars." She was not surprised that Sam had ignored her advice about moving

on, nor was she surprised that his segue —
if one existed in his head — was opaque to
her. "We talked about this two hours ago."

"What if it was Elliot? The person Doctor
Doctor expected to find his body?"

"Because of Beulah's gun? That's why Elliot?" Lucy gave Sam's theory some
thought. "That day was September eleventh.
Let's say Doctor expected Elliot to be the
first one there after he shot himself. There
are fifty fine reasons why Elliot wouldn't
have had time to keep a playdate in Eldorado. Sure, Sam, I could see it being Elliot.
But I can see it being people we haven't
thought about, too."

"How many times has Elliot pulled that
file?"

"I was about to tell you. The early years?
Three, four times a year. Then once a year,
always near the anniversary. But last year,
four times again."

"Why the sudden interest last year?"

Lucy checked for stray ears. "Lauren
Crowder checked out the file during the
middle of March last year. Gary said the
records staff had instructions to notify the
DA if anybody pulled it. He's sure someone
made the notification. Lauren pulled it
again after Labor Day, weeks before she was
shot. If you're keeping score, that was *after*

Jumble Guy found the bungee gun. That means Deputy DA Crowder knew about the bungee and the gun in the fireplace when she died."

"Those standing instructions were to notify the DA's office? Or the DA?"

"The man himself," Lucy said.

"The four times Elliot checked the file last year were all after mid-March?"

"Yes. It's reasonable to assume he was monitoring his deputy's interest in Prado."

Donna returned with more coffee for Sam. She told Sam his food was coming off the griddle. He smiled and offered a thumbs-up. She winked at him.

Sam's usual was a mess of food. It came on two platters.

Lucy's usual was a grapefruit and dry wheat toast. It came on two little plates.

Lucy said, "Do you eat any fiber? Ever? Do you even think about switching to oatmeal, Sam? From sausage and eggs and white bread and pancakes and —"

"Hash browns. Don't forget them. No, I don't know what Lauren was hoping to find. And, no, I haven't considered switching. Oatmeal is boring. I don't like to be bored at breakfast." He took his first bite. "Not so much at the other meals either. I eat oysters now. Did I tell you I like oysters?"

Lucy said, "What?" She assumed he was kidding. "First suicide I ever did as a detective. Before you. Thirty-four-year-old guy lived with his mother. He stuffed —"

"Wait," Sam said. "Is this a stuffing story? I don't want to listen to you making fun of my breakfast while I'm eating. Wait until I'm done."

"It's a Prado story," Lucy said. "The man stuffed his bedroom closet full of shit — I mean full-full, just about everything he owned — before he backed himself into the closet standing straight up so he could just manage to pull the door closed."

"You're describing OCD guy's worst nightmare," Sam said, laughing. "The Acura guy over in Sombrero Acres? He of the imperfect crime and the perfect privet?"

"Ranch, not Acres. Asshole. Don't interrupt me. The closet — it's a real closet, not a metaphorical closet — is so tightly packed with his shit that even after he shoots himself in his mouth his body can't fall down. He knows damn well the person who is going to come looking for him eight hours later when she gets home from work is his mother.

"Sure enough, Mom opens the closet door right on schedule. Rigor of the corpse is at max, which I think is no accident. His rigid dead body — by then it was white and gray and pasty and bloody, probably looked to her like Frankenstein with vertigo — falls forward right on top of her. Flattens her. Poor woman basically ends up in the missionary position frenching her son's corpse."

Sam was getting bored. Trying to be polite, he said, "What? You telling me the disappearing handgun was Doctor Doctor's way of saying 'fuck you' to Elliot?"

"It was Elliot's damn gun!" Lucy spoke too loudly. The packed room quieted as the other patrons at the Village waited to hear what she might say next.

She sipped tea like a lady until the room volume returned to normal. "Let's say Elliot went to Prado. Looked through a window. Or maybe he had a key. Doesn't matter. He sees the corpse, the blood. Maybe he knows Beulah's gun is gone. Maybe he thinks Doctor took it from him. Or maybe he loaned it to the guy for protection from all the critters in Eldorado. Mostly, Elliot is shitting bricks that it's possible his gun shot Doctor Doctor. Maybe he knew it was suicide. Maybe not."

"That is one big-ass boatload of maybes," Sam pointed out.

Lucy expected a harsher critique. "Well, Elliot's in a pickle. He knows the gun can be linked to him, but where the fuck is it? Who has it? Is it under the body? He can't go in and look because he knows he'll leave a trace behind. If it's gone, where is it? Without a weapon, he knows that the ME won't rule on manner. Elliot knows damn well the death will get investigated as suspicious, and that we'll be looking for a suspect. Where will we start? With the missing gun. And that day on Prado —" Lucy paused to see if Sam was paying attention.

Sam was trying to time the consumption of his meal so that he finished his last sausage and his last bit of egg yolk in the same bite. Simultaneously making sense of Lucy's maybes and pacing his ingestion was beginning to feel like trigonometry.

He forced his eyebrows up and said, "Yeah? What?"

"Elliot had no idea where the gun was. Why? Because the damn bungee had pulled it back up the fireplace. Ever since? Elliot's been waiting for the damn gun to show up and for somebody to put something in that file about it. He knows that eventually it will lead to him."

"But 9/11 had happened," Sam said. "That week? If any of your maybes were true — if all of them were true — Elliot had other things on his mind."

Lucy said, "I know that, Sam. I remember 9/11. But I guarantee that Elliot had self-preservation on his mind even then. He was already worried about Beulah's .38. Had to be. I would be. You would be. He was."

"Your theory, such as it is, means that Doctor Doctor was pissed at Elliot."

"He may have been. We don't know. My theory is a theory. Motive remains a loose end."

"I like the Elliot part, Luce. But that loose end? Kind of crucial. All the maybes stay maybes without it. The roommate? That could be your motive. Maybe Ophelia was right — they had some lovers' quarrel. Some isosceles problem with the gay tri-angle."

Lucy sighed. "I don't know what the hell that means. I'm pretty sure I wouldn't like it if I did." She pushed away her grapefruit. "I should have had the pancakes."

"Second rule of breakfast?" Sam said. He was confident he had resolved the pacing problem to his satisfaction. He would end up having just enough egg yolk for dipping his last sausage. "If in doubt you should always get the pancakes."

He raised his mug to Donna for more cof-fee.

Before Donna arrived with his refill he

lowered his voice. "Gary? In records? Did you have to, you know . . ." Sam stuck his tongue into his cheek, mimicking Lucy's provocative gesture from earlier in the day. He didn't glance at her face until he was done with the pantomime. "Back in the file room maybe?"

"That's any of your business?" she asked.

"Hey, I'm trying to be a concerned —"

"Asshole. Well, you succeeded — You are an asshole, Sam Purdy."

Donna splashed coffee into his mug. Donna said, "She's right, hon. Sometimes."

Sam didn't wait for Donna to depart. He said, "Rogaine and dumbbells, Lucy? Seriously? Has it come to that?"

Lucy grabbed the last sausage off his plate.

Sam said, "Man."

Donna said, "That's one brave woman."

62

ALAN

I sat paralyzed. My coffee was gone. I did not know what to do next.

My burner vibrated with a text. I didn't recognize the number.

Kirsten getting back to me? No. It wasn't her number.

Then I knew. It was Sam Purdy on his burner.

Call thisnumver

I left the tiny café and called Sam burner to burner as I walked in the direction of the Mall. I examined every person I saw. I looked for people in parked cars. Both sides of the street. I couldn't spot my tail.

It meant nothing that I couldn't. I knew that.

"I've been calling your other phone. I thought I'd try this one," Sam said.

I was alone on an island and knew that Sam might be at the helm of the only boat.

Despite the fact that I had exonerated him for killing Big Elias, I lacked the trust to climb on board. "My tracker's off. What's up?" I turned it back on.

"Had a late breakfast with Lucy at the Village. She got me thinking. The Elliot questions? His background? It's officially urgent. You have anything?"

Do you know about my imminent arrest? "What kind of urgent?" I visualized the Venn diagram of our overlapping interests in Elliot's professional history.

"I can't say, but I need whatever you have. Like now."

"Anything about Elliot goes both ways, or it goes no way."

Sam went quiet for ten seconds before he said, "There's an old case, an unsolved death. Elliot may have some peripheral involvement. *May* have. That's all I can say. This is really sensitive shit. You breathe a word and I'm —"

"Don't talk to me about sensitive shit," I hissed. I regained my composure. "I will give you a date. If your unsolved death took place within, say, a week of that date, then you tell me what is going on."

Sam said, "Deal." His tone was so dismissive he could have said, "Sure, guess."

I said, "September eleventh, 2001. 9/11."

548

Sam went silent. He exhaled in an extended *whew.*

My eyes were locked on a woman sitting on a bench twenty yards away pecking on her phone. I thought she might be my tail. Or that she might be some woman sitting on a bench pecking on a phone. I lacked a reliable way to tell the two apart.

Sam said, "How do you know that date? What do you have on Elliot?"

I said, "I have a guy who died on Prado on 9/11. What do *you* have?"

"We need to talk. Where are you?"

Without reaching a decision to be candid I blurted out, "I don't trust you, Sam."

He said, "I know you don't. It pisses me off. It really pisses me off."

"I don't know if my office is a good idea. I think Elliot is about to have me arrested. I can't reach my lawyer."

"And what? You think I'm going to report your location so they can pick you up? With what you have on me? You are the only person I trust with this. Lucy doesn't know. O doesn't know. I trust you with my *son,* Alan. My kid."

It was my turn to get silent. Finally I said, "I'm on the Mall near Oak. On Fourteenth. I may have a tail, or I may not. I'm too damn stupid to be able to tell. I don't even know which phone to use for what. I am . . . rattled."

Sam said, "Let me think." I walked west while he thought. "Head to your office. If you're being followed, and I doubt you are, or if they're tracking you, and they might be, that won't raise any suspicions. Lock the door behind you. I'll be inside."

"You can't get in. It's locked."

Sam laughed. He hung up. I didn't know whether I should power up my tracker to let them track me. Or not.

Someone experienced at being a target would know. Carl Luppo would know.

Lauren would know. *Fuck you, Lauren.*

Sam was sitting cross-legged on the floor in the short hallway between the offices and the waiting room. The interior space was dark and cool. I sat across from him.

"You pick locks? Is that how you searched my house for the gun?"

"People need hobbies. One of my CIs got me interested in locks. I wasn't honest with you about Ivy Baldwin. There was a metaphor."

"I thought there was."

"You and me. Murder. Tightrope walk. You think you've taken every precaution. You think you made a righteous decision, but from the day the deed is done the rest of your life is a high wire. Every step matters. Can't get distracted for a second. Any mistake is fatal. A misstep. A gust of wind. A loss of concentration. Boom. We're dead."

"Do you regret it?" I asked. "Frederick?"

"Not for a day. Want to know what I wish? I wish your wife was a better shot."

"I don't follow that."

"Michael McClelland. That night in Aspen, right after I met you? The very first confrontation in that house Lauren owned with her ex. If Lauren had known how to handle a gun back then, McClelland would've died. He never would have come after us. You and I wouldn't be out on that wire. I wouldn't have had to go to Frederick. We wouldn't be hiding in this hallway wondering how to keep our balance for one more fucking step."

He was right. But I didn't want to tell him he was right.

Sam said, "Wishes and horses? So tell me what you know about our DA."

I told him Lauren had been looking into Elliot's background for a long time. She had documents. I provided him with an overview of the facts she'd collected and with her conclusion. "Elliot came to Boulder to establish a political base. He had great options elsewhere, all the credentials. He could have done big law on either coast. He could have gone the AUSA route. But he wanted a political launching pad. Elliot picked Boulder, and Colorado, as places where a young prosecutor — even a gay one — could make a rapid political ascent. Lauren was certain of it."

"He wasn't running from anything back east? No skeletons? His political aspirations here — carpetbagger and all — made sense to her?"

"I just learned most of this. There are papers I haven't gone through. There's a box from her office from the Justice Center I haven't even opened. Andrew implied there may be more in there. But I know of no skeletons. The big question for Elliot was how gay tolerant the electorate would be. Jared Polis answered that. Elliot's been playing a long game, preparing for statewide office. That's what Lauren thought."

"Now tell me how you know about the Prado case on 9/11?"

The hallway was tight. Sam stretched out his legs. I kept my feet flat on the floor. My knees up near my chin.

"Lauren was assigned to a suspicious death investigation on Prado a few days after 9/11. Almost immediately she was pulled off. Something didn't feel right to her; she never let go. She kept notes about that week in the same envelope with the materials about Elliot's background. I assume she suspected a connection. Does that case ring any bells for you?"

"It was my case, too. Like her, I got reassigned. Last summer, before either of the fires, Lucy and I answered a call to the same house on Prado. We collected a new piece of physical evidence that we eventually linked to Elliot. No proof of anything, just a provocative connection. We didn't know the evidence would lead to him, so we did nothing to hide it. Elliot knows we know — he's been routinely monitoring the file. So he's aware of the new evidence — but he doesn't know we've linked it to him. It's not obvious. He may be praying we miss the connection."

I said, "Before the fires, Sam? Did Lauren know what you and Lucy found?"

"Yes. No doubt. And Elliot knew she knew. Is any of it important? I don't know. What Lucy and I learned on Prado might embarrass Elliot, cause him some political indigestion, but it's nothing criminal. At worst? Bad judgment. I've been thinking he was confident he could survive, I mean politically survive, if the Prado evidence

553

became public. But he's not acting that way. He's acting squirrelly."

"What are you thinking now?"

"He knew the men who lived in that house. The guy who died, and his roommate. That's clear. The new evidence that links him to Prado also implies the kind of bad judgment that doesn't reflect well on a candidate for statewide office. He may be able to finesse that, spin it. I'm not convinced it's a fatal mistake. My instincts say I'm missing something else. His behavior — the possibility that he had something to do with getting me and Lauren reassigned back on 9/15, his longtime adversarial relationship with her and with you, this apparent determination to take you down since she died — doesn't make sense unless there's some other piece. That search warrant at your house? Risky. Maybe it's something he's afraid you're going to discover. Could be unrelated. I don't know.

"But he's confident enough about where he stands to come after you openly. That may mean that he doesn't think you know whatever it is, or that he suspects you know but doesn't think you're smart enough to put the puzzle together. What's more likely? He may be feeling bulletproof because he thinks that the people capable of making the right connections are already dead."

"Lauren," I said.

"Yeah. Elliot knew she was monitoring the Prado file. I'm sure he was worried she knew something. Suspected something. Had something. Or would see something."

I asked, "Would the roommate from Prado know anything important? Lauren talked to him once. A few years ago. Were you aware of that?"

"I was not. Is he here? In town?"

"Don't think so. Lauren talked to him in Tennessee. Nashville, Knoxville? Knoxville. In 2007, maybe. He confirmed that Elliot was involved with the deceased."

"Involved involved?"

"Yes. He told Lauren it was his room-mate's first gay sex. Did you know that in 2001? That the deceased was sexually involved with a deputy DA?"

"Back then I didn't have anything linking Elliot to Prado. And I didn't know anything about anything gay. But I was pulled off the case after twenty-four hours." He paused. "You sure know a lot."

I had neither the time nor the inclination to go into the story of the elly-ott envelope with Sam. "Lauren left some papers behind. I've only recently learned what's in them. What's your gut, Sam? Did Elliot commit a

555

crime related to Prado? Is this one long cover-up? Was Lauren onto something at the end?"

"I'm not sure. We either don't know everything, or we don't recognize the importance of what we know. Elliot is acting vulnerable. But about what?" Sam shrugged. "Could it be something to do with 9/11? Long shot. The Prado death? Maybe. In 2001, he was young and single, and he was acting young and single. He was also gay. It may seem like ancient history, but remember, we passed Amendment Two in Colorado in 1992. Being gay was still a political liability here in 2001.

"Now? Elliot is reading different tea leaves. The current political environment is as gay friendly as it's been in his political lifetime. Yeah, Prado could be his Achilles' heel, but I don't see how the fact that he's gay becomes such a vulnerability today."

I said, "I'm not arguing that. Elliot wasn't involved in the Prado death, Sam. Not directly. He has a great alibi. He wasn't in town on 9/11, or the weekend before. He'd been on the East Coast. He was in the air on his way to DIA when the towers were hit. He got stuck in the Midwest someplace, drove back in a rental truck."

"I didn't know any of that. You're sure?"

"Lauren was. The papers she left behind? It includes his flight numbers. Truck rental info. I can get you copies." My tracker beeped. A text from LA Amy.

Black Cat. Boulderado. Bthere@8. BBB!!!

I silently added a fourth *B* for the orange bra. LA Amy and I had both been drunk the night before. Sober? Her desires and my intentions did not coincide. I flicked the phone to mute. I used my tracker to type a reply.

Can't. Sorry. Maybe another time.

Sam said, "You are a stronger man than me."

I didn't want to talk about LA Amy. I said, "Here comes me trusting you."

Sam looked me in the eyes for a few seconds. He nodded once. He understood.

I handed Sam the sheet Andrew gave me earlier that day. "Can you help with this? Lauren gave these notes to her assistant the morning she was shot before she came to see me. Andrew, her assistant, thinks Elliot stole the notebook these pages are from during the Dome Fire evacuation. Andrew had a copy. Elliot doesn't know that. I assume these notes are important, but I haven't been able to puzzle out the meaning."

Sam stared at the sheet. He looked on the

back as though he was hoping for a glossary. The back was blank.

He said, "Here comes me trusting you back."

I nodded once. I understood.

"The stuff on the left about Prado? Accurate. *Bungee* has to do with what Lucy and I learned last summer about Elliot and Prado. We recovered a bungee and a .38. It's a long story, but the .38 is the link to Elliot. Below that? These abbreviations are about a fractured index finger. From the ME's report. The part about Frederick? *I/E?* Don't know. *A4BCOP?* The BCOP part could be Boulder cop. If she wrote it after she saw Tres's drawing? Could be me."

"Yeah," I said. "It could. If she saw it after she saw Elias Tres's drawing, *I/E* could be Izza and Elias. *A4?* Our car is an A4, Sam. The Audi wagon. Lauren knew about you driving our car. A4-BCOP? That has to be it. What about on the right?"

ALIBI GOOD. 90801 ☐ HB&HBL BG ☐ Tog?? NoE IND. DEAD END??

Sam reread it. "Beyond 'alibi good' and 'dead end'? Gibberish. I got nothing."

"I might have a piece of this," I said. "I think HB is Elliot. Lauren used to call him 'Helliot.' Around me. With Andrew, too. With an *H.* So HB, not EB."

Sam smirked. "I like 'Helliot.' The rest? Whose good alibi?"

"Don't know. I was thinking that was either about Frederick — she may have written it the morning she came to see me — or maybe it related to the Prado notes. Which? Don't know how to tell. Is 90801 the address of the Prado house?"

"Not even close. It could be a zip code." He pulled out his phone. He searched 90801. "Long Beach, California. Mean anything to you?"

"I'm not aware that Lauren knew anyone there."

Sam started thinking out loud. "Okay, let's try the obvious. If it's a date — September eighth, 2001 — it fits our 9/11 story. The guy on Prado died on September eleventh. His body was discovered on the fourteenth. September eighth was what, the Saturday before the attack, which means the Saturday before the death in Prado?" He shook his head.

"Hold on," I said. "Lauren's papers indicate that Elliot's trip to Boston was on September — God — I think it was the seventh, not the eighth. Friday, not Saturday. It *was* the seventh. That's not it."

"You're sure?" Sam asked.

"I am. I looked at the papers this morning. They said the seventh. That puts Elliot in Boston on the eighth. One of the 9/11 planes took off from Logan, right? Is it possible Elliot has a connection to that?"

Sam made a skeptical face. "Both Twin Towers planes left from Logan that morning, not one. But I don't see how we get there from here. It's way too big a leap. What's HBL? What's BG? If they're initials they're almost meaningless. Could be anybody. If they're not initials? What? An acronym? Abbreviations? If they are initials — did she mean two individuals or a couple? It says HB — Helliot — *and* HBL. Or could it be two related things? Could the *B* be Boulder? Like in *BCOP*?"

"Boston gives us another *B* to consider. Since Elliot was in Boston on September eighth."

"Okay, what if it's Boston? *BG* could be Boston Gardens. September eighth is too early for the Celtics or the Bruins. Is Elliot a hockey fan?"

Sam would love to turn this into a hockey mystery. "I doubt it," I said. "And I don't know about t-o-g or n-o-e. Capital *I-N-D*? Individual? Independent? Or are they someone's initials?"

"Or wait . . . HBL is three letters. It could be an airport code. What about the arrows she used. Are those just doodles? Did Lauren use those arrows to indicate a progression of some kind? Do you know her doodles?"

I said, "I would say progression. But I can't make sense of it either way. Sorry."

Sam was back on his smartphone. "HBL is an airport code."

"There you go, that might —"

"For Babelegi, South Africa. I think we can rule that out. But this is interesting — the first Google link for HBL is Habib Bank Limited in Pakistan. Pakistan, Alan. What if Lauren tied Elliot to a bank in Pakistan three days before 9/11? That would be something that Elliot would not want broadcast. Hey, hey, wait — IND is an airport code, too. Indianapolis. Don't see how that helps."

"Maybe it does. That's where Elliot's plane was forced down on 9/11. That's where he rented the Ryder truck he drove back to Boulder."

"Was Lauren saying she ran into a dead end after that? After Indianapolis? If so, what does that tell us?"

"Who knows? Come on, Sam, listen to us. We've gone from Boulder to Babelegi to Pakistan to Boston to Indianapolis and back to Boulder based on some scribbles. We're making way too many assumptions. The simplest explanation is that the letters are initials. HB might be Elliot. But we don't really even know that."

"You're right. We're spinning our wheels. We need another piece."

I stood. "I need to watch the time. If Elliot is planning to pick me up for questioning, or to arrest me, I don't want to give the police any excuse to come in here. My patient files? Can't risk it. I should go out front and look for them. Or wait for them. I definitely don't want them to see us together. Clean hands and all that."

Sam nodded when I said "clean hands." "You're being smart. If you see Sengupta out there with uniforms, greet them loudly, keep your hands where they can see them. Don't come back inside. Don't invite them in." I was nodding nonstop. "Empty your pockets. Keys, phone, everything. I'll take it all. And silence, Alan. Not a word."

"I know how it goes." I emptied my pockets. Except for my burner. "Call Kirsten, please? Fill her in. Give her that page with Lauren's notes."

"Yes. Go."

"Take care of my kids, Sam."

"It won't come to that, Alan."

"Take care of my kids, Sam."

"I promise. Now go."

I stepped into my office to confirm that my files, and Lauren's papers, and my appointment book were locked up. Sam watched me from the hall. He asked, "What does Elliot have on you? What crime? What evidence? Do you know?"

"Not for sure. One of the murders, I guess. Lauren? Does it matter?" I moved back into the doorway. "Here," I said. "A parting gift." I was holding Tres's drawing of espíritu, the one that Izza had given me earlier in the day.

He recognized its significance instantly. "Where did you —"

"Don't ask. I am resigned to the fact that what happened in Frederick — what we did in Frederick — will never stop dogging us. That's fair enough. We needed to do it. We did it. But having this in your possession should make you less vulnerable. Maybe make us less vulnerable."

Before Sam could come up with a reply I closed the office door, confining him in the dark hall, out of sight. My lungs emptied involuntarily. I felt as though I might puke.

I stepped out the back door with a clear memory of a patient I'd had who'd left a session early out my back door after explaining to me that in the running-for-your-life business a fifteen-minute lead constituted a head start.

I was hoping I was getting a head start. After I hopped the fence at the back of the yard I called Carl Luppo on my burner. Sam had provided me with advice from the law enforcement perspective. I thought it would be helpful to get some counsel from a criminal who had spent some time on the lam.

A woman answered Carl's mobile phone as I reached the corner of Canyon and Ninth. My radar said something was up. I introduced myself. She then identified herself as Franco's daughter. She said she recognized my name as a friend of her father's. She paused. She told me she was in LA.

I said, "Okay." I knew things weren't okay.

She then said she thought I was calling because I already knew.

My trepidation swelling, I asked, "Knew what?"

She said she was sitting with a homicide detective in California. He was going over the contents of her father's personal possessions with her. His wallet. His phone. His luggage. She said I was on speaker.

I assumed she wasn't supposed to tell me I was on speaker, and that she didn't care.

She was her father's daughter.

I said, "What? Why?" I knew what. I knew why. All I lacked were the details.

She said her father had been shot to death two days before — her word was *assassinated* — while sitting in his car in Pacific Palisades.

Oh, Carl, I thought.

By the time I turned the corner onto Pearl Street I knew that Carl would have told me that he had earned this end. He had lived by assassination; he had died by assassination.

The wind was shifting. It was blowing into my face as I walked east. An upslope had started. The promised storm would ride in on the eastern wind's heels.

What have I earned? What end have I earned?

And what have I learned?

63

SAM AND JONAS

Sam met Kirsten Lord's car on the lane in front of Alan's home. When she'd returned his urgent call he insisted she join him in Spanish Hills.

She had complied primarily because she didn't think her apparently fugitive client completely trusted his old friend. She was hoping to get a clue from Sam about how to find Alan, and to get a sense of which side Sam was really on.

Kirsten started peppering Sam with questions the second she got out of her car.

Sam said, "Alan told me he was going outside to wait for Sengupta. I had no reason to think he was lying to me until I heard Sengupta pounding on the door ten minutes later."

"I should believe this why?"

"Believe whatever you want. I was snookered, Counselor."

Kirsten laughed. "Snookered?" Her next question was about whether Sam was on duty.

"I told my captain I needed some personal time to deal with my son. He knows I'm having issues with my kid."

"Your captain's not suspicious of the timing?"

"Of course he's suspicious. He's a detective. Hey, look northeast. I love how you can watch the weather coming from here. See those clouds? That's what's going to curl back at us. If the low sets up at the Four Corners, like they say? We're going to get blasted. Classic upslope."

Kirsten didn't care. "You don't know where Alan went? He's not up here?"

"He's on foot. His car is outside the office. I don't think he'd come here, but I checked. No sign of him. My first thought was that he went to your house or your office."

"I was home when you called. He hasn't shown up at the office. Let's get this done, whatever you have planned. Since he's not answering his phone, I'm at a loss. I should be downtown looking for him."

"Alan doesn't have his usual phone with him. If you hear from him he'll be on a burner. You won't recognize the caller ID.

It's a 720 number."

"That's what that number is. He called me earlier. Alan has a burner?"

"Yes. You know Alan won't say anything if he's picked up. He was married to a deputy DA. He's my friend. I assume he'll call you when he's ready to turn himself in. In the meantime, if you want live ammunition for your legal arsenal, we may find it here."

Kirsten said, "I was thinking he could be at Diane and Raoul's house. He knows it's empty."

Sam said, "That's a good thought. I wouldn't think to look there. I'll drive by there when we're done here."

He opened the front door with Alan's keys. Emily woofed a couple of alert barks before she reached some confidence that the intruders were friendlies. Fiji demanded attention.

Sam said, "Their office is off the master bedroom. We're looking for a box with Lauren's personal things from the DA's office. I'm thinking a file box. Like that."

Kirsten spotted a copy-paper carton near the doorway that led to a sitting alcove. The lid had Lauren's name written on it with a marker. Sam said, "Wait." He offered her latex gloves from his coat pocket. She pulled some on before she lifted the lid.

568

She said, "A couple of vases. A mug. Tea, three kinds of tea. Framed pictures. A bag of almonds." She fished around a little more. "Some artsy-craftsy things from the kids. It's all personal stuff. What am I looking for?"

"No papers or files? No personal notes? Let me look."

Looking didn't take long. At the same instant they reached an identical conclusion. They said, "The search warrant."

"This explains why it was drawn so narrowly," Kirsten said. "Damn."

Sam said, "Finding that gun would have been a bonus for Elliot during the search. He got what he was looking for in this box. That may be why he thinks he's in the clear and can move on Alan. Elliot thinks he has the high ground. Once he has Alan in custody, anything Alan alleges about Elliot will look like desperation. Or retaliation, or even vengeance. And Alan won't have whatever was in this box to back him up."

"Elliot's in the clear for what?" Kirsten asked.

"Lauren had some suspicions about Elliot. Alan has some suspicions about Elliot." Sam gave her the copy of the page from the yellow Field Notes book. "He wanted you to have this. I will let him tell you what he thinks it all means."

Sam phoned the DA's office from his burner. He asked for Andrew.

Kirsten whispered, "Who is Andrew?"

Sam packed as much Iron Range as he could into his words as he said, "Recognize my voice? Good. This is about your old friends. The couple?" Sam noted a lack of objection. "I'm at their home looking in a box you prepared for one of them. You gave the box to the other one. Are we clear?"

"Maybe."

"Maybe is fine. There is no paper in the box. Not a sticky note. Not a while-you-were-out slip. Is that how it should be?"

Andrew's voice went low. "There was paper. Plenty. A manila envelope with non-work things. Personal stuff, invitations, old birthday cards. Some personal mail delivered to the office that she hadn't carried home. Copies of personal emails. And there were some little stapled notebooks she always had with her to jot stuff down. On the cover they say FIELD NOTES. All caps. Most were blank. One wasn't. A yellow one. You know what I'm talking about?"

"Yes." Sam had seen Lauren use the notebooks a dozen times.

"What was in that notebook was important."

"Our friend told me one was missing. Was it that one?"

"No. There were two yellow ones. The one in the box was the first one. The missing one is the second one."

"Well it's not here, so both are missing. Anything else I should be seeing?"

Andrew said, "A small stack of other people's business cards — about an inch's worth — with a rubber band around them. A couple of those had writing on them."

"Gone," Sam said. "Should I be looking in her computer for anything?"

"Old emails maybe. I managed her work files. She didn't put anything important in .doc files. She didn't use the cloud for personal stuff. She said that other people were smarter about computers than she was. She didn't trust them for that reason."

"You have the password for her laptop?" Andrew didn't reply. "Want to tell me?"

Andrew said, "No. Not at this time." They both hung up.

To Kirsten, Sam said, "Lauren's assistant. He put this box together. There were papers in it. Important stuff. An envelope of things. One of those little notebooks she carried." Kirsten nodded. "Some business cards."

Kirsten said, "We have to assume Elliot instructed someone to grab any paperwork from this box during the search."

"I would also bet that you won't find any of it listed on the inventory."

"It appears we're a few days late with this errand, Sam. I should get back downtown."

"I am going to poke around a little more."

Kirsten dug her car keys from her shoulder bag. Offhandedly she asked, "Who is that with Lauren in the photograph? On top? She looks so young."

Sam glanced down at the framed picture. He said, "Not Alan." The photo had been taken from the dock as the couple was standing on the stern of a sailboat in a slip on the San Francisco side of the Bay. The north tower of the Golden Gate was visible in the background. The sailboat was named *The Cliché.* He said, "Lauren used to live there. Could be her ex. I never met him."

"Lauren had a framed photograph of her ex-husband on her desk at work?" Kirsten said. "That's not right."

Sam hit REDIAL on his phone. Andrew answered warily. Sam said, "The framed photo of your friend on a sailboat with a guy? Was it displayed on her desk?"

"God no. It was in the bottom drawer of her desk. On the side that locks. She showed it to me when she brought it here only weeks before she was shot. I never saw it displayed. I almost didn't include it in the box. To spare feelings." Sam thanked him.

Kirsten was inches from Sam, staring at him, eavesdropping. He stared back at her. He said, "She recently took it to the office. But never put it out."

"Doesn't smell right."

Sam lifted the photo. He examined the back of the frame. "Lauren thought that Elliot was going through her things at work," he said. "If she wanted to hide something in her office from Elliot, this would be a good choice. The photo wouldn't mean anything to Elliot, but it would get Alan's attention, right? A photo of the ex?"

Kirsten said, "If he ever opened the damn box. You and I need to slow down. If she was hiding something, was it about a case? Is it potential evidence?"

"Evidence? It's a framed personal photograph. Don't overthink this."

She sat on the edge of the bed. Her eyes fell on a brown shoe box with a scripted name on the lid: *Christian Louboutin.* Her eyes followed the perimeter of the room in a slow panorama as she recognized that the bedroom was arranged as an estate sale waiting to happen, with Lauren's personal things on display. Her eyes filled with tears. "He doesn't sleep here," she said.

Sam said, "What?" He didn't give a shit where Alan slept. He was dialing Lucy on his burner. "It's me. The Prado roommate? You have his particulars? Good. He may be in Knoxville. Try to find him, ask him about Beulah's nephew. And run him."

Kirsten said, "What's that? Who's Beulah?"

"Maybe a missing piece to a puzzle Lauren was trying to solve about Elliot."

She said, "I'm going to get some water from the kitchen. Want anything?"

He said, "I'm good, thanks."

Sam rotated the tension clips on the back of the frame. A section of a page of a newspaper was folded into a size that fit comfortably behind the photograph of Lauren sailing with her first husband.

The half page of newsprint featured a short column along with an accompanying photograph of seven young people smiling at the camera. And of one young man looking back over his shoulder as he exited the frame. The man exiting the frame was Elliot Bellhaven. None of the partygoers were identified; the column described a fundraising event the group had attended. Sam flipped the newsprint over to find a date. *September 8, 2001.* Three days before the attack.

"Nine-oh-eight-oh-one," Sam said quietly. "Bingo."

The newspaper was the *Boston Globe.* "BG," Sam said. Both flights that had flown into the Twin Towers had originated from Boston on the morning of September 11. "Bingo again."

The pieces were filling in parts of a puzzle that Sam had difficulty believing was what it was appearing to be.

Elliot? 9/11? Really?

By the time he joined Kirsten in the kitchen he had a semblance of a plan.

He showed her the newspaper photo. "Ms. Lord, do you know what time Jonas gets home from school?"

64

"First, tell me why they want to arrest him," Jonas said to Sam.

Sam had hoped to distract Jonas away from that line of inquiry. He was learning that Jonas wasn't easy to distract. "Detain. Where's Grace?" Sam said. "She's not here?"

"With Clare. They dropped me off. They're shopping or something. Why do the police want my dad?"

Sam said, "A misunderstanding. His lawyer and I are working on it."

"Don't bullshit me. I know about the guns. The new gun, too. I was here for the search, remember? That was me in handcuffs. What do they think Alan did?"

Jonas didn't look up from the keyboard of his laptop. His fingers were dancing. Sam was mesmerized at the kid's skill. He never seemed to touch the DELETE key. The DELETE key was Sam's best friend on the keyboard.

In similar circumstances Sam's son, Simon, would not have demanded more information from his father. He would have asked once, maybe. Sam would have said what he said to Jonas. Simon would have then told his father, "Whatever" or "I don't care" and then retreated to his room. The next day Sam might have found a fist-size hole in the drywall next to Simon's bed.

Sam was growing adept at drywall repairs.

But Jonas? He got right in Sam's face, just like his mother, Adrienne, would.

Sam knew Jonas's history. He had suffered way too much. Alan's troubles had to be terrifying to him.

Jonas stopped typing. "I'm waiting for an answer."

Sam said, "Those guns? You know where they are now?"

"If I do?"

"Hey, I'm sorry, Jonas. I'm anxious, too. I need to know if Alan has one with him. If he's armed. Jesus, I hope he's not armed."

"I can check. You stay here. You follow me or look out the window, I won't help you with your other problem."

"Okay. Got it."

"I mean it," Jonas said.

"Check the guns, please."

Jonas returned in less than a minute. "He's not armed."

"Thank you. You're not either?" Jonas glared at him. Sam said, "That was a joke. Elliot and your dad? Alan is a . . . person of interest. The DA thinks he knows something about Lauren's death that Alan kept to himself. I'm pretty sure Elliot wants to question him, not arrest him, but I'm not in the loop."

"Why doesn't Elliot arrange to question him through his lawyer? Or just come here? Lauren used to do stuff like that with witnesses all the time."

"Why? Intimidation basically. The DA may be trying to make a point."

"Alan could be charged with a crime so Elliot can make a point?"

Jesus. "It's possible. It's more likely he just has questions, for now."

"Likely?"

"Alan has good lawyers, Jonas. This will get resolved."

Jonas emitted a sardonic laugh. "You know he slept with one of those good lawyers last night."

"What?"

Jonas said, "Uh, yeah. After you guys were done drinking."

Sam couldn't get his arms around that.

Alan and Kirsten? "You — How — You saw them?" Sam's mind's frame was instantly filled with the texted photo from the beguiler in Aspen. *Not her?*

"Right there. On the couch." Jonas shook his head. "Slept slept, for all I know. For Alan, maybe more like passed out. How much did you two drink?"

"A lot. How do you know all this?"

Jonas was growing exasperated. "Diane shot my mom. Alan saw it. He told me. He's a witness. And a victim. What's Elliot's problem?"

He told you all that? He *told* you? Sam was recalibrating his judgment about Alan's parenting skills. *How old are you, kid?*

"Alan was the only witness, Jonas. Eyewitness testimony can be unreliable."

"Unreliable? What? Alan got really confused somewhere between 'she shot her' and 'I shot her'? That's your explanation for what Elliot's up to, Sam?"

Sam didn't want to continue the conversation. "Can we move on? Sometimes forensics can't settle all the ambiguities. Investigations can get complicated."

"That's crap. Elliot thinks Alan's lying. Why? What does he have?"

"Elliot is challenging Alan's initial statement. It's his job."

"My mom didn't trust Elliot. You know that?"

"I do know that."

"Now Elliot thinks Alan shot my mom? That's crap. He's setting him up. Why?"

Sam didn't want to go on record agreeing with Jonas. He said, "That's what I'm hoping you can help me discover today. The why. There's another crime that may be part of all this, too. The DA may want to question Alan about a woman who died in Weld County a few years ago."

"For a cop you don't lie very well. I thought you'd be better at it."

"Jonas, you're a kid. Anyway, I think you're a kid. I would rather not be discussing any of this with you. Do you get that?"

"When you want my help I'm a genius. When my questions make you uncomfortable? I'm a kid again. Must be real pleasant in your house for Simon."

Sam sucked his tongue to the roof of his mouth to keep from reacting to that taunt. He left it pasted there until the urge passed. He said, "The other crime took place while you were in New Mexico picking up your dog. Do you remember that trip?"

"That makes me Alan's alibi. Give me Elliot's number, I'll tell him myself."

"It's not that simple. I wish it were."

Jonas said, "If you have something to tell me, tell me. Don't pile bullshit on top of bullshit." He focused his attention on the keyboard. "Got it. This is a digital photo file — of that picture from the *Boston Globe.* I need it to do image comparison. Which guys do you want facial recognition on?"

"What's the difference?"

"Google Image will search the Web for matching images — photos in this case. Find another one just like this one. But I think what you want is facial recognition. You want software that identifies the same individual in different photos? Is that right?" Sam said it was. "That's different software. Which people?"

"All of them. Men and women."

"The guy on the right is Elliot." Jonas digitally cropped off Elliot's portrait, then copied and pasted it elsewhere on the screen. "If we're lucky they're all on Facebook. Facebook's software tags faces. Good accuracy, not great accuracy. I'll start there and then confirm the results with other . . . options."

"Do I need to understand what you're doing?"

"No. It's better if you don't. Turn around, Sam." Sam didn't turn around. Jonas took his hands from the keyboard. Sam started to protest. He turned around.

"Wait," Sam said. "Is there a Facebook archive? Maybe they were all on Facebook in 2001? Wouldn't that be easier?"

Jonas sighed again. "Do you go to the movies? The photo is from 2001. Facebook didn't exist until 2004." In seconds Jonas had a facial recognition match of the 2001 newspaper photo of Elliot's face with his current headshot on the Boulder County website. "Worked. You can look. *Ta da.*"

Sam's mouth dropped open. "It's that easy?"

"If I knew all their names, or if they were on Facebook, or if I knew where they worked — now, today — this might not take long." Jonas sat back. "But first you need to explain why it's me doing this and not some IT guy at the police department."

"I can't tell you that."

"I figured. Then this is when you need to leave. You can't be here. I may go places you won't like. I assume part of your job is to prevent . . . trespassing."

Sam considered reframing the nature of his profession for Jonas. He decided it wouldn't be appreciated. Instead he said, "For relaxation I pick locks. I think you do, too. No harm, no foul? I'm asking how long it will take to pick these locks. Best guess."

"You know how to pick locks? Where do you get 'em? Will you show me how?"

"eBay mostly. Some at garage sales. Maybe. I'll think about it."

"This might take five minutes, or five hours. The VPN I use can drag this time of day. I may need to . . . borrow some software. And I don't know what databases I will need to access if Facebook doesn't work. I can't get into some of the best databases. I won't go into others. I avoid traps."

Sam didn't know what a VPN was. He'd Google that later. "Stay in public databases, Jonas. If these people showed up once in the *Boston Globe,* they'll show up someplace else that's just as public. Remember, to help your father, I need names. Not just a match for the photos."

Jonas said, "My father was Peter Arvin. He is dead. We're helping my dad. His name is Alan Gregory."

Sam thought, *Wow.* He said, "Let's help your dad. What's your cell number?"

Jonas recited the digits as though they spelled out the letters of his name. Sam pecked the ten numbers into his burner and texted Jonas. "Text the word *done* to that number when you're ready. Don't use the landline. Don't call me. Don't email me. I'll come back when I get the text. Got it?"

"Is our landline tapped? Is your phone tapped?" Jonas asked. "Cool." Headshots were appearing and disappearing on the laptop screen faster than Sam could make visual sense of them. The progression became so rapid that the screen was a blur of fractals.

Sam let himself out the door. Under his breath he said, "Jeez."

65

Sam walked to the doublewide. He explained to Ophelia what was going on with Alan. He left out the part about Jonas and facial recognition and VPNs. He didn't leave out the part about Alan sleeping with Kirsten.

Ophelia thought that was nice, that Alan was finding some comfort. She sat beside Sam and pulled his head to her chest. They didn't talk. Five minutes became ten.

Lucy interrupted their moment with a call to Sam on his smartphone. He asked her if it concerned the last conversation they'd had. She said it did. He told her he would call her right back. Sam kissed Ophelia softly on the lips and walked from the trailer toward the old barn. He returned Lucy's call from his burner as he walked.

"The roommate in Tennessee is dead, Sam."

"Shit. Details?"

"Almost three years ago. Overdose. Anti-depressants and benzos mixed with one too many pints of tequila. Long history. In and out of rehab prior to his death."

"No foul play?"

"They didn't find any, but I doubt they looked very hard. It was an *adios hasta luego* death. Multiple arrests, including a couple for assault, all when he was high. He did eighteen months for cracking a guy's skull with an oar outside a bar in Wailuku. I'm sure I pronounced that wrong."

"No, you got that right. It's *oar.* Hawaii I take it?"

"Cute, Sam. Yes. Wailuku is Hawaii. What was your clue?" She said, "Sam?"

He had already pocketed his phone.

Jonas's one-word text — **Notdone** — arrived ten minutes later, twenty-five minutes after Sam had left the kid alone for his hack-a-thon. Sam had set a child's drawing on fire and was rubbing the ashes of the paper into the dirt with the toe of his shoe while his brain was busy trying to assemble a plan B, or C. He read the text message. He broke into a jog back down the lane.

Jonas was on a stool at the kitchen counter scooping peanut butter out of a jar with celery spears. Sam sometimes did the same thing with chocolate-covered pretzel sticks.

He could see how the celery sticks might be a healthier food choice.

"Clare and Grace?" he asked.

"You're a detective. Did you see a car?" Jonas said.

Sam again sucked his tongue to the roof of his mouth. "You find them, or no?"

"All but two." Jonas slid a few sheets of printer paper Sam's way. "Three of them have Wikipedia pages. That was like cheating. Two others have detailed profiles on LinkedIn. Slash you'll like this — one of those two is in a database of facial matches of people who are in amateur sex tapes or erotic photos online. And —"

"There's a database of people who are in online sex tapes?" Sam almost asked why Jonas knew that, and why he thought Sam would like that.

"Not by name, but by facial recognition. But from there you are only a quick step from a home sex tape to a Facebook tag or an ID on Instagram."

"I had no idea," Sam said. Degradation of personal privacy worked to cops' advantage. But Sam was beginning to think it had gone too far. Maybe way too far.

"Sexting is for fools," Jonas said.

"You guys still say 'sexting'?" Sam said.

"You guys do. And this doofus . . ." Jonas

laughed as he pointed at the guy in the middle of the original photo. "Is on JDate. Look at his profile" — Jonas clicked and brought it up — "I'm thinking he'll be dateless for a while. We're down to two people we don't know. This woman, this one here, has no facial recognition match in any of my databases."

"That means she didn't make any sex tapes," Sam said. "Good for her."

"She's not on Facebook. And the guy next to Elliot? Can't find him, either, so I'm thinking he's the one you want."

"Why?"

Jonas crossed his eyes. He said, "Life is like that. You haven't noticed?"

Sam tried to recall if he was that nihilistic as a kid. *Nah.* "I need them both."

Jonas asked, "Do you know anything more about them? I need new databases to search."

Sam took the jar of peanut butter from Jonas's hand. He said, "Stop eating. Please. For a minute?"

Jonas's face became a mask. He said, "Go on."

"This was right before 9/11. You know about 9/11?" Jonas winced. Sam said, "What? You were like a toddler then."

"It turns out there are references to that

event on the Internet."

Sam stepped away to compose himself. He recalled the search he'd done on the phone for *HBL* when he was sitting with Alan in the hallway of his office. "You want more information? Try 'Habib Bank Limited.' *H-a-b-i-b.* It's a big Pakistani bank. See if that gets you anywhere. Cross-check Elliot with the bank, too."

"I hope the website's in English. I don't read Urdu. Was the bank involved in financing 9/11?"

Urdu? "I don't know. Terrorism isn't my beat. I'm out of my comfort zone here."

"No worries. Easy to check," Jonas said. "Why a Pakistani bank?"

"The flights that hit the World Trade Center took off from Boston's Logan Airport. The guy you're having trouble identifying has features that —"

"I get it. He has brown skin. He looks Arabic-ish. We're looking for terrorists."

Sam couldn't tell if Jonas was being sarcastic. That bothered him. He also thought Jonas was growing a little hyper.

Jonas said, "I'll pull the original 9/11 terrorist photos off Google. You're thinking — or what, hoping — that this guy in your photo was a go-between with Al Qaeda's bankers or that he was partying with the terrorists in Boston before 9/11?" Hearing Jonas say it out loud made it seem absurd to Sam. He didn't know how to respond. Jonas let him off the hook. "Give me ten minutes. Then I'll tell you it's all a dead end."

Sam started to walk away. Jonas said, "But if it's not? Think about the attack ads against Elliot when he's running for governor. Every ad will be about him palling around with terrorists."

Sam had a thing for Sarah Palin. Politically and not politically. He continued to grieve the 2008 presidential election. He thought Jonas might be taking a cheap shot at Sarah with the "palling around with terrorists" quip. He decided not to defend her because he was worried Jonas had set a trap. "This is our secret. All of it. You can keep a secret?"

"Sam? My mother was bisexual. My father was murdered by a ghost in the Boulder Theater. You really want to know if I can keep a secret?"

Sam's face went soft. "Thank you, Jonas."

Jonas sighed. His shoulders fell two inches. "I don't have enough information. This won't work. We would have to find a link between the guy in your photo and the Al Qaeda assholes in Boston. I can't do that with what I have."

Sam stared off at nothing. "Check anyway, please. Look for any connection you can. Being right helps. Being wrong helps less, but it helps."

"Sam?" Jonas lowered his eyes to the keyboard. "Can I tell you something? Personal?"

Sam was wary. But he said, "Sure."

"Sometimes you can be patronizing even when you don't want to be patronizing. Might want to keep an eye on that around Simon. I bet he gets tired of it."

66

ALAN

I thought I'd weave through downtown on residential streets hoping to be invisible. My tentative route was Tenth to Spruce to Eleventh to Pine and then across Broadway until I got a better idea. I made it as far as Spruce Street without the better idea. My brain was too crammed with thoughts about Carl Luppo and deserved ends.

I paused at the corner to call Amanda from my burner, hoping to arrange to hide out in the incall. While I waited for Amanda to pick up, I spotted my ex-therapist on foot, turning the corner from Spruce onto Eleventh. She entered the door of some old brick row houses. I knew the building was full of therapists' offices. But not hers.

Maybe my ex-therapist is in therapy. No big deal. Many young shrinks are.

I spun away; I didn't think she had spotted me. If she did? So what?

Amanda answered my call. I asked if she had a minute. So many things could go wrong with my impromptu plan. Amanda not having a minute was only the first.

"I'm heading into a business meeting. Not an ideal time," Amanda said.

Ideal time? Ha. "Quickly? I would like to, uh, use the apartment on Pine Street," I said. "Now. Is it available?"

"You're sure? You didn't seem very comfortable there."

I could have explained that my options were constrained. I didn't. "I'm sure."

"How long do you . . . want it?"

"I don't know. A while. What's possible?"

"A couple of hours?"

"Of course. Sure. I'm not far away. Is the key still —"

"Yes, where I told you."

"I can count on your discretion?"

"I've always counted on yours," she said.

When Amanda and I were considering locations to meet the previous afternoon, she had texted me instructions so I could find the spare key. After we ultimately agreed to meet at the nearby pizzeria, I deleted that text. I thought it had said that I should walk behind the stairs that led up to the second-floor apartment where I would see a fake junction-box cover at chest height.

The faux j-box was precisely where a faux electrician would put it.

The futon was gone from the apartment along with almost everything else except the beat-up leather sofa. All that remained in the bedroom was a queen-size box spring and mattress in desperate need of linens. I wasn't counting the upside-down wine-box bedside table on which sat a bottle of lube.

It was apparent that the incall was being retired earlier than planned. For my purposes that was a fine thing. I grabbed a bottle of water from the refrigerator — the only other items in it were two containers of Noosa yogurt and a box of condoms — and I collapsed onto the sofa. I had a couple of hours to figure out what to do next.

I knew I shouldn't drag Kirsten any further into my mess. Sam had done what he could. Andrew had risked plenty on my behalf. Although I was tempted to view Izza as more of an ally than an adversary, I didn't see anything she could do that would save me from whatever Elliot was planning.

I accepted that I would need to turn myself in to the police. And soon. The question I hoped to answer during my time in the incall was whether I could accomplish anything useful before I did.

I was grateful that my new lawyer's number was already in my burner's call history. I would need his help arranging my surrender. As the call to his office was being completed I revisited the morning's monetary arithmetic in my head. I not only needed to find five figures of cash I didn't have to give to my new attorney as a retainer, I also might need to find five or ten times that much to post bond to get myself out of jail.

That was if Elliot arrested me and if — the second *if* was a large-size *if* — Elliot failed to convince a judge that I should be held without bond.

The attorney's receptionist answered. I identified myself and asked to speak with my lawyer. She didn't offer an update on her boss's daughter's condition. She said, "Just a moment, Dr. Gregory." I heard a key slide into the lock of the incall door. I hit END.

I cursed under my breath. My two hours at the incall were not up. Not even close.

67

DOCTOR LILA

"This is my first time in this building. It's lovely," I said to my new supervisor.

"Thank you. We like it."

"So much charm. My office has no charm. Not like this."

My new supervisor was not chatty. He said, "I assume you're not here to talk about décor. You said on the phone you have a pressing issue, something about two patients knowing each other. Should we start there?"

"That's correct. I only realized that they were acquainted after the initial few sessions I had with the second patient. When he mentioned the first one's name."

My supervisor shrugged away the news. I expected him to do that. He said, "Boulder is a small town. Patients being acquainted happens more often than any of us would like. What kind of relationship do they have? Does it present a conflict for you to treat them both?"

I said, "I do anticipate some conflict. But I should also let you know that coming here to see you presents a different problem for me. I made a commitment to one of the patients, the one I saw first, that I wouldn't seek supervision without notifying him."

He smiled, I thought, condescendingly. He said, "May I call you Delilah?" I nodded. "He asked you not to get supervision, Delilah?"

"He has concerns about other people knowing things. Content." *With damn good reason,* I thought. But I didn't say that.

"Did you tell him you were coming here? Does he have my name? That is not how this is supposed to work, Doctor."

"I did not tell him I was coming here."

"That is an odd request from a patient. I take it he is a therapist?"

"It wasn't a request. He made it a requirement for continuing treatment. I shouldn't have agreed. But I did. I also made another commitment to him — about anonymity. For that reason I am not comfortable saying anything to you about him, including what he does for a living, that might provide a clue to his identity."

"This patient has you tied up every which way. Whose therapy is it, Delilah? Have you

597

thought about that?"

My supervisor and my patient were contemporaries. It seemed my new supervisor was the more patronizing of the two, by a nose. Also the less dangerous, by a mile.

I didn't respond to his taunt. I did rethink my intention to disclose Alan Gregory's insistence about shredding and torching and rewriting my notes. Along with the fact that I had promised to do that, too. And the fact that I had not done it.

He crossed his legs and his arms. "An observation? You are rather cavalier about rationalizing away the first commitment you made to him — the one about supervision — but you seem to be squeamish about breaking the second, the one about his anonymity? I'm trying to understand the parameters of your sense of therapeutic fair play. They seem . . . elastic. Though I can't decide whether that is good, or bad."

"I'm aware of the inconsistency. I know. The first patient is no longer in my care. He terminated . . . abruptly. Regardless, I don't intend for this visit to be case consultation, per se. Of either therapy. I am hoping this can be supervision about a broader therapeutic issue."

"Per se?" he asked.

"It's Latin. It means —"

"I know what it means. Consider it a confrontation. I, not you, will be the one who decides the nature of this consultation."

The room suddenly felt too warm. "What I was saying? The patients know each other well. Their relationship goes back many years."

"Friends? More than friends?"

"Friends, but not only friends. Other things, associations not typical of friendship."

"I don't mean to be difficult, Delilah. But you are mincing words. I won't. I'm a supervisor, not an oracle. You may be comfortable with your patient dictating ground rules with you. But I am not comfortable with you doing it with me. Do you understand?"

"I apologize. I'm — I am seeking ethical guidance. I've been reading ethical casebooks and I've been unable to find a situation even remotely similar to the one I'm in. Your experience and your reputation in the community about ethical issues? That is what I hope the supervision can be about."

My flattery softened him. It had never softened Alan Gregory.

"Let's try that then," he said. "What is the ethical dilemma? Specifically please."

I didn't hesitate. "I think my two patients killed someone. Together."

68

SAM AND JONAS

Jonas texted **More** to Sam. Sam was back at his side in a minute.

Sam said, "You have something with the hijackers?"

"No, not them. You ready for this? The woman is related to a Saudi prince. I found a photo of her family with him in 2000. Distant relative — not sure she would be invited to the Saudi version of Thanksgiving at the prince's palace." Jonas spun his laptop toward Sam. The family tree was immense. Jonas had highlighted her name in the bottom third.

Her surname rang no bells for Sam. "What are you thinking this means?" Sam asked. He was certain that Jonas had digested the facts and reached a conclusion.

"You have your Middle East connection. Maybe not the one you expected, but most of the 9/11 crew were Saudi. Open minds?

My father used to tell me to see, not to look."

"Peter? Regarding . . . what?"

Jonas said, "Rock climbing and lumber picking."

"He died when you were really, really young, Jonas."

"Your point? You want to argue with me about my memories?"

Sam demurred. "Peter gave you good advice," Sam said. "We can put a Saudi prince's distant relative at the fund-raiser in Boston the weekend before September eleventh. So what?"

"You wanted a connection. She's there on September eighth. Elliot is there on September eighth. And you said to watch for a banking link. Her family is in banking. Bigtime."

"The Habib Bank Limited in Pakistan?" Sam felt hope.

Jonas said, "Nothing ties Habib Bank Limited to terrorist funding for 9/11. I did a search of the text of the report of the 9/11 Commission."

Sam exhaled. "Okay. We strike that off our list. That's how this process works."

"The prince has ownership in two Saudi banks. Big players in oil and transport."

"Lots of rich families are in banking. We

need to find a straight line that connects Elliot to something beyond that fund-raiser.
Maybe the guest list for the event has
another Arabic name. Maybe she was there
with someone from home. The guy next to
Elliot in the photo? We need to know who
he is."

"I looked for an attendance list. The
records aren't online. I could hack the
organization's server but there's no guarantee the list is there. Hell, 2001 was the dark
ages."

Sam said, "You have her name and her
family connection. Is there a way to use that
to get a lead on the man next to Elliot, our
maybe-Arabic John Doe?"

"I thought John Does had to be dead. Not
true?"

"No, just unidentified."

"Huh," Jonas said. "I'll go at it that way.
See if she shows up with him. Elliot could
have been at the event with her, not with
the guy. I'll look for both couples."

"Elliot is gay, Jonas. We should assume if
he's there with someone, it's a man."

"Oh. He's not allowed out with women?
Is there a rule I don't know about?"

Sam took a deep breath. "Sure. Okay.
Look for both couples. She and Elliot could
have been together. But I'm staying here.

I'm tired of running back and forth."

Sam sat on the sofa, his back to Jonas, his eyes on the Rockies. *Is the woman in the photo HBL? Or is John Doe HBL? Another leap too far,* he told himself.

Jonas stopped typing.

Sam said, "Can I ask you something? Unrelated."

Jonas said, "My connection is dragging. Shoot."

"You ever heard of Ivy Baldwin? Guy in Eldorado Springs a long time ago? I'm asking everybody lately."

Jonas's voice brightened. "Hell yeah. Ivy was one of Peter's heroes. My father. He loved Ivy Baldwin and Philippe Petit. He left me the book Philippe wrote."

Jonas's father, Peter Arvin, had been a legendary free-solo rock climber. Sam knew rock-climbing cops who remembered watching Peter work without ropes in Eldorado Canyon. They considered him to be the finest nontechnical climber they ever saw. "Who's Philippe Petit?" Sam asked.

"The guy who crossed between the towers of the World Trade Center on a wire."

"Your father's heroes weren't rock climbers?"

"No, funambulists. High-wire guys who worked in the wild. The rarest breed. There have only ever been a few dozen great ones. My mother said Peter tried and tried but he couldn't walk a wire."

"I'd forgotten all about the World Trade Center thing," Sam said. "That was a long time ago, too. Is that a real word you just said?"

"It was 1974," Jonas said. "Funambulist? Yeah, it's a real word."

"Which was harder to do? Did your dad — your father — ever say?"

"Petit was up higher by far, on the World Trade Center. But Ivy Baldwin went a greater distance by far. Both had to deal with wind and weather. A fall meant instant death for either. Ivy crossed Eldorado dozens and dozens of times. Philippe got only the one chance, but he nailed it. Adrienne said that Peter would tell me stories about what they did when I was a baby. He'd turn pages in books, pretending that he was reading about them."

Sam said, "I still can't believe Ivy Baldwin walked across Eldorado on a wire. Look at that canyon." Sam pointed at it. "That's nuts."

Jonas said, "I like that you know about Ivy Baldwin, Sam." He didn't look up from the keyboard.

They were both quiet for a while. A few

minutes later, to Sam's back, Jonas said, "You are way too concrete about this gay thing, Sam. You need to chill. Don't forget my mother. Straight, bi, gay. People are what people are. Have to give him room."

Sam would never forget Jonas's birth mother. Adrienne had been straight and married before she was lesbian before she was bi before Sam lost track of what the hell she was. He knew Jonas had a point. Sam felt he had done a lot of chilling about the gay thing, but acknowledged that he might have more to do.

He was about to admit to Jonas that there was probably some truth in what he was saying when he had a sudden awareness about exactly what Jonas was saying.

Have to give him room.

Jonas isn't talking about Elliot. He's talking about Simon.

My hockey-playing, weightlifting, zombie-loving, wall-punching, shoplifting, brooding, hulking adolescent-boy-in-all-ways kid?

Is gay?

69

ALAN

Amanda walked in the door. I was surprised that I was not unhappy to see her.

I considered explaining that I could be picked up by the police in the next little while, but I couldn't discern a way to share that news without jeopardizing the outcome I desired. Which was solace, and a clear head. Definitely not panic.

"You startled me," I said. "Your meeting ended early?"

"It's a consulting gig with one of my private equity contacts. I bill hourly so it was a short meeting." She sat beside me on the old couch. She frowned. "I didn't expect to hear from you again. Tough day? Or tough life, at least lately?" she asked.

I didn't answer. The question seemed too cumbersome.

"Hey?" she said. "You in there? Hello?" She gestured at my water. "Are there any more of those?" I nodded. She went to the kitchen.

I asked, "Why are there condoms in the refrigerator?"

She said, "Don't knock it until you've tried it."

Yeah? I couldn't tell if she was messing with me. I was immediately distracted by a noise outside. "Did you hear that? Out front?"

"The wind. There's a storm coming. Don't worry — this place is over. My friend has a new one up and running on Bluff near Folsom." She sat beside me again. "My question before? I'm curious why you called."

"Sorry. For me? Yeah, a tough day and a tough life lately," I said. "I needed to get . . . away. This seemed good." I smiled. "No one will look for me here."

"People are looking for you?" she asked.

I didn't want to explain. "I need a break. Let's leave it there."

"What would help?"

I didn't have an answer. That's how messed up things felt. I said, "This is fine."

She sipped water. I sipped water. Seconds later she stood. She faced me. She locked eyes with me, apparently saw something that looked to her like affirmation, and then in one graceful provocative motion she hiked her skirt up to her waist, wriggling her butt back and forth as she did, and lowered herself to her knees, straddling me.

She leaned forward, crossing her arms behind my neck. Her breasts were, literally, in my face. She smelled like spicy floral elsewhere. I will admit that in that instant it was as enticing an aroma as I could imagine.

Amanda had my complete attention. I had my break from my reality. She was offering me a potential solution to a lot of problems. Just not the ones I was having. In retrospect, I recognized I could have spared us both some awkwardness had I been a little less vague about the reason for my presence in the incall.

I managed to say, "Amanda," but before I could complete an explanation that I wasn't there for sex, someone else said "Amanda," too.

My "Amanda" had been muffled and soft. Apologetic. The other "Amanda" was firm. Demanding. If Amanda hadn't already succeeded in raising my heart rate, that voice from outside the front door certainly would have caused my pulse to jump.

"You have to go. Now!" she hissed into my ear. "That's — He's here!"

She hopped up and tugged down her skirt.

He who?

70

SAM AND JONAS

Sam had started to doze. The very idea of his son being gay exhausted him beyond his comprehension. He was trying to weigh the evidence. Each new piece put him back to sleep.

Jonas sat down on the sofa near him. "I got something. Wake up. You may not like it. You will not like it."

Sam tried to pretend he'd been awake. "What do you mean? Who?"

"What, not who. Because you're a cop. Because you're you. Our John Doe?"

Sam was trying to jump-start his brain. It wasn't going well. "I still don't know what you mean, Jonas."

Sam had an urge to talk about his maybe-gay son. With someone who had recognized the fact before he did. He wished he were awake enough, or courageous enough, to engage Jonas about Simon. He wasn't.

Jonas angled his laptop toward Sam. "This is your original photo from the *Boston Globe.* The guy closest to Elliot is the one we can't find. After this day he's a digital cipher. Never on Facebook. Or anything similar. No images or tags of him on the accounts of the other people in the photo. Nada. I was beginning to think he died right after the 9/11 attacks."

"Is that it? He's dead?" Sam asked. Sam's brain wasn't in a high enough gear for him to decide whether the guy being dead would be good news or bad news.

Jonas made a few deft swipes with his fingertips. "We have the woman's name. On 9/11 she was just starting her senior year at Boston University. And" — Jonas slid a new photo into place — "here she is in 1999 with a guy who might be our John Doe. It's a good photo of her, but he's in profile. I think it's him, but it's not a no-doubter." He arranged the images side by side. "What do you think? Him?"

"Does the facial recognition software think it's him?"

"The software matched her, not him. This JPEG is digitized from newsprint. Not ideal. And we're going back in time — real time and digital time — to 1999. For facial recognition newer is better. More pixels are better. Color is better. 3-D is best. Facial recognition is just a complex algorithm. Some variables — eyes, width of the nose — are crucial to the algorithm. Clarity aids measurement."

Sam's mouth was hanging open. "Are they in a classroom?"

"Yeah, the photo is from the *Crimson,* that's the Harvard newspaper — they're attending a lecture by some famous somebody in Cambridge. If — if — that's our John Doe he may have been a student, too. Maybe at Harvard."

Sam said, "Elliot went to Harvard. That could be where they met. Good work."

"I looked in some Middle Eastern databases where I could poke around in English. The guy shows up a decade later, but only once, and only briefly. And it's weird." Jonas dragged another picture to the row of photos on the screen. The photo was of a sheik speaking to another sheik. "Ignore the two sheiks in the center. That's our guy standing at the desk to the right. Next to the third sheik who's sitting. See?"

"What is a sheik exactly?" Sam asked. "Is that a religious thing? A tribal thing?"

"It's an honorific. It's not important."

"You're sure that's him?" Sam said. "I see some resemblance, but I wouldn't have . . ."

"The software is certain. Good straight-on facial shots. This is a recent photo, 2009. He's older. Hair is different. He has a beard. He's lost weight. It's him. The photo was taken in a town called Duba."

"I don't know where the hell Duba is," Sam said. "What's his name?"

Jonas said, "Neither did I. It's a resort on the Red Sea in Saudi Arabia. This puts him in Duba, I think maybe with one of his uncles, in November 2009."

"You know his uncle? You must have a name."

"The newspaper is in Arabic. This photo is from a cache of the print edition, but the photo is not in the online Arabic version, or in the English language edition. I used translating software on the caption in the Arabic edition, which isn't a reliable way —"

"Jesus Christ, Jonas. Please tell me his name."

Jonas rearranged the images on the screen. "Sometimes you find news articles online that aren't in print editions, but it doesn't usually happen the other way. There had to be a reason to scrub the photo from the digital editions. If I had time I could probably find a cache with the original page for confirmation."

Sam started pacing. He saw Clare's car pull to a stop outside. Emily barked twice to announce the girls' arrival. Sam said, "They're back. I need his name, Jonas."

"I should find someone who can confirm the translation. But it's sensitive — I don't want to just throw the question out online. Do you know anyone who speaks Arabic that you could trust with this?"

"Speaks Arabic? Trust with what? I can't wait any longer. Tell me."

"The newspaper is *Al Jazirah,* Sam. I think our John Doe is Haziq bin Laden."

71

HBL. "You're sure?"

"The software is sure."

"Those bin Ladens?"

"Them. I printed a family tree for you." Jonas switched the screen to an article in the *Washington Post.* "You may know this, but it turns out a whole mess of bin Ladens were in the U.S. on 9/11. U.S. National Security approved a Saudi government request to airlift them out of the country right after the attacks. I have links if you want. It's real."

"I remember. The mainstream media gave our president a hard time about it."

"Can't imagine why," Jonas said. "Haziq — our John Doe — was on the repatriation flight to Saudi Arabia with his extended family."

Sam said, "His relation to Osama?"

"Brother's son. Osama bin Laden's nephew. Another big family, by the way."

"Your theory about why the guy disappeared for all those years? Notoriety? Because of his name? I'm sure you have a hypothesis."

Jonas said, "The obvious one? Yeah, he was lying low. After the attack. Not the best time to be a bin Laden."

Sam kicked at nothing. "Other bin Ladens resurfaced long before 2009. This is too important to guess about. I need to see if any of this means anything to Alan." Sam began to compose a text to Alan, burner to burner.

Jonas said, "You told me you have Alan's phone."

"I have his smartphone. I'm sending this to his burner. From my burner."

"Wait, wait. Alan has a burner? You have a burner?"

"This is a Hail Mary, Jonas. I'm praying Elliot doesn't have possession of Alan's burner. If I'm wrong? I don't want to think about it."

Sam typed: **HB in MA with Osamas nephew? Mean anything to u?**

Jonas went back to his laptop. He flipped from a *New York Times* article to one on the Fox site. "You're right — various bin Ladens began showing up again in Western media long before 2009. One even wrote a book. That may not be why our guy was so low profile."

"Motherfu—" Sam said. "Shit. The connection between this guy and Elliot? All we really know is, what, that Elliot attended a fund-raiser with a Saudi prince's great niece and a bin Laden nephew prior to 9/11? Dozens of other people attended that event. The charity isn't controversial. It doesn't explain anything. It certainly doesn't explain why Elliot would care one way or another if the news got out that he was there."

From the front of the house Grace said, "Two bucks, two bucks."

Jonas told Grace to shut up. Clare told Jonas not to tell his sister to shut up.

Jonas told Sam he would keep looking.

Sam told everyone that he should have verified Alan had his burner before he sent the text.

Grace didn't care. She said, "Two bucks. Two bucks."

72

ALAN

I jumped as my burner vibrated twice in quick succession.

Amanda whispered, "*The Buffer.* Go!"

Raoul. I whispered, "Where?"

She pointed toward the bedroom. It didn't feel like a great solution, but options for hiding places were limited. I went.

I stood with my ear near the door as I checked the texts. *Not about the kids please.*

The first was from LA Amy. **BBB?? On my way. Confirm.** *What? Jesus.*

I heard Amanda say, "How did you find me here?" The bedroom door had the substance of a shoji screen. Her voice was as distinct as if she were in the room with me.

Raoul spoke next using his familiar voice, the one that played distant notes of his childhood in Catalonia. He had other accents for formal settings that scrubbed away those notes. A linguistic chameleon, he could sound like he was born in Omaha or Guadalajara. He said, "I've been trying to find you. You know that. A friend told me about your meeting at Gibbs and Brown."

"Tanya? Damn Tanya."

"A friend. I waited outside their office, followed you here. I thought I would learn where you were living, but instead —"

"Are you stalking me?"

"— this isn't where you live. Whom were you talking to just now?"

"I was on the phone."

"Let me see your phone. I don't believe you."

"No! You can't have it. Raoul, those days are over. I have moved on."

"They don't have to be over."

"Please leave. Now."

"Are you working here? I see two water bottles. Has it come to this for you? For money? We can go back. I am ready to go back to what we had."

"I'm doing a favor for a girlfriend, collecting some of her things. As you can see, this place is closed up." Her voice shook a little as she added, "I have retired from the business, and from you."

"Don't lie. The water in those bottles is cold. Atlanta? Corporate training? You'll make less than half of what I paid you. And you will grow bored, Amanda. Three months? Six? There will be no stakes, no risk. No reward, no passion. No adventure. That's not you. That's not your life."

"And you, you're my life? How did that work out for me? Leave. Please. Let me be. Let me go." Amanda's voice was firm. It was also sad.

Raoul didn't respond to her. They went silent. Neither of them seemed to move. I did not hear footsteps, or creaking floors. I imagined an embrace between them.

I checked the second text. It was from Sam.

HB in MA with Osamas nephew? Mean anything to u?

Elliot in Boston with Osama's nephew? I immediately wondered if Sam's text had been autocorrected, if he'd meant *Obama.* Obama was his parents' only child but he had a bunch of half siblings. Any of their sons would be his nephew. As would the sons of Michelle's brother. Did Michelle's brother have a son? I did not know. I typed:

???

A minute passed without a sound from the other room. I wondered what the hell was going on with Raoul and Amanda.

And with Sam Purdy and the nephew of

either Barack Obama or Osama bin Laden.

I tried to imagine how my life had progressed to a point where the answer to that question could be such a crucial consideration for me.

A gust of wind caused the glass to rattle in the bedroom window.

73

DOCTOR LILA

"You *think*?" my supervisor said.

"Yes," I replied. "Together my two patients committed a murder."

"That is quite an allegation. On what do you base it?"

"Bits and pieces from one therapy added to bits and pieces from the other therapy. One plus one. And news reports about the death in question. From Google. Given what I suspect happened, I need your help understanding my ethical obligations going forward."

He closed his eyes for a few seconds. I feared he was trying to rediscover his arrogant center. He said, "I am intrigued, of course, but also more than a little lost. Obligation to do what? Barring child endangerment, you not only have no ethical obligation to report a prior crime, but you also have no liberty to do so. That knowledge is protected by the patient's privilege. It is not a gray area clinically. Or legally."

"I understand all that," I said. "I am wondering about my obligation under the 'duty to warn.' "

He uncrossed his arms and uncrossed his legs. He leaned forward. "You're thinking *Tarasoff* applies to this? I must have misunderstood. I thought you were talking about a prior murder, not a threatened one. An imminent one."

"I am talking about both. A prior murder. And possibly an imminent one."

"We, as therapists, only have a duty to warn when we have a patient who has made an overt threat. Has either of your patients made a clear threat, one that could be considered imminent?"

I gave it some thought. "Clear? No. Not exactly. But I have reason to think they do intend to harm someone. Soon."

His posture relaxed. He thought whatever imminent threat I might pose had passed. He said, "Tell me about their intent to harm? Why?"

"Same answer as before. Bits and pieces from one therapy plus bits and pieces from the other therapy. News reports I got from Google. One plus one plus one."

He sighed. The sigh, I thought, was dismissive. He said, "Go on."

"The risk of harm to the new victim is high. It may not meet the letter of the current *Tarasoff* standards, but I believe I have a clear duty to warn in this circumstance. I know it's unusual. I wouldn't be here if it wasn't."

"Please tell me what you were told that you believe constitutes a threat."

"The first one said that he was looking for a way to take a specific individual 'down.' I clarified with him. I said, 'Down?' He said, 'Permanently, yeah. I have to find a way to end this harassment. I can't live like this.' That is close to an exact quote."

"But those words could mean a number of things. Most of them benign."

"But given their history? The earlier murder? I don't feel I can take the risk."

He contorted his face as though he had food caught between two molars. "Is there some countertransference we should discuss? Something that might be influencing your judgment about these men?"

"No. I understand that concern, but I am confident that I am perceiving these events without any . . . distortion."

He got up and walked to his desk. He checked his cell phone for messages. He returned to his chair. "So your question to me is about your ethical obligation to warn a potential victim based on, what, a little of this and a little of that and your clinical intuition that these two patients are planning to hurt —"

"Kill."

"— kill someone? Absent an overt threat? It's not a lot to go on. Clinically."

"The threat is implied. No, I think it is more than implied — to me it is almost clear — when I combine what I know from the two therapies. With what I've read online. These two men have demonstrated that they are willing to kill. The next victim? I believe he is at risk."

" 'Implied'? 'Almost clear'? 'Believe'?"

"Yes."

I expected him to argue. He didn't. He said, "What about immediacy?"

"It could happen at any time."

"Is that imminence, Delilah? Or speculation?"

"It's risk to someone's life. The stakes couldn't be higher."

"Are you able to identify the intended victim?"

"I am. It's the Boulder County district attorney, Elliot Bellhaven. He has been identified by both patients as their prime . . . focus and adversary."

74

SAM AND JONAS

Sam didn't find Alan's reply to his text — **???** — helpful. It provided Sam no confidence at all that Alan, and not Elliot, was in possession of the burner. He typed:

Verify Fijis original name?

Ten seconds later Sam got a return text from Alan.

Callie wtf?

Sam said, "Clare and Grace are downstairs?" Jonas nodded without looking up from his laptop. "You're sure?" Jonas nodded again. "Your dad still has his burner. He's not in custody."

Jonas said, "Jackpot. I searched for the names together. Get this: The Saudi prince's great niece or fourth cousin or whatever she is, and Haziq bin Laden were married in 2005 in Saudi Arabia. The same week Katrina hit New Orleans."

Sam thought for a moment. He said, "Our

guy is not gay? That changes things. I was thinking he was gay."

"What? We don't know that. He could be straight. He could be gay. She could be his beard."

"His beard?"

"Being gay isn't a great thing in Saudi Arabia. Or in Islam. He would need cover. A beard. A wife. Kids would help, too. They have three already."

Sam said, "How the hell do you know all this?"

Jonas said, "How do you not? If he's gay, it might explain his low profile. Right? And maybe why that photo in Duba was scrubbed. Haziq could have been there to see the sheik next to him in the picture? That sheik could be prominent, too. The scrubbing could have been because of the sheik, not Haziq."

"I hear guesses, Jonas. We have no evidence, either way. What else would cause Elliot to be so determined to keep this part of his life secret? And cause this Haziz bin Laden to keep such a low profile?"

Jonas said, "Haziq. Has to be. If Haziq bin Laden is gay it explains things. If he's not? This may all be a waste of time. All we may have is evidence that Elliot was at a fund-raiser with a guy who happened to be a relative of Osama bin Laden. Big whoop."

"Lauren thought it was important," Sam said. "She found that photo. She hid that photo from Elliot."

"Yeah?" Jonas said. "Then that might be it."

"Yeah." Sam put one of his big hands on each side of the kid's head. He touched his own forehead to Jonas's. He said, "I'm going to go do my best to help your dad. You keep all this to yourself. Thank you for all your help. All . . . your help."

"You're going with the gay thing? With Alan?"

"We're out of time, Jonas. I'm going to give it to him. Leave it up to him."

Jonas said, "I don't like it. Say Haziq is gay. Elliot's been an ass, but he shouldn't get crushed for being with Haziq. So Elliot was with a guy in Boston before 9/11? And maybe the guy was his boyfriend. That's not a crime."

"Wrong weekend. Wrong guy," Sam said. "Elliot might have a knack for wrong guys."

"But we found nothing that says Haziq is a bad guy. He had a bad uncle. That's not a crime."

"Politically? Other people won't see it the way you do, Jonas. You're smart. You know that. Elliot is smart. If he was involved with

Haziq, he knows what this news getting out would mean. It's the only theory we have that explains why he is so willing to throw your dad in jail."

"And you're what? You're going to out Elliot and Haziq as a couple? That's not right. It may not even be true."

"Alan won't tell anyone about this but Elliot. You know that. If it's not true they were a couple, it is what it is. We tried. We lost. If Elliot did have a thing with Haziq, Elliot will recognize his vulnerability. This isn't really about them being gay. It's about them being a couple. Politically, is it fair? No. But Elliot wouldn't get away with this news getting out if he was straight and his girlfriend was a Bin Laden niece. If he's gay and his boyfriend was a Bin Laden nephew? The public will definitely not forget that. That's Alan's leverage. It's why I have to tell him.

"Elliot's the one who started this war with your mom and dad. And I can't think of another way to help Alan stay out of jail today, right now, than to let him know that Elliot may have been hiding the fact he had a relationship with Haziq bin Laden."

"What if we're wrong?"

"If we're wrong? Alan's in trouble. We can't debate this any longer, Jonas. I have to do it now. I'm sorry."

Jonas said, "Haziq could be your kid. It could be his life."

Sam said, "Yeah." The tears in his eyes revealed that he knew that Jonas was not speaking hypothetically.

Jonas stood up. He said, "It sucks."

Sam said, "It does suck."

The second he got into his Cherokee, Sam used his smartphone to type "Beard" into search on Urban Dictionary. He read the definition. *Damn.* He started driving back to town but he knew Alan might not have the luxury of waiting to learn what Jonas had discovered.

He stopped the Cherokee near the mailboxes on the lane. He switched to his burner. The signal was one bar. Aloud he said, "If I'm wrong, I'm wrong."

He texted Alan one more time.

He opened the driver's side window a couple of inches as he pulled away. If he saw flashing lights in the mirror on his way back to town he had to be prepared to ditch his burner's SIM. Fast.

75

ALAN

I finally heard the front door open. *Raoul is leaving,* I thought. *And I am losing my chance to confront him.*

I heard a voice of caution in my head. *Do not do it. Don't talk to him, Alan.* The voice of caution was not Lauren's. It was Kirsten's. But I couldn't let Raoul go. I knew that moment might be my last chance to speak with him. As I grabbed the doorknob I heard Raoul say, "Please, come in. He's back there. Bathroom or bedroom, I'm not sure which. I heard his voice earlier. It's him. There's no back door."

That gave me pause.

Amanda said, "What the hell is going on? Who are you? Raoul, who is he?"

Raoul said, "This is when you should be quiet, Amanda." He shushed her.

I expected Amanda to protest. She did not. My burner buzzed again.

It was Sam, again, on his burner. Sam's previous text about our small dog's original name had baffled me. The new text read:

HB MAYBE with bf haziq bin laden — HBL — in Boston 9-08-01. Nephew of Osama. MAYBE BF! Found Laurens photo from Boston globe BG. Where r u?

Holy shit. That, I thought, *explains a lot. Maybe.*

Sam's *maybe* meant it might be time to gamble. I thought of Carl Luppo and his Powerball. *Maybe.* And the bullet that found him in Pacific Palisades. *Maybe.*

I thought of Ivy Baldwin dying peacefully in bed as an old man after a full lifetime of high-wire maybes.

But Sam's *maybe* meant caution was in order, too.

The page from the Field Notes book meant Lauren knew some of this, too. But she wasn't sure. She had her own maybe. I'd decided that *NoE* was her shorthand for *no evidence.*

Instinctively I knew, no matter what I did next, I had to protect Sam's clean hands. I took a moment to extract the SIM — and all its data — from my burner. I entered the adjacent bathroom and dropped the card into the toilet. I slowly ran water into the sink. I submerged the burner and held it under until it stopped bubbling.

I flushed the toilet. My burner was drowning, its memory was in Boulder's sewers. I could no longer reach Sam or my lawyer. Raoul and someone he knew were outside the door.

My degrees of freedom were officially exhausted. The sound of the flushing toilet announced my presence to Raoul and his guest. I opened the door.

Helliot was walking toward me. He stopped.

I felt serene when I saw him. I said, "Hello, Raoul. Hello, Elliot." Amanda looked baffled. "Amanda, in case you haven't been introduced, this is the Boulder County DA, Elliot Bellhaven. Don't be alarmed. He's here to see me, not you."

Raoul spoke to Amanda. "You are fine, cherie. We can go, find somewhere to talk. About the future. This doesn't concern us."

I looked at my old friend. "How is Diane, Raoul?"

My earnest question — I had feared that when I finally spoke those words to him they would not sound sincere — seemed to cause him to freeze as if in a still frame. For an instant he moved not a muscle. Then he glanced at Amanda before his eyes came back to me. He said, "My Diane is sick. The surgery — they operated to remove the glioma — could have gone better. That's what they said. The radiation they did? It's been hard on her. Toxic."

"Her prognosis?" I asked. "Are the doctors optimistic?"

"Some days I hear more hope than I hear on other days. Lately, less hope, I think. Certainly less than I would like. It could be my ears, not their words. Who knows?"

I expected to feel sorrow at Diane's plight. I didn't. I felt no glee, but no sorrow.

"I heard she is in Arizona. Still?" I said.

He sucked air through his clenched teeth. "You don't need to know that, Alain."

I was stung but managed to keep my voice cordial as I said, "Diane is why you are helping Elliot frame me?" I said. "To try to keep her out of prison? Does she know you're here in Boulder? What you're doing to me? To my children?"

Raoul went back into freeze-frame. He didn't reply. He didn't move. His eyes told me he couldn't believe I'd asked him that question. Again he looked to Amanda.

I suddenly realized he didn't know that I knew. He thought I was ignorant about the affair.

I understood protecting family. At almost

any cost. I had come to accept that I might be too comfortable rationalizing those particular costs. But Raoul didn't know that about me. He couldn't know that his motive to protect Diane was more palatable to me than had been his motive to seduce my wife.

I lost focus for a moment as I questioned my assumption. *Who,* I wondered, *had seduced whom?*

I forced myself back to the moment. Amanda's expression revealed that she recognized that a setup was in progress and that she didn't understand its parameters. She looked to me, not to Raoul, for guidance. "Should I go, Alan?"

I shook my head. "Please stay for a moment, Amanda. I think everyone should stay. Raoul, I don't believe she wishes to go anywhere with you."

Raoul had regained his equilibrium. He grinned. I had to admit that the man had a million-dollar smile. I felt an unpleasant urge to remove some of his perfect teeth.

Elliot grinned, too. He said, "I don't think what you believe is relevant, Alan. Do you fail to recognize your disadvantage? The gravity of why we're here?"

I assumed he meant my imminent arrest. I recalled Sam and the Kumamotos and the glass of rye teetering on his belly. That the only thing more alluring than the spectacle of success was the prospect of spectacular failure. That's where I was with Elliot.

I would either pull off this long shot or I would go down in dazzling flames.

I also heard Elliot's words as his acknowledgment, and his caution to me, that he was in possession of Lauren's missing yellow Field Notes.

Elliot didn't know that I, too, had a copy. Or that I had, courtesy of Sam, a recent annotated translation of the most pertinent line of Lauren's notes. *Well, maybe.*

I said, "I think I do understand why you're here, Elliot. The gravity? I may understand that better than you."

I held my hands in front of my body, tapping my inner wrists together to suggest my capitulation. I interweaved my fingers and placed my hands on top of my head. "If you wish to detain me, Elliot, do it. Before I hear Miranda I'd like to say something. Voluntarily. I'm sure you appreciate the value of having these two witnesses affirm that I am speaking to you of my own free will prior to being taken into custody."

I moved like a sloth toward Elliot to allow him opportunity to protest. The grin stayed plastered on his face. "Don't worry, I'm

637

harmless."

"I'm not worried," he said. "About you."

This isn't Flagstaff, this is the Morgul Bismark. We're not climbing big mountains. My territory, my advantage. You should be worried.

Maybe.

I felt a flicker of ambivalence about what I was about to do to protect my family and myself. If Sam was right Elliot had likely done nothing illegal prior to 9-11-2001. I thought it through. Because Elliot didn't expect the world to treat him fairly when they discovered his romantic relationship with a Bin Laden relative in Boston, he had decided on a take-no-prisoners approach since then.

When Lauren became too curious about Elliot's background, he made her one of his casualties. Elliot was eager to make me one of his casualties, too. And he was more than willing to allow my kids to become collateral damage.

Elliot's transgression? I saw blind ambition. And political self-interest. I had little tolerance for those motivations.

Despite the risk that Sam was wrong — that *maybe* — and that I was wrong, I felt a sense of calm.

All the doubt, all the options, would come

down to a binary outcome. What I was about to say to Elliot would either work. Or it wouldn't. I had Ivy Baldwin on my mind. No one knew binary outcomes better than Ivy.

I leaned toward Elliot so that my lips were inches from his right ear. He leaned away. I leaned forward some more. I was not fond of his cologne. I felt exhilaration that was almost equivalent to my fear.

Ivy had been right about the high wire. It was the greatest poison in the world.

One drop would kill me.

I enunciated with exaggerated care as I whispered into Elliot Bellhaven's ear, "Haziq" — I paused — "bin Laden."

I began to count to myself, something I do reflexively in moments of unbearable anticipation. By the time I reached three, my confidence began evaporating.

I held my lips where they were. I was so close to Elliot that had he turned his face in my direction we would have kissed. By my count of six I began expecting Elliot to laugh at me, a laugh I feared I would hear echoed for my eternity in state prison.

I reached eleven before Elliot took his next breath.

76

DOCTOR LILA

My supervisor said, "Your patients identified Mr. Bellhaven by name?"

They aren't fools, I thought. "By his role. His position."

"Specifically? The Boulder County district attorney?"

"No. In general terms. His legal authority."

"It won't work, Delilah. The duty to warn has never been interpreted the way you are suggesting. It has certainly never been invoked in a circumstance where the therapist's determination of an overt threat is dependent on knowledge from two different clinical cases combined together. Let alone based on media reports of unknowable veracity. About a victim whose identity is a clear leap of faith. The ethics don't back you up. The courts won't see it the way you see it."

I was prepared for that argument. I had rehearsed my response to it. "Prior to *Tarasoff* there was no duty to warn. But things evolve. That's the nature of our profession. Ethical standards are organic, just like diagnoses. DSM-III became IV. Soon it will become V. Pathology standards change. Ethical standards do, too. Child endangerment wasn't an exception to privilege in the first half of the twentieth century. *Tarasoff* will be superseded by an evolved ethical dictate about the duty to warn. You know that is true."

"So why not your case? Why shouldn't this . . . confabulation be the one that changes the world? That's what you're saying?"

Asshole. "Yes, why not this case? These cases. The consequences of inaction are immense. I don't feel I can ignore the risk. I am not looking to change the world, but simply to prevent a tragedy. In good faith."

"Hypothetically? Let's say I concur, Delilah. What do you propose you have an obligation to do with your conclusion that Mr. Bellhaven is at risk?"

"Warn him."

"You cannot. That's a clear violation of confidentiality."

I had done my homework. "Do you remember Michael McClelland? You were in town then. Practicing, I believe."

"McClelland? What does he have to do with this? That was a long time ago. I'm surprised you even know about it."

I said, "One of my professors knows Dr. Gregory, McClelland's psychologist. She told me some things about the case. She thinks, and I agree, that ethical missteps were made. Mistakes in judgment."

"By McClelland's therapist?" he said. "What missteps?"

"McClelland tried to kill Dr. Gregory's girlfriend. Did Dr. Gregory violate McClelland's privilege when he helped the police track him down to prevent that murder? Did Dr. Gregory violate his professional ethics by trying to protect someone he cared about?"

"Those were extraordinary circumstances. And I think a careful analysis of what happened would reveal that the therapist in that case erred on the side of confidentiality, not on the side of disclosure. My advice is that you should do the same."

I said, "I think we may be in agreement. See, that is the specific error in judgment I am questioning. How did his decision to be so protective of his patient's privilege work out for Dr. Gregory? Or for Michael Mc-

Clelland's future victims? I've read interviews with law enforcement officials who maintain McClelland continued to arrange murders from the state hospital and later, from prison."

I paused to give him a chance to contradict me. He didn't. I said, "I want to do what is right. I don't want those kinds of concerns chasing me because I failed to act. The men I am discussing have demonstrated a willingness to murder to protect themselves."

"You think," he said.

"I do think. Yes, I do. I am aware this is a judgment I am making."

He asked, "Do you feel any personal danger from either of your patients?"

I said, "I have not been threatened. But I do feel vulnerable. Anyone would."

I'd had supervisors like this man before. Pedantic ones. They were not my favorites. I had hoped to find an ally. I realized I wasn't going to get one.

He said, "Our job as therapists isn't to predict future wrongdoing by our patients, Doctor. You know that. The data show we are not good at it."

"I am not predicting. I heard a threat. I would be reporting what I know."

"You heard a generic assertion. You don't

know. By your own admission, you are surmising, linking disparate pieces of information. For some reason we both need to understand much better, you are reaching for a conclusion. Right now? You lack both the legal and ethical authority to take the steps you are contemplating."

I said, "Well, I appreciate your counsel."

"Is that capitulation? I'm surprised. You clearly disagree with me."

"We're not on exactly the same page. But I am here to learn." I forced a smile.

"The Michael McClelland situation? Years ago? You seem to know that history?"

"Yes," I said. I was curious where he was going.

"Review it, please, before we speak again. That therapist never broke his patient's privilege. He upheld our profession's ethical standards."

I said, "I am not in a position to argue that history with you. I wasn't there. But my understanding is that McClelland's therapist, Dr. Gregory, paid a high personal price for his decisions. And that other people — complete innocents — may have died because he decided to adhere to ethical standards that might have been outdated even back then."

I put air quotes around the word *ethical.* I

regretted doing that. Instantly.

I think that was what provoked him.

He went to his desk and returned with a leather portfolio. He began writing. "In my notes for today, I will make clear that I am advising you to act in a way consistent with applicable Colorado law, and to adhere to the *current* ethical standards of APA. You will get a letter by email later today reflecting that advice."

He was warning me. I said, "Even if it means someone dies?"

I thought he seemed tired. He said, "We aren't seers. We aren't detectives. Or cops. What we do is hard enough. There is no need to complicate our role."

"I think that if Alan Gregory had been more of a detective when he was treating Michael McClelland, and if he had been willing to involve the police earlier, the world would be a different and better place today."

His voice softer, he said, "Yes? No? I can't say. I do know that it is not our job. Think about what I've said. Please. Let's meet again on Friday. Two o'clock?"

I thanked him as I gathered my things. Frankly I'd expected better from him. At his door I said, "To be clear, today's meeting, between you and me? This is covered by the same privilege as psychotherapy, isn't it?"

His eyes told me he saw the trap I'd set. The ethics of our profession did not allow a supervisor to break privilege, whether or not a supervisee heeded his counsel.

He couldn't tell anyone we had met about my two patients.

"It is," he said. "But I urge you in the strongest possible terms not to act precipitously before we speak again."

"I wouldn't think of it. I will count on your discretion until then."

I had an appointment with Elliot Bellhaven at five thirty on Thursday evening. The outcome of that meeting would determine whether or not I kept Friday's supervision appointment.

I kept that fact to myself as I closed the door behind me.

Snow flurries fluttered across my vision when I stepped outside. I hadn't realized that a storm was on the way.

I pulled my phone from my bag at the corner of Eleventh and Spruce.

77

ALAN

Elliot took one step away from me. He turned to Raoul and Amanda.

He asked if he could "have the room."

I didn't know if I had won or I had lost. I was teetering on Ivy's wire, one foot in the air. My equilibrium no sure thing.

Amanda looked to me for direction. "Should I go?"

I took my hands from my head, hoping I could regain some literal balance.

I wasn't sure I had options. I was sure I was unprepared to have options.

A grad school professor had once taught our class that if someone is eager for a certain status, he should act like he already has it and see if anyone objects.

Why not? I began to act as though I had regained my balance, and as though I was in control. I said, "Would you like to leave here alone, Amanda? With a head start?"

She nodded. We embraced. I thanked her for her help. She kissed me on the cheek. She did it a second time. Amanda grabbed her things and hurried from the room. I was able to watch through the window as she climbed into a black Boxster on Pine Street. She drove away.

Until Elliot objected I would continue to act as though I had the power. I was cognizant that any opportunity I had with Raoul was a fleeting thing. Once he left the incall I would probably never again see him absent a roomful of lawyers. I went back and forth in my mind about my options. The trade-offs. The repercussions.

I decided that I needed to do something I could live with. Something prudent rather than satisfying. My overriding goal remained what it had been all along: clean hands. For my kids. For Sam's kid.

My anger at Raoul for all his betrayals threatened to burst from my chest. The rage screamed at me to ignore prudence. To seek retaliation. Better? Vengeance.

I waited a full minute — Amanda's head start — before I took a cue from her departure. I leaned forward and I kissed Raoul on one cheek and then on the other.

I said, "I know you were fucking her, Raoul. Now get the fuck out of my sight."

Raoul backed away. He did not understand what was happening. He looked at me and said, "Amanda?" I shook my head. His eyes grew dark as he realized that his long affair with Lauren was no longer a secret.

He faced Elliot and mouthed, *What?* Out loud, Raoul said, "What did he say to you, Elliot?" Elliot merely closed his eyes. "What is happening?"

Raoul had arrived in the incall expecting dual victories. To win Amanda. To vanquish me. Instead he was being shunned by his ally. At the door, he paused. He said, "Elliot, is there —"

Elliot said, "No, Raoul. Go. I have this. I'm good. I'll be in touch."

I waited until I saw Raoul reach the sidewalk on Pine. He looked back at the incall once before he turned west.

Elliot has this? Let's find out.

I said, "Elliot, take off your clothes."

Elliot looked at me. I looked back at him. Being with people in awkward silence was my forte. Elliot may have failed to recognize his disadvantage; testing me at that particular pastime was like challenging a snake to a staring contest.

Only half a minute passed before Elliot

relented. Thirty seconds was nothing to me; with resistant patients I occasionally sat in silence for forty-five minutes.

Elliot said that he would disrobe — his word — if I would.

I removed my shirt as he removed his. He was wearing an undershirt; I was pleased to see sweat stains below his pits.

It was only when he was naked to the waist, his belt loose and his trousers undone, that I began to allow myself to feel that I may have won.

Elliot insisted on examining the seams and buttons of my clothing for tiny digital devices. I did the same with his. My clothing convinced him that I wasn't wearing a wire. I wasn't as convinced about him. I asked him to remove the battery from his BlackBerry. His phone buzzed as he pulled it from the pocket of his jacket. For a fleeting second the screen was visible to me.

Caller ID was a number, a local 303 number, but not a name.

I thought I recognized the number. I tried to place it. I came up blank. I repeated the final four digits in my head in an attempt to sear them into memory.

Elliot sent the call to voicemail before he slid open the back of the device. I couldn't discern if he knew that I'd seen the screen. Or that he cared if I had.

Things were moving quickly. I had to keep my focus.

Elliot removed the battery from his phone. He asked me to do the same with mine. I explained it had drowned in the sink. I went to the bathroom to retrieve it, taking the opportunity to flush the toilet again to give the SIM an extra push on its journey to Boulder's sewers.

I returned to show Elliot the saturated phone and the empty SIM slot.

We placed our dead devices together on the center cushion of the leather sofa.

"You have a burner." Elliot said it in a way that made clear how much that explained to him.

I nodded. We dressed. We chose opposite ends of the old leather couch. I liked the irony that this protracted match between us was concluding in an apartment on Pine Street that had recently been the home of a drug dealer before it became an incall for industrious escorts.

Elliot and I would be only the latest criminals to conduct our business there.

"What do you want from me, Alan?"

"To be clear? This?" I pointed at myself and then at him. "Another one of our social

651

visits. Is that acceptable to you?"

"Yes."

"What do I want from you? Simple. To be left alone. What do you want from me, Elliot?"

"The same," he said. "And your promise of the same going forward."

"If that's all you want you should have asked. A year ago. Five years ago. Hell, ten years ago. I would have said yes in a heartbeat. There would have been no casualties. No blood."

"Back then it wasn't about you, Alan. It was about your wife. Lauren wouldn't have left me alone. It was not in her character. At the end? I think she thought she had me. She was relishing that she had me."

"You might be right about her, Elliot. In circumscribed areas Lauren had a more crystalline view of right and wrong than I do. But before I agree to leave you be, I need some questions answered."

"Perhaps I will answer them," he said. "That depends on the questions."

"And perhaps I will leave you be. That depends on your answers," I said. "Let's start with the .38 on Prado."

"I thought you would want to start on 9/11. Isn't that the juicy part?"

"Is it? We will get there."

"The gun was my aunt Beulah's. She lived in Iowa. She was the only one in the family who had guessed I was gay. She gave me her .38 Special a week before she died. She had synovial cancer. I didn't even know what it was. Anyway, Beulah thought I would need 'protection' because of my 'lifestyle.' 'Lifestyle' was her euphemism for homosexuality. For her, 'protection' didn't mean condoms. Beulah was a pistol.

"I didn't realize the .38 was missing from my apartment until I got back to Boulder after 9/11, which was days after Marshall had died. When I learned later that a gun had been involved, I had a bad feeling about what might have happened."

"How did you learn a gun was involved? That he'd shot himself?"

"You know, Alan, I don't recall. It was later, from the police, I imagine."

I detected a smirk. I asked, "You thought he used your gun to kill himself? Was Marshall angry at you?"

"Angry? I don't know. He was young. Younger than his years. Confused. He was upset that sex didn't mean forever. He couldn't believe that he didn't become the center of my life after we were together a few times. He was certainly unhappy that I went back to Boston to see Haziq. Yeah, I guess he was angry. Marshall was also a depressed guy. I knew that. When he didn't answer my calls from Boston? I admit I began to worry."

"The police didn't find your gun back then. In 2001. You knew that, too?"

"I knew. I followed the investigation." Elliot shook his head, bemused. "Marshall was a closet writer. Marshall was a closet a lot of things. He had written a draft of a short story, a mystery, that he insisted I read, weeks before 9/11. It was about a man who shot himself and died, and also about a disappearing gun that had stumped the cops. The story wasn't that good — he made the guy's suicide seem like a lark, not a tragedy — and Marshall hadn't been able to work out the part about exactly how the gun disappeared. Looking back, I should have seen the story as a cry for help. Instead I was an ass about it. I was . . . unkind to him about his writing. I did not need to be so cruel. But I was. I was pushing him away, probably."

"Because there was someone else," I said.

"Yes, Alan, there was. Later, when I heard the police couldn't find the gun, I knew he had finally figured out how to end his damn story. But I couldn't figure out how he did it, how he made the gun disappear. Ironic, huh? I had no idea where that gun was, but I was damn sure the disappearance wouldn't be permanent. I've been waiting for Aunt Beulah's .38 to show up ever since. And then last year, sure enough, it did."

I said, "Right when you were preparing to announce for statewide office?"

"Your friend Sam found the gun last year. You probably know that. And Lauren learned about it late last summer, not long before she died. It was just a matter of time before one of them traced it to Beulah and then to me. I knew that wouldn't look good politically. But I thought I could ride it out. I didn't do what was right back in 2001, but I really didn't do anything wrong. I actually thought the bungee part could help me. The bungee would be a distraction for the public. Do you know about the bungee, Alan?"

I didn't answer his question. "Why didn't you come forward and admit that you knew Marshall Doctor back then? That he had taken your gun? What was the downside? Were you still in the closet?"

He gave that question some thought. "I was in the closet at work. But that wasn't it. I didn't want an industrious detective to call my friends in Boston to ask them if I'd been in touch with Marshall. To question whether I knew what he was going to do. I couldn't risk someone digging around in that part of my life. The Boston part."

"The Haziq part?" I said.

"God yes. The Haziq part. If Haziq's name came up? That week? After 9/11? If our relationship had become public? God knows what would have happened to him when he got back to Saudi Arabia. I don't like to think about it."

I said, "And you? Your political ambitions in Colorado would have been over before they started?" He nodded. I asked, "At some point you began going through Lauren's things at work. Was that to find out what she knew about Marshall, or about Haziq? Or was it something else?"

"No comment. Next."

"Why did you search my house and my cars? It wasn't about the shooting in my office. Were you still trying to find out what Lauren had on you?"

"No comment. Next."

"Why are you threatening to prosecute me for killing my wife? What the fuck is that about?"

Elliot recognized that my composure was deteriorating. He became officious. "Prosecutors, like me, must often contend with conflicting witness statements. Early on the investigation was marred by breakdowns in police procedure and protocol, and by compromised forensics. Both witnesses had reasons to lie. That is all I will say. Next."

"You also have prosecutorial discretion?"

"Always. Always. Always. Next."

It was time for me to place a governor on Elliot's prosecutorial discretion. I said, "Let's go back to Haziq."

Elliot's eyes filled with tears. "He is not some symbol, Alan. He's not your 'gotcha.' He is an amazing man. You would like him. We were together for almost two years before I came to Boulder. I adore him still. I miss him terribly."

"Lauren said you gave up a clerkship with a feeder judge in the Ninth Circuit to stay in Boston? That was to stay near Haziq?"

Elliot smiled. Not at his recognition that Lauren had learned of his sacrifice, but that it hadn't been a sacrifice for him at all. "Haziq and I haven't spoken since 9/11. While I was in Boston the weekend before, we were working on schemes that would allow him to move to Denver. Grad school at DU. That awful week changed everything. If his name becomes public, even now, if the nature of our relationship becomes public? Lives will be ruined. Innocent lives. Haziq has a family. A wife. Children. This isn't

657

about my career, Alan. Innocent lives are at stake. Not reputations. In Saudi Arabia? *Lives.*"

Elliot wanted to shift the burden of protecting the safety of Haziq bin Laden and his family onto me. I wasn't about to accept that responsibility. Elliot had not demonstrated any compassion for my family or for my children or for their lives.

"Given the vulnerability of Haziq and his family," I said, "you must feel a huge personal responsibility to protect the truth about your relationship with him. To keep anyone from making it public. For *any* reason."

He stared, his contempt for me clear in his eyes. I also thought I saw some admiration, too. He had been counting on using the fate of Haziq's family to sway me.

I said, "I am done with you, Elliot. If you're not done with me? Know this: I will protect mine. You think Lauren was a bulldog? Try me."

I stood to leave. I told him I had to lock up.

He didn't stand. He said, "No. My turn. I have a question. Who knows what you know?"

I knew the danger was in appearing evasive. "Some of it? Lucy, Sam's partner. Most of it? Sam. All of it? I texted Haziq's name to two people from the bathroom."

"From your burner?"

"From that burner right there. You might be able to guess the identity of one of the recipients. The other? You will never guess. Thanks to my little burner? All your surveillance failed you."

He pondered my words for truth and lies. I hadn't had time to share the story with anyone from the bathroom. I would certainly do so before that afternoon edged into dusk. But I hadn't done it.

"What if I don't believe you, Alan? What if I think you're bluffing?"

Elliot might have suspected I was lying. But he didn't *know* I was lying. I was tempted to ask him if he knew about Ivy Baldwin. I didn't.

Would Elliot call my bluff? I thought, *One drop . . .*

Elliot said, "If I run for statewide office? For AG or for governor, do I have to worry about this . . . history becoming public?"

I didn't hesitate. I said, "I will never vote for you, Elliot. But if fate is kind to me, if I am left alone, and if those I love are left alone, I will feel no inclination to interfere with your political ambitions."

Elliot stood. He offered to shake my hand

to seal our deal. I stuffed both hands into my pockets to help contain an urge to strangle him as he walked past me.

Once he was outside he rushed down the stairs and around the back. I could hear his footsteps fading in the distance before I moved off the landing.

I savored the mental image of Elliot sneaking away down the alley, his head down, his collar high against the falling snow.

78

I slept no better that night.

But when I climbed out of bed the next morning I felt different.

I felt lighter, though not light.

I felt safer, though not safe.

I felt grateful, though not great.

The kids woke to a house that smelled of pancakes and bacon.

Grace had become a vegetarian overnight. And she was no longer eating white flour. She wanted to know if we had any spelt.

I offered her some coffee instead.

She said, "Yes, please." She had a couple of ounces *au lait* with her wheat toast and peanut butter. And her banana.

Jonas had earbuds in his ears. He brought a book to the table.

He listened and he read while he ate his share and Grace's share of the pancakes and bacon.

The music was Girlyman.

The book was *On the High Wire* by Philippe Petit.

Over my son's shoulder, I read, "Limits exist only in the souls of those who do not dream."

I didn't eat. But I felt full.

I felt good.

EPILOGUE
APRIL 1

ALAN

Emily barked her attention bark — an extended "Wooof" without much volume — as she raced from the bedroom to the front of the house. I heard the big dog slide to a stop on the slick wood floors. My breath caught in my throat.

Then . . . nothing. I exhaled.

She rocked her hips, just a little, to refocus me.

The motion caused her breasts to sway.

"Do you like them?" She rocked her hips a second time. The motion induced more sway. She knew it would.

The query wasn't about her hips.

"Is that a trick question?" I asked.

She shook her head, which caused more swaying.

That time the sway was inadvertent.

"I do," I said, "like them." I tried to imbue

intimate appreciation into the words because that was what I was feeling. I saw both
mischief and welcome in her eyes.

I didn't trust my appraisal. I had been
misreading women my entire life.

I asked, "Do you like that I like them?"

She wrinkled her nose. She didn't blink.
"Is *that* a trick question?" she said. "A
shrink thing?"

I said, "No. Sadly."

"You are a damaged man, aren't you?"
The sound had a ribbed texture that came
from deep in her throat, the volume a
whisker above a whisper.

Damaged? I didn't quarrel. She sounded
more compassionate than accusatory. Was it
possible that she was, just maybe, relieved
that I was not undamaged?

She said, "I do like that you like them.
Truly." She rocked her hips again. Physics
being physics, the sway followed, just a little.
She knew that would happen.

Truly. I began to feel buoyant, a familiar
sensation of intoxicating lightness, as though
I could begin to float away.

She may have sensed the danger. She
reached down between her legs and grabbed
me in a manner guaranteed to keep me
from drifting anywhere.

■ ■ ■ ■

The big Bouvier began barking again — *rat-a-tat-tat-tat-tat* — five times in quick succession.

Those were Emily's automatic-weapon barks.

My dog was seriously unhappy about something.

I am fluent in Bouvier. The deep ominous claps, roared without nuance, were Emily's I'm-going-to-maim-you-if-you-take-one-more-step warning shots. When Emily barked that way — she did it rarely — she first bared her fangs and lowered her hindquarters so she was prepared to leap.

No matter how distracted I was by other things — and at that moment I was maximally distracted by other things — those barks captured my attention.

I held my breath and I listened. At my five-count the big dog's initial warnings were chased by three barks of a slightly higher pitch, each one finished with a hint of vibrato. The barks' trailing rumbles were the result of hollows created when Emily's loose cheeks dropped to cover her fangs.

Vibrato barks indicated an all-clear. Once I heard the rumble I knew the alarm, whatever it was, had passed. The rumble meant that Emily had shifted her weight from her haunches and that her nub of a tail had begun its approximation of a wag.

I exhaled. Within moments I heard heavy footsteps on the hardwood floor and then the sounds of Sam Purdy's voice at an unexpectedly high volume: "Alan! You back here? You in the shower? Get out. We —"

"Sam, wait. Don't come in —"

The bedroom door was open. He walked in. He said, "Oh. Oh. Sorry. I didn't know you had — I didn't know you were —"

I was facing the doorway. She was leaning into me, her head buried at my neck. I said, "Bad timing, Sam. Go, Sam." He didn't. I said, "Turn around. Leave."

He turned around. He didn't leave. "This can't wait. We have a problem."

"Are the kids okay?"

"It's not the kids. The other thing."

God. The other thing is over. We won. Didn't we?

"It can wait, Sam."

"It can't wait, Alan."

"Go to the kitchen. I'll be right there. This better be important."

I pulled on some sweatpants and joined Sam at the counter.

"Did you really just bust into my house?"

"Bust in? The door was unlocked. Is that a good idea?"

"I live in the middle of nowhere. My neighbor is a cop who picks locks. What's your point? And what the hell is so important it couldn't wait?"

"I said I was sorry." He lowered his voice to a whisper. "Is that the beguiler in there? I couldn't tell from the back."

I shook my head. I opened my mouth. I shook my head again. I closed my mouth.

"Was that a no-don't-ask headshake or a no-that-isn't-the-beguiler headshake? Tell me. Who is it?"

"Move on, Sam. The emergency?"

"Kirsten? Jonas thought you and she were —"

Jonas? I shook my head again. "The emergency? Please?"

"Raoul's . . . friend? She didn't leave town?"

Sam's eyes were frowning, apparently at the thought I was with Amanda. He was not beyond a reflexive moral judgment.

"Or — holy shit," he said. *"I-z-z-a?"*

I didn't know why he felt compelled to spell Izza's name. I shook my head once more. "I'm not going there. What the hell is so important?"

Sam said, "We're seeing the same therapist. Did you know that?"

"I did not." *Damn.* "That is awkward." Other than awkward I wasn't sure how I felt about it. It did not feel like critical news. It was a problem that had an apparent solution, which made it one of my favorite kinds. I asked, "Why did you choose her for your therapist? She's young and inexperienced."

"I called a bunch of therapists for late appointments. After work. She was the only one with an opening."

I could have told him that was not an ideal screening tool for therapists. I didn't. Sam wasn't fond of water-under-the-bridge advice. "What am I missing? Why is this news worth busting into my house?"

He took me by the arm and led me as far from the bedroom as we could get. "Because she knows. Our therapist knows."

"She knows what, Sam?"

His eyebrows jumped. "That."

Oh God.

It was my turn to whisper. I said, "Frederick?" Sam nodded.

I said, "Haziq?" He shook his head. "You're sure?" He nodded. I looked him in the eyes. "Did you tell her about Frederick, Sam?"

"No. She added stuff up. A little from you.

668

A little from me."

And some from the Bing, I thought. "Does she have it right?"

"The details? Not at all. The big picture? Enough to cause trouble. She thinks we have another one planned. And that she has some obligation to stop us. Ethically."

"We don't have another one planned." *Do we? Sam?* "Who's the other one?"

"She thinks it's Elliot," Sam said.

I remembered the phone number I saw on Elliot Bellhaven's caller ID in the incall. *It was Lila's number. Our therapist's number. She had called Elliot. Fuck.*

My knees felt weak. "How do you know all this? What she knows and what the hell she thinks? Did she tell you?"

"God no. During my session last week she said some stuff that made me uncomfortable. Couple of things I should probably admit first. One, I have trust issues in relationships — so shoot me. And, two, the picking-lock thing? I'm getting good. That's the how. What do we do?"

"You broke into her office? Her files?"

Sam rolled his eyes. "Amateur hour. Cheap locks. No security. In and out."

Jesus. "You looked at my file?"

He shook his head. "I looked at mine. She has notes about some supervision meetings

669

she had. And a cover-my-ass letter from her supervisor. There's a lot of detail in that. He thinks she's off base. What is supervision, exactly?"

"For us? Not a good thing. I thought we were finally in the clear with Elliot. If she has already talked to him, though —" I began to war-game the potential outcomes in my head. This could get ugly for Sam and for me, fast. I asked, "Did you see any indication she's been in touch with Elliot? That they've spoken about us?"

"In her notes? No. Can she talk to him?" Sam asked me. "You never talk to anybody."

"Ethically? She can't talk. But ethics aren't black-and-white. She may view things differently than I do. She may have told Elliot her concerns. It's not like we can sue her, right? Let me think on this. Did you take her records?"

"Course not. I took photos with my burner. How bad is this for us?"

"Depends on what she knows. Who she tells. Damn. You know I fired her?"

"No. Why?"

"I got suspicious, too. I developed concerns about her judgment."

"Wish I'd known that. What do we do?"

"Well, termination probably, but it may make sense to wait."

"Termination? Yeah?" Sam showed instant consternation at my suggestion.

I recognized the problem might be semantic. "It doesn't mean that; it means you stopping therapy with her. I'll meet you over at Ophelia's in a little while. We'll walk and talk. Don't forget to lock the front door, you know, on your way out."

He whispered, "You going back for mulligan sex?"

"After this? I doubt it." Over my shoulder I added, "And next time, knock." I took one more step before I pivoted back. I lowered my voice to hushed-secret volume. "When you walked in on us who did you think I was with? Which woman?"

"I really couldn't tell from the door."

"Be honest. Let's say I was a . . . lucky guy and I got to choose from the women you named, which one do you think I picked?"

"You're serious with this?"

I nodded. "Yes. It's important to me."

Sam's eyes got sad. "You want the truth?"

"I do."

"Whoever it is in there" — Sam gestured toward the bedroom — "I figure you chose the wrong woman."

ACKNOWLEDGMENTS

A note about some not-so-factual facts in *Compound Fractures:* I take intentional liberties with geography, time, and jurisdiction in this book. Although readers outside Boulder County are unlikely to notice anything amiss, be forewarned that if you find yourself in need of law enforcement help near Eldorado Springs, the person who shows up to lend a hand will likely be an employee of the county, not the city of Boulder.

I have tried to present the early twentieth-century history of Eldorado, and especially that of Ivy Baldwin's remarkable accomplishments, with a nod to the truth. I apologize in advance for errors or omissions. Any mistakes are mine.

The staff of the Carnegie Branch Library for Local History provided assistance navigating the library's collection, as well as with that of the Boulder Historical Society. Philippe Petit, funambulist extraordinaire, inspired me to rediscover Ivy Baldwin. M. Petit also graciously permitted me to include a quote from his poetic *On the High Wire.*

For their help with this book, I thank Jessica Renheim for her guidance and patience, and Robert Barnett for his representation and for his wise counsel.

Jane Davis has long managed my presence on the Web, but I've come to rely on her instincts and judgment about my work and about crime fiction. *Invaluable* is an overused word, but it describes Jane. Elyse Morgan and Nancy Hall each brought a sharp eye and a sharp pencil to the manuscript. I am, as always, grateful for being saved from myself.

Compound Fractures marks the end of an accidental, unlikely series of crime novels. Although I am tempted to thank again everyone who was instrumental in assisting me over the last twenty-two years, I won't. Please know that the appreciation and affection I have already expressed has only deepened with time.

I close the series cognizant that I have the opportunity to write these final lyrics of acknowledgment because, at a time when my dreams required angels, a few people believed in me. The list of early advocates started with Patricia Limerick and the late Jeffrey Limerick. Their faith propelled my first manuscript — unagented, unsolicited — into the hands of the man who became my mentor and guide on this journey, Al Silverman. Dozens — no, hundreds — of writers will attest to what an extraordinary editor and publishing professional Al is, and I am thrilled to lend my voice to any chorus that sings praises about his skills or the quality of his character. But as the twenty-book adventure we started together comes to a conclusion, I find that I am primarily grateful that I still get to call Al my friend.

Two other groups of believers from those early days proved essential: the independent booksellers who hand-sold the first book, and the readers who took a blind-faith flier on a debut novel by an unknown guy with the misfortune of being born with a pseudonym. My deep gratitude to all. Without you, I am not here today.

I've written almost every one of the ten thousand plus pages of this series alone, with a dog or two at my side. Working in isolation for so long has been possible for me because my family has been there when I step away from the keyboard. I have relied on and treasured their support and love

while I've pursued this solitary passion.
From my heart, with my love, mahalo.

ABOUT THE AUTHOR

Stephen White is a clinical psychologist and *New York Times* bestselling author of nineteen previous suspense novels, including *Line of Fire, The Last Lie, The Siege,* and *Dead Time.* He lives in Colorado.

For more information, please visit author stephenwhite.com.

The employees of Thorndike Press hope you have enjoyed this Large Print book. All our Thorndike, Wheeler, and Kennebec Large Print titles are designed for easy reading, and all our books are made to last. Other Thorndike Press Large Print books are available at your library, through selected bookstores, or directly from us.

For information about titles, please call:
(800) 223-1244

or visit our Web site at:
http://gale.cengage.com/thorndike

To share your comments, please write:
Publisher
Thorndike Press
10 Water St., Suite 310
Waterville, ME 04901